PRAISE FOR THE NATIONAL BESTSELLER RITA MAE BROWN'S *HIGH HEARTS*

"This expansive novel of the Civil War contains what must surely be the first in-saddle marital squabble between two members of a Virginia cavalry regiment. . . . Rita Mae Brown's childhood fascination with Virginia battlefields—and her extensive research for this book—serve her well. . . . Fine comic scenes and smart-talking characters . . . Admirable."
—*The New York Times Book Review*

"A vivid and soul-searing picture of the psychological effects of war on decent and intelligent human beings. . . . She does a splendid job on behind-the-scenes power struggles in the Confederate bureaucracy."
—*Washington Post Book World*

"Brown's female characters, always her strength, don't let us down here: they grab their milieu and shake it till things fall out as they please."
—*Kirkus Reviews*

"An entertaining historical tale that presents the war between men and women as a subplot to the War Between the States. . . . Should keep readers turning pages."
—*Ms.* magazine

Books by Rita Mae Brown
Ask your bookseller for the books you have missed.

THE HAND THAT CRADLES THE ROCK

SONGS TO A HANDSOME WOMAN

THE PLAIN BROWN RAPPER

RUBYFRUIT JUNGLE

IN HER DAY

SIX OF ONE

SOUTHERN DISCOMFORT

SUDDEN DEATH

HIGH HEARTS

RITA MAE BROWN

BANTAM BOOKS
TORONTO • NEW YORK • LONDON • SYDNEY • AUCKLAND

HIGH HEARTS

Bantam hardcover edition / May 1986
3 printings through May 1987
A Selection of The Literary Guild of America, Inc.
Bantam paperback edition / May 1987

*Biblical quotations throughout the book are taken from the
King James version of the Bible.*

Library of Congress Cataloging-in-Publication Data
Brown, Rita Mae.
  High hearts.

  Bibliography: p. 460
  1. United States—History—Civil War, 1861–1865—
Fiction. I. Title.
PS3552.R698H5 1986   813'.54   85-48042
ISBN 0-553-26125-8

*Bantam Books are published by Bantam Books, Inc. Its trade-
mark, consisting of the words "Bantam Books" and the por-
trayal of a rooster, is Registered in U.S. Patent and Trademark
Office and in other countries. Marca Registrada. Bantam
Books, Inc., 666 Fifth Avenue, New York, New York 10103.*

PRINTED IN CANADA
COVER PRINTED IN U.S.A.

U   0 9 8 7 6 5 4 3 2 1

For my beloved Uncle,
Claude Brown

CONTENTS

CONTENTS

ACKNOWLEDGMENTS

One of the best parts of writing a novel is thanking everyone who helped you do it. My first thank you goes to Lawrence P. Ashmead for urging me to finally get to this story. My friend Wendy Weil, who is also my agent, gave me wonderful suggestions and support.

The following people gave freely of their knowledge and time, and I am indebted to them: Larry Rumley of Seattle; Elinor S. Hearn, Librarian of the Archives of the Episcopal Church in Austin, Texas; Sarah M. Sartain, Reference Librarian at the Virginia State Library; Sharon Gibbs Thibodeau, Archivist at our National Weather Archives; Robert E. Merritt of the Richmond *Times-Dispatch*; Colonel Joseph Mitchell, author of *Decisive Battles of the Civil War*; Richard Heinz; Carol J. Nicholas, Kentucky Reference Librarian of the Lexington Public Library; Eugene Genovese, Chairman of the Department of History at the University of Rochester; Jerry L. Russell, National Chairman of the Civil War Round Table Associates; Fritz J. Malval of the Hampton Institute; Mr. Dawson and Preston A. Coiner of Charlottesville.

Thank you to Edward Foss, Gloria Fennell, and George Barkley, also of Charlottesville, for providing me with information on foxhunting history.

The U.S. Weather Bureau, the Smithsonian Institution, the Cartographic Department of the National Archives and the fabulous Library of Congress were there when I needed them. Truly, these organizations are national treasures.

The Albemarle County Historical Society, friend to writers, historians, and the public at large, put up with me wandering in and out of their small library on Court Square.

Federal Express of Charlottesville literally kept me going.

Materials came in and materials went out at a fast clip, and I could rely on them one hundred percent.

I wish to thank Thomas Selleck for sending me the "No Negative Thinking" T-shirt which I wore while writing the novel. I also wish to thank Jan and John Alonzo for asking him to send it to me in the first place.

Muffin Spencer-Devlin, a competitor in a different discipline, cheered me on. I appreciate the assistance.

I also must thank Daniel Van Clief of Nydrie Stud whose beautiful stables, unbeknownst to him, gave me inspiration.

I send a big kiss to the city of Richmond. Here in Charlottesville if I wander through the streets or fields with binoculars, maps, and notebooks, well, they're used to me. "There she goes again" seems to be the prevailing attitude, but in Richmond they don't know me from a hot rock. Nonetheless, the citizens of that fascinating city were tolerant, kind, and helpful.

I am blessed to live in Albemarle County, not just because the citizens are fun-loving, but because it is a community that nurtures writers as well as other creative people. I thank everyone in my hometown.

I am also fortunate to live in a state whose first lady, Lynda Johnson Robb, cares deeply about preserving and sharing women's history. I hope other first ladies will follow her example.

Thank you, too, to Nightcap at The Barracks. Nightcap is a school horse. His generous temperament helped me go back to the typewriter, relaxed and refreshed.

Claudia Garthwaite, my researcher and right hand, was a part-time saint and I thank her.

For those of you who write me about my cats, I pass on the sad news that Baby Jesus died on October 6, 1982, at the ripe old age of seventeen. She was followed too soon by my mother who died August 13, 1983, at the age of seventy-eight. I console myself with the knowledge that they both had good, long innings.

I still enjoy the protection of little friends, and I would like to thank my mews: Cazenovia, Sneaky Pie, Pewter, and Buddha.

FOREWORD

Novels, like human beings, usually have their beginnings in the dark. *High Hearts*, a slight variation on this theme, was born in 1948 in blinding sunshine. My great-grandfather Huff, born in 1848 or 1849, was still alive. Breaking one hundred is not uncommon on that side of the family. He enlisted in the army at age thirteen or fourteen. In 1948 I was three and a half, so I recollect vaguely the details of his conversation. But I do recall his passionate need to tell me about the central event of his life. In this he was successful. I could not pass a battlefield without beseeching my father to take me through it. Fortunately, my father encouraged me in my pursuits. I often wonder how many times I took that poor man out of his way or made him late for an appointment. No matter, he cheerfully turned down dirt roads, put the car on the shoulder, and out we'd go to wander over pastures and through woods with our inadequate maps. Mother's contribution was to park me in the library on Saturdays so I could ransack the sections of books devoted to the War Between the States. I have always had the strangest sensation that I was not really learning anything but rather I was being reminded of something I already knew.

When you sit down to write a novel, old research and recollections aren't enough. You'll find a bibliography in the back of this book should you wish to further your own studies.

Walking battlefields is more difficult than when I was a child. Some, like Manassas, are carefully preserved. Others, like the Seven Days which took place around Richmond, are not preserved and the trenches, the dead, the forests have often given way to modern needs. If you attempt to retrace

Stuart's ride around Richmond, this will become apparent to you.

The characters in this book belong to the First Virginia Cavalry, and their actions often parallel those of the troops belonging to Colonel Fitz Lee.

For those of you who wish to read battle reports, allow me to warn you. The Union officers often did not bother to file a report if they lost a battle. They habitually inflated Confederate numbers and then screeched to President Lincoln that they needed more men. Does this sound familiar? The more things change, the more they stay the same.

The Southern officers created a variation on this theme. Their assessment of enemy numbers was usually closer to the mark, but if they did not fare well in an engagement, they wrote florid reports in which they praised their personal favorites.

Julius Caesar started the rage of congratulating one's military exploits in print. By the time of the Civil War almost 2,000 years later, men had perfected it to an art. In reading these reports, you can immediately spot the man who has an eye to future public office. Nothing has changed there either.

You must consider anything written by a Southerner after the Civil War which attacks General Longstreet as corrupt. The fortunes of that man are too complicated to address here, but suffice it to say he was made a scapegoat and much abused by everyone except for Robert E. Lee.

This novel is written entirely from the viewpoints of Virginians. They did not think as Georgians or South Carolinians. Virginia, then as now, nurses its own peculiar vision of world events. Sometimes we are prophetic, other times dead wrong, but we are always Virginians. While I admire a novel that attempts to explain both sides of a story, that was not my intention. My concern is what happens to the main characters. You see things as they saw them. To give them credit for our world view would be a slander on them and on me.

Which brings me to the problem of slavery. No one alive knows what it is like to be a slave. We may know what it is to be downtrodden, despised, deflected, and determined to win despite the odds, but not one of us knows what it is to be owned. Since I could interview no one, I sifted through records. For the most part, the records are written by the owners of the slaves. Even after the Civil War, few former slaves could read or write. Franklin D. Roosevelt created the WPA Program, and one of those projects enabled writers to go out and interview former slaves. These interviews, unedited, poorly typed, and of varying quality, exist in eighteen volumes. They are only available in libraries designated as Federal record depositories. Claudia Garthwaite, my researcher, and I poured over these volumes. I spent the summer of 1984 in Alderman Library at the University of Virginia reading the direct word of slaves. We also read *A Classified Catalogue of the Negro Collection* in the Huntington Library at the Hampton Institute. Aside from a few religious fanatics interviewed, volume after volume reveals individuals who could laugh at the world and themselves. Some were servile. Most were not. All were curious, caring, and filled with a rare perspective due to their phenomenal experience. What was most impressive was their ability to love and to even love and extend forgiveness to the very people who possessed them. This takes a rare spiritual courage, all the more remarkable since so many of the subjects expressed it. These people did the best they could with what they had. Do I pity them? No. I'm proud of them.

The language of the slaves would be difficult for many readers, regardless of background, to comprehend. Language is a means of maintaining power; it is also a means of resistance to power. The white owners did not want the slaves to speak as they did. An argument can be made that the language issue is not resolved to this day. This is a novel, not a book on linguistics or the politics of language. I can't write a novel set in 1861 and 1862 and have most slaves speaking like graduates of Yale. That's an insult to everybody. Slaves revealed their status through their speech the same as everybody else. What I have done is slightly modify the speech so that it is easier to read, but I haven't strayed too far from the original. Obviously, the speech patterns of the white people also reveal their status.

Some of you may know that less than ten percent of white males throughout the Confederacy owned more than two slaves. However, that class of men controlled the Southern legislatures and the written word. Since slavery was part of the economy of the South, it isn't an easy issue to separate from the other issues, although today the Civil War is taught in that simplistic fashion. It is inconceivable that ninety percent of the white men would fight so that ten percent could remain rich. On top of that, there were 93,000 blacks serving in the Confederate Army. Why did the poor whites and blacks fight? To state the obvious is a deceitful temptation. I'll let you figure it out.

The real assault on our senses is the fact that this conflict is presented as inevitable. What happened was that fanatical and irrational elements on both sides of the Mason-Dixon line slowly gathered their power over the three preceding decades. Politics began to take on a hysterical tone. No man could run for office without ruthlessly being grilled by these special interest fanatics. A moderate candidate in Massachusetts or Alabama would be cut to ribbons. Then as now, moderates fade away in the vain hope of being left to private concerns. They cultivate wealth instead of solving the problems of their nation. Within the span of two generations, politics no longer attracted men like Washington, Adams, Jefferson, Franklin, Madison, Monroe, and Jackson. The legacy of gifted public service disappeared with them. Today as in the middle of the nineteenth century, the brightest and the best for the most part avoid politics like the plague. We paid for it then, and we're paying for it now.

When the Civil War finally did come, it degenerated into a disastrous struggle. The Civil War was the last of the old wars and the first of the new. Not even the most rabid secessionist could have foreseen the toll it would take on both sides. Once the war ended, men on either side had a stake in declaring it inevitable. God forbid they should take responsibility for the horror they created.

If this war were not taught as inevitable, it would force students of all ages to question methods of government, to question the morality of powerful lobbying groups forcing their will on the majority as well as to encourage the student to formulate strategies. Why bother to see if we can negotiate these old issues? Aren't they dead and buried? Not exactly.

In the first place, if you and I and millions of other Americans entertain a sense of history that is fatalistic, we're in terrible trouble. If we believe that great forces—first embryonic, then fully developed—move on a collision course, then nuclear war is inevitable, as inevitable as the War Between the States. The past is prologue.

The ultimate blasphemy is that the hundreds of thousands

of dead did not solve the problems. The slaves were freed. That was a partial solution although the North hardly made life easier for them. But the central issue of who controls your community is alive and well. Do you control your community or do a group of men in Washington? Do you have the right to sell your product anywhere in the world? Do you have the right to buy the products of another country without excessive tariff added to the price of the item? Do you have the right to sell your labor at a fair price? Is industry more important than agriculture? If we are a Union, then are our taxes sent to the Federal government and fairly redistributed among the various states? What do we do when women enter the labor force? Now white men have competition not only from black men but from women as well. This is one of the hidden issues in the South during the aftermath of the war. It is now an issue everywhere. Another issue, usually expressed in the past in mystical terms by Southerners, is today expressed as quality of life. Just how do we want to live? Is commerce everything or is the life of the spirit equally as important? If it is equally important, how do we give it its just due in our society? The issue of environmental control began to surface between the two regions, too. If you take the time to read original sources and not anthologies, you are going to find that much of what vexes you today was clearly expressed then.

Finally, no nation or people can go to war without the tacit support of its women. In the case of this war, some women disguised themselves as men to fight. There were no physical exams. Today, a woman is denied the right to combat under the guise of "protecting" her. Margaret Mitchell, before she wrote *Gone with the Wind*, researched this phenomenon among Georgia women. The two Northern women often cited for becoming soldiers were Frances L. Clalin of the Fourth Missouri Heavy Artillery, later of the Thirteenth Missouri Cavalry, Company A, and Doctor Mary Walker of New York state who passed as a male surgeon. There isn't space to list the Confederate women. Then, too, for every woman who came forward after the war and revealed herself, there is no way to know how many melted back into society to continue life as a man or to quietly change back into a woman. As to why so many Southern women chose to fight, your guess is as good as mine.

Behind the front lines, women and slaves worked for the war effort. It was my privilege to read unpublished family papers, if I promised to maintain the family's privacy. The courage of these individuals is breathtaking. Sometimes, in my darker moments, I wonder if we have it today.

One brief aside: Most academic research on this period focuses on politics or military operations. There is precious little about the bonds between men and women. Heterosexual relationships were not a luxury in those times, they were a necessity. Finding a suitable mate was a serious undertaking. People needed one another in a way they do not seem to today. I would love to see research conducted in this area since I think we can profit from it.

Also, there is little psychiatric research applied to this time. Aside from the jolt to everyone's psyche, other problems became evident. Many men, permanently disabled or disfigured, committed suicide. We have no statistics on this since it was almost always covered up. In fact, this is often one of the reasons families want their papers kept private. Suicide remains a terrible stain. We also have little information about mercy killing. I bring this up in hope that it will spur someone into a new area of inquiry and also because it was discussed in my family. We also have no statistics on subsequent addictions to alcohol or morphine. We know it existed, but how wide the scope? How did the sight of a maimed and sometimes chemically incapacitated generation affect their children?

To the best of my knowledge, there is not one monument in the South to commemorate the sacrifice of our women nor is there even so much as a plaque paying tribute to the slaves for their contributions. Here in Albemarle County we have a fine monument of a Confederate soldier in front of the courthouse, a splendid statue of Thomas Jackson beside the courthouse, and another good statue of Robert E. Lee. In a lovely graveyard off Alderman Road there is a statue over the massed graves of those who died from their wounds. So many perished that we buried them in trenches. The earth still gently rises over the bodies so we know where they are even if they lack markers. At the rotunda in the university is a plaque listing the men from the school who died during the conflict. Yet nowhere in my hometown is there mention of the sacrifice of women and blacks. Some paid with their lives, all paid with their worldly goods, many paid with their health, and no one, no one was ever the same again. Until such time as we correct this oversight, let this book stand as their monument.

6 March 1985
Rita Mae Brown

Charlottesville, Virginia

I

THE DECEPTIVE CALM

APRIL 11, 1861

"Girl, my fingernails could grow an inch just waiting for you." Di-Peachy leaned in the doorway to Geneva's bedroom.

"If they grow an inch, you'll work them off tomorrow." Geneva yanked a shawl out of her bureau, twirled it around her shoulders, and breezed past her oldest friend and personal property, Di-Peachy. At eighteen Geneva Chatfield was the tallest girl in Albemarle County as well as the best rider. She stood six feet in her stocking feet. Towering over Di-Peachy, who at five feet six inches enjoyed some height, Geneva banged down the stairs.

"Last one to Auntie Sin-Sin's—"

Geneva was interrupted by Lutie Chalfonte Chatfield, her mother. Lutie had the metabolism of a hummingbird and the nerves, too. "Calm yourself!"

"Yes, Mother."

Di-Peachy tiptoed up behind Geneva. Lutie flashed like a sheet of heat lightning. "You're going to be married tomorrow, and you're running around here like you're in a footrace."

"Yes, Mother."

"I know you haven't the sense God gave a goose, Geneva, but"—Lutie turned to Di-Peachy—"you do! What are you doing galloping down the steps? Is there no one in this house with a sense of proper decorum?"

Portia Chalfonte Livingston, Lutie's younger sister at forty-one, strolled out of the parlor. A huge harp gleamed behind her. "Lutie, don't rile yourself. This will all be over tomorrow, and things will return to normal."

"Normal, Poofy, normal! We've got a lunatic president in Washington, another lunatic in Montgomery, Alabama, who says he's president, my son crows he can't wait for a war, and my daughter is getting married. Normal? I tell you nothing will ever be the same and I feel pulled around backwards." Lutie returned her attentions to her fidgety daughter. "In the face of all this chaos, I would appreciate it if you would play your part and act like a bride!"

"Yes, Mother. May I be excused now?"

Imperiously Lutie waved her hand, and that fast Geneva shot out the door with Di-Peachy in hot pursuit.

Poofy took her sister's elbow in the palm of her hand and discreetly walked her down the long hallway of the Georgian mansion that was the pride of the Chatfield family since 1796 when the cornerstone was laid. Under no circumstances was Poofy about to allow Lutie to strain herself. She'd begin talking to Emil and, well, the less said about Emil, the better. His name was not to be mentioned at this wedding.

The house was jammed with guests, family, and shirttail relatives. More would come from Charlottesville itself on the wedding day. Portia Chalfonte Livingston left Bedford, New York, a month ago to assist Lutie in preparing for the wedding. Their brother, younger by nearly twenty years, T. Pritchard Chalfonte, arrived from Runymeade, Maryland, a week ago to help out. Everything was under control except for Lutie and Geneva. Poofy sighed to herself. "Lord, just let us get through tomorrow."

"Do you think there's going to be a war?" Lutie shook Poofy out of her musings.

"How can we avoid it now that the radical tail shakes the dog? My husband will raise up a regiment for New York State and your son will enlist for Virginia and our brother will join the South. If I were a man, I don't know what I'd do. Living all these years in Bedford gives me a different perspective."

"Oh, perspective? I'd like to know how anyone can have perspective on murder, pure and simple!" Another flash of sheet lightning.

Poofy decided against a long discussion with her volatile sister on the merits of tariffs and the protection of industries versus slavery as a base for agricultural wealth. Portia smiled. "It's going to be a splendid wedding."

"I hope so. I feel this is the last time we'll all be together. Henley is more nervous than Geneva, I think. He says he wishes Sumner married first. You don't have to give your son away. That would toughen him up for Geneva."

"He's a wonderful father, your Henley."

"And a lackluster husband," Lutie snapped.

Portia dismissed this. "Sometimes I don't like my husband, but sometimes I don't like myself. Men—" Portia sighed again, "are different."

"Different? I'll tell you what's different between men and women, sister mine: There's one set of rules for us and another for them. I suppose my poor girl will find out just like every other woman!"

"Nash Hart is a good young man, and he loves Geneva."

"Loves her! They all love you in the beginning. Oh, Poofy" —Lutie wrung her hands—"I've started to tell her so many times, tell her about the way things really are between men and women, about the way your heart shatters or maybe it disintegrates like a fine powder."

"Don't start. Geneva will find out things in her way and in her day. What good would it do you to tell her? Would she listen? Does any young person listen to an old one?"

"I'm not old—not yet!" Lutie appeared in command again. "I must put Di-Peachy further from the front than Geneva wishes. She'll overshadow the bride."

"Now, Lutie."

"Don't waffle. We both know that girl is the most beautiful female God ever put on this earth—to torture me, I suppose!"

It was true. Di-Peachy was lustrous in her beauty. The only way a man couldn't get a hard-on around her was if he was stone queer or dead. She had almond-shaped eyes of light hazel. What a contrast those eyes were against her coffee-colored skin and her long curly hair. Her breasts stuck straight out like hard melons, and her hands were as aristocratic as a queen's. At seventeen Di-Peachy was still far away from her full power, yet she defeated other women simply by drawing breath.

While not immune to the effect of her beauty, it brought her no pleasure. She learned to read and write even though whites thought slaves were best kept in ignorance. The only way Lutie could get Geneva, a lackluster dull student, to do her lessons was if Di-Peachy did them with her. What she learned did not make her position in life easy to bear. Her bondage, like her beauty, was a burden whose weight increased yearly. Her thoughts of freedom conflicted with her love for Geneva who up until now had been the compass of her young life.

"Geneva is a healthy, happy, young woman, and she'll shine at her own wedding." Poofy cooed.

"I gave birth to a plain girl, but she's the best horseman in the whole country. What good will it do her?"

"A great deal, honey. She and Nash will continue Henley's breeding programs. She's going to make a good wife, and her skill with horses will serve her well. Just you wait and see."

In a moment of anguish, Lutie squeezed her sister's bejeweled hand. "Poofy, I don't want the world to rudely cross my threshold. Not tomorrow! Not on my baby's wedding day."

Poofy sighed a great sigh and kissed her sister's freckled hand. Lutie smiled. "I wish you'd stop that damn sighing! It sounds like respiratory martyrdom!"

The clouds nearly touched the treetops. A strange light seemed to shine through them this early evening. Geneva and Di-Peachy skipped over the green, spring lawn. A few brave crocuses popped up their heads and the forsythia threatened, but winter and spring still played tug-of-war. Easter was eleven days ago and spring seemed late. The magnificent stable, the pride of the Chatfield family, loomed in the half-light like a candle.

Normally Geneva would wander into the stable. If she wasn't on a horse then she was around them. But tonight she skirted the stables and made for the slave quarters. These faced the stable instead of the main house, which was the custom. Each quarter was a two-story, frame dwelling with a pitched roof and a front porch. Behind each house was a garden. Since Henley Chatfield concentrated on horses rather than crops—he had hay, of course—he could streamline his business to thirty slaves and the various children produced. In the number one house resided the powerful Auntie Sin-Sin. Sin-Sin was aide-de-camp to Lutie. She didn't so much seize power as she accreted it. Of course, Lutie never addressed her as Auntie Sin-Sin which would indicate that both women were growing old. They'd each die before they'd admit that. However, Geneva and Di-Peachy had to address Sin-Sin as Auntie, her due respect.

"Auntie Sin-Sin! Auntie Sin-Sin!" Geneva shouted as she ran.

The door to the white house opened, and Sin-Sin barked, "Couldn't stand it no more? Well, get in here. Both of you get in here."

Geneva thundered across the porch. Di-Peachy was more dainty about it.

"My bones'll rust in this weather." Sin-Sin closed the door. "Sit by the fire, missy." She turned to Di-Peachy. "You, too."

The house was full of pots—big red pots, little bright green ones, a black one with snakes on it, another one filled with sunflower seeds. You could barely move but for bumping into a pot. The pot of honor, a blazing cobalt blue, sat square in the middle of a well-made table.

"Don't you come in here with the searching eye, missy."

"Auntie, I wouldn't do that," Geneva protested.

"Ha! I knowed you since you was in your mama's belly. I can still box your ears! Don't weasel me."

"Can't I have my wedding present now?"

"No! You turns around and get right out of here if you're goin' to start that."

"Just a peek?"

"Next thing, you'll be wanting to speak at the groom. You pay heed to superstition. That's old wisdom. Don't trifle with it."

Di-Peachy grinned.

"Tell me about your husband, Auntie," Geneva said teasingly. They'd heard about Marcus Armentrout a million times.

"I promise to obey the man but before I finish, it was cussing, honey." She slapped her thigh and laughed. Sin-Sin couldn't abide taking orders from anybody, any color. Even Lutie carefully phrased her "requests."

Geneva fixed her eyes on the cobalt blue pot. "I've got to find something blue."

"That's not it," Sin-Sin replied. "Borrow a blue garter from your brother."

Di-Peachy poked the fire. "We were hoping you could tell us something about the wedding night."

Sin-Sin's eyebrows darted up to her peacock blue turban. She always wore a scarf around her head, reserving red for Christmas and special occasions. Once Lutie gave her a white silk scarf from Paris. When Sin-Sin didn't appear wrapped in it the next morning, Lutie's feelings were hurt. Finally Sin-

Sin told her that white was for when one died. She put the scarf in her small dresser, top drawer, and instructed Lutie to wrap her in it should the Lord call her first. Lutie agreed, secure in the knowledge that Sin-Sin was indestructible.

"Your momma kept that to herself?"

"Mother and I don't talk very much." Geneva said this without rancor.

"Well, your momma is a Chalfonte, honey, and they run to brilliant, and your daddy, he's a Chatfield, and they run to practical. You take after your daddy. But Nash—he's almost like your momma. He has a rhymin' turn of mind."

"You do like him, don't you, Auntie Sin-Sin?"

"Like him? Why I think he's the best young man in this entire county!" Geneva's relief was so visible that Di-Peachy laughed. Sin-Sin growled at Di-Peachy. "Soon enough, you'll be moonin' about some buck, too."

"Never!" Di-Peachy was emphatic.

Sin-Sin polished the pot with the snakes on it.

"I mean it, Auntie." Di-Peachy's eyes crackled like the fire.

"Girl, every man sees you wants you—Mr. Nash and Mr. Henley being excepted naturally. Sooner or later you gonna fall!"

"I will never, ever fall in love, and if I do, may God strike me dead." This was said with such force that both Geneva and Sin-Sin stared at Di-Peachy. Di-Peachy warmed to her subject. "I'll never be the slave of a slave!"

"Watch your mouth," Sin-Sin warned. "Losing most the light. You two best burn the wind gettin' back to the big house."

"But tell me about the wedding night!"

"Thass the best part!" Sin-Sin laughed.

"Does it hurt?" Geneva tried not to sound as anxious as she was.

"Sometimes it do, sometimes it don't. But the first time is, well, hard on the nerves."

"My monthly shows up when it shows up. Half the time, I don't get it at all. What if I can't have children? Oh, there has to be another way to do all this." Geneva nearly wailed.

"That'll even out when you gets older. See that big green pot over there? That's the baby pot. When you wants a baby, you come on in here and we rub the pot."

"What if you don't want a baby?" Di-Peachy inquired.

"What's got into you, Miz Peaches? I never heard such talk."

Di-Peachy shut up. Sin-Sin's raptures over her pots and their magical impregnating qualities were a tried and true topic. If she launched into it, they'd never get out of there. "Geneva, let's go before it gets black as pitch."

A silver softness enshrouded the back meadows. The two girls walked side by side. Di-Peachy felt displaced by Nash. She'd run the new frame house Nash's people built on the seven hundred acres Henley gave the couple. As it adjoined Henley's own land, the breeding operation would go on as before. She'd watched Auntie Sin-Sin and Lutie, so Di-Peachy knew she could run an estate. She'd have to or Geneva would wind up in the poorhouse. Geneva didn't know jack shit about running a house, and she didn't care. All Geneva cared about was horses and Nash, though Di-Peachy wasn't sure in what order. Nash was smart enough, but he was a dreamy sort. Some of his poems had been published in the literary journal at the University of Virginia, where he attended with distinction. Di-Peachy hated that he could attend school, but she could not. She was smarter than these white people, and it drove her deeper and deeper into a frozen rage, frozen because she dared not express it. Why did Geneva have to fall in love and spoil everything? At least when it was the two of them, life was tolerable. Now she'd have to take orders from Nash and worse, watch Geneva take them, too.

A pack of black and tan hounds tore across the deep meadow, baying in metallic, thin voices. The moisture in the air seemed suspended like tiny pearls.

"My God, where'd they come from? Nobody hunts with black and tans around here. Not for years." Geneva gasped and stopped talking. Twenty-some riders blasted hard on the hounds. The horses glided over the pasture, muscles straining. Geneva didn't recognize any of the riders. A straggler on a magnificent seventeen-hand gray rode up to her.

"Ladies." He swept an old-fashioned cap off his head.

He was a big man, and his shirt, open almost to the waist, revealed a torso that could have been carved by Michelangelo. His boots were also old-fashioned. They could have covered his knee, but were rolled over once. He looked like a cavalier. Possessed of an enigmatic radiance, he spoke to Geneva. "Each person you kill is a soul you must bear like an unseen weight." He clapped his hat back on his head, wheeled the huge horse away from them, and sped off as silently and swiftly as he came.

Geneva felt a chill. He was swallowed in the noctilucent mists.

Di-Peachy pulled on Geneva. "Let's get out of here."

"They're crazy. You can't foxhunt in this weather. There's no scent."

Geneva froze. She stopped and shivered. "Di-Peachy, that was the Harkaway Hunt! They come for you when you die or at a time of great crisis. Momma said she saw them when my little brother Jimmy died."

Di-Peachy, a fervent rationalist, wanted none of it. "We'll ask people at the wedding."

Geneva seized Di-Peachy's left arm. "No! Don't say anything to anybody! Whether you believe the Harkaway Hunt legend or not, plenty of people around here do. They'll take it as some omen—what with conditions."

"All right, Geneva, all right."

" 'Each person you kill is a soul you must bear like an unseen weight,' " Geneva said, repeating his prophecy. "I'm not going to kill anyone."

"Forget it. Maybe it's indigestion."

"I'll never forget it—and neither will you."

Di-Peachy pushed Geneva forward. She wanted to get back. The two raced toward the big house. They were glad to finally see it, anchored on the edge of the meadow like a great ship laden with treasure.

APRIL 12, 1861

The clouds, to spite Lutie's entreaties, hung fat with rain. It was a matter of time until they spilled it over yet another cool April day. The Chatfield house hummed, an overexcited hive. The servants scurried about, sticking ribbons into the twisted, dried grapevines which were wrapped around the stairway and the mantelpiece. Others groomed the carriage horses until they shone like patent leather. Lutie determinedly set about her morning Bible lesson. No day, no matter what day, could begin without a reading from the Bible. The inscription from Ephesians on her *Episcopal Church Almanac* was Redeeming the Time, and she wasn't going to waste a precious second. Today's lesson was Judges 2:1–11 and Luke 22:31.

Henley, tall and slender like his daughter, read: "And ye shall make no league with the inhabitants of this land; ye shall throw down their altars: but ye have not obeyed my voice: Why have ye done this?"

From the kitchen Sin-Sin's bellow catapulted Lutie and Geneva out of their seats. "You're so dumb you ain't even ignorant!"

Lutie went to see what all the fuss was about. Geneva, Di-Peachy, Poofy, and T. Pritchard Chalfonte escaped by every available exit. Henley smiled and closed the Bible. He couldn't keep his mind on the lesson anyway. He quietly left as well and walked down the hall toward his daughter's room.

Sin-Sin was throwing salt on the cook, Ernie June. Scattered on the floor of the kitchen were the pieces of a beautifully glazed red pot.

Lutie roared in. "What goes on here!"

Sin-Sin blindly continued to throw salt at Ernie June. Ernie June, not the easiest person to get along with, behaved herself remarkably well for her. She slung whole handfuls of pepper at Sin-Sin.

"Put back your skin, witch," hollered Sin-Sin.

"No more than yourself, and pepper will catch you jes as good." Another handful dotted Sin-Sin's white apron, starched stiff and placed neatly over her black dress.

"How can you give in to vile superstition when I'm having my morning Bible reading?"

"It be true. She's a witch." Ernie June spat. "When a witch starts to shed her skin, you throw pepper—"

"Salt!" Sin-Sin commanded.

"—pepper to catch her."

"Now you've got two messes to clean up, Ernie June," Lutie said.

"Three, after I clean up the floor with you!" Sin-Sin started for Ernie.

"Sin-Sin, I have enough on my mind today without you cuttin' a shine."

Sin-Sin put the salt shaker down, but folded her arms across her ample bosom. She wasn't giving in yet. "I made a lucky pot for Miz Geneva. Ernie June with her big brown eyes and feet to match done tripped me as I was comin' into the kitchen with my weddin' present."

"You wasn't lookin' where you was goin'!"

"You so fat, Ernie, that half of you is in the next county." Sin-Sin relished this particular insult since she had kept her figure. It was true that Ernie's elbows appeared as dimples in her arms.

"When a man got his arms around me, he knows he got somethin'."

"A lardass, thass what he got."

"Will you two stop it!" Lutie yanked a pan from overhead where it hung on a big, wrought-iron hook. "Someone is going to have a flat head!"

Sin-Sin, carefully not looking at Lutie's eyes, untied the sparkling white handkerchief around her neck and shook it out. Ernie June yanked open a closet door and pulled out a broom. As she walked past Sin-Sin, she pulled the end of Sin-Sin's turban. Sin-Sin kicked her in the butt.

Lutie brandished her pan. "I've got a daughter gettin'

married at noontime, and why do I have to contend with two crazy girls in my kitchen!"

Ernie began to vigorously sweep up the mess. Sin-Sin picked up her pot bits.

"Ernie June, don't tell anyone that you broke Geneva's wedding pot." Lutie now spoke soothingly.

Ernie scowled at Sin-Sin, whose face was flushed with both anger and sincerity. "You 'spect me to believe 'bout yo' old pots?"

"Remember, Ernie June, Geneva does share Sin-Sin's belief in the magic of pots. If she thinks her marriage pot has been broken, it won't sit well with her." Lutie quickly spoke before they started fighting again.

"You always takes up for her." Ernie pointed the broom at Sin-Sin.

"I am not taking up for her. I am trying to keep the peace with little help from either one of you!"

Sin-Sin gathered the red bits and pieces in her unfolded neckerchief. She sashayed toward the door. "Me and Miz Lutie go back a long ways, Ernie June. You can't fight time!" With that, she banged the door and left.

Ernie steamed. Lutie pacified Ernie. "When I married Mr. Chatfield, Sin-Sin was one of his gifts to me. I was sixteen and didn't know beans about running this place. Sin-Sin was the greatest help to me. It isn't that I don't value you; after all, you are the best cook in all of Virginia. In fact, do you know that fine-looking fellow who visited here from Mississippi offered me a small fortune for you?"

Ernie June's eyes bugged out of her head. Lutie rolled on. "But I told him your price is beyond rubies!"

Lutie left the room with a nod. Ernie was lavishly complimented, and Sin-Sin's power was reconfirmed.

A stunning bridal gown, French lace from head to long, long train, hung on the wooden torso in Geneva's bedroom. Di-Peachy had gotten accustomed to seeing it but today, The Day, a lump formed in her throat. Geneva threw on riding clothes and didn't notice, but then Geneva wasn't as sensitive as Di-Peachy. Geneva was contented with the surface of things. If Di-Peachy told her something, she would respond; otherwise, she'd just go about her business.

"I've got to get out of here. If Mother comes looking for me, tell her I'll be right back."

"It's going to rain, Geneva. Don't get wet and mess up your hair or your mother will mess with me."

"I need a half-hour ride, even fifteen minutes will do. My God, Di-Peachy, I want to get married and get it over with. I can't stand all this carrying on."

"May I come in?" Henley stopped at the door.

"Daddy!" Geneva kissed him.

"I'll see to your shoes." Di-Peachy plucked two shoes out of an enormous wardrobe and left the room.

"I hate to give you up, baby." Henley put his chin on the top of Geneva's head. About six inches taller than his daughter, Henley was the tallest man in the county with the exception of Big Muler, a servant of Nash's. "If that boy ever lays a hand on you, you tell me."

"He would never!"

"I hope so." He kissed his daughter again. Why tell her how someone so right can turn out so wrong? Not that Lutie was a bad wife. He'd been fortunate in most respects but the fire burns out, people change, usually they grow apart. "I want you to be happy."

"I am, Daddy." She pulled her old sweater from underneath a pillow on the window seat. "Want to take a short ride with me while I'm still a Chatfield?"

"You'll always be a Chatfield, honey." Henley put his arm around her, and they snuck down the back stairway and headed for the stables.

A light drizzle kept the servants busy as they dashed out quickly to carriages to cover the dismounting occupants with huge umbrellas. By 10:30 A.M. one hundred fifty people gathered at the Chatfield home. Laughter filled every room. Daniel Livingston, Poofy's genial husband, was the object of much attention. There were few Northerners at the wedding, all of them being family in some way, but everyone was acutely aware that Virginia was neither fish nor fowl. She had not joined the seceding states. If Lincoln pressed for troops to squelch the insurrection, as it was referred to in Washington, it seemed inevitable that Virginia would go with the South. No one wanted Daniel to think there was any animosity toward him. Most of them had known him for upwards of twenty years, and they hoped he understood that the bragging of the young men about whipping five Yankees with one hand tied behind their backs was not directed at him. Henley was upstairs with the bride so the pleasant task of being the host fell to Daniel. T. Pritchard Chalfonte also did his duty. Sumner apparently was upstairs with his mother. No one thought he'd come down with a case of nerves but he did. Nash Hart and his father stayed sequestered in a downstairs room at the end of the long hall.

Sin-Sin paraded through the front door carrying a cobalt blue pot. She nodded to all and sundry. Sin-Sin was not coming in through the back door on Geneva's wedding day. She entered the library, rich with the smell of leather-bound books, and placed her brilliant blue pot smack in the center of all the silver gifts.

The ballroom filled with guests. It was now quarter to twelve. The orchestra played in the balcony overhead. Satin and silk crinkled. Swallowtails were flipped up so that the gentlemen could sit down without wrinkling their coats. Waistcoats and ladies' dresses, all in soft pastels, were a garden of colors. Daniel herded everyone inside. At twelve o'clock Nash took his place at the altar. Sumner Chatfield, his best man, towered over the groom. The Very Reverend Franklin Manlius beamed at the congregation. He adored being able to stand before his own flock plus those wayward souls that were Methodists, Lutherans, Presbyterians, and even, shudder, Catholics. There was one of everything out there, even a Jew. Lutie walked down the aisle on the arm of Increase Hart, Nash's father. A murmur of sympathy and affection greeted Increase, because Mrs. Hart had given up her ghost to consumption a scant year ago.

At last, the orchestra struck up the wedding march. Di-Peachy sat in the back with Sin-Sin, tears streaming down her high cheekbones. Sin-Sin held her hand and patted it. From the other end of the long hall, Geneva walked with her father. As she entered the ballroom, the crowd whispered their approval. Henley gravely looked forward, fighting back his own tears. Geneva entered the room like a christening, full of hope. Nash turned his face from facing the altar to behold his bride. He was well pleased. The entire room could feel the spark, the heat between Geneva and Nash. No, she wasn't the prettiest bride in Albemarle County but she was radiant, and the man she chose truly loved her. As she stood by his side, she glanced over at him. His face was slowly turning bright red underneath his sandy, straight hair.

The Very Reverend spread his hands, his vestments catching the candlelight. "Dearly Beloved," he began. Very Reverend Manlius gave a fantastic performance. In spite of his histrionics, he was a good pastor, otherwise Christ Episcopal Church would have clamped down on his theatrics a long time ago.

Nash said, "I do," in a voice that would roll back the tide. Soft laughter rippled through the room because his voice betrayed so much eagerness. The Very Reverend allowed a smile of understanding to flow over the audience. Geneva spoke her words clearly and firmly. Di-Peachy sobbed. Lutie sobbed. Sin-Sin sobbed. Henley cried quietly. Increase Nash held a handkerchief to his eyes. But when the ceremony was finished and the groom had kissed his bride with tremendous enthusiasm, the families leapt to their feet with the rest of the congregation and applauded. As the couple walked down the aisle, the room thundered, it shuddered, it shook.

After a feast worthy of Henry VIII, the guests returned to the ballroom, where colored streamers with small flowers knotted at the ends had been added to the garlands. Di-Peachy, who played her harp through the dinner, stood against a wall while the orchestra played. Her slave status should have kept the men away publicly, but Di-Peachy was a goddess in human flesh. One by one, the men paid her their compliments. She smiled and returned their admiration with polite restraint. Reddy Neutral Taylor, the owner of a hardware store and crooked as a dog's hind leg, was persistent in his attentions. Sin-Sin very pointedly told him that one Miss Caroline Metzger needed a dancing partner right now. Reddy took the hint.

"Girl, give these men a rest. Let's see if we can make Ernie June drop a tray of champagne. She ought to be put out with the heifers. Her head's too big to be in the house."

Ernie June was exalted this Friday because each guest loudly proclaimed the excellence of the food. Sin-Sin detested Ernie's prominence at this occasion, and Ernie knew she had Sin-Sin dead to shit this time.

As the bride was exhausting herself dancing with every man in the room, Lutie was likewise twirling about. Finally, she had to release herself from the grasp of her brother, T. Pritchard, and repair to the punch bowl. Poofy was also there catching her breath.

"You're as light on your feet as a fairy." Poofy knocked back the punch.

"Where'd the time go, Poofy? I feel like it was only yesterday that I danced at your wedding."

Just then Jennifer Fitzgerald tacked over. Jennifer reveled in insulting people. It gave a glory to her life since she so fabulously succeeded. She was married to Sean "Big Fitz" Fitzgerald, an important horseman in the county, so she couldn't be ignored.

"Why, Lutie, this wedding rivals anything I've ever seen."

"Thank you, Jennifer," Lutie replied, thinking to herself that Jennifer had probably seen the wedding of Hades and Persephone.

"And, Portia, I can't tell you how good it is to see you. By the way, Lutie, how old are you?" That was just like Jennifer. Sock you without warning.

"Thirty-eight." Lutie coolly smiled.

"Now isn't that the oddest thing? I just spoke to Sumner not two minutes ago, and he told me he was twenty-seven."

"Well, he lives his life, and I live mine," Lutie airily countered, then wheeled off to collar her son.

"What's the big idea of telling Jennifer Dogmeat Fitzgerald how old I am? I am shocked at your revelation of personal information."

"My age is not personal information."

"Mine is!"

"Mother, who cares about the years? You're the prettiest lady in this room, and Jennifer Fitzgerald, I mean Jennifer Dogmeat Fitzgerald, seethes with jealousy. Do you see anyone asking Jennifer to dance, except for her unfortunate husband, of course." Sumner hummed maliciously.

"Sumner, giving birth to you was one of the best things I ever did." Lutie shed two decades as Sumner twirled her around the floor.

The bride and groom slipped out the back door at the height of the festivities. They would spend the night alone at their new house with no servants inside until the morning. They were scheduled to catch the train to New York in the afternoon, and from New York they would sail to France.

On into the night the party continued. Lutie generously distributed her personality. Sumner got drunker than a boiled owl. His friends carried him to the stable and left him in a stall covered with blankets. A bucket was by his side. No sense in having him ruin any of the rugs at the big house. Henley, Daniel, and T. Pritchard continued to see to the needs of their guests, which grew more eccentric as the night wore on. Reddy Neutral Taylor actually offered Henley one thousand dollars to sleep with Di-Peachy. Henley put him out of the house. Poofy crept up on the tail end of this.

"How could he do such a thing?"

"He doesn't have the sense God gave a goose." Henley closed the door.

"That girl will never have a minute's peace unless she becomes fat or disfigured." Poofy shook her head.

"Great beauty, like great wealth, is not always a blessing." Henley put his arm around his sister-in-law's shoulder. "Please don't mention this episode to Lutie. You know how she is about the girl."

"Yes, I know." Portia's voice dropped.

They rejoined the festivities arm in arm. Finally, guests dotted the rooms like fallen blossoms. Those that could stagger home did. Those that couldn't, stayed put.

Lutie climbed into bed, exhilarated and exhausted. She had kissed her husband good night at the door, hugged her sister and brother-in-law and was now blissfully alone. She wore her loveliest nightgown and blew the candle out next to the bed.

"Emil, is that you?" Lutie whispered. "They've done everything to keep us apart. I'm dying to talk to you."

Rain poured outside. A fire cast golden light over the large bedroom. Geneva perched on the edge of the rice bed and listened to the downpour. She liked her new house. It wasn't fancy but it exuded warmth, and Geneva was happy to have something that was hers alone. Nash came in after seeing that Bumba, his man, had taken the horses to the small stable. Water dripped onto the small Bukhara rug, which Poofy and Daniel Livingston had given them.

"I think I'll get out of these clothes." Nash shook his arm, sending a light spray sizzling into the fire.

Geneva rose from the bed to help him. He started to move

away from her, but she held him. Silently she unbuttoned his beautiful waistcoat and threw it on the floor.

"Geneva—"

She moved around in front of him and kissed him on the lips before he could finish his sentence. She bit his neck. Nash shuddered and held her close. She felt an unfamiliar but welcome hardness bump into her groin. She peeled off his trousers like shucking corn. He wore beautiful silk underwear of bright white. She could see his penis outlined against it. He looked better than anything she'd seen in the stable. She was a little afraid to go on.

Nash kissed her again much harder, wrapped his arms around her waist, and picked her up. He put her down on the bed and quickly removed the many layers of sumptuous traveling dress off her. When he got to the corset, he stopped for a moment. Nash had enjoyed the favors of a few women. The women he'd slept with had been servants or the occasional whore. He didn't think about it. That's the way things were.

"Cut it," Geneva suggested.

He leapt over to the pile of clothes and retrieved a small, flat pocketknife from his waistcoat. As he charged across the room Geneva noticed how slender he was. His sandy hair appeared more fair in the firelight. The soft hair on his chest was in the shape of a golden T, the tail end of the T mysteriously disappearing into his silk shorts. There was nothing wasted on his elegant frame. Everything about Nash was refined, even his fingers. As they slashed through the stays, they looked as though they should be playing a piano or writing a poem. Her corset fell off like a split turtle shell. Nash stopped for a moment to stare at his wife. This was the first time he would make love to her, and he wanted to remember every second. He'd never made love to a woman he loved. Everything pounded; his cock throbbed, his heart slammed against his rib cage, his temples banged, his knees shook.

"Geneva, Geneva, you're wonderful." He gently placed himself on top of her and kissed her.

Nash kissed her again. He kissed her tiny breasts. He nibbled her broad shoulders and put his hands under her armpits; he ran his fingers down to her nonexistent hips. Geneva was long, lean, and boyish. He found her more exciting than the overweight women he'd known. He felt her legs, which were more heavily muscled than his own, but then she would have legs like that, for no one could touch her riding ability. He came back up her body.

Nash whispered, "Can I touch you?"

"You're my husband. You can do anything you like." He cupped her genitals in his hand.

"Geneva, I don't want to hurt you. I want to go inside. If it hurts, tell me and I'll come out. It might take you some time to get used to me."

"I want to spend the next one hundred years getting used to you. I want to do this every night." She placed her hands behind his neck and entwined her fingers.

Afterwards, Geneva said, "I want to do it again."

"Now?" Nash was stunned.

"Now." She rolled him on his back and kissed his body as he had kissed hers. Nash moaned. He thought he died and went to heaven. After that surprise, he pulled down the covers of the bed.

"Let's get under the covers. It's a wicked night."

Geneva darted under the goose down quilt. He crawled in next to her. She kissed him some more. He laughed. He put his arm under her neck, and she snuggled into him like a kitten at the breast of its mother, and so they fell asleep on the first night of their marriage. Nash thought as he drifted off, God sure knew what He was doing when He said, "Be fruitful and multiply."

APRIL 13, 1861

Littered with remembered kisses, Nash awoke the next morning enjoying a stupendous erection. He peeked under the covers to inspect himself. It must have grown in the night. He jumped out of bed, sucking in his breath as his bare feet hit the cold floor. The fire was out, and the servants wouldn't come into the room until he asked them. Naked, he trotted down the hallway to his dressing room and toilet with the ubiquitous bucket of lime.

Bumba, shining Nash's travel boots, worked hard at not being impressed with his master this morning. Nash grinned.

"Might you build the fire in our bedroom? Mrs. Hart is still asleep." Mrs. Hart. That was the first time he'd used those words. They tasted like honey.

"Mrs. Hart's wide awake, and she's starved." Geneva, in a heavy robe, interrupted his shave.

Nash kissed her. She emerged from this embrace with a white moustache. "For a woman, you don't look half bad in a moustache, but then you don't look half good either."

Once downstairs, Granville, Nash's cook, greeted them with hosannas and hot coffee. The grits, sausages, eggs and biscuits with redeye gravy shortly followed.

Nash swallowed a sausage whole. He paused. "Do you hear that?"

Geneva remained still for a second. A low muffled boom filtered into the kitchen. Then church bells pealed, followed by more booms. They lived five miles west of town. The sound carried even on this soggy morning.

"It's in honor of our marriage." Nash delicately kissed Geneva's hand.

"Cannon?"

Before he could answer, hoofbeats clattered in the small courtyard. The front door flew open, and Sumner burst in. "Geneva!" he shouted. "Fort Sumter was fired upon yesterday!"

Nash dropped his cup of coffee.

"Is this it then?" Geneva asked, betraying little emotion.

"Yes, thank God, this is it! No more pussyfooting! No more waiting around! War, sister, war at long last!" Sumner was jubilant.

Nash quietly took charge. "Geneva, get your coat. I think we'd better go up to your parents' house."

Breakfast, lavishly served, covered the lovely table set in Lutie's breakfast nook. Many of Sin-Sin's bright pots were filled with blooming flowers and covered the windowsills. Daniel, Poofy, Lutie, Henley, and T. Pritchard quietly ate their meal. Lutie couldn't touch a bite. Sumner strode in with Nash and Geneva behind.

"Sit down, darling." Lutie pointed to a chair. Nash pulled it out for Geneva. He sat next to her. Everyone exchanged greetings.

Sumner hit his chair like a large rock. "I'll enlist today. One summer of hard riding and hard fighting, and I'll be back by fall!"

"Don't gloat, son." Henley placed his large hand on Sumner's bulging forearm. Sumner, exuberant as he was, was not entirely insensitive.

"Aunt Poofy, I'm sorry." Sumner's face blotched with embarrassment.

Lutie's eyes moistened. "This is the last time the family will be together."

Portia, seated next to her, caressed her hand. "This family will always be together, Lutie."

"Oh, Poofy," Lutie said in a trembling voice, "we're at war now."

"We will each do what we think is right, but we will always love one another."

Lutie raised her delicate face. "I shall pray nightly for all of you."

"And I shall also pray for each of us." Portia's deep, melodic voice touched everyone. "I pray that the Lord keep thee and bless thee, that the Lord make his face shine upon thee and be gracious unto thee and give thee peace."

"Amen." Henley spoke for them all.

After breakfast, Nash pulled Geneva into the library. "Geneva, I must offer my services to Virginia. She'll secede now."

"Don't go!" Geneva felt a panicky beating of her heart.

"You wouldn't want a husband who was a coward." Nash bowed his head. How could he go from such intense joy to such profound misery within the space of twenty-four hours?

Geneva straightened herself. "You're right."

The men rode into Charlottesville while Bumba drove a wagon to the station to retrieve Geneva's trunks.

The women stayed at the Chatfield house. Lutie and her sister packed Poofy's things as she would be leaving on the afternoon train.

"It's those rodent bankers." Lutie slammed a carefully folded nightgown into the trunk. "Money starts all wars. Or the principle of money. If we measured our wealth in turtles, then this war would be fought over turtles."

Portia's languid eyes, the color of cognac, the same color as her niece Geneva's eyes, softened. "Does it matter anymore? The reasons are only excuses. Events are moving at a tragic velocity."

"I can't bear the thought of being so far from you, Poofy."

"The distance to Bedford, New York, is the same as it always was. Some five hundred–odd miles."

"You live in a different country now."

Poofy held up a piece of Belgian lace. There wasn't enough light on this overcast day to make a pattern on the wall. Disappointed, she placed it in the yawning trunk. "I've never lived through a war before, Lutie. I don't know what to expect. If I should be boiling over about great issues, I'm not. I'm worried about Daniel, about our brother, about you and your family."

"Me, too."

"We're getting older. I worry about that, too."

"Don't beat about the bush, Portia. What you really mean is what if I die."

"I could die, too."

"You're the younger sister. Younger sisters never think they'll go first."

A slight smile tugged at Portia's mouth. "Perhaps."

"I'm not afraid to die. I don't want to die, don't misunderstand me, but I am not afraid. The seasons pass; why shouldn't I?"

Tears filled Poofy's eyes. She hugged her sister who, like herself, had begun to cry.

Downstairs, Di-Peachy played her harp. Geneva observed her companion and thought how young Di-Peachy was. Someday Di-Peachy would be initiated into the secrets of womanhood, but for now, Geneva had the edge.

"Do I look different?" Geneva teased.

"No, why should you?" Di-Peachy replied.

"Oh, Peaches, you'll find out in time." Geneva said this with an air of sophistication.

"I'm not in any hurry."

"You know, you can be a real old maid sometimes."

"Geneva, I can still break crockery on your head, so watch your mouth."

Sin-Sin appeared. "Miz Geneva, honey, I heard Nash say he's goin' to enlist." Sin-Sin put her hands together as if in prayer. "Lord, what's to become of us?"

"We'll knock those goddamned Yankees into next week, and then life can return to normal."

"Uh-huh." Sin-Sin nodded.

"Auntie Sin-Sin, you gave me the lucky pot. It's the gift I love the most."

Sin-Sin beamed. "You knows I love my Neevie. And don't you worry none about Mr. Nash goin' to war. You tell him to kill the first snake he sees in the spring, then his enemies won't get the best of him this year."

"I'll be sure to tell him."

"Explain me this. Why are the mens downtown formin' up companies when we ain't even at war? You knows them South Carolina folks is hotheads. Remember when that skinny girl come up here to take care of Miz Jennifer's babies? She insists she be called 'Dah,' then she talk that crazy talk. Those chillun never be right. I wouldn't give you two straws for anyone from South Carolina."

"I think the abolitionists drove them to it." Geneva figured the abolitionists were rich men who wanted to drive the South into poverty. Then they'd control politics.

"Sin-Sin, I need you," Lutie called from upstairs.

"Herself calls." Sin-Sin bowed low as if to a pasha and walked to the door. She bowed low again and wiggled her fingers. Geneva laughed loudly.

"I'd like to know what you have to laugh about on a day like this, Geneva Chatfield Hart," Lutie reprimanded from upstairs.

Sin-Sin ascended the stairs with various motions of derogation.

Geneva grabbed her friend's hand. "Oh, Peachy, I'll die if he leaves me. I'll just die!"

Upstairs, Lutie and Portia finished the packing. Sin-Sin, who'd come in, tied up the last of the trunks.

"I'll get the boys to bring these out." Sin-Sin was satisfied with her work and started to leave for the door.

Portia called her back. "Sin-Sin, I don't know when I will

see you again. I'd like you to know that my husband and I will think of you fondly."

"Miz Poofy—" Sin-Sin broke down. She hated to cry.

Seeing Sin-Sin cry set Lutie off. "Poofy, I can't bear it. My heart is breaking."

Portia and Sin-Sin wrapped their arms around her. Lutie sobbed.

"Now, sister, we're Chalfontes. We shine in adversity, even if we are on different sides."

"This is worse than adversity. This is the end of the world."

"This isn't England or France, honey. We're Americans. We'll be more sensible about our civil unrest," Portia babbled, worried over Lutie's outburst.

"Sensible! My God, if we were sensible, it wouldn't have come to this!"

Neither Portia nor Sin-Sin had an answer for that one.

"I'll tell you what this is." Lutie's brain felt like ice; everything was crystal clear. "This is a bolt of lightning over a nation of quicksand."

Sin-Sin rubbed Lutie's back.

"I want to talk to Emil," Lutie demanded.

"No, you don't want to talk to Emil." Portia was firm.

"He understands me."

"You can talk to Sin-Sin."

"But Sin-Sin hasn't been to Constantinople."

Lutie maintained the stoicism of a Roman matron as the train left the little station. She waved to her sister, tears streaming down her face. Henley kept his arm around her and held her close. Geneva, Nash, and Sumner appeared stunned. Slowly, the enormity of events seeped into their pores.

Nash put his name forward for the cavalry, as did Sumner. Sumner felt sure his engineering degree would prove useful. Even the cavalry needed engineers. T. Pritchard left for Runymeade, Maryland, where he hoped to raise a regiment for the defense of Virginia. Henley also offered his services to the state. Due to his age and the fact that he did not attend military school, it was tactfully suggested that he be a commissary officer. As he would be given the rank of colonel, the sting wasn't so bad, and to Henley's credit, he possessed good powers of organization.

"Your father is making arrangements to ship the best brood mares and stallions to Kentucky." Nash leaned against a pillow.

"Why?" Geneva was incredulous.

"Because if they stay here, they'll be used for cannon fodder, and that will be the end of a lifetime of bloodlines. He's going to give the geldings and average stock to the cavalry."

"Why is he doing it now?"

"Within a few days every train will be used to carry troops. It's now or never."

"Nash, let's not talk about this anymore. We have a few nights left. Kiss me until sunrise."

He did, and they made love with an incendiary passion.

APRIL 14, 1861

Hosea, chapter 13, was the lesson for the morning along with Acts, chapter 3. Lutie found the Hosea passage exceptionally revengeful. After all, making silver and golden idols didn't seem too much worse than making naked statues, and the museums were full of those.

"I will meet them as a bear that is bereaved of her whelps, and will rend the caul of their heart, and there will I devour them like a lion: the wild beast shall tear them."

"O, Israel, thou hast destroyed thyself; but in me is thine help."

Lutie read on. Devout as she was, she never found the Old Testament consoling. But Acts brightened her. She particularly liked the part where Peter spoke to the lame man begging for alms at the temple. "Silver and gold have I none;

but such as I have give I thee: In the name of Jesus of Nazareth rise up and walk."

Miracles pleased Lutie. She'd never seen one. She thought perhaps medical miracles died out with the apostles. Miracles of the heart, yes, she believed in those. She felt the gradual return of her affection for Henley after he had betrayed her those many years ago was a kind of miracle. She never wanted to speak to him again when she found out about his affairs. She recoiled at his touch. How could he lie with other women and then come home to her? She hated him. Hate was too good for him. She'd read in one of her travel books about the Oriental death of a thousand cuts. That's what he deserved. He stopped running around either because he understood how it ripped her to shreds or because he tired of it. But the damage was done. She never again would love Henley as she had when they were new to each other. That she loved him now, though in a muted fashion, was a miracle of the heart.

Imagine saying to St. Peter, she thought, Peter, I have been betrayed. My husband is unfaithful. Can you cure this disease? Somehow she couldn't imagine any of the saints addressing this manner of pain, but they were all men, and Lutie had noticed quite early in her life that men stick together. Why should saints be any different? It never once occurred to Lutie that men might say the same thing about women.

"Mother, you read beautifully." Sumner complimented her after she finished the passage. "I can't imagine getting up with the sun and not hearing your voice. You and Aunt Poofy speak like musical waterfalls."

Lutie reveled, but kept her pride under straps. "I'll speak to Very Reverend Manlius and see if he has an extra copy of the almanac. You can start every day by reading, too."

Sumner, like most sons, loved his mother despite her peculiarities. He could tell her almost anything. He respected his father, but said little to him. "Is it wrong for me to be so excited about war? I want to drive out the invader."

"They haven't invaded yet."

"They will. Mother, it's the spirit of 1776 again, and I'm going to be a part of it."

Lutie closed her Bible. Maybe the Old Testament was bloodthirsty because people are bloodthirsty. Hate, revenge, murder—what a pathetic legacy. "Sumner, why is the fighting so important? You'll be asked to kill people."

His face mottled. "I don't actually think I'll have to kill anybody. I'll be building bridges."

"War means killing. Do you think you're going off to some grand adventure?"

"My God, it's better than sitting around here, one day like the next, one season following the other. It's so relentless."

"Someday, my fine young man, you will pray to great God Almighty for such peace and contentment as we have been blessed with here in these foothills." Lutie was getting heated.

"Mother, I never meant for an instant that you were boring."

"Maybe I am; maybe I've forgotten what it's like to dream the dreams of youth. My dreams were of love, of children, of sumptuous Thanksgivings and Easters, of Christmas pudding and Halloween pumpkins. Simple dreams."

"Do you think we're going to war?"

"We haven't a choice, have we?" She opened and closed her Bible again. "I'm frightened, Sumner, in a way that I've never been frightened before. I've felt desolation and grief. But those were personal sorrows, sorrows that come to everyone when God wills it. They test us, but this is different. This is the sorrow visited upon a people."

"We'll win and that will be the end of sorrow."

"We'll win and the dead will still be dead!" Lutie stood up. Although much smaller than her energetic son, she seemed much taller. "Sumner, I'll be goddamned if I want someone telling me how to live. People like Thaddeus Stevens up there in Washington have the grotesque bad manners to meddle in our affairs. And I'd fight if I could, but don't ask me to celebrate this war or any other war. I will never understand, not even on the day I die and meet our Saviour, why people can't let one another alone. Live and let live, that's my motto."

"Are you sure your mother won't mind that we missed her reading this morning?" Nash asked as he and Geneva rode across the rolling meadows.

"She knows we haven't much time left, and after you all go, she and I will do nothing but spend time together. Mother has her ways, but she's fair."

"We're going to church, so that should satisfy her."

Geneva slowed Gallant, her 16.2-hand, steel-gray gelding to a walk. She stuck in the saddle like a burr. Long legs gave her an advantage, but it was Geneva's hands that made her a superb horseman. She could feel the slightest change in her fingertips, and she possessed that rare ability to make the horse want to please her. By the time Geneva was ten, Henley realized that the gods had granted her a gift with horses. He stopped worrying about her after that. She could ride horses that would kill other riders. She encouraged the timid, calmed the wild, and bent them all to her will.

Nash Hart had known Geneva since they were small, but as he was six years older, he didn't pay much attention to her. Shortly after he graduated from the university, he noticed her on a hunt. He fell in love with her on that day. Gawky and lacking in feminine graces off a horse, she was transformed into a graceful, mesmerizing person on one. He courted her with poetry until he discovered Di-Peachy had to explain it to her. He squired her to the dances and parties in the county. He accompanied her to church as much to please Lutie as Geneva. He applied himself to winning over Henley, who viewed any male in the vicinity of his precious daughter with suspicion. More, he seriously began studying equine husbandry. Success with horses enhanced anyone's reputation throughout the South, and breeding horses wasn't grubby like trade. He'd slit his wrists before he would lower himself or his family name to trade. Still, money had to be made somehow, and this offered hope. He could write poetry in his spare time. He thought it best to keep that to himself.

Sunlight flooded the undulating meadow, fresh with spring grass. "I think of this meadow as the place where the rainbows fell," said Geneva.

"What a beautiful expression, my love. You've a bit of the poetess in you." He leaned over in his saddle and kissed her. Geneva decided not to tell him Di-Peachy said that years ago. She wondered if not telling him was the same as lying. It was such a little thing.

APRIL 15, 1861

Cloudy and cool, the day depressed everyone who hoped that yesterday's warmth was a sign that spring had arrived at last. Sumner and Nash checked their tack.

"I'm taking extra stirrup leathers. They'll break before anything else." Sumner squeezed the soft, thin, well-worn strips of leather.

"I haven't heard anything about firearm specifications, have you?"

"No. I'm taking two pistols, one rifle, and one saber. Put the ammunition on a pack mule, I guess."

"I don't have a saber." Nash stroked his chin.

"Maybe you can buy them at camp."

"What a mess! Do you think the Union is as mixed up as we are?"

"Since most of the senior officers went with the South, I'd say they're all beshit and forty miles from water."

Nash laughed in agreement. "Hard on the women though—running the farms without us."

"They've got the servants. Besides, we'll be home before the frost's on the pumpkin."

"What if the servants run off?" Nash's right eyebrow twitched.

Sumner dropped the blanket in surprise. "What are you saying? You lost your mind? These people will never leave us! They belong to us! They belong to Chatfield!"

"Some do and some don't."

"What are you talking about?"

"Everyone's a little different from everyone else. Some of them are going to shoot out of here on a dark night and run like a scalded dog."

Sumner faced Nash, who disturbed him with unwelcome worry. "You know, Nash, I am beginning to realize there's a lot about you that I don't know."

Nash and Geneva attended Lutie's evening lesson which was 6 Judges: 11–25 and 4 James. Geneva read the lesson tonight. Lutie took faint heart in the story of an angel of the Lord appearing to Gideon at Ophrah and telling him he could drive out the Midianites. When Gideon says, "If now I have found grace in thy sight, then shew me a sign that thou talkest with me." She again plunged into worry. She'd prefer a heavenly sign herself. She was fixing to send off a son, a son-in-law, and a husband. Her brother had already departed as well as her brother-in-law. A sign would do nicely. Still, Judges offered hope. James, chapter 4, with its admonishments against adulterers, seemed tactless in light of her prior experiences. Henley displayed no discomfort during the reading. That was all very well until Geneva reached the part that said, "Whereas ye know not what shall be on the morrow. For what is your life? It is even a vapour, that appeareth for a little time, and then vanisheth away."

Lutie cried, "I don't want to hear about vapours. I want to hear about life everlasting!"

"Mother, that's what it says. It's today's lesson."

"I don't think much of today's lesson, and I fully intend to take up this disturbing matter with Father Manlius."

Sin-Sin, who had been dozing in the rear of the room, awoke and said, "Amen."

Lutie took this to mean her own logic was so moving that even Sin-Sin vociferously agreed. She turned around and bestowed radiance upon Sin-Sin who bestowed it right back.

After the lesson, Lutie and Sin-Sin strolled down the hall together. Sin-Sin wore a dime on a string around her ankle to keep cramps out of her leg. These fluctuations in the weather and the cold dampness drove her wild.

"How's your leg, Sin-Sin?"

"Fine," Sin-Sin lied. She'd never admit one of her cures failed.

"Ernie June fretted herself sick today with her rheumatism."

"Too bad the rheumy don't leave her legs alone and go infect her mouth."

Lutie giggled. "Sin-Sin, we've come out of our Bible reading, and you display no charity for Ernie June. What kind of Christian does that make you?"

"A smart one." Sin-Sin tapped her head. "I don't never hear the name Ernie June in the Good Book. When I does, I'll consider it."

Steam moistened Geneva's nostrils as she gulped her hot chocolate. Expensive and delicious, Geneva preferred this luxury to jewelry, but Lutie assured her that as she grew older, she'd develop a taste for stones. Nash sat across from her in his worn university chair. She slumped down in the rolling arms and cushy seat of a fat chair stuffed with horsehair.

"The Maupin boys joined the infantry. Turners, too. The five Huff brothers signed for the artillery." A slight tone of excitement snuck into his deep voice.

"Jennifer Fitzgerald informed Mother that everyone she knows is sewing uniforms."

"What color, I'd like to know."

"Homespun, I suppose." Geneva savored another rich swallow.

"That makes sense." He exhaled. "Little else does. I'd feel better about going if I knew you were with child."

Geneva's eyes got bigger. "Nash, don't say such a thing. You'll come home, and we'll have lots of babies. I'll throw them like litters. It might take me a while, you know."

He appeared puzzled. No, he didn't know. Was the advent of children yet another female mystery? "I'll attend to that each and every day."

She smiled. "I have little doubt on that score, but I'm not always on time. In fact, I can go months without my friend. There's no rhyme or reason with me about that, but Mother says it's just because I'm young. My insides will settle down later, I suppose."

"You look lovely in your dress and shawl tonight." His eyes glittered.

"You knocked back a whiskey. Anyone looks good then." She teased him.

True, he indulged, but he was working up his courage to tell her about the day after tomorrow. Somehow the prospect of war seemed easier than this.

"Stone sober, I would find you equally alluring." He crossed over to her chair, bent low, and brushed his lips across her hand. Then he turned her hand over and ran his tongue along her palm. "You have a long lifeline." He licked her palm again.

Geneva felt a rush of blood to her temples. Nash held her hand in his left hand, put his right behind her head, and kissed her. "I like seeing you in long dresses. I like imagining what's underneath." He bit her neck. "Let's go upstairs."

In the firelight he slowly undressed her. First he removed the shawl and twirled it around her shoulders. Then he unfastened her dress from behind. When the dress was open, he put his hands on her shoulders and moved the dress downwards so the fabric hung around her waist like petals. He performed the same motion for her silk chemise. He kissed the line of her neck down to her small breasts and then down to her navel. He reached under her petticoats and touched her inner thigh. Then he peeled off the dress and the petticoats, layer after layer. He thought his cock would rip right through the fabric of his trousers.

"Under the covers," he said breathlessly.

He propped the pillows up against the headboard, leaned against it, and placed her on him while he sat upright. He pulled the blankets around her shoulders, then he slid his hands under her buttocks. He liked to feel her tight little ass. As Geneva kissed him, she ran her fingers through the thin line of hair between his pectoral muscles. When Nash came, he had visions of a volcano erupting. It couldn't be this good for other men, he thought. Nothing could be this good.

Cuddling under the covers, he kissed her nose and her eyebrows and her earlobe. He'd avoided telling her as long as he could. "Honey, we're mustering in the day after tomorrow."

She stared at him, speechless.

"The infantry fellows are going to catch a train on April seventeenth, and we're supposed to leave, too."

"Where are you going?"

"No one knows or maybe no one is telling because there might be Northern spies about."

"Does this mean Sumner, too?"

"Yes. I'll take Bumba, of course. He's happy to go. We're taking two mounts each, plus a pack animal and a horse for Bumba and Sumner's man."

"Why don't you take Big Muler? He's near to seven feet tall. He'd be worth his weight in gold."

"I wouldn't take Big Muler to the corner store. He's surly. Besides, Bumba wants to go. He's been my sable playmate since childhood. I can rely on Bumba."

"Do you think I'll have trouble with Muler?"

"If you do, talk to Sin-Sin. She'll walk on down here and put the fear of the Lord in him." True enough, no one messed with Sin-Sin. "Actually, I think Di-Peachy has a bit more to worry about concerning him than you do."

"What do you mean?"

"The boys up at your father's stable were laughing about him. He's laid claim to her. Says if another man touches her, he'll kill him."

"She doesn't want any man, Nash. She told me she'd die before she'd be the slave of a slave."

Nash frowned. "Di-Peachy better come down off her high horse. A woman's got to have a man."

"And a man's got to have a woman." Geneva nibbled his upper lip.

"Yes, thank Jesus!" He kissed her hard.

Geneva lay on top of him, her head between his breasts. "I think I'll die without you."

For a terrible moment he thought he would cry. He couldn't give way. She needed him to bolster her. "I'll be home as soon as I can, if I have to walk every step of the way. I love you, Geneva."

She held him and sobbed.

He never felt more rotten or more loved in his life.

APRIL 16, 1861

Golden bubbles popped in the cast-iron pot. Boyd, Ernie June's fourteen-year-old daughter, called to her mother.

"Corn's boiling."

Ernie leaned over her daughter's ear and whispered low so Tincia, her other helper, would not hear. "Keep stirring, slow down the boil, no big bubbles. And I want you to stir in a handful of sugar and a pinch of cinnamon." She grabbed the expensive, refined sugar and threw it in. Boyd plucked some cinnamon between her fingers and added it to the delicious smelling concoction. Being a political creature, Ernie June then spoke louder for Tincia's understanding. "Girl, don't never want to hear you talkin' 'bout cups and measurements. That don't make a good cook. That make a chemist."

Corn pudding, favored by Sumner, would grace the table tonight. She'd heard the news, the men were leaving tomorrow. Well, Ernie would play her part. Boyd carefully stirred the pudding, and Ernie returned to her two other ovens. One was a huge hearth. She stepped down into it. On either side of the hearth were long bread ovens cut into the stone. With an efficient crew, Ernie could keep the bread ovens humming enough to feed over one hundred guests on special occasions, such as Geneva's wedding. The floor of the hearth Ernie kept in hot ashes. One of her secrets was burying vegetables in the hot ash and then hours later retrieving them. A small, new iron stove also functioned. Ernie thought this wood-burning stove good for coffee, but to her way of thinking, no great cook would dream of roasting meats in such an oven. The griddle was an improvement over the old method, yes, she would admit that, but meats needed an open fire, the flavor controlled by the wood chips and spices

mixed into the fire. Ernie passed these practices on to Boyd as
though administering holy sacraments. Boyd, plump already,
displayed her mother's appetite for culinary distinguishment.

Ambition coursed through Ernie June. As cook of an important estate, she too had power, but not enough. One
obstacle blocked Ernie's ascension: Sin-Sin. As long as Sin-
Sin lived, Ernie couldn't get around her, she could only hold
firmly to her number-two spot. Sin-Sin owned Lutie as much
as Lutie owned Sin-Sin. The fact that Sin-Sin bore a child
that died drew the two even closer together. Hearing the
little girl's pitiful whimpers as she tossed on her straw pallet
was the only time Ernie felt pity for Sin-Sin. When the child
finally left this earth, relieved of its terrible suffering, Sin-Sin
smeared white ash on her face, made pots, and refused to cry.
For one week she kept to her cabin, firing her kiln like a
woman on fire herself. Ernie June lost no time in taking over
Sin-Sin's duties. Sheer ugliness drove Sin-Sin back to life.
She washed her face, walked in the back door of the house,
and took over. Sin-Sin's husband died of the same suffering
some seven years before the little girl. It was a tiredness, an
evil in the blood. Ernie wished Sin-Sin would get it. But
Ernie would outmaneuver Sin-Sin in the long run. She knew
that, because she had two children and Sin-Sin had none.
Boyd would inherit both her mother's cooking ability and
position. Braxton, her oldest son at twenty-two, marked sums
when he wasn't at the stables. Henley perceived the young
man was good with numbers and taught him to keep books.

With both her children in the house or stable and not in the
fields, Ernie expanded slowly. She'd worked too hard to hang
back. She ate the same food the master did and so did her
children. She never stood in line on Saturdays for the rations:
four pounds of wheat flour, one pound of sugar, one pound of
coffee, a peck of corn meal, four or five pounds of pork, a
quart of blackstrap molasses, tobacco, and all the potatoes
and vegetables one could grow in his own garden. Ernie June
would never, ever bend over a patch behind her cottage.
That was for field niggers. If the master ate quail, so did
Ernie June. Not one carrot passed through the kitchen but
what Ernie June did not decide its fate. She was consulted
each time a pig, sheep, or cow was slaughtered.

Yet her greatest power, her left-handed authority, came
when she distributed riches from her kitchen to the other

servants. Ernie June was courted hotly by every black soul, save Sin-Sin and Di-Peachy, on that property, all four thousand acres of it. Sin-Sin knew what Ernie did, but she couldn't cross her on this. Sin-Sin had sense enough to turn a blind eye. However, after such distributions, Sin-Sin would wear Lutie's keys around her waist to remind everyone that she, Sin-Sin, held ultimate power. Ernie hated the jingle of those keys. Like a sixth sense she knew when Sin-Sin was wearing them instead of Lutie. Lutie's gait, light and skipping, rang down the hall. Sin-Sin walked like Napoleon. Someday, someday before she died, Ernie would wear those keys on her belt. And when the mistress designated her, no one, no one would meddle with Ernie June.

Ernie untied her neckerchief and wiped her brow. It was eighty degrees in the kitchen and forty-two outside.

Sin-Sin majestically strolled through the door to the main rooms. "Ernie June, this is a sad supper for the family. Let's keep our feelin's to ourselves tonight."

Pure D hate shot through Ernie. That conniving bitch, coming into her kitchen, telling her that this is a sad night, as if she's a dandelion, but too dumb to know it, and then ordering her how to act. "You tends to your business, Sin-Sin; I tends to mine."

Sin-Sin glared at her and then walked out. Boyd giggled and Tincia laughed. Ernie swelled. She had her troops, by God. Just who would stand beside Sin-Sin when the time came?

Sin-Sin, her ginger cake skin shining and bright, informed Lutie and the others that dinner would soon be ready, and they might want to refresh themselves. Geneva and Nash came through the front door as Lutie, Henley, and Sumner retired to their rooms.

"In time for the fixin's." Sin-Sin smiled.

"Thanks, Auntie." Geneva dutifully pecked her on the cheek. Sin-Sin noted how pale the girl looked. Nash looked peaked himself. Poor babies, she thought, they can't stay together long enough to warm hands.

Conversation stumbled along. Sumner babbled. Henley said little. Nash and Geneva jollied Lutie, who appeared stricken throughout the meal. When the table was cleared, Henley called for the brandy. His toast was simple: "May we serve our nation, our state, and our house with honor." Lutie gulped the fiery brandy, which brought tears to her eyes.

"Ready for the evening lesson, Mother?" Sumner asked.

"I read it before dinner. More Judges. More Gideon. More battles. I'd as soon forget it."

"Well, then, why don't we go into the peach room and enjoy ourselves?" Henley suggested.

The peach room, small with a black marble fireplace, was Henley's favorite room. The walls, covered with peach moire silk, glowed in firelight. It lifted his spirits. Sin-Sin sat in the corner on a hassock, and Di-Peachy threw cherry wood on the fire. Ernie June, enthroned in the kitchen, was not part of these gatherings. She fumed, but brought in a devil's food cake with thick, vanilla icing on it.

"Daddy, tell us about the Harkaway Hunt." Geneva wanted entertainment even as she unconsciously wanted confirmation of what she had seen on the meadows.

Lutie, never one to back off from telling a story complete with embellishments, started, "They ride at dusk, the hour between the dog and the wolf."

Henley took over. "So they say. The Harkaways settled in Albemarle County at the time of the Monacans. Now you know the Monacans were a fierce Indian tribe that simply disappeared from these parts. Not a trace of them was ever found, not even on the other side of the Blue Ridge. But before they vanished, the original Harkaway, a man called Randolph, violated the chief's daughter, a daughter the chief dearly loved. The child was so distraught that she killed herself, and the chief laid a curse on the Harkaways. He said their line would be extinct within three generations. Each male of the line would die a violent death at the hands of a woman, and the clan would ride forever, never to rest and never to capture their quarry."

"Henley," Lutie interrupted, "remember when we went to the Indian dances at the burial grounds in 1840? I think those must have been the descendants of the original Monacans."

"They come through here, big as life, and ast the Coles iffin they could dance." Sin-Sin contributed to the story. That dance caused a sensation in the county, and now everyone alive in 1840 claimed to have witnessed it.

"But what about the ghosts?" Geneva pressed.

"They ride. I know they ride." Lutie spoke quietly. "I saw them the night your brother died, and I don't care what anyone thinks or says about me in this county. I saw them."

Henley added, sounding as judicial as possible, "Many people have seen them or heard them. I've never seen them as has your mother, but I've heard the dogs." He tapped his pipe on the inside of the fireplace. "Of course, one could say I heard any pack of dogs but these gave a mystic tongue, like an old bell."

"And the chief's curse came true. Randolph was murdered in his bed in 1746. His wife said she was visiting a friend but everyone knew she did it. Randolph dallied in the Tidewater." Lutie's voice fell when she mentioned this.

"I don't remember this part of the story." Geneva caressed her husband's strong hand.

"Well, dear, you weren't a married woman then."

"And Casimer, the son, fought valiantly in the Revolutionary War. He was on General Washington's staff. They say Casimer was the handsomest man west of Richmond's boundaries, big and powerful with the chest of a bull. He was the one I saw. It couldn't have been anyone else," Lutie stated matter-of-factly.

"Why is that, Miss Lutie?" Di-Peachy's upper lip twitched slightly.

"Had his shirt open. Rode right up to me. He looked like a piece of Italian sculpture." Lutie enjoyed this part of the memory. "He said, and kindly, too, 'Death is the tribute we owe nature.'"

"He was shot through the head by a woman dressed in black," Henley continued. "His son, Lawrence, lived to about 1797 when he was killed in a duel over a lady of questionable virtue. But legend has it that she fired at him from behind a tree and hers was the killing bullet. So the chief's curse held true. Lawrence left no heirs, male or female, and the line died with him. I never met him, but my father remembered him. Said he was a passionate huntsman of both foxes and women."

"And they hunt with black and tans, a pack started before the Revolutionary War with hounds from the west of Ireland." Nash held Geneva's hand.

Sumner said, "I still think it's a good story for a cold night."

"Jennifer Fitzgerald doesn't believe in the Harkaways," said Geneva.

"Well, anyone who'd marry Big Fitz can be forgiven. She doesn't have a brain. She has a cerebral tentacle." Lutie smiled in delicious malice.

The little group gossiped, indulging in mild backbiting and telling of other tales. No one wanted to leave, but Geneva and Nash, desperate for their last night together, finally broke the spell. Lutie kissed her son-in-law and wished him luck. As they walked to the door, Nash sought out Di-Peachy. "Di-Peachy, please look after my wife for me while I'm gone."

"I will." Di-Peachy's almond-shaped eyes glistened. She wasn't sorry to see Nash go, although she felt sorry for Geneva. It seemed to Di-Peachy that every emotion she had was quickly pulled in the opposite direction by another conflicting emotion.

Lutie lingered by the fire after her daughter left. Time was when recalling the Harkaway Hunt frightened her, but as the years receded, the strange power of that moment would both haunt and illuminate her. What manner of magical events or creatures lurked between our version of reality and the creation of Almighty God, she wondered. Perhaps unicorns, centaurs, and griffins existed side by side with us just like the Harkaways and a tremendous jarring of our ordered existence would open our eyes and we would see them for an instant. Perhaps this war would shake the earth like a mighty earthquake. Who knew what creatures will emerge from the fissures?

"Lutie, I'm going to bed now." Henley placed his pipe in his pocket.

"I'll join you, if you like."

"Yes. I'd like that."

And so Lutie slept beside her husband, a thing she rarely did now since she reserved these nights, in her heart, for Emil. But Henley needed her, and God only knew when she would see him again. She turned under the covers and wrapped her arm around his sagging but still massive shoulders.

In another bed, down the tree-lined drive to the Chatfield estate, Nash and Geneva surrendered themselves to the night's sacraments. They made love with as much hysteria as passion, neither one sleeping and each one feeling the first glimmer of dawn as a knife to the heart.

APRIL 17, 1861

Snow covered the mountains which looked like big, sugared gumdrops. Nash felt even more desolate when he saw them. Bumba knocked softly on the door.

"I'm awake, Bumba."

"Fine." Bumba discreetly left.

Unfurling her heavy robe, Geneva walked to the window. "This is eternal winter. Maybe we'll get snowed in and you won't be able to set foot outside the house. I don't want to be apart from you." She grabbed him. She was strong and squeezed the breath out of him.

"I've got to get ready."

Reluctantly she released him, and he padded down the hall to his dressing room. She flung herself into her own modest dressing room. Ice clogged her water pitcher. She cracked it with a nutcracker hammer. The cold water slapped her awake. She brushed her teeth, washed her private parts, and hurriedly toweled dry. The cold weather was heartless. She walked quickly through her closet, deciding to put on a velvet dress of deep burnt orange. Nash liked her in fancy clothes, and it would keep her warm. She wanted his parting memory of her to be lovely. She combed her thick auburn hair, set it on top of her head, and raced down to the kitchen where Nash was already drinking his coffee. He stood when she entered the room.

"No sunrise shone more radiant than yourself."

She kissed him again and again, oblivious to the servants around her, each trying to prepare the food or take out Nash's satchel and one trunk.

He had wrapped a plaid shawl around himself. She took it off. His uniform startled her.

"Where did you get this?"

"Jennifer Fitzgerald organized the women down at Town Hall. They've been sewing since April thirteenth, night and day, as I hear it."

A tartness crept into her voice. "Why wasn't I told about this?"

"Because we didn't want to upset you, darling."

"I could have sewn the uniform."

"Geneva, look at the braiding on the sleeve. You're not a professional tailor."

"Neither is Jennifer Fitzgerald!"

"The ladies performed the cutting, and the tailors put on the colors, the braidings, and so forth. See, I even have a stripe on my trousers."

"You look very handsome." She choked back a sob. The uniform somehow made the war real. "Shall we enjoy our breakfast?"

Waffles and molasses languished on Geneva's plate. Nash gobbled his food.

"How will I write to you? Where will you be?" Geneva's voice forced through her constricted throat.

"As soon as we're quartered, I'll get word to you. Don't worry, Geneva. The Yankees aren't going to attack anytime soon. They're probably as disorganized as we are." He paused. "Thank God."

"Do you know where you're going?"

"Not exactly."

Bumba, smart-looking in tight breeches, a heavy woolen jacket, and a cape, came into the kitchen from outside. "Everything's ready."

The sound of hoofbeats came through the open kitchen door with the cold. Bumba shut the door. Nash rose, drained his coffee cup, and put it down so forcefully it broke. "I'm sorry." He was embarrassed at his own nervousness.

"Break it all." Geneva smiled at him. He threw his arms around her and kissed her with all his might. "I will come home. Don't worry."

She hung on to him and sobbed. Bumba turned away. He nodded to the men outside. "Master."

Nash straightened himself. "Yes, of course."

Bumba handed him his Remington pistol and holster. Nash strapped it on. He snatched a navy greatcoat from a peg on the wall and threw it over his shoulders. Geneva could see outside the kitchen window that her father and brother waited. "Let me walk you outside."

He kissed her again, then they pushed open the door.

Sumner smiled at his sister. He, too, was in a uniform. The facings of his frock coat were bright yellow. Henley's cuffs and collar were a soft blue.

"Little sister, you'll catch your death!"

She raced over and kissed him, and then turned to her father, stiffly bent over. "Daddy, why are you wearing light blue on your sleeves and collar when Nash and Sumner are in yellow?"

"Theoretically, I'm in the infantry. They're in the cavalry."

"Just remember, I'm an engineer in the service of the cavalry!" Sumner burst with enthusiasm.

Geneva lifted her face up to her father, who seemed in his uniform as gray as the sky. "You won't fight, will you?"

"Only if I have to, sweet lamb. But don't fret over it. Look at me. I'm fifty. My eyes aren't too sharp, and I've been given strict orders to find and transport provisions. I think I'll be denied the whiff of gunpowder." Slight regret laced his deep, resonant voice.

Bumba gave Nash a leg up and then joined Sumner's servant with the string of extra horses and the two pack mules.

Henley gravely instructed his daughter. "See to your mother. You are her strength now."

"Yes, Daddy." She bowed her head. The tears wouldn't hold back.

"Geneva, we'll all be back by fall. Don't cry. This is the most exciting thing to happen to me in my entire life! I wish you could come too!" Sumner thought this viewpoint consoling.

Her eyes glittered. "So do I." She put her hand on her husband's boot. Supple, he leaned down and kissed her one last agonizing time.

"What's to become of us?" she cried.

Nash said gently, "Some things are in the hands of God. We're like dice thrown on the plains of destiny." With that he wheeled and trotted away, not looking back. Henley and Sumner followed. Geneva watched until the mist and the snow swallowed them up. Half-frozen, she went back into the house and cried until she thought she'd throw up.

*   *   *

As the men rode toward town, other men joined them, riding down the long country roads from their estates. Poorer residents of Albemarle County walked toward the train station. Sumner, joyous, chattered with friends, then mindful that he would soon be separating from his father, rejoined Henley and Nash who headed this scraggly, ever swelling column. The sun, pale and loitering, offered no warmth. The snow slowed. Sumner reached in his greatcoat and pulled out Darling Fanny Pan Cake. He cut a plug of this Myers Brothers tobacco and popped it into his mouth.

"Sumner, gentlemen smoke tobacco. They don't chew it," Henley chided.

Sumner, now in the army, such as it was, didn't feel like taking any more orders from his father. "It calms my nerves. Besides, how can I get a light on horseback?"

Henley frowned. "What do you have to be nervous about, my boy? You have no rank, and therefore, you have no responsibility."

Stung, Sumner replied, "If I earn a rank, I'll accept it. We all decided to go in as privates."

Henley couldn't fathom why most of the sons of good families chose this path. Any man who had attended military school automatically received a junior officer's rank. Any man formerly in the United States Army retained his rank. In Henley's day, a scion enlisting could depend upon automatically being granted a lieutenancy. Now it was fashionable to be on the bottom of the heap. He shrugged his shoulders and ignored his son.

Sumner, determined not to let his father whittle him down, pressed on. "I'll finish this war as a captain, the hard way."

Henley turned slightly in his saddle to look at the set face chewing his Darling Fanny Pan Cake. "I hope so." The braid of colonel gleamed on his sleeve and so did the three stars on his narrow collar band. Henley, not a military man, gladly accepted his status as senior officer. He needed weight in order to force some of these tight farmers and sly merchants to comply. He assumed that the government, once settled, would commandeer the railroads. He also needed authority over engineers, switchmen, and the riffraff that ran the trains. Rank was his only protection.

Sumner, so like his sister in many ways, bore no resemblance at all to Geneva when it came to responsibility. Sumner, groomed to inherit a great house and a great stable, dallied with ladies of Richmond. He was happier throwing up a rough bridge over a friend's creek or dancing all night than learning the rigor of scientific breeding and the management of an estate. Why Henley had to sit on him for three months just last year to get him to go to Kentucky to buy yearlings. Geneva, on the other hand, soaked up horse genealogies. Henley only had to tell her once. Her gift as a rider was the most remarkable talent Henley had ever seen. A pity Geneva was a woman. She couldn't race, but she could train them at home. That was some consolation. He thought about changing his will before leaving today, but Sumner and Geneva loved one another. He found no fault with his son there. Sumner was a devoted brother. The children would never fight over the disposition of their inheritance. Sumner would care for Lutie if anything happened to him. God knows, the boy loved his mother. Natural, he supposed. Fathers and sons look out the same window but don't see the same tree.

Nash noticed the sudden pallor on Sumner's face under his father's scrutiny. The loud and cheerful arrival of Greer Fitzgerald, Jennifer Greer Fitzgerald's son, turned his attention away from the Chatfields. Greer rode up and down the line of men, shouting, whooping, slapping hands. He stopped short of Henley and saluted, then rode a trifle more quietly.

When they reached the outskirts of town, Henley bid his son, son-in-law, and friends good-bye. The men assigned to cavalry units, not yet named or numbered, turned north and rode toward Culpeper. Nash grumbled that they could have been loaded on a train; after all, this was 1861. The Culpeper train station was at least two days away, even riding at a reasonable pace.

Henley split off and rode into the town, which was buzzing with morning activity. At the station he handed over his mount to Timothy, one of the young stable boys he had brought along with him, and told him to return home to Lutie. He gave the boy money to buy a large box of sweets for Lutie. Timothy, a reliable twelve-year-old, would spare the candied peaches but demolish the chocolate. Henley, remembering Timothy's weakness, rewarded him with two dollars to thoroughly indulge himself. The boy, thankful, pressed Henley's hand and wished him a safe journey.

The small train station crawled with young men in various, ill-coordinated uniforms. Noise bounced off the walls. Henley accepted a few salutes with the air of one accustomed to deference. Their urgency for excitement would be fulfilled within twenty-four hours. Henley knew these boys would be loaded on a train headed for Harper's Ferry. A secret communication from John Letcher, the governor, informed Henley about this. This was a courtesy due him as one of the senior officers in Albemarle. The legalities and formalities of secession as well as declaring war were not yet on paper, but Letcher, an intelligent man, grasped the importance of seizing the arsenal at Harper's Ferry. The South's supplies of ball, cannon, gunpowder, and artillery were nil. Letcher said, "Go." These boasting, high-spirited young men were going to do just that, unbeknownst to them. The authorities in Richmond tapped out false telegrams declaring the destination of the train as the Portsmouth Navy Yard.

When Henley finally boarded a train heading east for Richmond, he looked back at the youths crowded on the platform and wondered who would be alive tomorrow night. He slumped in his seat. He lied to his wife. He knew the war would never be over by the fall. Henley had spent too much time in Boston, New York, and Philadelphia not to understand what Northern industrial might would mean in a conflict. All we want to do is be left alone, he mused. Why in God's name won't they let us go in peace? We can be good neighbors.

These thoughts still haunted Henley Chatfield as he arrived at the Spotswood Hotel at the southeast corner of Eighth and Main Streets in Richmond. Without washing up he made his way to the capitol building. He suffered few illusions. He would choke in red tape, bureaucratic vanities, younger men hungry for name and fame, older men tired and irritable, all of them the woop and warf of politics. It was a game Henley Chatfield despised. But his country needed him, so if that meant working side by side with baboons, he was prepared to do it. Chatfields accept and discharge duty; they do not evade it.

The throng of people outside the governor's office seemed tighter than the Gordian knot. Henley edged into it. Gregory Lawson, an old friend, shouted over the heads of others, "Chatfield, you're here!" He pulled Henley outside the antechamber and handed him scribbled pages. The proclamation wasn't even typeset. When Henley read it, he felt that he had been handed a thunderbolt. Instinctively his right hand rubbed his chest. The repeal of the ratification of the United States Constitution was short and to the point. As the Constitution was ratified on 25 June, 1788, so it was dissolved on April 17, 1861, awaiting ratification by the voters of Virginia on the fourth Thursday in May. Henley read in disbelief. Of course, these things needed to be tied up, written down, but why did it hurt when the ordinance declared that the federal government had perverted its powers. Perverted? Well, if we are going to war, I guess we need strong words, he thought.

Henley handed the scrawl back to Gregory. "The western counties will go."

Gregory shouted above the din, "I think so, too."

"I've got to get as many supplies out of there as I can while they're still under the laws of Virginia." Henley ran his fingers through his thick, gray hair. "Who will command the armies of Virginia?"

"We haven't anyone yet."

"Jesus H. Christ on a raft."

The fact that 120,000 followers of the two Midianite Kings Zebah and Zalmunna were killed by the sword and the remaining 15,000 were pursued by Gideon and his scant band of three hundred men failed to cheer Lutie. Given that the North boasted a much bigger population than the South, Lutie might have drawn a parallel. Instead, she snapped her Bible shut and glared at Sin-Sin.

"Don't be rough with the Good Book. Your voice would soothe all the givin' saints."

"Flattery is a vice, Sin-Sin, and you're riddled with it." Nonetheless, Lutie read John, chapter 2, which was an improvement. This time Christ threw the money changers out of the temple.

"I likes that. I likes when Marse Jesus fluffs his feathers."

"Still, it's so full of anger and violence. What a bloodthirsty book this is. I really must take this up with the Very Reverend Manlius."

"I don't know how the Reverend keeps all that knowledge in his little head."

"He does have a little head, doesn't he?" Lutie put the book down. She peered out the window. "At least the snow's melting. I guess Henley's in Richmond by now. Always a little warmer there." She sighed and started to say something but changed her subject. "Geneva's worked seven horses since this morning."

"Got no sleep. Looks like a raccoon."

Lutie's delicate, small fingers touched her own face. "I didn't sleep much either. Do you know, Sin-Sin, there's not a man in this house? Not one. Poof! Gone."

"They be back."

"After breakfast I found myself in the library breathing great gulps of air. Henley's pipe tobacco lingers there. Eventually the odor will disappear. I hated it when he smoked in the house. Now I miss it."

Lutie strode into the kitchen with Sin-Sin close behind her. Ernie June and Boyd were sifting flour. Tincia washed pots. Ernie smiled at Lutie. Sin-Sin folded her hands across her breast. Ernie refused to acknowledge Unredeemable Sin.

"Ernie June, I'd like to ask your advice about something."

"Yes, ma'am." Ernie gloated. Her advice!

"There's no point in that ancient-of-days cooking for Geneva. Nash brought precious little to this marriage other than his undying devotion for my daughter—and the new house, of course. I'm going to strongly encourage my daughter to move back up here. If I do that, I can't discharge that poor cook, Granville. She can barely see. Might you find some use that won't tax her or make her feel out of place?"

Ernie pretended to turn this over in her mind. "I can gives her sittin' duties."

"I knew you'd think of a solution, Ernie." Lutie beamed.

Ernie swelled like a frog about to croak. Sin-Sin wanted to poke her in the gut and say, "Blow it out, lardguts."

Lutie swept out of the kitchen to the hall. She put on her navy blue coat, her everyday coat with the worn sleeves and shiny elbows. Sin-Sin grabbed her heavy scarlet shawl and ambled out. The two women headed for the stable, the light snow crunchy underfoot in the shade and sloppy in the sunshine.

"Geneva won't come back to the house," Sin-Sin observed.

"How do you know?"

"She's mistress of a house."

Lutie slowed. "But it's so much more practical for us to live together."

"Maybe Di-Peachy can honey her into it."

"Geneva can listen to her own mother."

"Since when?"

Lutie shot her a glance. Sin-Sin took the hint.

The stable boys huddled inside the tack room. Only Geneva and Lorenzetto, a small-boned young man, worked outside.

Lorenzetto saw Lutie and Sin-Sin before Geneva. He bowed to Lutie, who rarely came to the stable. His eyes twinkled. "Auntie Sin-Sin, you look good in red."

"You make a girl's heart beat faster." Sin-Sin favored the boy. She favored his father even more.

"Mother, Auntie, you'll catch cold."

"That's why I'm here—to see that you don't."

"I'm fine, Mother."

"You're not fine. Looks like you rubbed a pencil under your eyes. You've suffered a sad jolt. Come on, let the boys finish up here, and you come back to the house."

"I've got the dun to ride."

Sin-Sin glowed in Lorenzetto's direction. "You can do it, can't you?"

"Oh, yes, Auntie!" Lorenzetto wanted the chance to work the hot-blooded dun.

"I really should be here."

"Geneva," Sin-Sin commanded, "you'll do your mother no good by getting sick, and when your husband hears about it, he'll be worried to death. Now git!"

Geneva allowed as how Sin-Sin was right. She handed the reins to Lorenzetto. He sprang on the animal like a cricket. Lutie and Sin-Sin flanked the tired, young woman and walked her back to the house. As she stepped inside the door, she broke into uncontrollable sobs.

Lutie wrapped her arms around her. "There, there, honey, this is hard for you. Come on now. Come on." She nodded at Sin-Sin, who made for the kitchen.

"Ernie June!"

"Sin-Sin, I ain't deaf."

"Mix up a hot toddy for Miz Geneva and make it a strong one."

Before Ernie could snarl, Sin-Sin was in the main room where Lutie had the distraught young woman on a davenport. Di-Peachy, who was packing her own things upstairs, hurried down. At the sight of her friend, Geneva burst out again. "He'll die! Five days, that's all we had. I can't live without Nash!"

Di-Peachy sat at the foot of the davenport and massaged Geneva's cold feet while Lutie managed to get her boots off. Lutie patted her hands. Sin-Sin put a plaid throw over her cold legs.

"What'll I do?"

"Courage, my darling. Courage. Men have their brand and we women have ours." Lutie fought back her own tears.

"Miss Lutie, do I have permission to play the harp? I think we'll all feel a little better if I do."

The golden harp resting on her shoulder, Di-Peachy played a short Mozart piece that Geneva liked, and soon she stopped crying.

Ernie June delivered the hot toddy. Sin-Sin started to take it from her, but Ernie turned her shoulder and brushed by her. "Miz Geneva, here's something to warm you on up."

Geneva swallowed the huge hot toddy like a greedy child. Since she'd eaten nothing that day, it hit her with the force of a sledgehammer. Before she dropped off, she murmured, "I can't live like this, Momma. I'd rather die with Nash than live without him." Lutie held her hand until she fell asleep.

"Poor baby." Sin-Sin stood up. "Blankets." She left for the linen closet and returned with blankets and a pillow. Lutie and Sin-Sin arranged these items to their satisfaction. Di-Peachy continued to play.

"She'll be herself by tomorrow morning," Lutie said, assuring herself as much as the others.

APRIL 18, 1861

Geneva awoke, miserable with a headache. Was she going blind? The world looked pitch. She groaned and noticed a layer of scarlet and gold embers in the fireplace. A grumble on the floor startled her. She reached down and touched Di-Peachy's beautiful rump.

Geneva listened as Di-Peachy rolled over on the floor. She'd slept with the sound of that breathing from infancy. Odd that she didn't miss Peaches one bit when she slept with Nash. Nash. My God, where was he? Maybe he was shot. Maybe a marauding Northerner wanted to start his own personal war. He crossed the Potomac and—she sat upright. I can't live without Nash. I've got to go to him. If he dies, then I'll die with him.

The exquisite grandfather clock, carefully shipped over from England in 1727, ticked in the grand foyer. Night's silence enlarged the ticktock. Ticking away the minutes of my husband's life, Geneva thought.

She crawled over the end of the davenport. Another cold night. She wrapped a blanket around her. How could Di-Peachy sleep? She peeked over at the curled form on the floor. My husband could be dying, and she's asleep. Geneva walked across the foyer, the black and white marble nearly freezing her feet. The clock said 4:10. A first quarter moon smiled on the top of the clock face. She scampered into the kitchen, each footstep splitting open her head.

Ernie June would pitch a fit if she knew Geneva fiddled around her kitchen. Well, Ernie June could shut up as well as talk. Geneva figured her headache was more important than getting one of Ernie's precious pans out of place. She poked into the huge hearth. A small flame licked up through the

ashes. She pitched on some kindling. Within fifteen minutes
a decent fire warmed her blue toes. She ransacked the kitchen
until she found a small coffeepot, but she realized to her
dismay she'd have to stick it on the top of the new cast-iron
stove. Geneva clanged and clattered. Why did Lutie indulge
Ernie June with this contraption? Ernie June could hang a
coffeepot over the hearth as easily as mess with this monster.
Bitching furiously under her breath, Geneva slowly figured
out how to get a fire going in the stove. She ground up beans,
put the sweet-smelling coffee into the tin container, dropped
it into the coffeepot, and slapped it on top of the stove. If
only Sin-Sin would come to work early. Sin-Sin carried the
cure for everything. Geneva pulled up a ladderback chair and
waited by the fire for her coffee. She wondered if anyone
ever died of a headache. She might be the first.

The smell of coffee snatched her from depressing reveries
about her death, Nash's death, the hellacious boredom of
staying in Albemarle County while a war was being fought.
The coffee perked so quickly that Geneva considered revis-
ing her opinion of the new stove.

She heaped honey in her coffee. The bees of Chatfield
produced vats of clover honey. One swallow of coffee jolted
her stomach into awareness. She hadn't eaten in a day and a
half. She gulped down the coffee, poured herself more, then
poked around the pantry for food. Sugar cookies big as pan-
cakes, cured ham, and yesterday's bread tasted better than
her wedding feast. Geneva ate standing up in the pantry,
then realizing she would not die from headache or starvation,
she carried the food to the long, smooth maple table in the
middle of the kitchen.

She tossed hickory wood on the fire, and it smelled like a
barbecue. Geneva felt alone in the entire world. The darkness outside the kitchen, the quiet of the house seemed to
seal her inside. A scratch at the outside door startled her. She
got up and opened it. Cazzie, a huge tortoiseshell cat, pranced
in, a mangled rodent in her jaws.

"For me?"

Cazzie purred triumphantly. Geneva, not without some
malice, decided to let the remains desecrate Ernie's kitchen.
Both she and Cazzie would vacate the premises before Ernie
marched in with the ever present Boyd. Ernie hated rodents.
This ought to send her through the roof.

Cazzie graced Geneva's lap while Geneva fed her bits of ham.

The door to the dining room swung open. Eyes half-open, Di-Peachy shuffled to the coffeepot and drained the contents. Di-Peachy glared at the paltry sum of liquid. "Selfish."

"How was I supposed to know you'd wake up?"

"You know the smell of coffee always wakes me up—that and the fact that it sounded like a blacksmith was working in here."

"This stove, have you examined this piece of work?" Geneva pointed to the stove even as she was making another pot of coffee for Di-Peachy and herself.

"No, but I see a piece of work on the floor over there." Di-Peachy indicated Cazzie's prize. "Ernie June'll turn white." The cat ignored this comment and continued to eat ham bits.

They laughed while Geneva poured coffee for both of them. The sugar cookies disappeared along with half the ham. All the more reason to get out of here before Ernie June arrived.

"I don't know where Nash is."

"He knows where you are. That's something." Di-Peachy couldn't fathom Geneva's carrying on about her husband. As near as she could figure, love was a disease shared by two.

"Don't get smart, Di-Peachy. I hate it when you're smart. Also, I've got a headache."

"Bet Lutie's got powders around here somewhere."

"I'll ask her when she gets up."

"There won't be any fighting for some time, Geneva. Don't worry."

"But I'm so lonesome," Geneva wailed. "I'm going to join him."

"That's wonderful. I'm going to be appointed Secretary of War for the Confederacy." Di-Peachy licked her fingers and picked up spilled sugar crystals from the table.

"I'm going." Geneva's lower lip jutted forward.

Di-Peachy stared her in the eyes. "Now look here, girl, stop this foolishness about going to see Nash. Other women are in the same boat you are."

"They don't love their husbands the way I love Nash." Geneva breathed passion. "I've thought it over. I know I can't go as a woman. I'll enlist as a man."

"You are out of your mind!"

Geneva's eyes narrowed. That was never a wise phrase to use at Chatfield. "Don't count on it!"

"You can't do this."

"I can ride better than any man in this county. Better than any man in the state of Virginia! You can cut my hair."

"You haven't got a beard. Your voice is high. They'll laugh you right out of camp!"

"Not when they've seen me ride. The South needs every one of her sons, even the boys."

Di-Peachy, dumbstruck, stared at Geneva. She was tall and lanky. Her breasts were very small. If she cut her hair like she said and rubbed some dirt on her face—well, it was possible but crazy.

"I'll say I'm eighteen, which is true. They'll think I'm lying and about fourteen. But they'll take me—once I find Nash's regiment, that is."

"You can't do this to your mother."

"My mother has Sin-Sin and you, so she'll be fine. Mother has her marriage and I want mine!" Geneva displayed no charity on this point.

"What makes you think Nash will go along with it?" Di-Peachy slowly began to believe Geneva. "If I were your husband, I wouldn't let you fight a war because I loved you."

"You haven't felt what Nash and I feel. He needs me."

"Don't be surprised if he sends you back."

"He won't. No one can make me do what I don't want to do!" The defiance in Geneva's face was the defiance of the South.

"Someone has to run your house and this house."

"Mother and Sin-Sin can run anything. You can take charge of my house."

"Geneva, this is crackbrained. Even if you get away with it, why risk being killed?"

"My place is with my husband. I took a vow before God, man, and my entire family: 'In sickness and in health, for richer or for poorer, for better or for worse until death us do part.'"

That was hard to fight. Di-Peachy folded her hands. Geneva was dead set on going. Di-Peachy couldn't change her mind, so she might as well make the best of it and help. "Let's get out of here before Ernie comes in. It's dawn."

The morning lesson was Judges 9: 1–22. Gideon finally

died but not without leaving behind seventy sons. Fortunately, this excess of progeny was not the work of one worn-out woman. Gideon disported himself amongst many wives. The Bible neglected to say how he maintained his energy. Apparently, the wives proved insufficient and he carried on with a concubine who bore him a son, Abimelech. So when Gideon went to his heavenly reward, exhausted by these earthly labors, Abimelech, no fool, killed the legitimate sons except for Jotham, the youngest son, who hid himself. Jotham, after registering complaint once out of danger, ran to a place called Beer. That's where the lesson ended and Sin-Sin wondered if beer came from Beer.

Sin-Sin wore a string of briars around her neck to keep the chills off. As an added precaution, she put red peppers in her shoes. She enjoyed the Bible readings. If Gideon could have himself a passel of wives, she could have herself a passel of husbands. Sin-Sin liked men. She had sense enough to keep this happy idea to herself ever since Lutie had lost her delight in the male sex two decades past. Sin-Sin walked through the hallway thinking what a pity that was. God made men and women to enjoy one another, and Lutie just closed down, pulling in the shutters.

Loud cursing in the kitchen brought Sin-Sin and Lutie running. Geneva and Di-Peachy had disappeared after the morning lesson.

"Miz Lutie, Miz Lutie, I been mocked!" Ernie's eyes bugged out, making her look like a locust.

"What seems to be the problem, Ernie June?"

"I finds a rat. Well, I cleans that up." Of course, Boyd cleaned it up. Ernie wouldn't touch the thing. "Now I finds half my ham gone. The one I cured with brown sugar! My cookies been et up! I won' stan' for it!"

Lutie, senatorial, said, "I don't blame you for a moment, Ernie. I have no idea how a rat found its way into the kitchen."

"Horrible. Head chewed to bits!"

Lutie flinched a bit. "How awful for you, Ernie June."

Ernie lapped up the sympathy.

"As for the foodstuffs, I believe Geneva must have gotten up in the middle of the night. You know how terrible yesterday was for her. She didn't eat a morsel. She probably couldn't help herself."

"Coffee on my new stove!"

"I'm sure you understand, Ernie. These little moments happen to all of us."

Ernie, having vented her spleen, settled herself. "Poor thing, losin' her man without hardly knowin' him."

"Maybe she's better off," Lutie blurted out.

Both Sin-Sin and Ernie June laughed. Then they saw one another laughing and stopped.

"Girls, don't you dare repeat a word I just said." Lutie's hand flew to her mouth.

Naturally, Sin-Sin and Ernie June would tell every other woman on the place. A comment like that was too good to keep to oneself.

"Not one word," Ernie promised.

"Uh-huh," Sin-Sin agreed.

Nash's clothing dotted the room. Geneva and Di-Peachy searched for items Geneva could wear: socks, underwear, shorts. Geneva wanted to ride off this instant. Di-Peachy hammered some sense into her head. She had to talk to her mother, no matter how much she wanted to avoid it.

As Geneva was six feet tall, taller than her husband, his pants came slightly above her ankles. The shirts fit.

"I'll go into town and see if I can't get parts of a uniform, anyway. I can get a cap. They cost two dollars."

"How do you know that?" Geneva asked.

"Sumner."

"I'm still mad that everyone kept their preparations from me."

"They thought it best."

Geneva pulled her boots out of the wardrobe. "Better take two pair." She sat on the floor and scanned the debris. "Let's pick this up and then cut my hair."

Di-Peachy cried as each lock of thick hair fell from Geneva's head. Geneva wasn't fazed. "Stop crying. It'll grow back."

"Hair is a woman's crowning glory."

"I'm not a woman anymore." Geneva smiled.

"I don't think that's funny. You could get killed."

"I can also die getting out of bed in the morning! Keep cutting."

While doing as she was told, Di-Peachy continued to talk.

"You could have at least waited until after you told your mother. This will kill her, Geneva."

"No, it won't. She'll run upstairs or walk out to the back meadows and unburden herself to Emil. For the first time in my life, I'm grateful to Emil!"

"Sometimes, Geneva, you can be cruel."

"Sometimes, Di-Peachy, you can be a pain in the ass."

"Your mother is very high-strung."

"My mother is soft as a grape."

"I don't know how you can talk like that about your own mother."

"Since when do you walk on water? She's never been warm to you. What do you care?"

Di-Peachy considered this. Lutie was never ugly or hateful to her. She didn't especially criticize but she didn't praise. Di-Peachy wanted Lutie to like her. She never knew her own mother. No one, not even Geneva, could worm out of Lutie and Henley any information about Di-Peachy's mother. For mothering, Di-Peachy turned to Sin-Sin. Sin-Sin and Geneva were her two points of emotional reference. Henley was kind but he was distant to everybody but Geneva. Di-Peachy answered Geneva's question with another question. "What about your father?"

"We won't tell him."

"You expect your mother to lie to him?"

"No, I expect her to say nothing to him. She's been doing that for years."

"I hate to lie to him."

"Someone has to!"

"The servants will talk." Di-Peachy was stubborn.

"No one will know but you. I'm not leaving this room except in the dead of night. Not even Auntie Sin-Sin will know. You bring Mother here. I'd rather talk to her in my house anyway. And when it's dark, bring me Gallant and Dancer. I'll ride out. No one will know the difference."

The last strand of long hair hit the floor. Di-Peachy worked another twenty minutes shaping Geneva's hair. Finished, she put her hands on her hips.

Geneva got up and looked at herself in the mirror. Stunned, she mumbled, "I look just like Daddy."

"Yeah, I guess you do."

Geneva inspected herself. She threw on Nash's shirt. "I'll pass. I'm going to do it!" She was jubilant.

Di-Peachy felt wretched. "I think you just might."

That afternoon Di-Peachy collected what odds and ends she could from the ladies at Town Hall. She paid twelve dollars for a short jacket with yellow facings on the sleeve and collar to indicate cavalry. Jennifer Fitzgerald and the ladies had only made one greatcoat, so Di-Peachy bought it just in case. That put her back twenty-five dollars. She lied and said it was for Sumner. The shirts went for three dollars apiece, but Di-Peachy thought some of Nash's shirts would suffice. The color combinations were as confusing to Di-Peachy as anyone else. Someone better come forward soon or Jennifer Fitzgerald and her seamstresses would write up army regulations for dress. Trousers were light blue and nine dollars. Di-Peachy figured two pair of Nash's black pants would be as good as blue. After all, Geneva could tire of her charade and why be out all that money? Di-Peachy was naturally tight.

She piled the goods in the light, two-wheeled gig, painted bright red and gold. When she picked up the reins and lightly touched the whip on Exeter's brown rump, the little cart jerked upward and off they went. The town, quiet on a typical day, hummed with people. About one mile out of town and four from Chatfield, she spotted the enormous form of Big Muler walking alone on the road. She stopped for him.

"Come on."

He squeezed all seven feet of him next to her and proceeded to stare at her. Peaches hated that so she chatted as best she could. "If I'd have known you were coming into town, I'd have given you a ride."

"Sin-Sin gave me an order for Reddy. Just pushed me right out the door. Don't need no pass in the daytime. I likes that."

Di-Peachy agreed. At night, the servants needed passes to leave the estates. Patrollers, called patters, swept the county searching for wandering or runaway slaves.

Big Muler, carved from obsidian, said nothing more. Di-Peachy realized that this giant was awestruck by her. For some strange reason, she wanted to laugh.

While Big Muler reported to Sin-Sin, Di-Peachy dropped off the clothing at Geneva's house. She then squared her shoulders, walked in the big house, and told Lutie that her daughter wanted to see her. Lutie thought it perfectly ridiculous that Geneva wouldn't walk up the hill, but finally she relented and strolled down to the house.

As Lutie entered the small foyer, Geneva came down the stairs in her bits and pieces of uniform, her wrists sticking out of the sleeves.

Lutie, speechless, beheld this apparition. Geneva looked like her father as a young man, just slightly more feminine.

"Mother, I'm going to war." Geneva took the offensive. "And, no, I am not crazy."

Lutie exploded, "In the house of the hanged man don't mention rope, and what in God's name have you done to your beautiful hair!"

"I'm joining Nash. This way I can pass myself off as a boy."

"Your hair! Your beautiful hair!" Lutie almost said, "it's the only beautiful thing about you, but she bit her tongue. Even in her shock she had some control. Lutie walked into the living room.

Di-Peachy shrugged her shoulders at Geneva and followed after Lutie. "Miss Lutie, would you care for something to drink?"

"A good stiff shot of gin would do wonders, thank you."

Di-Peachy retired to fetch the drink. Geneva, amazed at her mother's sudden calmness, joined her in the front room. "I can't live without Nash, Mother."

"So I gather." Lutie folded her hands.

"I love him. I never felt anything—"

"You needn't explain. I once loved your father like that."

The idea of Henley and Lutie sharing a passion as scorching and pure as Geneva and Nash's seemed ludicrous to Geneva. She decided not to pursue that subject. Di-Peachy came in and handed Lutie her drink. She then excused herself.

"I'm pleased you're so understanding, Mother."

"I don't know if I am. But I know I can't stop you. I'll be without my husband, my son, my son-in-law, and now my daughter."

"Sin-Sin's here."

"Yes, thank God."

"And Di-Peachy."

Lutie squirmed. "I expect she'll handle your affairs."

"She does, anyway. May she call upon you if she needs anything?"

Lutie assessed her daughter then spoke crisply. "Why not? Haven't I been good to her in the past?"

"You've never really cared for Di-Peachy, Mother. She's been my shadow since I was born, it seems."

"Let's just say you can get but only so close to the help. You young people do things differently than we did. Sin-Sin and I are respectful of one another. I know what it's like to feel gratitude and affection for a servant, but you and Di-Peachy act as though there are no boundaries between you. You must preserve your position, Geneva. Perhaps you're too young to understand what position means."

"She's my friend."

"She's not your friend; she's your servant."

"She's my friend!" Geneva spilled over with anger. "I was never what you wanted, Mother. You wanted a beautiful, golden daughter. Look at me. I'm not very pretty, but at least it means I can join my husband. No one will mistake me for a lavish female."

Since Geneva brought it up, Lutie plunged in. "Beauty is a gift from God. Apparently He favored Di-Peachy over all the women of the earth. One can neither take credit nor accept blame for beauty, but one can act like a lady. All you want to do is ride horses—and now that you have Nash, you follow after him like a penny dog."

"I love him!"

"Good!" Lutie pounced on 'good.' "But let me give you some motherly advice, not that you'll listen. Love makes the time pass and time makes love pass." Lutie knocked back her gin. "When are you leaving?"

"Tonight when everyone's asleep."

"How will you find him?"

"I figure he's at Culpeper or Harper's Ferry."

"How do you figure that?"

"Well, the wires said that we took Harper's Ferry but the Federals destroyed the arsenal. Di-Peachy heard that in town this afternoon. I know Nash and Sumner rode north. So I figure they've got to be wherever there's a good railway junction or some action. Besides, once I get on the road, all I have to do is ask."

"I see while I've been worrying, you've been thinking."

Lutie sighed, sounding like her sister Poofy. "I hope you come to your senses and turn around."

"I want to be with my husband, and I want to see what's going on."

"You're not afraid?"

"No. I believe in Fate."

"So do I." Lutie was surprised that she didn't feel more surprised now that the jolt of seeing a shorn Geneva had worn off. "I suppose you don't want anyone to know about this."

"No. I can't take the chance of word getting out in my regiment, whatever regiment that might be."

"Your brother will recognize you."

"Let's hope I recognize him first."

After twelve midnight, Geneva kissed her mother goodbye. Lutie had stayed at the house for the rest of the day and had even helped Di-Peachy pack Geneva's saddlebags. Lutie retrieved one of Henley's new Colt pistols from the big house. Mounted, Geneva looked like a cavalryman. She leaned over and kissed a crying Di-Peachy, then waved and rode off, swallowed by the faint light.

Lutie started to walk up to the main residence but Di-Peachy asked her to wait. She got a lantern and walked Lutie up the hill.

"Miss Lutie, I thought you'd put up a fight."

"Nothing could stop her. She's in the grip of an emotion I've almost forgotten and you've not yet felt."

"Did she tell you about the Harkaway Hunt?"

"No," Lutie said, filled with curiosity.

"The eve of her wedding we both saw the Harkaway Hunt, way in the back meadows just as you described it. The big man, Casimer, rode straight up to Geneva and said, 'Each person you kill is a soul you must bear like an unseen weight.' "

Lutie shuddered involuntarily. "First we saw the aurora borealis in the sky this winter and then that gigantic comet streaked across the sky and now I come to hear Casimer Harkaway spoke to my daughter. We've been given a talisman of insight and yet we can't decipher it."

Di-Peachy silently walked alongside Lutie.

"In highly intuitive beings, Fate and free will are the same thing. Never forget that," Lutie said.

Di-Peachy thought to herself that Fate was invoked to

explain human stupidity. And then, too, it was always the weaker ones, the chattel of this earth, that believed in Fate so as to explain their misery. Not her. Di-Peachy was too arrogant and too young to know that Lutie wanted to give her something. She was also too rational to know that Lutie could see around corners.

APRIL 19, 1861

Geneva rode through the night. She pressed on toward Culpeper even as the cold dew drenched her and the horses. She had to get far enough away from Albemarle County so that when she enlisted, no one would recognize her. At sunup, exhausted, she spied a run-in shed. After unsaddling Dancer and Gallant and giving them enough rope to contentedly graze, she crawled in the shed with her blanket and went to sleep.

"My father could sleep through the day like that. Don't know how you can do it."

"Huh?" Geneva awoke.

"Said, 'Don't know how you can do it.' Me, I'm up at the crack of dawn. Fly out of bed like a barn swallow." He dismounted by swinging his right leg over his horse and dropping to the ground.

Blinking, Geneva beheld a scrawny fellow somewhere between thirty and fifty. His age would be anybody's guess. A half-bald head encircled by a ring of curly brown hair gave him a jovial appearance. "Who are you?"

"Banjo Cracker. Yourself?"

"Gen—James, James Chatfield." She took the first name that popped into her head, the name of her deceased little brother.

"Good morning, James. Kin I call you Jimmy?"

"Yes." Geneva squinted at him. "I rode through the night. I don't usually sleep this late myself."

"See your cap has cavalry colors. Aim to enlist, do you?"

"Yes, sir, I sure do."

He smiled broadly. "Me, too. You're a green little sprig. Don't rightly know if they'll join you."

Geneva threw off the blanket and stood up. She towered over Banjo. "They'll join me."

Banjo measured from her toes to her head with his eyes. "Mebbe yes and mebbe no. You're a big 'un, but you're still a young 'un."

"I'm as good as anybody and better than most!"

He laughed. "All right, boy, don't git your feathers ruffled. I see your vanity is cut to your size. I hope they do take you."

She walked over to her saddlebags. Lutie had packed cheeses, smoked sausages, and bread. Geneva tore into the sausage, then remembered her manners and offered Banjo a bite.

"Thank you, no." He shifted to get his weight on his left leg. "I'd be joining the cavalry, too, but as you kin plainly see, I'm no gentleman. By the look of your horses I kin see that you are."

Geneva was taken aback by this. "Mr. Cracker," she sputtered, "a gentleman is a gentleman from his heart. Money's not so important."

He howled with laughter. "The world don't think like you do, son. You ran away from home else you'd have a servant with you," he slyly observed.

Geneva was beginning to realize how hastily she had left. No wonder Lutie had let her go. She thought she'd be unmasked in the first twenty-four hours. It was only forty degrees, yet she started to sweat. "Well, I did go off in kind of a hurry."

"So I gathered. Afraid your momma would stop you?"

"Well . . . uh . . ."

"Don't worry, I'm not going to send you back." Geneva breathed obvious relief, making him laugh all the harder. "I do have a terrible price though."

She automatically put her hand in her pocket.

"No, not that kind of price. First off, you write to your

momma and tell her you're safe and sound. You kin write, can't you?"

"Of course I can write."

"Well, I can't, so don't get flat righteous about it. Second, you and I enlist together and you tell the officer that I'm your hired man. They'd go for that. You get what you want, and I get to be in the cavalry."

She pondered this. "I'll do it."

He shook her hand. "Agreed!"

She turned to go back through her saddlebags and found a church almanac and a Bible which Lutie had slipped in. She pulled it out.

"Now mebbe I'll learn somethin'. You brung the Good Book and I brung a pack of cards." He reached inside his coat and withdrew a deck. "Keep it over my heart. Don't know why. Just do. You about ready to go?"

"I just need to saddle up and . . ." She didn't know how to excuse herself for her toilette.

"So, go." Banjo shrugged. Why didn't Jimmy get on with it?

"In front of you?"

"I haven't got a ruler on me."

Bright red, she spun on her heel and stalked off behind a shelter of bushes and trees, Banjo's laughter stinging her ears. She was quick about it because she didn't want to hear anything more on the subject.

"Shy little bugger, ain't you?"

"You want to be my man or not?"

"Yes, boss." Good-naturedly he waved his hand and climbed back in the saddle.

The gods watch over impetuous youth and falling down drunks. Unbeknownst to her, they'd sent Geneva her guardian angel.

Sin-Sin put her feet toward the fire. She'd worked her fingers to nubs today. Lutie suffered one of her organizing fits. Each spring and fall one of these spasms of inventory seized her like malaria. Sin-Sin was glad to be home with her pots. Another blue pot sat on her table but she thought the glaze not as bright as the one she gave Geneva. She munched on a praline. A Georgian relative of Henley's sent up huge tins of the candy for Geneva's wedding. A knock on her door brought Sin-Sin slowly to her feet.

"I hears you."

Sin-Sin opened the door. Braxton, followed by his mother, Ernie June, glowered behind two of the younger slaves, Alafin and Peter. Without a word, Braxton pushed the two men inside. He followed and closed the door.

"We got troubles," Braxton said gravely.

"What kind of troubles?"

Braxton held out his hand. An emerald brooch glittered against his calloused palm. Sin-Sin grabbed it.

"Miz Lutie's bar pin for her scarves! She's been searching high and low for this." Sin-Sin turned on the men. "You crazy, boy. What you want to do a thing like this for?"

Alafin answered. "I never got in the big house."

"Shut up!" Peter spat.

Braxton collared both of them and forced them to the floor. "Sit down, goddammit. You thinkin' of nobody but yourselves. Lotta people could get hurt over somethin' like this."

Di-Peachy, called to attend this hurried meeting, closed the door and placed the open mouth of a large kettle against the door. It was believed by everyone but Di-Peachy that this kettle would capture the sounds so no whites could hear.

"Let Di-Peachy enjoy her evening. Older heads be needed here." Ernie cooed.

My, Sin-Sin thought to herself, she gets her big foot in the door, and already she's trying to kick out Di-Peachy.

Di-Peachy, angry, started to speak, but Sin-Sin cut her off. "Ernie June, Di-Peachy reads. If we can't settle this amongst ourselves, Di-Peachy will haf to search the books for answers."

Ernie accepted this. Under questioning Alafin revealed that he and Peter fought over the favors of Tincia. Sin-Sin was like a hawk, circling around and around, getting closer to her mark. Finally she struck. "This pin got nothin' to do with poontang. You think we wet behind the ears, Peter!"

Peter, tired from the incessant questioning, cracked, "I need money. Once outta here, I need money."

Braxton cuffed him. "Fool!"

By midnight they'd reached a solution. Peter would have jeopardized every slave on Chatfield had he run off, but Alafin had hurt only Peter. Yet a servant stealing from a servant soured everyone. It was one thing to take from the master; it was quite another to fleece another slave. Although Peter's crime would have immediate physical effect on everyone, Alafin's would have a corrosive, psychological effect.

Sin-Sin spoke. "Alafin, you works an hour every evening in Peter's garden."

Alafin nodded his head.

Sin-Sin continued, "Peter, come harvest time, Braxton and I gonna take half your garden and give it out, but we ain't tellin' nobody that it come from your garden. You tellin' nobody either. You gotta think 'bout others!"

Braxton added, "If we catch you, if anybody catches you again, we'll turn you over to Lutie."

Peter laughed derisively. "That crazy ole fool! She can't do nothin' to me."

"You shut up, nigger!" Braxton growled. "Now git outta here 'fore we change our minds. We been easy on you."

Long after everyone had left, Sin-Sin sat deep in thought. Sin-Sin valued Di-Peachy's mind but for what had to be done next, well, she wouldn't tell Di-Peachy everything. After all, the girl was still young and filled with choked bitterness over being a slave. Sin-Sin knew that Lutie's authority must be reasserted. With the men gone, Lutie had to prove she could command. Through Lutie came Sin-Sin's power.

Even Ernie June realized what side her bread was buttered on, and Ernie's ambition expanded like yeast. She'd twist and turn every which way she could to get out of reporting to Lutie the misdeeds of another servant. Ernie had each foot planted on the back of two different horses. She wanted Lutie going her way, and she wanted every slave on the place going her way, too.

Sin-Sin knew only too well what Ernie was doing in that kitchen. Having lived for over half a century, Sin-Sin took some pride in her judgment of people. The emerald brooch rested on the table. Peter'd try again. Not tomorrow or even the day after tomorrow but sometime. Sin-Sin rocked in her chair. She was going to set down a trap of many teeth—and then wait.

APRIL 20, 1861

Lutie awoke to a brilliantly clear morning. Outside the earth, covered in ice, shone like a glazed doughnut.

"Emil, last night I dreamed of a black sheep with golden hooves! What do you think of that?"

She clapped her hands and hopped out of bed. Babbling as she washed her face and hands, Lutie pushed back the rising thought that she was in this enormous house alone, no children, no husband and a war on. Some war. Where was it? How could either side fight? She wasn't going to worry about it today anyway.

"Do you think it's an omen? The golden hooved black sheep? It's not the golden fleece. No, it's quite different. It was so vivid I could have reached out and touched his black curls."

"Miz Lutie, you stirrin'?" Sin-Sin's deep voice penetrated the closed door.

"Yes."

"Who you talkin' to?"

"You know who I'm talking to!" Lutie whispered under her breath, "Emil, sometimes I just can't stand it!"

Without further embellishments or politeness Sin-Sin opened the door. "Good mornin', cold as it is."

"Good morning, Sin-Sin." Lutie brushed her thick auburn hair, now half gray. "You know, Sin-Sin, you forget yourself. Say hello to Emil."

"Hello, Emil." Sin-Sin nodded at the window.

"He's behind me, Sin-Sin."

"He knows I'm minding my manners no matter where he is," Sin-Sin pouted.

"Today Emil is wearing his scarlet turban shot through

with an indigo blue strip and edged with gold thread. His outer robes match, and his inner robe is robin's egg blue. Every morning I wake up and wonder, What will Emil wear?"

Sin-Sin cleared her throat. "Miz Lutie, now that the men be gone, you and me be the only ones talkin' to Emil."

Lutie wheeled around on her stool. "Just what are you saying? We're the only two who ever talk to Emil!"

"The others can hear us peepin'. We got to be more careful."

"You don't believe in Emil, do you? And don't get your nose out of joint, Sin-Sin. I can't bear it when you go moral on me!"

"I believes in Emil. He's a pasha from Africa! He be king of Persia."

"Persia and Africa are two different places."

"He the boss man wherever he be." Sin-Sin folded her arms.

This reply pleased Lutie. "Quite right."

"We gots to be careful."

Sharply Lutie said, "Do the others think I'm crazy?"

Sin-Sin diplomatically replied, "People like cloth, Miz Lutie. Some is fine and some is coarse. It's the coarse one we got to be wary of. Gots no imagination. They doan understand you when you get above them in speakin' and imaginin'!"

"I never talk to Emil in front of anyone but you, Sin-Sin."

This genuine outburst touched Sin-Sin. "I knows it but folks overhear and you know that girl of yours be makin' fun of Emil when the devil gets hold of her tongue."

"You're right, Sin-Sin." Lutie stopped twirling her hairbrush. "I don't know what I'd do without you."

Sin-Sin smiled. Then tossed off as though it was of no consequence, "I gots eyes. Miz Geneva flew the coop! Why doan you tell me?"

"Oh, Sin-Sin, don't be hurt. I really can't tell you yet what she's up to except to say it's foolish and perfectly in keeping with her impulsive character!"

"That girl's a wild one. She galloped out of the womb."

"I should have known when I gave birth to her . . . more pain than I had with the other two put together." Lutie rarely mentioned Jimmy anymore. She glanced up at Sin-Sin's dark eyes. "Could it have been that long ago?"

"Yesterday, yesterday in my heart."

They were startled out of their mood by Di-Peachy. "Jennifer Fitzgerald is here."

"What?" Lutie hissed. "That python's crawling up here, and it isn't a receiving day!"

"I indicated as much, ma'am." Di-Peachy shared Lutie's opinion of Jennifer.

"I suppose she's sitting down there in my front parlor like a snake on a hot rock."

"Oh, she's not only sunning herself by your fire, she's rooting around in your knitting box."

"Well, I never!" Lutie, always enlivened by crossing swords, grandly threw on her most sumptuous morning dress. Lutie's clothes, sewn in Paris, were the envy of every woman who saw her. She may have thickened with the years, in fact, she was plump, but her clothes amplified her good features: beautiful complexion, thick hair, and magnificent carriage. Lutie swooped down the stairs. Sin-Sin was two steps behind.

"Jennifer, what a welcome surprise!" Lutie gaily lied through her teeth as Jennifer stood up, clumsily scattering the sewing box, yarns, threads, and needles all over the inlaid floor.

Jennifer had the presence of mind not to dive on the floor to clean up the spillings. She took Lutie's outstretched hand instead. Sin-Sin, spitefully, for she couldn't abide Jennifer, sailed past the parlor toward the kitchen. Sin-Sin made no effort to clean up the sewing box. Di-Peachy began to move toward the debris when suddenly Sin-Sin's iron grip paralyzed her elbow. Mute, Di-Peachy allowed herself to be dragged off to the kitchen.

Sin-Sin pushed open the kitchen door and bellowed, "Ernie June, we gots a fine lady in the parlor. Load her up on jams and teas and coffee and whatever else you hoardin' here."

Ernie called over her shoulder as she was tending the grits, "Di-Peachy done told me."

"Well, I'm telling you again."

Di-Peachy, weary of their squabbling even though she recognized the stakes, said, "Today in 753 B.C. Romulus founded the city of Rome."

"Pin a rose on Romulus," Sin-Sin grumbled.

Back in the parlor, Lutie and Jennifer gathered up the contents of the sewing box. Jennifer squeezed a large blue ball of yarn. "Ouch!" She carefully played with the yarn until she extracted Lutie's emerald bar pin. "Look." She handed the pin to Lutie.

"I went through the sewing box!" Lutie exclaimed. "Thank you, Jennifer, I've been looking for this for over a week now. I know I looked through this box."

"It was stuck in the middle of the yarn."

"How on earth could it have gotten in there?"

"Maybe the clasp is loose, and when you leaned over, it fell in."

"But in the middle of a ball of yarn?"

"Strange things do happen. Why, I used to berate my cook, a poor imitation of your Ernie June, because I thought she was stealing sweetcakes. She told me she didn't do it. One day I walked in the pantry and saw a little raccoon, a tiny one, mind you, and that little fellow would open the can! Saw it with my own eyes, a pygmy raccoon!"

"Perhaps you're right."

Just then Ernie entered with her tray of treats. "Good mornin', Miz Jennifer, it's good to see you."

Jennifer viewed Ernie's handiwork with envy and pleasure. "How beautiful!"

"Di-Peachy told me we has an important guest." Butter would melt in Ernie June's mouth.

Sin-Sin, lurking in the background, heard enough. She put her hand to her mouth as though clearing her throat. "Humph." Ernie, after more compliments, retired.

"Sin-Sin, Jennifer found my emerald pin!"

"I doan believe it."

Lutie handed the pin to Sin-Sin. "That's it."

"In the middle of the ball of yarn," Jennifer added.

Sin-Sin shook her head. "Doan that beat all."

"Well, this is a lucky day, Jennifer, and I have you to thank for it."

The two rivals buttered toast, gobbled jams, and plied one another with the conversation of the county. Jennifer, because she had organized the sewing brigade, was enjoying special prominence. Lutie couldn't sew worth a damn. It killed her to see Jennifer reap so much praise. Everyone in Albemarle County was carrying on about sewing uniforms.

"—and so you see, dearest Lutie, the situation could be quite serious." Jennifer's voice dropped into the terribly sincere key.

"Of course, I see. But not a shot has been fired." Lutie waved her hand. "Maybe both sides will get tired of this before it starts and go home!"

"With Abe Lincoln in the White House? He'll drive us into battle. It has to happen, and we have to be prepared for it."

"It's certainly not going to be here, Jennifer. There's nothing in Charlottesville those abolitionists want. We breed horses and tend to our business. Why, we don't even have an important railroad connection."

"How do you know the Northerners won't go on a rampage? What if they burn everything that stands and shoot everything that moves?" Jennifer was truly frightened.

"They're gentlemen! My brother-in-law is one of them. You've entertained Northern people in your superb home. Why I remember only too well the harvest party you had for the Aethelreds, those charming people from Maine."

"They're the exception that proves the rule."

"I do hope you're mistaken." Lutie's hand fluttered to her breast. "I can't believe the Yankee army will make war on women and children. Jennifer, our boys will whip the daylights out of them!"

"Yes, but our boys can't be everywhere at once, and they will need your help. You've had so much experience." Jennifer referred to Lutie's skill at nursing the servants and her sad ordeal with the dying Jimmy. "Why don't you set up nursing classes so we women will be ready to do our part on the battlefront?"

Trapped, Lutie didn't take long to answer. She had to accept the challenge or she'd forfeit her lead in the community. She'd lost ground, thanks to all the sewing! "You know I'll do it." Lutie began to fill with her task. "We'll start up here, of course. Each week we can move to another suitable house. I suppose we'll need to conduct some classes in town, too. I'll expect to see you and our ladies this Thursday then, the Feast of Saint Mark."

"Splendid, Lutie. Shall I have one of my servants leave cards for everyone at their home?"

"No, Di-Peachy can do that."

"I'm sure Geneva will be a big help."

"Geneva has gone away for a bit—the shock of Nash leaving so soon and all. Jennifer, I tell you this in strictest confidence, I sent her over to England. I didn't want anyone to know as it might look like I feared for her in this turmoil. She'll return in a few months. She was possessed of such grief, of such" —Lutie cast her hands skyward and smiled seraphically—"young love."

Jennifer smiled as though understanding, but she didn't at all. Jennifer Greer married Big Fitz for her days not for her nights.

The moment Jennifer Fitzgerald was gone, Lutie grabbed some sheets of paper, called for Di-Peachy, and the two began planning nursing classes.

Before nightfall, the women, white and black, in Albemarle County knew, knew for a fact, that Geneva Chatfield Hart was on the Atlantic, sailing toward England.

APRIL 21, 1861

"Proclaim ye this among the Gentiles; Prepare war, wake up the mighty men, let all the men of war draw near; let them come up." Joel 3:9.

Sitting in St. Paul's, Ninth and Grace streets, admiring the chaste interior, this third day after Easter Henley thought the lesson for the day wretchedly topical. So did the reverend. At appropriate moments he would swing out his arm, his flowing robes creating a mild breeze.

Henley knew that back home Lutie would be ensconced in her front pew at Christ Episcopal Church on the corner of Hill Street, or Second Street as younger people called it, and Jefferson Street. She'd be listening to the same lesson and fretting over war. Unfortunately, Geneva would be no help since she didn't seem to give a fig about the war. Henley doubted if his daughter comprehended the enormity of what was about to descend upon both the Union and the Confederacy. He wasn't sure he grasped it himself.

Henley knew wherever Sumner was, he'd take out his Bible and read the lesson. He had promised Lutie he would devoutly follow his church almanac, and he would. Sumner would always keep a promise to his mother. A pity he hadn't promised to stop drinking and playing cards.

The reverend belabored the phrase "wake up the mighty men." He was referring to the gentlemen assembled inside St. Paul's, over half of them in uniform. Henley rather enjoyed being referred to as a mighty man. The fact that the gray coat of his uniform called attention to his thick silver hair pleased him, too. Thank God I didn't go bald, he thought, and then offered a prayer to the Almighty whom Henley imagined as a gigantic man with long silver hair and flowing beard to match. One couldn't have a bald God, after all.

This deeply spiritual moment was riven to shreds by the alarm sounding from the bell tower in Capitol Square. St. Paul's, close to the square, shook with the noise. Before the reverend could finish his sentence, the uniformed men stampeded out of the church. Henley, sitting in the front, couldn't get out that fast. In the few seconds between blasts, the congregation panicked. The main aisle was clogged with terrified adults and screaming children. One ten-year-old boy led his weeping mother by the hand telling her not to worry; no Yankee could kill her because he'd kill the Yankee first.

Henley finally broke through the crowd and dashed out the front door into the mild, sunny light. He smashed into a woman, and they both tumbled on the ground.

"I'm so sorry, madam." Henley scrambled to his feet. He then offered his hand to the woman as she gathered up her luscious, pale pastel skirts. When she took his hand and finally gazed up at him, he wanted to faint. Staring him straight in the face was the most beautiful woman he'd ever seen in his life. Her rich blonde hair curled around her shoulders. Her becoming church hat framed her perfectly formed face. Her skin glowed like an unplucked peach. Her features bespoke fine breeding, but it was her eyes that destroyed him. They were bright cobalt blue, not pale blue or ice blue or watery blue but blazing, deep cobalt blue. Only once in his life had Henley ever seen a woman equal to her beauty, but she was a slave, Di-Peachy's mother.

"Colonel, I apologize. In the excitement I didn't look

where I was going." Her low voice soothed him like honey in whiskey.

"The fault is all mine." Henley offered his arm to this goddess. "Allow me to escort you to my carriage. I regret that I cannot see you home, madam, but as you can plainly surmise, I am needed elsewhere."

"You're both gracious and generous, Colonel. I have my own carriage, and I'd be obliged if you'd walk me to it."

The light pressure of her hand on his arm drove him wild. Here he was, a man twice her age and then some, and he felt like a satyr, a bull, Zeus beholding Leda.

Four perfectly equipped bay horses calmly stood amid the pandemonium. Henley sucked in his breath. She was not only beautiful, she was rich. Those were the best bred Cleveland Bays in Chesterfield and Henrico counties.

A man running by bellowed, "It's the *Pawnee*! The Feds sent a warship to bombard our city."

Henley walked her to her carriage. "If they have the range, they'll aim for the Tredegar Iron Works. Failing that, I think our Northern foes will settle for sowing misery where they can. Please be careful. Don't linger by any government buildings."

"I'm not afraid of the Yankees, Colonel." A crooked grin spread across her face. Her teeth were perfect. "I think the Yankees ought to be afraid of me!"

"I'm glad to hear it." He lifted her up into the carriage. "Madam, like Helen you could launch a thousand ships."

"Or oyster boats!" She laughed.

He laughed along with her. She was beautiful, but unconcerned about it. He loathed vain women. The fact that he could spend half an hour perfecting his beard did not qualify as vanity. That had to do with looking respectable. "Forgive me for not introducing myself." The commotion grew steadily worse. "I'm Henley Chatfield from Albemarle County."

"The famous horseman! Why, I've always wanted to meet you. My husband and I spent years in Europe, and we'd heard of you there. It's Fate that we should meet, Colonel Chatfield."

"The Fates are kind."

"Let's just say the Fates did not give us eyes in the back of our head." She smiled. "I'm Kate Vickers."

"I'm honored." So this is Kate Vickers, thought Henley. No wonder men fought duels over her.

"I receive on Thursdays after two. Won't you please come by? We might even be able to hear ourselves talk." She gestured at the panic around her. "I'm sure, too, that the other guests would be thrilled to meet Virginia's most successful horseman in person. I regret, of course, that my husband Mars won't be there. He's training a cavalry regiment somewhere in the western counties."

Henley didn't regret Mars Vickers's absence a bit. "Until Thursday." He raised his hat as the splendid carriage, driven by a fully dressed coachman, wheeled and turned. Walking with a calm, deliberate pace, so as not to appear frightened, Henley made his way through the mob of well-dressed citizens to the capitol. Men poured into the streets with pistols and shotguns. Many of the town's finer ladies headed for Chimborazo Heights. If there was going to be a display of fireworks, they fully intended to witness it.

Once inside the capitol, Henley found other officers. Nobody knew what was going on. At least one man had the sense to order the howitzers down to the riverbank. If the *Pawnee* came up the river, the artillery was ordered to fire upon it.

Henley, disgusted by the tangle inside the capitol, worked his way toward the legislative chamber. He picked a desk and sat in it. An ad hoc committee of men without offices filled the room designed by Thomas Jefferson. At first, concern over the projected damage a Federal warship could do dominated their conversation. As time went by and no sickening booms were heard, the men turned their minds to other matters. The Confederacy had a president. Virginia had a governor, a good one. But the army of Virginia had no commander. They'd heard that Governor Letcher had sent word to Robert E. Lee. Colonel Lee on April 18 had been offered command of the United States Army by General Winfield Scott. He declined.

Henley knew the Lees. He was four years younger than Robert, aged fifty-four. Henley hoped Robert E. Lee would soon take command. Richmond couldn't afford many more Sundays like this one. It was all the more upsetting in an odd way because the *Pawnee* never did steam up the James River. It was a false alarm.

APRIL 22, 1861

"How long do you reckon?" Geneva asked Banjo.

"If the weather holds, another day," Banjo cheerily replied.

The clouds crowned the top of the Blue Ridge Mountains. The world was wrapped in cotton candy, fairy floss as Lutie called it. The two companions had ridden steadily since dawn. At last the weather behaved like a mild April, and the morning temperature was in the low sixties.

The thought of seeing Nash soon made Geneva's heart pound. She dreamed of him night and day, but she was careful not to discuss him with Banjo. She had mentioned that she hoped to be reunited with her childhood friend, Nash Hart, and maybe she would even find her brother Sumner.

Banjo's presence was a tonic for her. She was spared those thousand and one false courtesies men shower upon women, at least Geneva thought them false. The only time she was happy was on horseback. Then her skill weighed more than her sex, her family name, her family wealth. Geneva never examined why she needed to prove herself physically against all comers. Geneva rarely examined anything. As far as she was concerned, she loved horses and she possessed a gift for them. What else was there to know?

"See that stump over there?" Banjo pointed. "Hit it."

Geneva, grateful for his attention to her marksmanship, pulled out her father's pistol and fired. The first shot went wide, but the second sank into the rotted trunk with a satisfying thud.

"Not bad, boy, but you'll have to keep practicing." Banjo pulled his own sidearm, and the slender barrel flashed. He had found his target. He dismounted, tied his horse, and walked over to the stump. Banjo rooted around the ground, finding four big pinecones to put on the stump. "Now, Jimmy, you stay off to the left here. Watch what I do, and then you do it." Banjo hopped back in the saddle, headed off about one hundred yards. He turned and cantered back toward the stump, then when forty yards from it, he turned parallel. He pulled his pistol, urged his horse on, and blew every pinecone off the stump without wasting a bullet.

Geneva applauded.

"You do it."

Dutifully, she retraced his route, turned, and then galloped. She emptied her gun and hit the stump, but not the reset pinecones.

"Keep your eyes on the target!" Banjo instructed. "Stare so hard at those pinecones that you see each little petal. Do it again."

This time she focused on those goddamned pinecones so intently her eyes ached. She hit one, but missed the others.

Breathing hard, she rode up to him. "I'll practice every day."

"Funny, isn't it, how we see but we don't see? If you think about nothin' on this earth but those pinecones, you see 'em for the first time. You can't hear nothin' if you do it right. If I was to fire a shot when you was riding in on them like that, you oughten to hear it. Everything you got has to be directed at those pinecones."

"I understand." She beamed. "And I'm grateful to you for taking time with me."

Surprised, he said, "Hell, boy, I'm your man. I got to take care of you. You shoot the Yankee before the Yankee shoots you."

They continued in their northwesterly direction.

"I been thinkin' about the Bible lesson you read me this morning."

"Judges." Geneva was sick to death of Judges.

"Seems to me like Samson didn't have the sense God gave a goose—gander, in this instance, when it came to women."

"Guess not."

"First he gets himself hot up over the woman of Timnath. His folks and people give her rat week, and then she finagles the answer to a riddle out of him, course she had to 'cause her own people said they'd kill her. Anyway, she gets burnt up in her house. Samson gets het up ass over tit. Then he recovers himself and visits a harlot. Didn't get far there. Then he finds Delilah. Next thing you know, Samson's shaved clean as a billiard ball and has his eyes put out. Now I ask you, Jimmy, was he a fool for women or not?"

"Don't you figure all men are fools for women?" She slyly winked at Banjo.

"If they're lucky!" He tipped back his head and roared. "I had a wife once, and I tell you, Jimmy, the sun rose and set on that woman. When I would call to her, she would always smile at me like an angel. I swear to you on my heart that woman was a blessing on the earth."

"What happened?"

"Died three years past. Like a little colt takin' colic, she curled up in a ball, and Jimmy, that fast she was gone. I called the doctor, but he couldn't do nothin'. A good man, warn't his fault. Before she left, she looked up at me and said, 'Forgive me.' 'For what?' says I. The woman never uttered a cross word in her life. 'I left you no children,' she says. Oh Lordie, Jimmy, I took her sweet hand, I held it, and I cried. I cried 'til I was sick myself. If'n I had me a little girl or even a little boy, I'd have me a bit of Mary left." Tears ran down his unshaven cheeks.

"I'm so sorry, Banjo." Impulsively, she rode next to him and patted his shoulder, a distinctly feminine gesture.

Banjo nodded his head and reached up to touch her hand. " 'Preciate your kindness, boy."

Geneva withdrew her hand. They rode on in silence for a while after that. If Nash died, she'd kill herself. Love was a terrible thing. She knew she couldn't live without it and wondered why it hit her so. When she met Nash, he didn't make a big impression on her. First off, he wasn't a good rider. Adequate, yes, but nothing special. He was determined to have her, and he paid court. Albemarle County marveled at how he paid court. She didn't believe he cared about her dowry all that much. The few suitors she'd had before Nash had cared about it a great deal. Soon she noticed how the light glowed on his sandy hair. She admired the cords and muscle in his forearms when he worked outside. He wasn't a tall man, but he was well built. His voice, so deep it made her backbone tingle, sounded like a melody. Before she knew it, she was as much in love with Nash Hart as he was with her.

She thought on these things as she rode ever closer to her husband. It never occurred to her that she would find another man attractive.

APRIL 23, 1861

From frost the temperature turned dramatically upward. The day wasn't half over, yet the thermometer climbed into the low eighties. Sin-Sin grumbled. She spent the last three days feeding hard woods—hickory, mulberry, heavy oak, and even some walnut—into her firing barn. The fourth day was critical and here it was hotter than Tophet. The boys dropping in the wood began to lose pace.

A bright yellow turban on her head, the white handkerchief tied around her neck already soaked, Sin-Sin chewed them out. "You gonna wisht you was somebody else!"

"Yes, Auntie Sin-Sin." Timothy moved a trifle faster.

Arms folded across her bosom, Sin-Sin could have been Scipio Africanus. These troops would obey! She was making an unusually large pot, and she was nervous. The glaze was a difficult color, almost a cerise, and would be mixed with fire streaks. She prayed the pot wouldn't crack.

As a young woman, Sin-Sin gathered as much information as she could about pottery, ovens, and glazes. She constructed an underground oven twenty-eight feet long. At the end, a huge mound with a hole in it provided a draw. The project had taken one entire summer.

She'd been using the oven for thirty-five years. Every year she learned something new about her craft.

Lutie joined her. "Ernie June chased after Boyd today with a broom."

Sin-Sin vastly appreciated this indication of familial dishar-
mony. She paused to bellow at Timothy, "Haul, boy!" He
trotted over to the woodpile. "Those chillun like to drive me
wild. I never could understand why God made chillun. What'd
Boyd do?"

"She forgot to put the raisins in the raisin bread," Lutie
gossiped.

"Ha! Mebbe that'll shut Ernie June's trap for a spell. I'm
worn out from hearin' what a wonder Boyd is."

Lutie fanned herself. "Sin-Sin, if we don't get out of
Judges soon I think I'll go mad. We've been reading that for
weeks. And I count on the New Testament to make me feel
better. Today's lesson was just awful."

"That business 'bout people talking from their graves on
Judgment Day?" Sin-Sin shook involuntarily. A vision of
graves yawning open, spilling out their contents made her
sick.

"No, today's lesson. That was yesterday's."

"I doan want to be talkin' to no dead people!"

"You'll be dead yourself then."

"I still doan want to be talkin' to no dead people even if I
is dead! Then I be wearin' a white turban!" Sin-Sin emphati-
cally nodded her yellow-turbaned head.

"Sin-Sin, I don't think this is an immediate worry." Lutie
fanned Sin-Sin as well as herself. "It was the part about the
wells without water and clouds carried with a tempest that
bothered me. Peter 2, Sin-Sin."

"Our well never runs dry."

"They were talking in symbols."

"Then why get your bowels blocked over it? It's not your
well!"

Lutie stomped her foot. "I hate it when you get bullheaded with me!"

"Youse the one being bullheaded."

Lutie stormed off. Sin-Sin stayed at her oven for another
ten minutes so as not to look too worried. She then went back
up to the big house. Lutie was pacing the long hallway with
the floor-to-ceiling windows.

"Lutie, what's got into you?"

"Nothing." Lutie knew she was being unreasonable.

Sin-Sin sat down in a pretty wooden chair, painted white.
She waited.

"I told you nothing was the matter with me."

Sin-Sin said nothing.

"Well, I got a letter from Poofy. Daniel left. He equipped an entire regiment, if you can believe that. The wealth of those Livingstons!"

"I knows you miss your sister, but I doan see as how that gets you wrought up."

Lutie paced. She stopped. "Sin-Sin, I have to break a confidence. Oh, I hate to do this!"

Sin-Sin leaned forward. Lutie rested her hand on Sin-Sin's shoulder. "Geneva cut her hair and ran off to war disguised as a man to be with Nash."

"No!"

Lutie sat across from her servant. "Didn't Di-Peachy tell you?"

"That girl didn't tell me nothin'. Di-Peachy keeps her word." Sin-Sin defended her.

Lutie's eyebrows raised. "Well, I was just checking. I promised Geneva I wouldn't tell, but, Sin-Sin, I haven't heard a word from her! You're the only person around here with sense. Besides, I can never keep anything from you."

Sin-Sin gloated. "Uh-huh. Why she want to do a crazy thing like that?"

"Says she can't live without him."

"Lord, I 'spect I felt that way over my first man, but I can't remember it." She sighed. "Sure not goin' to feel that way ever again, and I thank the good Lord, too."

"I thought she'd be turned back. I thought someone would see through her."

"She's tall and lean. She might could do it."

"Sweet Jesus, Sin-Sin, I don't want her going to war!"

"You can't stop her."

"Someone will find her out. It has to happen."

Sin-Sin folded her hands. "She has a mind of her own. Mebbe she'll tire of it or him."

Lutie tacked. "Do you know what Jennifer Fitzgerald said to me at Geneva's wedding? I was talking about how people are drawn to one another, and I said, 'Men fall in love with their eyes; women with their ears.' And do you know Jennifer said, 'Not this time.' I could have shot her dead."

"She got a mean tongue in her head."

"Well, she and her mean tongue will be here in two days."

"As is the way of Barabbas." This was Sin-Sin's stock phrase for somebody ignorant.

"We can't let anyone know what's happened here. We've got to start making up stories about Geneva in England. Surely, I'll have some kind of letter from her soon."

"We gots to be careful of Jennifer Fitzgerald coming about with the searchin' eye." Sin-Sin patted her turban.

"Don't I know it!"

A salmon-colored sunset softened the sky. Banjo calmly chewed on his Little Swan Rough and Ready plug. If he didn't have time to sit and enjoy his pipe, he would jam tobacco in his mouth. Banjo couldn't live without tobacco or a deck of cards. He kept both in the pocket over his heart. He attempted to initiate Jimmy into the delights of chew, but the boy didn't take to it. With cards he was more successful. He reckoned that Jimmy wasn't a day over fifteen. Not a hair on his cheeks, and his voice, while not high, hadn't cracked into a reassuring baritone. He looked at the Shenandoah rushing into the Potomac. They'd have to pick their way down to the river and take a ferry over to the town.

Banjo could see the railroad tracks emerging from a mountain. Getting in and out of Harper's Ferry was no easy task.

Geneva kept unusually quiet. Darkness enveloped the river; a light mist curled skyward. The two friends waited by river's edge along with others. Women in good cotton dresses chatted with soldiers and civilians. Some of the men wore full uniforms, complete with facings to indicate their branch of the service: blue for the infantry, gold for the cavalry, red for the artillery. Others made do with no uniform at all, but since they carried firearms one assumed they were soldiers. Banjo happily struck up a conversation with these fellows. Geneva spoke to no one.

Men grunting and laughing were heard before the outlines of the ferry revealed itself. Slowly its squat prow jutted out of the silver mists. A lone, towering figure stood forward, a huge rope coiled in his hand. His face wasn't visible. As the ferry pulled closer, another figure labored at the rear. Geneva thought of Charon ferrying across the river Styx. Was she being taken from the land of the living to the land of the dead? Wasn't war the ultimate harvest of death? But quickly her thoughts turned to Nash. It was just as well.

When Geneva and Banjo reached the outskirts of the camp, whatever fears they may have harbored about the state of the Confederacy were confirmed. Men sat in the open around fires. Tents dotted the landscape but in no discernible order. No sentry barred their passing into this haphazard military area. The first man they came to was a black man carrying a sack of grain. Banjo asked him where the cavalry was. The man pointed left and continued about his business.

The moon, a day from full, flooded the camp with light. When Geneva and Banjo got to the cavalry area, they were relieved to find that one corner of it was organized. Tents, like corn, were pitched in straight rows. Horses chewed contentedly in square corrals. Behind every five tents was a small fire pit.

"Hey," Banjo called to a white man bending over a trestle table. On one side of him were piled calfskins. Lanterns covered the table. He was sewing and mumbling to himself. He glanced up from his task with irritation.

"We're looking for Nash Hart. Do you know where we might find him?"

"What makes you think I know everybody in this camp? I've got enough on my mind."

"Jes what you doin'?" Banjo queried.

"Lining the inside of these britches with leather. Goddamn Mars Vickers, Major Mars, wants everyone under his command to have it. Says they'll stick in their saddles like a burr. Well, I can tell you where I'd like him to stick it. He spent ten years in Europe in their armies. Says the Fifth Hussars and the First Lancers in France have a leather inseam. Do you know how long I've been in the army? Twenty-one goddamned years. I don't care what they do in Europe. I'm beginning to think I would be better off in the Yankee army. Least I wouldn't have to sit up night and day and sew!"

"Yeah, but look at the company you'd haf to keep." Banjo grinned.

The balding fellow smiled. "You got a point there. Who'd you say you were searching out?"

"Nash Hart."

Geneva found her voice. "He's a nice-looking fellow with sandy hair."

"And wet behind the ears like all the rest of 'em?" asked Bob.

"He's old. He's twenty-four," Geneva said.

Banjo and Bob looked at her, then at one another and laughed.

"Well now, you might find him anywhere. That's a pretty general description for such an old man." Bob poked a skin with a big needle. "What's he ride?"

"Short cropped, rose gray with a black tail."

"Why didn't you say so? Horses I remember. The men all look alike. Go down the third line of tents, and you'll find him."

Banjo tipped his hat. "See you tomorrow."

"I ain't going nowhere," the tailor replied, pointing to the pile of skins.

Geneva put her forefinger to her head in a quick salute and fought the impulse to gallop wildly to the third row of tents.

"Banjo, once we find Nash, would you take care of the horses while I surprise him that I'm here?"

"Surely. That's my job now, ain't it? First thing tomorrow morning, we got to find this Vickers fellow and enlist proper."

They rode slowly past each tent in the third row. The flaps were open. She saw Nash writing a letter.

"That's him." Geneva swung her leg over the saddle. "Banjo, come find me in the morning." She handed her reins to Banjo, who nodded and rode toward the end of the row. The servants and seconds had to be around there somewhere.

Geneva walked into the tent. Nash looked up. At first he didn't recognize her. "Hello."

"Nash, it's me."

Dumbfounded, Nash looked at his wife. He whispered, "Geneva?"

"It's me!"

He moved behind her and dropped the tent flap. "What are you doing here?"

"I can't live without you." She flung herself into his arms.

Too surprised to respond with words, he hugged and kissed her. "I can't believe it." He pushed her away and looked at her. "You cut your hair!"

"I'm going to enlist. Can't very well have long hair."

"You're what?"

"I'm going to enlist so I can be with you."

"Geneva, you'll do no such thing." Nash sat on his camp bed. She joined him.

"No one will find out. All I have do is stand up and sign my name."

"I can't allow you to submit yourself to such danger."

"I'll die without you! Really, I will!" Tears ran into the corners of her mouth. "I'd rather be fighting a war than sitting home and pining away."

He touched her cheeks and wiped away the tears. "How could you love me so much?" He wrapped his arms around her. "Look, why don't you just live at the camp? Some of the officers' wives are here. We'd have time together."

"No." She grew hot. "No, I want to go where you go and do what you do. I'm not afraid. It beats hearing Mother tell me what to do or listening to Sin-Sin and Ernie June fight or dragging into town every Sunday to die of boredom in a church pew. No! I won't go home. I'm staying with you!"

"Geneva, you could get killed!"

"So could you."

"I'm a man. It's my duty. You have different duties, darling. Everyone has a purpose in life, and it isn't your purpose to risk your person in such a violent fashion. Childbirth is risk enough."

"I want to be with you. I don't care if I get killed. I have to be with you!" Geneva boldly put her hand on his crotch. He responded immediately. She unbuttoned his trousers, got up and fastened the tent flap, then returned to a bewildered but excited Nash. She touched him; she bit his ear. She wiggled out of her boots and pants and pressed her body next to his. Nash melted. He longed for her, ached for her. He wanted to howl with pleasure, but he had to be scrupulously silent. They made love and talked half the night. By sunrise Nash saw things Geneva's way.

That night Banjo bedded down with other servants, most of them black. He curled up in his blanket and felt a tad lonesome. He'd gotten used to sleeping beside Jimmy. He realized he thought of the boy as a son. He shut his eyes to close out the tears. As the years sped by, he felt the lack of children more and more. Well, Jimmy'd be half a son. Banjo fell asleep talking to his dead wife. He did this every night. He felt she heard him.

APRIL 24, 1861

A loud cannon boom sounded by Geneva's right ear. She scrambled out of bed, struggled into her pants and boots, grabbed her pistol, and dashed outside the tent. No enemy approached, but she saw a puff of smoke a mere hundred yards from the tent, and she smelled gunpowder. She ran back into the tent.

"Nash, wake up! The Yankees are coming!"

Nash opened one eye halfway.

"The Yankees are coming! Our boys fired a cannon at them!" She sat on the side of the cot, her heart pounding.

He closed his eye again. "That's the artillery telling us it's time to get up. Guess we have to give them something to do."

"All right, you walleyed sons of bitches, get up and get moving!" a rude voice shouted in a singsong voice.

Furious, Geneva bolted out of the tent and squared off against an unshaven man with bright red hair. "This is a military camp, not a brothel. Watch your tongue!"

"Who the hell are you to tell me what to do, sister boy?" He glared at Geneva, an inch taller than he but suspiciously sleek.

Geneva blew up. "I'm no sister boy!"

Contemptuously he pushed her out of the way and kept walking. "Get up and get moving, you walleyed sons of bitches."

Geneva put her boot smack in the small of his back and sent him sprawling on the ground. The redhead was a slender man in his thirties, but he still outweighed her by twenty pounds. He leapt up and collared her.

"I'll teach you, you little pissant."

"Foulmouth!" She bit his arm. He howled and released her. Then he advanced, his fist cocked. He lunged at her and she dodged the blow, tripping him as he fell. She didn't grow up with brothers for nothing.

The redhead's pride was scorched. This skinny flit dared correct him and push him in the dirt. He ran at her like a bull and caught her by the legs, throwing her across his shoulder. Her head dangled down his back. She reached her long arms around his body and down into his crotch and yanked his balls as hard as she could. Stunned and hurt, he dropped her. While he was doubled over, she smashed up against him with all her weight, and he fell down. Then she jumped on him and tried to hold him down, but he was too strong. She pinned his arms with her weight. He rocked from side to side, managing to throw her off because she was so light. Then he jumped up and smacked her upside the head. Blood trickled down the side of her face.

"Mr. Poist, that's enough." A melodic tenor voice, drenched with command, rang out.

The redhead lumbered a step backward. Geneva stood beside him.

A tall, well-built man with curly auburn hair and a luxurious moustache to match looked at her with laughing eyes. He wore blue trousers with a gold stripe down the side. His boots were highly polished. The inside of his pants were lined with roughed leather. His gray tunic top with a double row of gold buttons was opened, revealing a white shirt underneath, also opened. The hair on his chest matched the hair on his head, and it spilled over his muscled chest. A yellow foraging cap sat back on his head, the leather visor freshly oiled. His stand-up collar, like all his facings, was yellow with gold braid trim. A single star stood on each collar flap. He reeked of masculinity.

"Major, this sister boy started a fight."

Geneva knocked him on the ground again. "Don't call me sister boy!"

The next thing she knew, two powerful hands under her armpits lifted her up, and she found herself staring straight into Major Mars Vickers's light brown eyes. "Hot tempered, aren't you?"

Held in midair like a helpless pup, Geneva replied, "He's got no right to call me a sister boy."

Mars put her down. "I reckon he doesn't." He was sensitive to adolescence and to the varying developmental rates of young men. True, this young fellow left a great deal to be desired, but he had time to fill out. "I reckon he doesn't."

The redhead waxed eloquent. "Major Vickers, I was waking the men and this—individual—flies out of Hart's tent and gives me a Sunday sermon on my colorful employment of language."

Mars smiled, his white teeth glistening. "Mr. Poist, I believe you have considerable powers in the vocabulary of abuse."

Poist puffed up. "Thank you, Major."

"Now, sir, why don't you continue on your rounds so I might have the pleasure of torturing these gentlemen after their sumptuous breakfast."

Poist sauntered down the row of tents. "Get up, you lazy jackasses! Let me see your face, unless you think you can piss up a rope!"

As men with profound lack of enthusiasm greeted the sunrise, the dew cold on their bare feet, Mars turned to Geneva. "If cussing offends you, wait for Jackson to come to camp. He neither swears nor drinks nor smokes. I don't know if he'll live longer than I do, but it will seem longer."

Geneva mumbled, "I want to serve with you."

"You do, do you? Young man, I doubt you've been in school long enough to read Caesar's *Gallic Wars*."

"I read 'em, and I'd rather decline two drinks than one verb." Geneva caught on fast.

Mars threw back his head and laughed. "A boy after my own heart. What's your name?"

"James Chatfield, sir."

"Kin to Henley and Lutie Chatfield in Albemarle County?"

"Son."

Mars stuck out his big hand. "Finest horses I ever saw, your father's. Never had the pleasure of meeting him, but I've seen Chatfield's colors in many a race. I hope you'll give him my regards."

"I will, sir. He's in the army, too."

"Does he know where you are?" Mars asked casually. Geneva fumbled, but said nothing. "I thought so. Look, Mr. Chatfield, I applaud your patriotism, but you're too young. You ride back home now."

"No, sir. I want to fight."

"I can see that."

"I'm the best rider you ever laid eyes on." She said this with a touch of defiance.

"Big words for a little fellow."

"I'm not so little." Indeed, she was tall.

Mars thought a bit, then brightened. "I'll tell you what. I'll set up a course—timber, hazards, and brush. We'll provide the boys with some entertainment after breakfast. You race me. If you win, you're on." He stuck out his hand.

"I'll take that bet, Major Vickers."

As he walked back to his tent, Mars laughed to himself. He was the best rider in the camp. He had ridden at Samur, Sandhurst, and the Spanish Riding School in Vienna. The kid didn't stand a snowball's chance in hell.

Geneva burst through the tent.

Nash said, "He'll bury you, sugar."

Geneva's eyes widened. Her own husband didn't believe in her. "I'll win, and you can just goddamned stand there and watch me!"

Nash got out of bed and admonished her. "I won't have a wife of mine using foul language."

Geneva started to say something, but then graciously agreed. "You're absolutely right, Nash. I do so apologize. I will, however, beat Major Mars Vickers."

Banjo found Geneva eating her breakfast and drinking strong coffee with Nash and the men of four surrounding tents. Mars had organized them into units of five tents for cooking.

"Jimmy, you gonna do it!" Banjo slapped her on the back.

Nash started to rise to put this man in his place. How dare he touch his wife? A sharp look from Geneva caused him to reconsider, and he sat down.

"Nash, this is my man Banjo Cracker."

Banjo good-naturedly stuck out his hand. "Pleased to meet you, Mr. Hart. This here boy sets a store by you."

Nash accepted the offered hand. "I'm glad to meet you, too, Mr. Cracker."

"Banjo!" He pumped Nash's hand. "Now, Jimmy, you know Mars is the best rider in this army. But you're gonna lick him, Jimmy boy! I jes know you are."

The other men scoffed. Banjo challenged them. "I been

riding with this boy. He's a wonder, I tell you! I'll bet each and every one of you ten dollars that Jimmy skunks Major Mars."

"I'll take that bet," several men called out. "If you want to part with your money that bad, we'll help you."

A lump knotted in Geneva's throat. "I won't fail you, Banjo."

"What if there's a draw?" Nash asked, as he put his ten dollars down. He had little choice.

"The odds are so much against a draw, I think we ought to consider it a win for your fella," one man said. The others agreed. They could afford to be generous.

The artillery men with their heavy draft horses helped Mars set up the course. A few low carts without sides were used for jumps. Hastily constructed fences of whole timbers dotted the course; brush jumps a good four feet tall added to the difficulty. The course included a rushing creek at the bottom of a treacherous slope. Mars exuded high spirits.

The light haze dispersed about ten in the morning. The temperature hovered in the midsixties, perfect weather. Word reached the regiments in the camp, and most of the men gathered to enjoy this new diversion.

The officers climbed up on a platform that was moved over from the infantry field, and the rest of the men eagerly lined the course. Men in artillery units commanded the back by the miserable water jump. The infantry crowded along the middle of the course, and the cavalry took pride of place, the homestretch and finish line, since it was one of their own competing.

Banjo and Geneva worked both her mounts that morning. Gallant, the gray, seemed springier, so they decided to go with the gelding. Nash nervously inspected her tack. Why in the world did he let Geneva convince him to be silent about her enlistment? And now this? He wanted her to win, but he thought it was impossible. Well, this race would end it. She'd go back home, which was probably just as well.

Riceland, Major Vickers's handsome black servant, came over to Geneva. "The major is ready, Mr. Chatfield."

"Good." Geneva's grin was infectious. Riceland grinned back.

Banjo ran on ahead and worked the crowd. He picked up

two thousand dollars in bets. His boy was gonna thump this flashy major. Men smiled as though they were taking candy from a baby as they traded hastily made chits. Banjo had colored pieces of paper sticking out of his hat, his pockets, up his sleeves, in his belt, in his boot tops.

Mars sat astride a big bay mare that had hindquarters that screamed power. The mare was already foaming at the mouth. Mars sat deep in his seat, long stirrups in the correct jumping position.

Geneva cantered up, crouched on Gallant's neck. Her stirrups were much too short, and her toes lay alongside his flanks instead of properly sticking out. To the crowd, her riding style appeared ridiculous.

Mars appraised her seat. "Boy, you're perched up there like a dragonfly."

Banjo and Nash wriggled up to the finish line.

"That Major Vickers is a fine-looking man, ain't he though?" Banjo said admiringly.

Nash shrugged. With Mars Vickers it was hate at first sight. Nash didn't know why he couldn't bear the man, but he couldn't. However, he was assigned to Vickers' cavalry and he wasn't going to make a spectacle of himself by trying to skin out of it.

An artillery officer in dress uniform stepped up to the starting line. A saber rattled by his left side. He raised his right arm. The thousands shut up on cue. Geneva calmly waited. Mars's moustache twitched. Bang!

The course was two miles. The riders were side by side. The first jump, a simple three-foot timber on flat ground, was easy. The next jump was brush taken on the rise. Geneva felt Gallant's hind hooves tick the brush. The land rolled now, and the grass was cut on part of it. Those jumps were relatively easy, even though the height varied. Two twelve-pound cannons were placed side by side for a jump of breadth. The artillery troops went wild as both the gray and the bay sailed over the cannons. Caps waving, they shouted the riders on.

Mars, cool and confident, didn't push his mare. He didn't turn his head to see Geneva, but he felt her on his left shoulder. The kid was tough.

The water jump loomed ahead, inviting and frightening. Many horses don't like to jump water or even walk in it.

Gallant put his ears back as he approached. Geneva squeezed him, and he obeyed.

Tall grass didn't slow her but it beat against Gallant's flanks like thin whips. Horse and rider flew into the woods. Mars made this a complete test. If the kid wanted to be in the cavalry, then Mars would show him what cavalry conditions were like. Mars also figured he'd have lost Jimmy by the artillery jumps or he'd be so far ahead it wouldn't matter. He also had the advantage since he had laid out the course.

Woods were difficult to gallop through, but neither rider could afford to slacken the pace. They hit the homestretch. A hedge jump of four feet awaited them. The animals would hit the ground on the other side, take two strides, then have to jump a timber of four feet. Gallant was as graceful as a ballet dancer. The noise of the soldiers drowned the sound of thundering hoofbeats, even though the animals were racing flat out now. Banjo jumped up. Nash's knuckles were white, and he felt sick.

The last jump presented itself. An overturned supply wagon, traces and all, was the obstacle. It tested the courage of both horse and rider because it was high and wide and was the last jump on a rugged course. Neck and neck, Geneva and Mars glided over, and as they did, a volley of rifle fire blasted in their ears. That was Mars's further contribution to make this steeplechase somewhat martial in effect. He neglected to inform Geneva of this.

Geneva didn't flinch. She urged Gallant with everything she had. She had the gift of making an animal believe in itself. Mars couldn't shake the gray. The two opponents blasted through the finish line in a dead heat.

Men shrieked with excitement. Banjo was hoarse from shouting.

As they slowly cantered to cool down their mounts, Mars called over, "You can ride, boy."

"Thank you, sir. Now will you write my name?"

"No, I said you had to beat me. We finished in a dead heat."

Geneva felt as if she'd been hit in the gut. "Then I'll make you a second race, Major Vickers. Only this time we ride without reins."

"What?"

"You heard me, Major. Without reins."

Swallowing, he called back, "Well, I don't see how I can refuse."

Banjo skipped with pleasure up to Geneva. "I know'd you for a wonder! I am so proud of you, boy!" He reached up and patted her hand.

Nash reached up and shook her hand. How odd to shake her hand. He wanted to pull her off the saddle and kiss her.

She told them of the new wager.

"Don't do it. Don't risk yourself like that!" Nash said worriedly.

"Jimmy can do anything!" Banjo boasted.

Mars explained the situation to the officers on the platform. The officers spoke among themselves with excitement. Banjo ran up and down the lines and took new bets even as he collected on the first race. The bettors weren't as cocky this time. Nearly half of the men had swung their allegiance to Geneva, and the chatter was loud and lively.

Geneva walked Gallant over to Mars. "Should we change horses?"

Mars replied, "No. If we were being pursued by the enemy, we couldn't change horses."

She turned her body toward him. "You could have warned me about the rifle fire at the last jump."

"I could have." He smiled.

Again they took their places. The reins were knotted and dropped on the horses' necks. The crowd murmured. Few men there envied either rider.

Again the artillery officer raised his arm. Again the pistol signaled the start of the race.

This time Mars pulled ahead on the bay. He had legs of steel, but so did Geneva. Gallant fell in just behind the bay's left hindquarters. Everything was fine until they came to the water jump. The path was slippery. The bay's rear went out from under her as she attempted to gather herself for the jump. She went down with a thud and slipped into the water. Mars fell into the water, too, but he quickly got up and grabbed some mane. He hauled himself back on the saddle.

Geneva was now far ahead. She restrained the impulse to shout and holler and push her horse faster. Gallant already had a full day of it, so she dropped the pace to save him.

She took the last jump, the rifles fired again, and the crowd went berserk. Three minutes later, a wet Mars Vickers gamely finished the last jump. As he crossed the finish line, he untied his reins and walked his mare over to Geneva. He stood up in his stirrups and called to the crowd, "Boys, I'd be a fool not to take him!"

The crowd roared approval. Mars dismounted and turned his soaked animal over to Riceland.

Geneva dismounted, and Banjo slapped her on the back repeatedly. "Jimmy, I never saw anything like you!"

Nash pulled him off.

Banjo's eyes blazed. "What's the matter with you?"

Nash stammered. "He must be dog-tired and ready to bite. I didn't want you to knock him flat."

Banjo squinted at this tepid explanation, then waved his hand to dismiss the subject forever. "You made me rich!" he said to Geneva.

"I'm glad." She walked over to Mars. "Major Vickers, might I have another favor?"

"Ask me."

She pointed to Banjo, collecting his winnings. "Might my man enlist—not as a servant but as a cavalryman? He can shoot the eye out of a turkey at one hundred yards, I swear it!"

"I think we've had enough demonstrations for today. You tell him to come on down to my tent, and I'll put his name on the roll."

"Thank you, Major, thank you."

APRIL 26, 1861

Geneva woke an hour before dawn. She had disappointed Nash last night because she was so exhausted she had fallen onto the cot still wearing her clothes. He rolled over as she snuck out of bed, her feet hitting the cold earth.

Ground fog lay between rows of tents which looked like dropped handkerchiefs. Getting up before the others was a necessity for her. No latrines had been dug, but there was a tacit agreement about the area used to relieve oneself. She figured she'd become the world's fastest evacuator.

She rummaged through her belongings and pulled out the church almanac. Geneva paged through her small, fat Bible to Judges, chapter 19. A Levite visits his wife's father-in-law and tarries there. That was pretty boring. Then he and his wife begin his journey back to his dwelling place but the sun sets, so he lands in Gibeah. Gibeah belongs to the Benjamites and he can't find a place to stay. A kindly old man gives him lodging. In the middle of supper a group of rowdies, sons of Belial, pound on the old man's door and holler that they want the stranger brought forth. They said they wanted to know him, but Geneva suspected they wanted to bugger the fellow. So instead, the gallant Levite hands over his wife. The sons of Belial abuse and rape her the entire night. She crawls back to the old man's house and drops with her hands on the threshold. Her husband hauls her up on an ass and takes her home. Once home he seizes a knife and divides her into twelve parts, bones and all, and sends one piece to each of the twelve tribes of Israel. Naturally, this offends his neighbors.

Geneva snapped the Bible shut. She failed to see what this gruesome story had to do with her spiritual life, and she couldn't believe the husband was such a coward. Lutie would have a fit reading today's lesson. Geneva turned to the New Testament lesson. Fortunately, it provided more hope. John said we'd all be forgiven. Geneva again closed the Bible, more respectfully this time. Forgiven for what? She didn't know that she'd done anything. Maybe she wasn't the most obedient daughter, but she never really did anything wrong—well, not too terribly wrong.

She was a good wife but she hadn't been at it long enough to be otherwise. She was a good citizen; she was even willing to die for her country. She considered that again. She had come for love of her husband, but when she saw those thousands in uniform, amassed for the deliverance of their nation, she realized she was part of that great purpose. For the first time in her life, Geneva had a goal outside her own self. She felt magnified, important, useful.

"Rise and shine, my little morning glories," Poist shouted,

just as the cannon fired. "Get up, lovelies. I've seen more action with stinkbugs in a pile of horseshit." When he sauntered by Geneva, he stopped. "Some ridin', boy. I misjudged you."

After breakfast, the three hundred men under Major Mars Vickers assembled on a flat meadow, now called the parade ground. They were on foot. Geneva fell in, her husband on one side and Banjo on the other. Mars stood facing them.

"Drop!" Mars commanded.

The men fell flat on the ground. Geneva remained standing, then saw what was happening and quickly fell to the ground alongside Nash and Banjo.

Nash growled, "You're going to be sorry. He's flaming out of his mind." He shut up because he needed his breath for push-ups.

Next came sit-ups, then special stretches and leg exercises which Mars had developed for cavalrymen. The most painful ones involved sitting on the ground facing a partner. Each man took turns placing his legs around his partner's legs while his partner tried to open them.

Geneva took Nash. Both of them sweating, they pushed against one another. Geneva's legs were stronger than her husband's, although she couldn't match his torso power. He grunted, his face red and sweating, and he glared at her for winning. After exercising, the men ran. Soldiers from other regiments tormented them as Vickers's troops plodded along their three-mile jaunt.

"Thought you boys were horse soldiers!"

"Where's the bridle?"

After this torture, the noon meal was a godsend. Geneva, Nash, and Banjo ate their boiled beef in silence. Major Vickers walked up.

"Banjo Cracker, I think you ought to skip riding this afternoon and go to Harper's Ferry. Put that money you won in the bank."

"Yes, sir, but I don't trust banks, sir." Banjo smiled his snaggletoothed grin.

"Then put it in gold or land. You hear?"

"Yes, sir."

Mars walked off.

Nash jabbed at the beef. "He had no right to tell you what to do with your money."

"He's jes lookin' out. What makes a man a true leader, I guess." Banjo stiffly got up.

That afternoon Banjo purchased three thousand acres of rich land. A strong stream ran through it. Half of the acreage was in timber; the other half had already been cleared and the soil was rich. The family that owned it had slowly died off and no one was left to care for it. Banjo figured come hell or high water, and Harper's Ferry knew both, he'd be able to make a living when this war was over.

APRIL 27, 1861

Mars watched his troops ride in the afternoon sun. This was their first day wearing the pants with leather on the inseam. It made their legs sweat but even the loudest complainers could grip the saddle more tightly.

Divided into groups of ten, the best rider in each group took the inside position as the groups wheeled in circles. From the circle they rode in a line single file and then back to a circle again. They had to respond both to voice commands and to a bugle.

"Parade ground stuff," Nash grumbled, within hearing of Mars. Mars was definitely beginning to form an opinion about this sandy-haired slender man, and it wasn't a good one. On their first meeting, Nash had said, "Defend Rome by striking Carthage." It galled Mars that a university boy thought it necessary to chop such pretentious talk into the conversation. Mars could read Latin as well as anybody, and this boy still had a thing or two to learn in real life.

"Drop your stirrups. Now drape them across your horse's withers," Mars directed. "Circle."

Within minutes horses bumped into each other, and men cursed.

"You aren't even at a trot. What are you going to do in the field if you lose your stirrups at a gallop while under fire?" His face darkened. "Leg! Leg! If we have to do this for fourteen hours a day, then that's what we'll do!"

A collective groan rose from the dust.

"Single file." He squinted as they unfurled into a line again. "Reverse." Jimmy Chatfield was the pivot man on his team of ten. Mars admired the boy's even temper with horses. Occasionally Jimmy would call out to his group, and a rider would respond. Only Nash bitched at the boy. Why Jimmy wanted to stay in the same tent with that man mystified Mars. Why didn't the boy pick Banjo for his tent mate?

"Circle. All right, drop your stirrups. Form three squares of one hundred men each. Chatfield, you ride first left on the first square; Benserade, first left, second square; I'll take first left, third square."

For another twenty minutes, they walked, trotted, and cantered in big squares. When the bugle sounded halt, both men and horses were relieved to head back to camp.

Geneva, Nash, Banjo, and Sam Wells, also from Albemarle County, rode to the makeshift stables. When Sam had left to attend the University of Pennsylvania, Geneva was still a little girl. Sam had remained in Philadelphia to pursue his business. He accepted that she was the younger Chatfield boy, although he only vaguely recollected the baby and thought he'd heard that the boy died. Well, whenever his mother supplied him with the news, her definition, gossip, his, he promptly forgot most of it.

Riceland, Mars's man, brushed by her with Mars's horse behind him. " 'Scuse me, Jimmy."

"I'm too worn out to get out of your way," she said with a smile.

"You ain't seen nothin' yet. Major Mars givin' you the easy stuff. Don't worry 'bout it. You'll do fine. You're the best rider I've ever seen. Never thought I'd see a better rider than Major Mars, but he's complete. Knows everything there is to know about horses, and everything there is to know about men. Got no sense when it comes to women though."

Geneva shrugged. "Bet the ladies worship the handsome Mars Vickers."

"Yes, sir, that they do." Riceland leaned closer. "But the major is poisoned by his wife. Sweet poison. The major is miserable sick with love. He commands everyone but her. She looks like a goddess. Be easier if she was ugly."

"But if she was ugly, he probably wouldn't be married to her."

Riceland clapped Dancer's neck. "Jimmy, you said a mouthful."

APRIL 28, 1861

"Micah 5 exhorts me 'O daughter of troops' to go to war once again—for the Lord, of course," Lutie chattered. "Why do I bother telling you, Emil? You're a Muslim. You probably kneel on my Persian carpets when I'm not looking and bow your turbaned head toward Mecca. Sin-Sin wears turbans but I can't feature her kneeling on a rug. It's quarter to seven, and I'd better get this house running."

She fastened her shoes. She'd rather go barefoot but then she'd get splayed feet. That's what her mother, Diddy Elizabeth Simms Chalfonte, told her. Diddy Simms, born in 1798, exercised notions, one of which was that she could tell who had the Third Eye of Prophecy by the number of times they blinked within a minute. Those that blinked but once possessed the eye or had paralyzed eyelids.

"I'm hoping that Jennifer Greer Fitzgerald throws her May party. I fully intend to ride on a lavender ostrich. You're conspicuously silent, Emil. I hate it when you flout superior airs. It's all those luxurious silks and satins that you wear."

A bottle green cloud so dark it was nearly black drew Lutie's attention to the window. She peered out, then threw open the door to her room and hurried down the long hallway. "Sin-Sin! Sin-Sin!"

Ernie June answered her from the kitchen. "Sin-Sin ain't in the house, Miz Lutie," she called out.

Lutie reached the kitchen. "Ernie June, look out the window!"

A terrible howl began. Ernie June opened the kitchen door, and Cazzie, the cat, barreled by her and hid in the pantry. A treacherous funnel mesmerized both women.

Coming to her senses, Lutie pushed the door shut with Ernie June's help.

The front door opened, then slammed shut. "Miss Lutie! Are you here?" Di-Peachy's usually deep voice rang shrill.

"Yes. Come on down to the cellar."

"My Boyd's out there with Braxton," Ernie wailed.

"He'll take care of his sister." Di-Peachy comforted her.

"Where were you?" Lutie asked.

"I was shutting up Geneva's house when I noticed everything was still. I saw a dark cloud, maybe half a mile off but moving fast. Big Muler closed the back of the house, and I closed the front and ran for you."

A horrifying rumble overhead shut them up. A great cracking reverberated outside of the house. The roar then drowned all other sounds.

"Lord Jesus, this ole nigger woman ain't done nothin' wrong," Ernie prayed. "Take me 'fore you take my babies."

Listening to Ernie's sincere prayers, Di-Peachy remained calm, and Lutie found an inner strength in the face of the tornado that amazed herself.

The howling finally faded. "I think it's over. Let's go back upstairs," Lutie ordered.

Ernie showed no signs of moving. "Come on, Ernie, it passed." Di-Peachy offered her a hand.

"The devil's straw, a whirlin' storm! Stick you head up too soon and whoosh, off it go to a big stewpot in hell."

Lutie and Di-Peachy were in the kitchen before Ernie put one foot out of the cellar. From the kitchen window everything appeared fine.

Lutie opened the door and stepped outside. "Holy Mary, Mother of God!"

Di-Peachy followed her. A path about seventy-five feet across had been cut clean through the property. A tornado had veered off to the right and had torn down a woodshed as well as two servants' houses. The brick chimney had been knocked down at another servant's quarters.

Sin-Sin, picking up her skirt, ran toward Lutie. She was so worried she forgot to call her Miss in front of the others. "Lutie, Lutie, you all right?"

Lutie ran for her. Meeting midway in the backyard, the two embraced. "I'm all right. What about you, Sin-Sin?"

"Never saw anything hurl itself outta the sky so fast. Di-Peachy, I see you in one piece."

Behind them, Ernie bellowed at the top of her lungs, "Boyd, Braxton!" Both emerged from the stables.

"Let's inspect the damage." Lutie grimly headed toward the servants' quarters. She passed a three-story-high chestnut tree, one mighty limb dangling like a broken arm.

The women and Braxton reached a flattened house. "Anyone in there?" Di-Peachy called. Nothing stirred in the rubble.

Braxton observed the flattened house before them. "Be firewood now. Lucky thing Peter down at the stable. This one's his."

"Where were you?" Sin-Sin asked, as Tincia and the other women came up behind the quarters.

"Mess of us hid in your pots' oven, Auntie Sin-Sin. Everybody there but the house folk and the barn folk."

"Thank God," Lutie sighed.

Di-Peachy opened the door. She blanched. "Auntie Sin-Sin, you'd better come here. You, too, Miss Lutie."

Sin-Sin pushed through the door, but Lutie saw him first. She knelt over the twisted body of Alafin. His skull was smashed in. Bricks were strewn about. Braxton looked in and then turned around to keep the others away.

"Braxton, tell Timothy to saddle up and get Father Manlius. And tell him to come up as soon as he can." She reached in her skirt pocket, pulled out a pass, and gave it to Braxton. "Even though everyone knows Timothy, we can't take chances. After all, it is wartime."

Braxton left. Di-Peachy observed a brick. Hair and brains covered the end of it. Lutie took it from her. "I don't think a tornado did this."

"Wind does strange things. Heard tell of a reed bein' driven through a tree." Sin-Sin grimaced.

"Alafin made enemies." Lutie laid the brick by his crumpled body.

"Peter, for one," Di-Peachy said.

"Couldn't keep it in his pants." Sin-Sin crossed her arms across her bosom. "Ran after women, especially Tincia. Even Frederica, and her bein' married didn't faze him. Di-Peachy, too."

"Everyone notices Di-Peachy." Lutie waved that off.

"He'd get all randy and rub up against the girls."

Lutie looked at Di-Peachy, who nodded her confirmation.

"Miss Lutie, you have enough on your mind. We women-folk watch out for one another."

Lutie stared at the lifeless body. Poor dumb fool, she thought.

Sin-Sin leaned over and felt his wrist. "Still warm. He was kilt within the hour."

"During the storm." Di-Peachy shuddered.

"Who would search him out in that terrible wind?" asked Lutie.

"Someone who hated him beyond reason."

Sin-Sin muttered a rhyme under her breath, the rhyme she'd used to admonish Geneva and Di-Peachy when they were children.

"Right is wrong
And wrong is right.
And who can know it
All by sight?"

Sundays in camp were a mixture of piety and drunkenness. Banjo was working on the drunkenness.

"Banjo, if I put a torch to you, you'd explode." Geneva sat down next to him.

"Christ died for my sins. I got to sin as much as I can, else he woulda died for nothin'." Banjo took another pull.

Mr. Poist, Sam Wells, Banjo, Benserade, Nash, and Geneva sat around the open fire in varying states of inebriation.

"Did you vote?" Sam asked Nash.

"Sure. Breckinridge and Lane."

"I voted for Bell and Everett," Benserade chimed in. "Family's always been Whigs. We wouldn't be in this war if they'd won."

Sam replied, "I don't know. I've been living in Philadelphia for years now. Voted up there. Lots of votes for Lincoln. And even if a Whig or Democrat got in, we'd still have those fanatics in the Senate like Thaddeus Stevens from Pennsylvania, I am sorry to say."

"Someone should of shot that son of a bitch abolitionist years ago." Poist folded his hands.

"They should of jammed him back in the womb." Benserade poked at the fire.

"That's what you hear down here. Up there," Sam reminded them, "they hear nothing but stories about wild secessionists in South Carolina and slave beaters in Mississippi. You wouldn't believe the talk."

"Small choice in rotten apples." Banjo rocked back and forth on his hunkers.

"What do you mean?" Nash asked.

"Crooks. Never saw a politician yet that wouldn't steal the pennies off a dead man's eyes."

"Hear! Hear!" agreed Mr. Poist.

Nash's brow wrinkled. "Some of them are good men. Can't go around thinking the worst of people."

"I don't think the worst of people. I give 'em the benefit of the doubt, and they prove my thinkin'. The higher a monkey climbs, the better you can see his little red ass," said Banjo.

Sam smiled, and Nash spoke again. "Nobody thought there was even one Republican in Albemarle County, so they printed up Constitutional Union ballots and Democratic ballots. Then along comes old T.W. Savage."

"T.W.'s still alive?"

"T.W.'s been alive since the French and Indian War, I swear it. Anyway, he came down and told the clerk to cry his vote. Fine. But T.W. says, 'Lincoln.' The clerk wouldn't cry it. They laughed T.W. out of the courthouse. Course T.W.'s disgrace didn't last long. After all, everyone is entitled to a few mistakes, especially an old man."

"This old man thinks all politicians are as crooked as a dog's hind leg." Banjo spat in the fire. "I say let the rough side drag."

"Huh?" Geneva asked.

"You know," Banjo explained. "Let them go to hell. Now if Bob, the tailor, will lend me his banjo, you'll find out how I got my name."

Banjo returned with a banjo and Bob, who carried a guitar.

Soon after they began to play, soldiers ran over from other tents, and the party started in earnest.

"Let's dance!" Poist nimbly kicked up one leg. He grabbed Benserade, and they galloped around the fire. "Come on, boys, grab a partner. If you take off your neckerchief and wave it in the air, you can be the girl."

This suggestion was met with a burst of laughter. Some of the men untied their neckerchiefs and played the lady's part. A few were graceful, but most were not.

"Let's dance," Geneva whispered in Nash's ear.

"I'm afraid I'll hold you too tight."

Sam Wells hauled Geneva to her feet. "Come on, little Jimmy Chatfield. Let's see if you can dance as good as you can sit on a horse."

"I don't want to be the girl," Geneva protested.

"You're the youngest. Come on, don't be touchy about it." He slapped his right arm around her waist and off they went.

Three other men joined Banjo and Bob. One had a mouth organ, another had a banjo, and the third joined in with his fiddle.

The dance finished. Each man sipped a drink or other refreshment. Banjo and his crew began to play another tune. This time Nash asked Geneva to dance. He trembled when he held her. They couldn't look into one another's eyes.

Mars Vickers, walking with a few of the staff, stopped to enjoy the merriment. He pushed his way to the inside of the large circle.

Poist, wild with music and whiskey, released his partner, who twirled into the crowd and landed flat on his ass. Poist clicked his heels in the air. The men cheered. He tiptoed over to the major and bowed low. "Major Mars, may I have this dance?"

Mars bowed equally low. "Mrs. Poist, I'd be honored."

Yelling and whooping, they trotted into the fray. Poist waved his hanky in a fit of exaggerated femininity. Now all the men were dancing, except those too drunk to stand. At least five men were sprawled flat on their backs in the grass, out cold.

The band began to play.

Mars released the enthusiastic Poist and walked over to Geneva. "Might I have a dance with my conqueror?" His moustache twitched.

"I don't want to be the girl."

"Jimmy, I'll gladly be the girl. In fact, if there's reincarnation, I want to come back as a woman." He held up his arms as would a lady, and she clumsily put her hands in the right places. She began to push him around like a barge. "Come on, Jimmy, I'm not that bad."

Nash leaned against a tree, arms folded across his chest. He despised the very air Mars breathed.

Geneva stumbled; Mars righted her, quickly switched positions, and seized the lead. She followed him naturally. He was a bigger man with a heavier build than Nash. She could feel the huge muscles in his shoulders and smell the sweet odor of whiskey on his breath. He loved to dance, and he was light on his feet. He whirled her around, picking her up on one pretty pass. A few of the men cheered. Geneva blushed.

"You aren't half bad, Jimmy."

"Thank you," she stammered.

"Up we go." He lifted her up again, and the music picked up tempo. Despite Nash fuming on the sidelines, she couldn't help but enjoy herself. She threw back her head and laughed. That inspired Mars even more, and they tore through the group like a cannonball. There was something about Mars Vickers that made people watch him. He provoked strong emotions, either love or hate. Fortunately for him, most people loved him. His men would follow him into the jaws of hell. And deep in his heart, he knew that's where he would be leading them.

The music stopped. Mars released Geneva. He pulled a flask from his hip pocket and offered her a swallow.

"No, thank you, Major."

"Gotta learn sometime, boy."

"Why'd you say you'd come back as a woman?"

He licked his lips and handed the flask to her again. "Because women are beautiful. Because if a woman even looks at a man, he's defeated. We work, die, even kill for women. I hope never to be a second in another duel as long as I live."

"I think women are silly."

"What?" He laughed at her.

"They sit around and sew and gossip and nurse the sick. You're better off as a man."

"Jimmy, all the guns of the Confederacy aren't as powerful

as one kiss from the woman you love." He paused and then laughed. "Or the one you don't love. Come on, yearling, let's dance." He placed his strong hand in the small of her back before she could retreat, and they slammed back into the mob.

Nash wiggled his way between the dancers. He tapped Mars on the shoulder. Mars turned around to behold his least favorite recruit.

"What do you want, Hart?"

"I'd like to dance with Jimmy." Nash grabbed his wife. Mars didn't appreciate his roughness.

"Don't do me like that, Hart," Mars said, his voice sharp, "or I'll give you a knockdown answer."

"I don't much care one way or the other," Nash caustically replied.

Geneva slid between them. She turned her face up to Mars. "We've all been funnin' and drinkin' too much. Don't hit him, Major."

He was one of the few men taller than Geneva. He stared into her cognac eyes. "You're right, Jimmy, I won't hit him. If I did, I'd have to touch him." He turned on his heel and stalked off.

"Let's go back to the tent," Nash growled.

They cut through the crowd. Banjo, wobbly as he was, watched the entire episode. Doe to stag, he thought to himself. Get 'em nothin' but trouble.

Inside the tent Nash extinguished the lamp with one hand. Then he bit Geneva's neck and backed her onto the cot. Angry at the scene he'd made, she refused him. Furious, he cursed and rolled over on his cot, turning his back to her. Geneva felt like the tent was spinning, but she also felt another kind of queasiness. She was learning some things about her husband which she didn't like. He was different outside of their circle of friends, family, and servants. But then so was she. Did other married people harbor doubts about their mate?

APRIL 29, 1861

"Man that is born of a woman, hath but a short time to live, and is full of misery. He cometh up, and is cut down like a flower; he fleeth as it were a shadow, and never continueth in one stay.

"In the midst of life we are in death; of whom may we seek for succour." The Very Reverend Manlius's voice floated up to the thin clouds.

The population of Chatfield gathered around Alafin's grave. The tombstone of servants dating back to the very end of the seventeenth century bore mute witness to their claim on this land. Like the Chatfields, they were of Albemarle County. Unlike the Chatfields, they did not own any piece of it.

Last night, the women dressed Alafin. They tied his legs together and his arms to his side. They closed his eyes by placing pennies underneath the lids. They tied his jaw shut with soft ribbons. Rigor mortis would set in within seven hours and sometimes earlier, so they took care to dress him promptly and properly.

The nights were still cool so the body was left in the death house built inside the earth near the ice house. In the winter the ground was too hard to dig a grave. Bodies—as many as four—were placed in shelves on the mausoleum dug into the side of the hill. When spring thaws came, the bodies were removed and put into the ground. Winter deaths were not as dreaded as summer deaths. Even if the body was packed in ice, it would go off quickly. No matter how much money was offered to the children to fan the bodies to keep the flies off, they were too frightened to sit next to death. On a blistering July or August day, Lutie insisted the bodies be buried within three hours. If Father Manlius couldn't preside, she or

Henley would do the honors. The stench so demoralized
everyone that getting the body buried took precedence over
an ordained minister. Alafin was lucky; he died in the spring-
time and got the benefit of the Very Reverend Manlius.

Big Muler moved the coffin to the grave site with no help
from anyone. He hauled it on his back from the death house
over the blooming meadows to the neatly maintained graveyard. His performance of power had the desired effect on
other young men at the ceremony. Big Muler stood behind
Di-Peachy. Her jaw was tight.

Lutie turned her head and glanced at them. Thank God for
Big Muler, she thought. The murder of Alafin shook her. Not
that she liked him. Alafin was obsequious to whites and
treacherous to blacks, but he was also a young man in his
prime, and his labor was valuable. Lutie surveyed the faces
surrounding the grave. It occurred to her that news of the war
might strike them differently than it struck her. Even though
Jennifer Fitzgerald had hinted darkly at an uprising, Lutie
did not believe her servants would murder her in her bed.
Yet, one of her people had killed Alafin. She stared at each
face: Braxton's clean, strong features already creased with
care; Sin-Sin; Tincia, creamy brown, pretty and empty-headed;
Peter, too pretty for Lutie's taste; Boyd, a fat little moon
face; Ernie June, dark as walnut stain; Frederica, long and
narrow like a silent flame, her baby in her arms. The others,
heads bowed, wouldn't kill anyone, but they might run off,
one by one.

Lutie believed that these people had been entrusted to her
care. She was the mistress of a great house, one of the finest
homes in Virginia, which was to say in the civilized world. To
her befell their religious training, assignment of duties, rou-
tine, and reward. It never once crossed her mind that the
white race might not be superior to the black, indeed, to all
other races on the face of the earth. Surely this was God's will
or why would the whites have conquered the others?

Henley had said that someday he wanted to free the servants. Lutie, whatever her reservations about slavery, had no
reservations about the cost of such an action. How could they
afford to pay these people a wage? Henley said that if you
paid them, then you didn't have to take care of them. In fact,
it would be cheaper to free them. Lutie's argument was, Free
them for what? Where would they go, and what would they

do? One would pay them a wage, but still be responsible for them. With a few exceptions, such as Sin-Sin and Di-Peachy, these people couldn't think for themselves. She, Lutie Chalfonte, was responsible for them to her peers and to God. Lutie never asked anyone if they wanted to be taken care of, but then she wouldn't have gotten a straight answer. No, Lutie was convinced no matter what, no matter when, the white race would have to care for the black.

She hated funerals. Her mind went back to Jimmy's funeral. The services for the burial of a child are exquisitely painful. She could hear Very Reverend Manlius intone, "O Merciful Father, whose face the angels of thy little ones do always behold in heaven; Grant us steadfastly to believe that this thy child hath been taken into the safekeeping of thine eternal love; through Jesus Christ our Lord. Amen."

A wail from Tincia brought her back to Alafin's funeral.

The Very Reverend Manlius finished. "Suffer us not at our last hour for any pains of death to fall from thee."

Peter placed a restraining hand on Tincia's heaving shoulders. He had no sympathy for her grief. He was glad Alafin was dead. He wanted Tincia all to himself.

Frederica handed her infant over the open grave to Boyd, who was standing on the other side. The five other small babies of Chatfield were likewise passed over the coffin. The servants believed that if this ritual was not performed, the soul of the dead would snatch the babes and force them to accompany him on his journey to the afterlife.

Following the service, Lutie and the Very Reverend Manlius walked back to the big house. Sin-Sin and Di-Peachy followed at a discreet distance.

"Thank you for officiating, Father Manlius."

"A duty, no matter how sad, that brings me to your beautiful home and your bracing company."

"Thank you, Father. I, too, look forward to your company. I'm hoping we can discuss the scriptures over lunch."

"Indeed. This is the twenty-ninth, is it not?"

"Yes," Lutie replied.

"This is the day Noah was believed to have quit his ark."

"I expect the poor man ate so much seafood his stomach rose and fell with the tide."

MAY 9, 1861

Ascension Day may have gotten Christ off the earth, but Geneva was stuck right here. The smoke confused her. She didn't mind the whine of cannon overhead, but she didn't reckon with the huge clouds of smoke that artillery fire creates. Coughing and sputtering, she kept the reins in her left hand and held her empty pistol in her right. Her squad trotted through the noise of war games organized by Mars Vickers. Clods of earth were shot into the air on her left, just far enough away to give her a margin of safety.

"Tighter, boys!" Captain Brown shouted, rallying his group. They trotted on only to see Benserade's men come riding toward them at a hard gallop. The earth rumbled underneath Geneva. Even though she knew another large cavalry force was coming, she wasn't ready for the tremendous vibration or the shock of horse slamming into horse. She didn't generate equivalent force. A horse at a trot is no match for a horse at a gallop. Dancer squealed. A forearm caught her on the chest, but she stayed mounted.

"Hard right!" Brown bellowed.

She heeled and moved through the throng at a diagonal. They'd never get out of this without getting the shit beat out of them. To her surprise, Captain Brown's diagonal movement worked, and she was clear of the melee. The entire operation took only four minutes, but it seemed much longer.

"Assemble on the parade grounds," Brown ordered.

The men, still on horseback, lined up by company on the parade ground. Mars, sweating, faced them on a roan he had picked up from a West Virginia farmer a couple of weeks ago.

"Brown, you did the right thing. You wheeled in time to make the blow a glancing one. If you'd met Benserade's men head-on, there wouldn't be one of you sitting on a horse. Now I know some of you boys want to draw sabers and charge. Let the Yankees do that. They don't know jack shit about cavalry warfare anyway." Some men laughed. Mars wiped his arm across his forehead. "This time I want Brown's men to reconnoiter Area Red. Okay, boys, ride on."

As Geneva, Nash, and Banjo slowly rode off, they strained to catch word of their opponents' war game orders. Today they bore the brunt of the action. Tomorrow it would be their turn to be the hunter.

Major Vickers displayed his genius by simulating every conceivable battle condition, short of live ammunition and death. He infuriated his men by insisting they no longer turn over their mounts to their servants. Each man had to rub down his own horse and inspect his own tack. Mars said repeatedly, "Your life depends on the condition of your body, the condition of your horse, and the condition of your tack. You can have the best horse in the company, but what good is it if your girth breaks while you're under fire?"

One night during a hard rain and without warning, Mars ordered them to mount up. The men staggered out of their tents, saddled up, and rode in the driving rain for two hours. Vickers's men were gaining a reputation as the toughest unit in the cavalry. They swaggered before the infantry and artillery. The sight of another cavalry command produced instant challenges. Mars finally had to forbid betting on racing or jumping against other cavalry units. He let it be known unofficially that he didn't want to embarrass the other officers and men. This endeared him further to his troops.

Mars kept counsel. Any man in his command could walk in and present an idea or grievance. No need was too small for his attention. He walked the lines at night; he questioned the servants as to the health and condition of their masters. Moreover, he never asked a man to do what he himself wouldn't do.

Area Red, thick with woods and hedgerow, was a cavalryman's nightmare. Brown told the men to break formation and string out over the terrain. They were to search for any sign of the enemy. A low road cut through the woods. Geneva moved away from the others and headed toward the edge of the road. A rifle cracked over her head.

"You're dead." An infantryman spat tobacco on the ground. "Tie the red bandanna around your cap."

Furious and somewhat frightened, Geneva shouted, "What makes you think you'd be that good a shot!"

"Like a demonstration, precious darling?" His voice dripped with sarcasm. He put his rifle to his shoulder and aimed it straight up. "Throw your cap in the air, snot nose."

Geneva tossed her yellow cap up as high as she could.

The rifleman bagged it. Triumphantly, he retrieved the cap. "Tie a red bandanna around it!"

She did and trotted back to Captain Brown.

"Dead?"

The rules were that she couldn't say how she had been killed. If the others didn't see the death, then they would have to draw their own conclusions.

"You shouldn't have strayed so far," Nash chided.

As they emerged from the woods, three supply wagons rested on a road cutting through a meadow. A slight rise on the far side of the meadow could conceal troops.

Brown peered through his binoculars. "Could be a trap. Sam, take Nash and Banjo and investigate."

Banjo and Sam led the way; Nash lagged behind.

No signs of life greeted them. Sam waved his hat, and the other men in the company joined them.

"Grab everything you can out of the wagons. Fast!"

Mars had told them never to try and move a wagon, but rather to sling grain and other supplies over the front of their saddles and ride off. Any papers or maps were often of the utmost importance and should be placed inside the saddle-bags. Money or other valuables would be shared equally among the troops.

In the middle of pillaging their booty, Nash saw a movement in the woods. He called softly to Brown. "Ten degrees off your right, Captain."

Brown looked through his binoculars. He saw infantrymen moving from tree to tree in the woods he and his men had just ridden through, but they were too far away to be a problem.

Suddenly Banjo shouted, "Here they come!"

A small detachment of cavalry appeared on the meadow's rise. Brown's unit couldn't flee back into the woods. They'd have to make a run for it over open fields.

"Back to the camp!" Brown ordered.

Forty men and forty horses burnt the wind getting back to camp. They discarded much of their fake booty in the process. Their pursuers caught up with them in fifteen minutes' time.

Mars, leading the pursuers, dismounted and clapped his hand on Brown's back. "What'd you learn today, Captain?"

"To post a lookout. My eyes were bigger than my belly."

Mars caught sight of Geneva. "Who killed you?"

"An infantryman hidden in the brush by the low road."

"What were you doing that far from the others? That's the edge of Area Red, Chatfield."

"I didn't hear anything, and I didn't see the harm in extending the line a little."

"Well, now you know, don't you?"

"Yes, sir."

"And take that ridiculous bandanna off your cap. I don't like to think of you dead."

MAY 10, 1861

Last night at Kate Vickers's home, Henley sparkled. He charmed the ladies while maintaining strict propriety. He felt young again. He adored Kate Vickers.

He also made some progress with other commissary officers yesterday. Everyone agreed that the state should be divided into districts of supply. Henley argued that certain wealthy businessmen and tradesmen should be made commissioners, civilian counterparts to the military officers. He thought that by using the businessmen as commissioners, the thieves would police the thieves.

Northrupp, head of Commissary listened but old Jacob Barnhart from Williamsburg nearly expired upon hearing this

suggestion. Southern gentlemen profiteer from the war? Never!
Every man would willingly give his grain, his cattle, his sons,
and himself to the cause. Henley bit his tongue while the old
man spun his illusions. Jacob Barnhart had never dealt with a
tradesman in his life. He had no appreciation for the mercan-
tile instinct which seeks profit in all things, even death.
Henley, because of his horse breeding business, understood
it only too well. The eight other officers in the stuffy room,
most of them considerably younger than Barnhart, winked at
Henley. Jacob was born right after the Revolutionary War.
The others were modern men, most of whom had spent time
in the North. They would consider Henley's proposal for
civilian commissioners.

What stuck in Henley's craw was the fact that the important ordinance officers were those assigned to weaponry. They'd
set up offices out at Tredegar Iron Works. No one said they
were that important, but the buzzing in and out of Lee's
offices in Mechanics Hall proved the point. Lee had assumed
the Virginia command that Governor Letcher had offered. As
each state was raising troops and putting a favored son in
charge, it was confusing. Beauregard and Johnston appeared
the most likely candidates for an overall command if the
Confederacy could get organized.

Henley felt he deserved better than the Commissary Department. The lavish compliments on feeding the troops
sounded sour in his ears. To hell with it, he wanted to fight.
After all, he'd read and absorbed Henri Jomini's *Summary of
the Art of War*. He knew his military history. On this day in
1796 Napoleon had defeated the Austrians at Lodi. Henley
left his card at Mechanics Hall. The new commanding officer
would get to it in time. Henley fully intended to ask an
already tired Robert E. Lee for a field commission.

The sun rolled over the horizon like the red rim of a wagon
wheel. Henley reached into the small desk made from cherry
wood and took out his Bible and the pamphlet of lessons.
Lutie would be doing the same and so would Sumner and
Geneva, wherever they were. It was curiously satisfying to
know this.

The Old Testament lesson was 1 Samuel 15. God told Saul
to kill the Amalekites, to massacre them, men, women, and
children. God even told Saul to extend his heavenly wrath to
the oxen, sheep, camels, and asses. Saul murdered the peo-

ple, but he and his men saved the best of the stock. This
didn't go down with the Lord, and Saul was bounced from
being king of the Israelites.

Before Henley could ponder the significance of the lesson,
a light rap on the door saved him.

"Colonel Chatfield." A bright boy held out a silver tray
with three letters on it.

"Thank you," Henley said, handing him a coin.

The first letter, on plain white stationery, was from Colonel Charles Venable, aide-de-camp to General Lee. The
general would be happy to see him on Thursday next.

The second letter was written on pale blue stationery. The
initials KLV were centered in dark blue block letters at the
top of the page. Henley liked that. Most women wallowed
around in script.

> Dear Colonel Chatfield:
>   You did so enliven us by your presence.
>   Might I prevail upon your good nature to ask you to
> accompany me, when duty permits, to inspect a gelding
> offered me for hunting? If you haven't time I do under-
> stand, and I hope you will forgive me for making so bold
> as to ask.
>
>   Yours, Sincerely,
>   Mrs. Mars Vickers

Whistling, Henley folded the letter back into the envelope
and placed it inside his breast pocket.

The third letter was from Geneva. She had written on
Chatfield stationery, a creamy bond with the name of the
estate in forest green. She was in London with the Bennetts
and hoped he was well. The Wells and Ryders, also in
England and old friends of the family, were fine. She received many invitations for visits to country estates. Right
now she was enjoying the city. She missed Nash so much she
could die, but she would be home by fall.

The salutations were most affectionate and the handwriting
far prettier than he remembered, but when was the last time
he had seen her hand? She had even sealed the letter with
dark green wax. Henley couldn't recall Geneva being that careful. Assuming Geneva was homesick, Henley wrote her a long
letter full of Richmond gossip and posted it before breakfast.

MAY 11, 1861

Colonel Thomas J. Jackson's headquarters throbbed with activity. Mars, fresh from a quick conference with the odd Jackson, walked over to his horses. Smartly uniformed men were coming and going. Every officer had brought his own batman, a personal servant who washed his clothes, ironed his shirts, polished and boned his boots, brushed his braid. Mars laughed to himself. This is the damnedest prettiest army I've ever seen at camp, he thought. Mars knew what it was to stay in the saddle for weeks at a time, without a bath or a change of clothes, without food. Enjoy it while you can, he thought.

"Jimmy Chatfield, what are you doing here?" he bellowed at the long, lean boy.

"Looking for you. The new mounts arrived, Major Vickers."

"Let's go then." Mars eased into the saddle.

As they rode along, Mars studied Jimmy. Jimmy wore his foraging cap cocked on his head, a yellow neckerchief tied in a knot at his throat. High summer wasn't upon him, but he was as tan as his saddle. His legs had bulked up a bit. Superb rider though he was, the extra work put more muscle on him. Still too thin in the chest, though. The other young men in the camp grew beards or moustaches. Facial hair was all the rage, though for those who didn't like to shave in the morning, it was laziness. Jimmy cultivated no moustache or beard. And while he got along with everyone, the boy kept to himself for the most part. Jimmy Chatfield was the only man who'd proven himself a better rider than Mars, so the major had a special interest in him. There was a sweetness and straightforwardness about the young man that touched him and made him regret the sons he'd never fathered.

The only thing Mars didn't like about Jimmy was Nash

Hart. The boy acted silly over Hart, and Mars couldn't understand it. As far as Mars was concerned, Nash Hart was so far behind everyone else he was lonesome. Yet Jimmy seemed to worship the man. Mars hoped it wasn't a physical relationship, but he was a worldly man. Sometimes a boy does swoon over a grown man before he becomes a man himself with a grown man's responsibilities. But it turned his stomach to think of Hart taking advantage of this youth, if in fact he was. He didn't want Jimmy used that way, and he thought the boy was too young to know what he was doing. On the other hand, Hart seemed jealous of the boy while simultaneously pretending to ignore him.

"When are the Yankees going to attack, Major Vickers?"

Mars smiled. "Why? You getting anxious?"

"A little." Geneva patted Dancer's neck.

"They'll have to attack us, because we aren't going to attack them. Now that the government is being moved from Montgomery, Alabama, to Richmond, they'll probably strike for Richmond."

"How do you think they'll make their approach to Richmond?"

"Well, there are a variety of ways they can attack: by water, straight down from Washington by land; or if they're feeling clever, they'll send out a body of men in one direction and the main force in another. However, I don't think they're that clever."

"Are you anxious to fight, sir?"

"Fight? It's my profession. But I've seen enough to know there's no glory in it, and I've seen enough to know it will never end."

"We'll beat their pants off, and that will end it." She jauntily trotted forward.

"What I mean, Jimmy, is after this war, there will be another war, and one after that. Man is more ape than angel."

"But if the abolitionists had just left us alone, there wouldn't be any war."

"Oh, hell, boy, that is just the excuse. This war's been brewing since I was in the cradle. I'd a damn sight prefer it if the real reason—greed—was put forward for once and not this smarmy abolitionist hypocrisy."

Geneva's forehead wrinkled. Surely Major Vickers didn't mean that the South was greedy. We only ask to be allowed to live in peace according to our creed. He must mean the North. But Geneva remembered her Aunt Poofy and Uncle Daniel. They weren't greedy people. They were good people. They were fighting for the North. This knowledge burdened Geneva.

"Independence! That's the real reason for this fight, Major Vickers. Doesn't matter what the abolitionists say. We know why we're fighting."

"What really matters, Jimmy, is who wins this war. Then the winner's reasons will become the official reasons."

"Well, they aren't going to win it." Geneva was defiant.

Up ahead, they saw Banjo perched on a hastily constructed fence, about seventy horses behind him.

"Let's see what we got." Mars dismounted.

For the next several hours, the three soldiers inspected each horse. A few would be turned out to pasture or sold cheap in town. Most of them, though, would do and even the rough broke ones would bend to Vickers's will.

"Major, why don't we attack Washington?" asked Geneva, as they finished their task.

"Because the troops are green. Because we are not yet a fully functioning army. Because we don't have enough provisions even if we did take Washington."

"Maryland is on our side," Banjo chimed in.

"Maryland's caught between a rock and a hard place. Listen up. There's something very different about this war. We could haul ourselves right over the Potomac and take Washington. In fact, it would be easy to take that stinking swamp city. The inhabitants would give it away, but that isn't going to end the war. This isn't a European war. Over there, those countries are so small that if you take the capital, it's over. If you take Washington, the Federals can withdraw into the vast countryside. On either side, city after city can fall, but it won't put a stop to the fighting."

Geneva stopped feeling a horse's foreleg and stood up. "I thought the war would be over before Christmas."

"This war will only end quickly if something miraculous happens. We're in it but good." Mars smacked a buckskin's hindquarters to get him out of the way. "I know you're younger than you want me to know. Do you want out?"

Geneva's face flushed. "No, sir."

"Look at me," Mars whispered. "Is it Southern independence you believe in or is it Nash Hart?"

Her face was now bright red. "I don't know what you're talking about."

"Let me tell you something about your friend. War is going to come as a terrible shock to your Mr. Hart. He's not cut out for it."

"He's no coward!" Geneva's temper frayed.

"I didn't say he was a coward," Mars said, raising his voice. "I said he wasn't cut out for war."

Tears came to Geneva's eyes. She was too angry to say anything. She focused on a bay horse.

"And another thing, Chatfield, I wish you'd stop looking at Nash Hart like a moonstruck cow."

In silent fury, Geneva kept working. Banjo, while sympathetic, thought the major was right. He was afraid Nash was carrying the boy a little fast.

There was enough electricity between Mars and Geneva to start a thunderstorm. Oddly enough, one did roll over Harper's Ferry in the late afternoon.

When Geneva returned to camp, she didn't tell Nash what happened. There was enough bad blood between him and Mars as it was.

MAY 12, 1861

Sunrise turned the mountains from deep purple to darkest blue. A thin ridge of brilliant scarlet outlined the peaks.

Ernie June, up early because the master was coming home today, had already supervised the killing of an especially fat pig. The hot blood was spilling into a bucket, held without enthusiasm by Boyd.

"Stir slowly!" Ernie June yelled. Blood pudding was a

favorite of Henley's, and she wanted to please him. Boyd grimaced.

"Girl, I done worse than that." Ernie June put her hands on her hips. "Slow. Soon as it's full up, keep turning the ladle. We gets it up the house, and then I shows you the rest."

"Momma, the smell makin' me sick," Boyd protested.

"I gonna make you good and sick!" Ernie took a threatening step toward Boyd. Her daughter backed off the protest. Ernie yanked the bucket from Boyd and started for the big house.

Boyd, twitchy, scurried after her huffing mother. "Momma, I kin do it. Gimme the bucket. I jes doan likes the smell."

"You gots to do a lot of things in this world you doan like, girl." Ernie slammed the heavy bucket into Boyd. The daughter sniffled and followed.

When the women came into the kitchen, they heard Lutie chattering upstairs. Boyd bent over the odious bucket and stirred anew. "Miz Lutie wakes up like a blue jay. Squawky, squawky."

"Miz Lutie has her ways."

"Some say she's 'teched."

Ernie lowered her voice. " 'Teched or not, she's the mistress here. You hear me? Miz Lutie's a good woman as them people go." Ernie's voice was barely a whisper. "She got a familiar, but that don't mean she's 'teched."

"What you talkin' 'bout, Momma?"

"You're too young, I reckon."

This made Boyd see pure red. "I am not!"

"You shut your trap else I shuts it for you!" Ernie hissed, "And lower that cow voice!"

Stung and curious, Boyd fell into step. She had to know what the big secret was. "Tell me 'bout this famlar."

"Familiar." Ernie waited and stalled to drive Boyd wild. She bustled around the kitchen collecting spices. She paused in front of the window to see if Sin-Sin, the bitch, was coming up from her little house.

"Momma!" Boyd's hushed voice rang desperate.

"You promise to be still 'bout it?"

"I promise. I promise." She stirred the bucket with what appeared to be delight.

Lawdy, Ernie thought to herself, what I go through to get a good day's work out of this girl. "When Jimmy died—"

"I 'member. I was—"

"You 'member nothin' much 'ceptin you was too big to be handed over the grave."

Sullenly Boyd responded, "I do so 'member."

"I thinks I be workin' in silence today. Got me a woolly-headed, nasty girl."

"Momma! I ain't nasty. Tell me, Momma," Boyd pleaded.

"If you shut up and listen. No sound squeaks outta this room." Ernie put her finger to her lips. Boyd nodded in agreement. "When Jimmy passed on, Miz Lutie jes close up like a turtle. She doan hardly eat. Me and Sin-Sin got to pry open her mouth. How we worried with that woman. Henley, he sick to death and scared she gonna follow that little boy to kingdom come. Well, she be like that for four months. Then she come out of it, but she doan talk to nobody but Sin-Sin. Why she want to talk to that ole muleface, I doan know, but Miz Lutie always been blind in that direction. What she say to Sin-Sin then Sin-Sin say to rest of us. She doan say much. We starts to hear Miz Lutie yakking her head off in the mornin's. I think it be Henley. Sin-Sin thinking it be Geneva and Di-Peachy. Ha, I say to that muleface. When you hear Lutie say two good words strung together to Di-Peachy? Comes to think on it, when you hear Lutie say three words minus one growl to Geneva? She be hard on those girls. I be right."

"Momma, you generally right on such matters." Boyd buttered her up.

"So one mornin' I goes upstairs like I hafta bring some tea. I make some raspberry cakes, puts 'em on a tray, and stands outside Miz Lutie's bedroom. She talkin' and talkin'. No Henley. No Geneva. No Di-Peachy. She talkin' to someone else. I opens the door likes I hearin' nothin'. She glares at me. Girl, I coulda burnt a hole in my stockin'! I 'pologizes and sets down de tray. That's when I knows she talkin' to herself but makin' it up in her head. Sin-Sin get mad at me for bargin' in. Say she know all along. Toad turds! She know nothin'. But then she say this talkin' be to a familiar. That's a person you imagine and he eases your heart."

"Could I have one?"

"Somethin' cruel hafta happen first. But see, she up there

now, and she liftin' her heart. No harm in it. I thinks she talkin' to her little dead boy. She love that little boy. Sweet chile. So much sufferin' at the end. He hurt down in his bones, and he lay on his big, soft bed, and he bite his lips till they white. He wouldn't cry in front of his momma. That make her wanna die, seein' his brave face. Miz Lutie easin' her mind. Sin-Sin go 'round me blowin' off 'bout this familiar called Emil. I say, doan matter what his name, in his spirit he be kin to little Jimmy."

"Momma, you think spirits come back here?"

"Course. That's why you keep a respectful tongue in your head! They hears everything; they sees everything." With that admonition, Ernie June lightly swatted Boyd across the back of the calves with a fly swatter. Then she started singing, and soon Boyd joined in.

Upstairs, Lutie flew about her room, babbling rapidly. Henley's expected visit stirred her up. She'd misplaced her lessons for the day and that put her nose out of joint. By the time she found her church almanac, her inner receptivity to the Lord's word was suspect. The readings from Joel 2 and John 17 barely scratched her consciousness. She told Emil about her dream where a bat wore ruby earrings and sang Mozart.

She allowed herself a fleeting, uncharitable thought about Jennifer Fitzgerald: she passes opinions like gas. The fact that the nursing program forced her to see Jennifer once a week tested Lutie to the core. Last Thursday, Jennifer asked if she'd gotten a letter from Sumner. Well, yes, she had. But before Lutie could quote her son's lucid observations of camp life, Jennifer burst into a rapture about her own son Greer, the military boy wonder. It was a wonder Greer stayed sober long enough to write Jennifer a letter. It was a good thing Jennifer loved Greer because nobody else would, Lutie thought. Then again, he was easy to manage. Some shrewd harpy would marry him for the Fitzgerald fortune.

Worse, far the worse, Jennifer peppered Lutie with questions about Geneva in England. Lutie felt that Jennifer was a touch too interested in the affairs of her daughter. She feared Jennifer was implying that Geneva's excessive grief over Nash's enlistment revealed some instability on the girl's part. Lutie curtly told Jennifer that Geneva took after Henley's side of the family, not the Chalfontes. Jennifer bluntly observed that Chatfield women were not especially good looking; Chalfonte women were gorgeous. Bitch, Lutie fumed to herself, I'll get her yet.

"Rise and shine," Sin-Sin called from the other side of the door.

"I'm up. Been up with the sun."

"Master's coming home today." Sin-Sin opened the door.

"I know. Let me fortify myself with roped coffee." She swept out of her bedroom like Catherine the Great preparing to see Potemkin once again. Lutie was ready.

Before coming to the big house, Henley stopped briefly at Geneva and Nash's house. Di-Peachy, despite Lutie's nagging, kept it open. Di-Peachy said she'd move to the big house when winter returned, but in the meantime there was no sense in Geneva's house smelling like old horsehair.

Big Muler lived in the barn and that bothered Lutie greatly. She didn't like any servant living where she couldn't see him. Di-Peachy vouched for Big Muler's character, which made Lutie certain she was sleeping with the giant. Her edginess around Big Muler seemed to confirm that point.

Henley wanted to get the facts for himself. He had other plans for Di-Peachy, and he couldn't believe the girl would be foolish enough to carry on with a field hand. Someday he'd find a high-yellow freedman, an artisan with some business sense. That kind of man would be best for Di-Peachy.

Di-Peachy, if possible, had grown more beautiful in his absence. He delicately asked her about Big Muler; her answer satisfied him that Lutie's imaginings were off-center.

He spent the rest of the day questioning his slaves. He talked to Boyd, Tincia, Peter, Timothy, Braxton, and Frederica, all separate from one another. Big Muler gathered up the field hands and Henley questioned them in a group. He even grilled the children. Oftimes, little ones see plenty even if they don't know what it means. He thought if one of the children had been frightened into silence, he could tell, but they seemed fine.

Ernie June, Boyd, and Braxton stuck together like three burrs. Their mimicking one another irritated him, still he had no cause to believe they knew more than what they were telling him.

One point stood clear: Everyone but Tincia despised Alafin.

Sin-Sin, however, proved the biggest surprise. She volunteered little. Henley pressed her, and she replied that she thought it best to let sleeping dogs lie. If life returned to normal, she explained, the killer would get careless. He'd show his hand.

Henley had to agree there was merit in the woman's logic. Sin-Sin, in her resonant voice, allowed as how Mr. Henley was off in Richmond, and Miss Lutie was running this huge estate. Everyone's hands were full. If the master and the missus would let her have her way, she thought she'd catch him. She needed only one thing: a pass, a pass good for more than one day. Trusting Sin-Sin absolutely, he wrote out the pass, leaving the dates blank. Sin-Sin placed the valuable document in her bodice and returned to her task, which appeared to be harassing Ernie June in the kitchen.

"You gots your own kitchen!" Ernie exploded when Sin-Sin imperiously flopped a small iron pot over the large fireplace.

"Makin' somethin' for Mr. Henley."

"I makes the food around here. You git your black butt outta my kitchen!"

"Master's pulled his back again. I be mixin' mullein flowers, poke roots, alum, and salt here in a high boil. Make the best liniment you ever heard tell of, witch."

Ernie fulminated. "You kin mix it up in your sorry excuse for a kitchen, sloppy tits."

Ordinarily this remark would provoke a fistfight. Today Sin-Sin paid no mind.

"Gettin' hot and sweaty here. I better be careful." She craftily removed the pass from her bodice and placed it on the kitchen table. Ernie couldn't read, but she knew an official document when she saw one, and she knew Henley's signature. Sin-Sin turned her back on the pass and stirred her brew.

"What you doin' with somethin' like this?" Ernie's tone had shifted from fury to appeasement.

"None of your business, selfish witch. 'Sides which, you can't read no more than a sheep." Sin-Sin half closed her eyes and crumbled poke root in her large hands.

"I knows the master's hand. You uppin' to no good, Sin-Sin. You stealin' somethin' here?"

"I doan steal, Ernie June. I doan take neither, if you catch my meaning."

Ernie snarled, "I ketch it, slut face."

Sin-Sin sniffed the dried mullein flowers and said nothing.

Sensing the paper was more important than her feud, Ernie turned sweet. "Well, if you workin' so hard for Mr. Henley, least I kin do is give you a hot cinnamon muffin and my best coffee."

"Believe I will." Much as Sin-Sin deplored Ernie, she was not immune to her cooking. Sin-Sin munched in silence for a while. "Ernie, sugar, you is the best cook. I believe if you needs it, master will give you a pass, too. Jes for the day, of course."

" 'Zat what this is? I seen passes before, Sin-Sin, but this has red on it. Doan 'member no red."

"This be a special pass."

"What for?"

"For days and weeks at a time. Mr. Henley and Miz Lutie already burdened double with this war."

"And not a shot fired." Ernie smirked.

"It will be, Ernie June. The Lord workin' his wrath on mankind."

"Uh huh." Ernie fed her another cinnamon roll.

"So, Mr. Henley give me this pass allowing me my comin's and goin's into the town, into Richmond iffin he needs me. Gotta lot of extra duties now." Sin-Sin affected newly earned weariness.

Ernie's eyes bugged out of her head. A pass like that, free passage! Ernie had no eyes for striking north, but she surely had eyes for free passage to other big houses, other kitchens, even Richmond! She felt faint. Damn that Sin-Sin! "I kin help you when it get too much. We could go to Richmond together." Ernie smiled broadly.

"Uh huh," Sin-Sin said, as though she agreed. "Ernie, I tells you this 'cause even though we get on like a cat and a dog, we the head folks on this place. We kin be fightin' 'bout the little things but not the big ones. We got to be quiet 'bout this pass. Create green jealousy in the others. You know what I mean."

Ernie nodded vigorously. "Uh huh."

When Sin-Sin took her liniment to Henley, Ernie June nearly broke her ankle bolting out of the kitchen door. She found Boyd and Braxton in the smokehouse making scrapple. She whispered the forbidden news to her children and implied that at some future date she would accompany Sin-Sin on a trip, quite possibly even to Richmond, as Sin-Sin's duties were too much even for Sin-Sin.

Braxton was impressed. Boyd scowled that she wouldn't go to the outhouse with Sin-Sin. Ernie shushed her and swore them both to secrecy. The secrecy lasted until someone appeared whom each wished to impress. Boyd told Tincia. Even though she didn't like Tincia, the news made Boyd important. Tincia told Frederica, and Frederica was a walking gazette. When word of this extraordinary extended pass reached Di-Peachy, she raced to find Sin-Sin. Sin-Sin laughed until she cried, but she did manage to tell Di-Peachy that yes, the gossip was true.

The trap was set.

Lutie laid rags soaked with liniment on Henley's broad back. The sun set two hours ago, and he was tired and sore. He'd have to get up early tomorrow and take the train back to Richmond.

"Thank you, dear. Your advice and praise soothes me as much as this liniment." He sighed. "I was wondering, my darling . . ."

Lutie waited. "My darling" was reserved for special occasions.

"Before travel becomes too impossible, I was wondering if I might bring down the Windsors and also their dear friend Kate, Mrs. Mars Vickers, for a few days? I think a respite from war fever would do everyone good."

"Yes, of course." Lutie rubbed his back. "Did I tell you Sumner is with the engineers? He's already a lieutenant. He thinks his unit will be assigned permanently to Colonel Jackson's regiment. I also heard from Poofy."

Henley sat up, winced, and then plopped down again. "What's she say?"

"She's fine. Bedford's gripped with war fever. Daniel is in Washington. Lincoln wants him in the capital but Daniel beseeches him to stay in the field. After all, he raised and equipped an entire regiment. Poofy thinks Lincoln will give in, so she's worried sick. Says it's a perfect spring up there.

You know, it doesn't seem like we are at war, does it? This whole thing is a dream."

"It wouldn't be so dreamlike if you were in Richmond." He paused. "But until we engage, time is oddly suspended, a kind of hibernation."

The liniment improved Henley's spirits, and he indicated to his wife that physical enjoyment would be welcome to him if it would be welcome to her.

Afterwards, they drank some homemade wine, a tangy white, and nibbled on some of Ernie June's sweetcakes.

Lutie looked ten years younger after making love. Henley admired his wife. He liked her plumpness, for it befitted her age and station. He liked her sense of responsibility and her wit. He had made a good match; no one could deny that. But what he had learned through the years was that living with a woman wasn't the same as being in love with a woman. He had felt only one great passion in his life, and it wasn't Lutie. He had paid dearly for that. Now seventeen years later, he again felt that strange, terrifying rumble deep inside, but not for his wife. Yet he loved Lutie. He was sorry he'd hurt her once. He was sorry he might hurt her again. He and Lutie Chalfonte were a team, but love wore thin under daily scrutiny, at least for Henley.

"Is she as beautiful as everyone says?" Lutie asked.

"Who?"

"Kate Vickers."

Henley fumbled. "I—yes, she is rather handsome, although I can't say that I've noticed her all that much. You'll see for yourself, dear."

Liar, Lutie thought. She was quite eager to see for herself.

MAY 14, 1861

Geneva and Nash, finished with drill for the day, snuck off to a meadow about four miles from the camp. The late afternoon sun scorched overhead. They tied their horses, then tore off each other's clothes. They were two people physically attuned to one another. Whether they were attuned in other, deeper realms only time would reveal.

Whenever Nash ejaculated, Geneva was amazed at how quickly his penis shrank and slid out of her. It made her sad. He lay beside her, sweating and happy.

"Geneva, how do you do that to me?"

She kissed him. "I love you. I want to make you happy."

"Happy?" He laughed. "You make me ecstatic!" The blond stubble on his cheeks glistened like gold in the bright sun.

"Do you hear that?"

He held his breath and put his ear to the ground. "Hoofbeats."

He tossed on his shirt. Geneva wiggled into her pants and put on her shirt. Nash climbed up a big hickory tree.

"There they are. Four of them. And they're going like a bat out of hell toward the camp."

He jumped out of the tree, scooped her in his arms, and squeezed her. "You do make me happy. I'll be glad when this war is over. Then you won't pretend you're a man, and we can make love in our big feather bed every day, until we're so old we're in pushchairs."

The four riders showed up at Mars Vickers's tent. Mars had refused a house in town. If his men lived in tents, then he'd live in a tent, too. An old friend of his, J.E.B. Stuart, had reported to camp with the rank of major. Mars was both delighted and curious because Stuart had the stomach for politicking and Mars did not. Stuart's father-in-law stayed with the Union Army as a general. Mars did not envy him that anxiety. But the arrival of Stuart meant Mars had an ally. He could have his regiment and let J.E.B. contend with the senior officers since Stuart was so hot to become one himself.

While Mars was a fighting man, he was not ambitious in the conventional sense. What he really wanted to do was write a book on modern warfare. His years in Europe taught him that the staffs of those armies looked backward to Napoleon. Mars believed in industry, railroads, and improved artillery. Rifles could fire with accuracy up to five hundred yards. In Napoleon's day, the range was a mere one hundred yards. He believed progress outstripped the military's ability to assimilate it. He wanted to incorporate his thoughts on new weaponry and strategy into a book. That would wait until after this war, if he lived through it. His ambition, then, was to provoke thought, to prepare his country for the future.

"Mars!" Sam Wells burst through the tent flap. He placed a packet of letters on Mars's camp desk. "From your wife, sir."

Mars glanced at the packet. "You didn't beat your shadow here for that. I thought you were to stay in Richmond another week."

"I called upon headquarters there. They gave me permission to ride up the lines. After calling upon Mrs. Vickers, I rode through Fredericksburg. Then I kept on the main road toward Washington until a few miles from the Potomac. Every time I saw anyone, I asked if they'd seen any troops cross the river."

"Sam, our people have been watching that river since Fort Sumter."

"I know that, but I wanted to see for myself. I rode by the river, keeping it to my right and got maybe six miles west of Alexandria. I camped without a fire by the river. Around two in the morning I heard voices, Yankee voices. A scouting mission, I reckon."

"So?"

"Yankees on our soil!" Sam was exasperated that Mars did not grasp the import of his message. "I say we take the whole army up there, mass on the banks of the river, and blast those sons of bitches to kingdom come!"

"We can't do that, Sam."

"Why the hell not?"

"We want them to cross over to Virginia soil and initiate hostilities. They are the ones who are going to start this war."

Livid, Sam shouted, "Then what was Fort Sumter about?"

"That was South Carolina. And if you want to get technical about it, you could argue that South Carolina was pushed into cleaning out the fort. We did not initiate hostilities."

"Horseshit!"

"I agree with you, Sam, but we aren't making policy. We're carrying it out. Jefferson Davis runs the army."

"We should hit them now, Mars, right now. We can end this goddamned thing in a week."

"With what?"

Crestfallen, Sam sat down in a folding chair. "Hell, Mars, I want to fight. I'd be happy to go call out a Yankee and have at him."

"This is a war, Sam, not a duel. Now go wash up, have a good supper, and get some sleep."

Wearily, Sam stood up. "You're so logical about it."

"That's the point, Captain."

Mars opened his wife's letters and read them. She reported the doings of the town, already swelled with about twenty thousand newcomers and more on the way.

His wife's fragrance lingered on the letters. She liberally dusted them with her perfume. The smell of the woman drove him wild. But Mars knew he'd been betrayed by his cock when he married the sensational Kate Louisa Carpenter. Before the first year of the marriage ran out, he'd known he'd made a terrible mistake. She rarely endured him physically. He was reduced to begging for it. Though her sex drive was low, her ambition was high. If Kate ever found out he had turned down an offered colonelcy, she would probably kill him. She wanted to be a leader of political society. Mars wanted to be left alone to think and to have a family. They couldn't have children. She blamed him for it. He blamed her. Mars was a tool to Kate. He knew that, and it cut him deep inside. But then what was she to him? He wanted a beautiful woman. He got one. Too late did he understand the meaning of the word partner. Well, he suffered for his foolishness. He remembered his Greek: Those whom the gods wish to destroy, they first make mad. He thought it should be, Those whom the gods wish to destroy, they first make fall in love.

Nash walked in. "You wanted to see me, Major Vickers?"

"You're on guard duty tonight and the password is love's labor lost."

Nash smiled. "I did not take you for a literary man, Major Vickers."

Mars bristled. "I did not take you for a military man, Private Hart."

MAY 15, 1861

By three in the morning, the chill had secreted itself into Nash's bones. Posted on the northern edge of the camp, he pulled a horse blanket around him. Loud rustling off to his right bolted him wide awake.

"Who's there?"

Nash could feel the sweat running from his armpits down his sides. He picked up his rifle and placed his thumb on the trigger. "Say the password!" The noise grew louder, and then he heard hoofbeats heading for the camp.

"Stop! Stop or I'll shoot!" He fired into the air, then fired again. He wanted to leave his post and run back to the camp, but he remembered Mars's instructions: "Obey orders, no matter how ludicrous they seem; you don't see the whole picture." Nash hoped to God an advance party of Yankees wasn't on his right, heading into the camp. He was at his post stone alone. They'd kill or capture him for certain. Nash continued to fire in the air. After what seemed a very long time, he heard noises far away in the camp. He emptied his pistol. Feverishly he jammed shells into the hot chamber. If they rode on him now, he was defenseless except for a knife. The sound of his own breathing crashed in his ears. He held his breath. No more noise. Gulping air, he held it again. Silence around him, but noise in the camp below.

He heard men shouting and horses neighing. He thought he could hear an order shouted from time to time. Then he heard a new sound—laughter. Hundreds of voices, laughing! His regiment had captured the Yankees, and here he was stuck on the edge of nowhere. Well, he had warned them. He sat down and thought how unfair the world was.

Hoofbeats alerted him again. A figure wearing a slouch hat approached. It was Benserade, Mars's right-hand man.

"Say the password," Nash said sternly.

Captain Benserade answered, "Love's labor lost. Did you fire off those shots, Hart? We thought they came from you."

Proudly, Nash said, "Yes, I did. How many Yankees did you get? I heard one mounted man, but there may have been others."

"You did, did you?"

"Yes, Captain."

"What you heard, you silly ass, was a pig."

Stunned, Nash swallowed hard. His deep bass voice cracked. "A pig?"

"A pig with a curly tail. You must have scared it, Mr. Hart, because that pig moved faster than anything I've seen since I got here. I expect, sir, you were not fully awake"—his voice dripped sarcasm—"when you heard the hoofbeats."

"I—" Nash could not look into Benserade's mocking eyes.

"Well, Private Hart, you can go back to the camp now and get your beauty sleep. I'll take over here."

"Does everyone know I fired those shots?"

"Came from your sentry station. The answer is yes."

Nash placed his rifle alongside his saddle. He rolled his blanket up and put it behind his saddle. Then he slowly walked his horse back to camp. Benserade's chuckles assaulted his ears.

Inside the camp, his humiliation was complete. Oinking sounds were all around him. Even Bumba, his servant, laughed at him. One of the men called out "Private Piggy." Another crooned "Piggy Woo!" Fighting back his misery, Nash stalked into his tent where Geneva waited for him. He brushed off her consolations and lay on his cot. He languished there with his eyes open and vowed to make good during the first battle.

When Mars bumped into Nash the next morning before drill, he addressed him as Private Woo. Piggy Woo stuck. Only Geneva, Banjo, and Bumba called him Nash after that.

MAY 17, 1861

Lutie felt wonderful today even though a low, yellowish haze hung over the meadows, refusing to burn off. The lesson for the day was chapter 28 in the first book of Samuel. Saul and the Israelites prepare for battle against the Philistines. However, God keeps a tight lip. So Saul, worried, wants someone to tell him what to do. Even though he has banished wizards and people who have familiars, in desperation he goes to a woman of Endor who has a familiar. He asks her to call up the spirit of Samuel, who had recently died. Samuel came to him and asked why Saul had disturbed him. Saul wanted some military advice, and Samuel, maybe he was crabby at being brought back to the fractious land of the living, sounded like the voice of doom. He told Saul that the Lord was done with him and that by tomorrow he'd be right there where Samuel was because the Philistines would do him in and Israel would be delivered into the hands of the Philistines. Saul probably wished he'd left Samuel with the dead. He felt weak and wouldn't eat. The woman of Endor, a kind heart, forced him to eat something.

Lutie liked the fact that a familiar was mentioned in the Bible and rather nicely, too. Naturally, the woman didn't know what Samuel would say when she called him up so she was hardly responsible for him being a wet blanket.

The great bulk of Big Muler crossed Lutie's line of vision.

He was carrying sacks of rice from Reddy Neutral Taylor's wagon.

"He's never far from you." Lutie pointed out the window to Di-Peachy, who was enjoying the Bible lesson.

Di-Peachy shrugged. "He's respectful."

"He's in love with you. They're all in love with you."

Di-Peachy bowed her head. "Don't say that, Miss Lutie."

"Why, does keeping my mouth shut make it any less true? That giant out there would follow you to the ends of the earth. Has he given up trying to sleep with you?"

Di-Peachy bit her lip and said nothing.

Lutie flounced her skirt. "But I forget. My husband doesn't want you carrying on with the help. I'd like to know just where you're going to find a husband good enough."

"I don't want to get married."

"I sometimes think that my husband and I were cruel to allow you to read. Your head is full of ideas, and where can you go with them? Life is unfair—for each of us in our various ways. Perhaps it's easier to see injustice with you. I'd advise you to make a good match while you're young."

Di-Peachy said nothing.

Frustrated, Lutie left the room. Di-Peachy was holding something back.

Outside, Reddy Neutral Taylor lounged in his wagon. As the owner of the hardware and provisions store, he usually did not make deliveries. However, he hoped for sight of Di-Peachy.

He called out to Big Muler. "Boy, where's that gorgeous piece of black ass lives up there?"

Big Muler slung another sack over his shoulder.

Reddy, like a terrier chasing a rabbit, ran on. "You know who I mean, boy. Di-Peachy. Nature's dusky goddess, I say. I'll bet Sumner Chatfield has enjoyed her delicacies!" He hooted.

Big Muler walked over to Reddy. He dumped the sack on the ground, stood by the wagon, and picked it up. He shook the wagon as easily as if he were shaking out a dust rag.

"Hey, hey! What you doin', nigger?" Reddy shouted.

"Doan like such talk 'round here." Big Muler gave the wagon an extra hard push and dropped it.

Reddy, tremendously impressed by this display of raw

strength, replied, "Chatfield niggers, Chatfield whites. You all think your shit don't stink up here. But I take your point, boy. I truly take your point. You take mine. You're a young buck. Lots of history here you know nothin' about. Won't do you good to ride a high horse, and won't do you good to think jes 'cause you're a Chatfield nigger, you're better than a workin' white man."

Impassively Big Muler stared at him. "Doan be talking that way 'bout Di-Peachy." He picked up the sack and returned to his chores.

MAY 30, 1861

The city of Richmond exploded overnight. The influx of government officials, those seeking posts and hangers-on, had swelled the population to forty thousand people, if anyone could keep count. Aside from those wishing to latch on to the cornucopia of government, there were the countless thousands of riffraff, drunks, lunatics, and failures that flocked to Screamersville just west of town. Whores cleaned up and so did the bartenders who cheerfully served rotgut. A few wags dubbed it "Disease Depot."

But on this day, every church, civic group, and musical consortium flocked to the train station or lined the avenue by which Jefferson Davis would make his jubilant progress to the Spotswood Hotel. Living at the hub of activity was a mixed blessing to Henley. Josiah Gorgas, Chief of the Ordnance Bureau, told Henley he hoped that he would press forward the needs of the department at every conceivable opportunity to the president. Henley liked Gorgas but he distrusted every department head, civilian or military, hovering over the budget, such as it was, like so many flies at a picnic.

Whatever thought Henley nursed about fostering good relations with Davis and his cabinet dashed out of his head when Kate Vickers appeared in the doorway of his makeshift office.

"All work and no play makes Jack a dull boy. Our president arrives and no matter how heavy the burdens of your office, you should celebrate."

"Mrs. Vickers, you're a heavenly vision." He courteously stood and offered her a seat.

"Some would place my status a bit lower, sir." She took his arm. "Now, come on. You can't expect me to brave these hooligans alone."

"How did you get here?"

"I put my servants in a wedge and ran for it." Her pale gray glove matched his uniform tunic. "Shall we?"

Henley and Mrs. Vickers left the building by the front entrance, already heavily crowded.

The day was a pickpocket's delight. Even the humblest of Richmond's citizens turned out in their finery to impress the President and his entourage.

A roar started at the other end of the boulevard. The sound rolled onward until it crashed over Henley and Kate. In the distance mounted figures could barely be seen.

Musicians preceded the cavalcade. By the time the handsome Jefferson Davis passed where Henley and Kate stood, people were hysterical with fervor. Each voice was united in one paean of approval, unity, and hope. Even Henley felt a surge inside. We are one people, he thought. One purpose. One heart.

As the president passed directly in front of him, Henley thought that he was a man in his middle years, much like Henley himself. To have such acclaim and such power, surely it must warp the senses. Henley caught himself whispering what the man in the chariot repeated over and over to each Roman general as he made his triumphal procession through Rome: "Remember, thou art mortal."

As she lay on her bed that night, Lutie thought what a strange time this is. Those who live through it will forever remember this lull, this rosy prelude to whatever shall follow, she thought. We laugh too readily. We speak more openly to one another than before. Perhaps we say things that would better be left unsaid. The smiles are brighter, and the men are more gallant. Is anyone as afraid as I am? The grain of destiny is in the wind.

She got out of bed and padded over to her window. Outside, the crickets sang to one another, a frog burped down at the pond, the night sounds of the country were so gentle. She heard a whinny from the back meadow, the meadow where the rainbows fell. Without moonlight the night shrouded her, more mysterious than before, each pinprick of light a blaze of questions; each constellation a gathering of unknown forces. She was forty-six years old and what did that mean? Time was a teardrop in an inky sky. What was time to a star or the passing of a comet in its eternal rounds of the sun and her planets? Without a heartbeat there is no time.

Instinctively she placed her hand over her heart. "Thank you, God, for my hardships and my blessings."

II

THE ANVIL OF GOD

JULY 21, 1861

Dawn licked the mountains fifteen minutes before 5 A.M. Lutie awoke with first light, as she had done since childhood. She washed herself in the basin, threw on a light cotton undergarment and a thin cotton dress. Even at that hour she knew the day would be a stinker. Lutie loved hot, sticky days. Her aches and pains had already disappeared. She'd drunk enough of Sin-Sin's rheumatism cure, white sassafras root tea, to float away her kidneys. On a day like today she felt young again.

She opened the family Bible. Inside, beautifully drawn, were the family trees of the Chalfontes and the Chatfields. The first Chatfield stepped on these shores from the *Mayflower*. Lutie thought to herself that the *Mayflower* was a small boat that brought thousands to the New World. Even Jennifer Fitzgerald claimed her people were on it. The Chalfontes, Lutie's people, arrived with Lord Baltimore. Lutie derived enormous pleasure from this. If she were descended from Puritans, she'd slit her wrists. Bloodlines, so dear to Henley, interested her, but she didn't set too much store by them. She'd seen splendid people produce vile children, and she'd seen walking horrors beget good people. Lutie thought the human race chaotic and curious at best. Breeding did not seem to improve its silliness as far as she could tell.

The thin pages crinkled under her forefinger and thumb. She turned to Exodus, chapter 14. Now this was why Lutie read the Bible. What a story. Moses and his people were camped at Pihahiroth by the sea. Pharaoh tore out after them with six hundred chariots. Despite God shaking his finger at Pharaoh by putting down a pillar of fire and by fiddling with the chariot wheels, Pharaoh was not to be deterred by a Jew God. After all, Pharaoh had gods of his own, thank you.

"And the Lord said unto Moses, Stretch out thine hand over the sea, that the waters may come again upon the Egyptians, upon their chariots, and upon their horses.

"And Moses stretched forth his hand over the sea, and the sea returned to his strength when the morning appeared; and the Egyptians fled against it; and the Lord overthrew the Egyptians in the midst of the sea."

Lutie closed the book. Pretending to be Moses, she held out her hands. The water in her wash basin did not part.

Lutie believed the miracle happened, but she found it strange that after this robust display of heavenly power, Pharaoh did not turn in his Egyptian gods—falcons, owls, and rams—for this God. If she'd been Pharaoh, she would have swapped in a hurry.

The big house ran like a Swiss clock. Ernie June pounded dough in the kitchen. Cazzie the cat licked an egg that fell on the floor. Boyd drew clear water from the deep well next to the summer kitchen. Sin-Sin sang her favorite song, "Annie Laurie," as she organized the day's housework.

At 6 A.M. a deep, resonant boom captured everyone's attention. The sound came from the northeast. Normally, thunderstorms crept over the mountains from the west, though sometimes one would sneak up from the south. Lutie couldn't remember when she'd seen a big storm come in from the northeast.

The boom was soon followed by another. The reverberations were precise, rhythmic. Lutie walked out to the middle of the backyard and stood next to the chestnut tree and listened. The leaves of the great, three-story magnolias that ringed the lawn glistened.

Sumner had written that they had to keep Manassas Gap open so the railroad could keep running east and west. Everyone figured the Federals would attack Harper's Ferry or some other position along the railroad which terminated in Manassas; either that or they'd make a beeline for Richmond. Sumner filled his letters with details that made her laugh. He called his hard biscuits "mummies." Sumner's letters chattered on like the man himself: gay, energetic, never thinking about tomorrow. He liked the other men. He worked harder than he'd ever worked in his life. As an engineer, he was highly valued. In his last letter, two weeks ago, he had told her not to worry. They were on the move. Once he had a minute, he'd tell her everything.

The roar continued. By now, most of the servants at Chatfield gathered on the lawn. Braxton and the men down at the stable silently stood in the middle of the racing ring. Even the horses paused and looked up from their ceaseless grazing.

Ernie June wrung her hands. Sin-Sin listened as intently as a blind woman.

How long it took her she didn't know, but Lutie finally realized it was cannon fire. She heard the voices of the Old Testament Yahweh calling for blood.

"No!" Lutie screamed. She ran for the rainbow meadow.

Sin-Sin ran after her. She wasn't fast on her feet, but she ran as hard as she could.

Braxton jumped on a black gelding and rode up alongside Sin-Sin. He halted the horse and held out his muscled, lean arm. "Come on, girl." Sin-Sin grabbed his arm, and as she jumped off the ground, Braxton lifted her up. Sin-Sin liked to look at horses, not ride them, and she squeezed Braxton so tightly he could barely breathe.

Lutie raced into the meadow. Her sedentary ways caught up with her. Her lungs scorched like fire, and she knelt down in the grass, sobbing. The sound of approaching hoofbeats terrified her. She thought it was Casimer from the Harkaway Hunt. She got up and tried to run again.

"Miz Lutie! Miz Lutie, stop!" Sin-Sin called to her.

Mad with fear, Lutie stumbled forward and tried to keep running. Braxton cantered beside her, then pulled slightly ahead of her. When she saw it wasn't Casimer, she stopped and fell down. Sin-Sin, none too gracefully, slid off the horse and grabbed her mistress. "Miz Lutie, what's got into you?"

The cannon boomed dully.

"My babies are out there! Oh, Sin-Sin, my babies!" Lutie screamed. She shook Sin-Sin's shoulders. "My babies are out there! Why can't they leave us alone? It's the war, Sin-Sin. My God, I thought we'd get out of it. I thought they'd come to their senses. Why can't everyone live in peace?"

"Seems like peoples always fightin' over somethin'." Sin-Sin wondered what would happen if the Yankees won. Would she be a free woman? Why should she think a Northern white man would keep a promise—whites is whites. Except for Lutie. She loved Lutie. "We gwine beat 'em today. Thass the end of it," Sin-Sin said with authority.

Lutie began to cry again, "But my babies—"

"Now, honey, once chillun get to wheres they can talk back, they do as they pleases. Everything gwine be fine." Sin-Sin put her arm around Lutie's waist, and they slowly walked back to the big house.

Braxton rode back to the stable, gave his mount to Timothy, then quickly ran to the kitchen. There he quickly told his mother what happened. Ernie June's eyes narrowed. She didn't know what it meant or even if it was important. After all, Lutie had been hysterical. However, too many strange things were happening and she vowed to keep alert.

Later that morning, cannon still rumbling incessantly, Ernie June asked Sin-Sin, "What'd she mean 'bout her babies?"

"She half outta her head. You knows Sumner be the apple of her eye. Jes babblin', Ernie June." Sin-Sin knew that wouldn't satisfy the cook, but she couldn't think of another answer.

Gray fingers grasped the night, slowly tearing it into day.

On cooking duty for her group of five today, Geneva started a fire. Most of the men, exhausted from forced marches, still slept soundly as Geneva slipped away to fill two buckets of water from a stream which fed into the larger Bull Run. The lesson for the day provided a happy omen for her. Moses escaped the tyranny of Pharaoh. Surely the people of Virginia and the rest of the South would escape Lincoln.

The last four weeks had hardened her. Geneva had been in the saddle from dawn to after dusk nearly every day. Mars had even drilled his troops on retrieving their bridles and saddles if their mounts were cut down. She was beginning to understand the wisdom of his methods. The war was no longer a lark, no longer parade drills or mock battles in the camp. Although she'd witnessed no real battle yet, she participated in the harassment of Patterson's outposts.

The camp moved to Winchester from Harper's Ferry. Her regiment was now under J.E.B. Stuart, who commanded the First Virginia Cavalry. Mars's men were supposed to patrol three hundred miles around Winchester. From the north,

General Patterson crawled toward them, but as yet provoked no battle.

Geneva's regiment had covered sixty miles in two days, arriving at Manassas on the night of July 20. July 19 it rained so hard that the men called to one another while riding so as not to get lost.

Nash carried on as best he could. He bore the grueling pace with no complaint, but he was not excited by it. Geneva, however, was thrilled.

As the gray gave way to a pale pink and then a rich rose, she prayed, "Thank you, God, for letting me live to fight this day."

While bacon fried in the pan, Geneva made biscuits. Even tasteless they'd be welcome. She also put up enough strong coffee to stiffen the weariest constitution.

"Jimmy, as a cook, you make a good rider." Banjo tiptoed beside her.

Nash threw off his blanket. He stumbled past Geneva and Banjo without a word. It generally took Nash a good hour to function.

The Confederate Army seemed to rise like an awakened cat, stretching this way and that, and then blinking with that unnerving alertness so peculiar to felines. The massed clamor of voices sounded like a low, rolling chord.

Breakfast was hasty.

Sam Wells called, "Mount up!"

Geneva sprang into her saddle. Mars trained them well. His regiment formed up within ten minutes.

A deep, loud explosion silenced everyone. It was 6 A.M. Every head snapped in the direction of the sound.

Mars rode down the line. The initial deep report was followed by others in the background, slightly higher in timbre. The battle was on. Mars paid no attention to the cannon fire behind him. He wore his major's tunic with the top unbuttoned. It was hot even at this early hour. His foraging cap, cavalry yellow and gold, dipped rakishly over his right eye. He wore no gloves, although a pair was folded over his belt.

"Do you have a sheath in there?" Mars pointed to a knife handle sticking out of Nash's left boot.

"Yes, sir."

"Good. Let's hope you don't have to use it."

A mounted Lutheran pastor by Mars's side offered a brief prayer before the battle. The pastor ended his appeal with the words "and may God take care of our women."

Nash muttered, "Our women can take care of themselves."

Mars trotted to the head of the column. The men moved slowly until they came to Sudley-Manassas Road. Although the bombardment was closer now, Geneva thought it was only two or three miles away. Having never been in a battle before, Geneva had no experience judging distance from the sound of artillery.

They rode into broad fields; Stuart and his aide-de-camp rode at the head of the brigade. Mars rode at the head of his unit, about five hundred men. The confusion in the hastily organized army as to how many men made up a company, a regiment, and a brigade didn't bother Mars. Whatever the numbers were, he'd command them.

Mars told his men to dismount. They languished for hours, listening to the battle grow steadily fiercer. Stuart, livid that he might be missing something, sent off spasms of couriers. Mars, equally distraught, paced.

At 11 A.M. Mars begged Stuart to let him take a small force and scout the terrain. Their maps had roads and streams marked, but no elevations. J.E.B. Stuart, pleased with his old friend's spirit, nonetheless informed Mars he'd already sent out such a party.

By noon, Stuart, impatience personified, mounted and rode off himself. Mars angrily threw his hat on the ground, then aware that every eye was trained on him, sheepishly picked it up and dusted it off.

When Stuart returned, the noise behind him was metallic bedlam. The smoke twirled up in black and deep yellow columns. Geneva stared at this sight, not comprehending what it meant. The dust from thousands of marching feet, feet she sometimes heard but didn't see, made her eyes tear.

The temperature was already in the 90s. She untied her kerchief and wiped her face. It was grimy and she hadn't fired a shot yet.

Nash, next to her, was conspicuously silent as he read and reread the Bible. Two hours passed, and Geneva realized Nash hadn't turned the page.

Banjo played solitaire. He enjoyed an imaginary conversation with his deceased wife. He prayed to her each night before falling asleep, and now he found himself talking to her in broad daylight. When he thought of goodness, he thought of her. He had difficulty imagining Jesus, but he could imagine her gentleness, kindness, and understanding. He figured that was as close as he would get to the exalted Christian virtues. He found himself suddenly fervent, and he prayed, "Sweetheart, if I die, it won't be so bad because I'll see you again."

The air was now blue and sulfurous. The men and horses coughed. Mars harassed Stuart once more. Jubilant, he returned to his men.

Benserade called out, "Mount up. Dress left."

For one quivering moment all five hundred men, stone quiet, stared at Mars. With a big smile, he shouted, "Remember your wives and children. If you don't have a wife, remember mine." The men cheered him.

Geneva's heart pounded. Instinctively she reached for Nash's hand. He touched her hand, but dropped it quickly. She wasn't afraid. She only wanted to touch Nash, to reassure him. His face was gray. Banjo smiled through his stubble. He was ready.

The troops moved at a light trot. It was about one in the afternoon. They passed fields, a tiny orchard, and the guns grew closer.

They moved toward their left and ten minutes later passed the hospital station. The yellow flag with the large green H hung limply in the stifling heat. Inside, Colonel Jeffrey Windsor was already overloaded with wounded and dying. The screams of the wounded chilled Mars's regiment, even in this inferno. Outside the hospital station, a huge pile of limbs, at least two feet high, shocked the onlooking cavalrymen. Jeffrey sweated, cursed, and cut. Spattered in blood from head to toe, he looked like torture incarnate. Each time an arm or a leg was tossed on a pile, a cloud of flies buzzed up like an evil umbrella and then gracefully settled down to their feast. The stench assailed Geneva's nostrils, yet she remained calm, quite at peace with herself. Nash's teeth started to chatter.

Everywhere signs of tobacco were in evidence, either to calm nerves or to kill the smell. Cans of Nature's Ultimatum, Diadem of Old Virginia, Wedding Cake, and Sumner's favorite, Darling Fanny Pancake, caught the light before being thrust back into breast pockets.

They passed wounded men straining to get to the field hospital. Someone said they were Fisher's men from the Sixth Infantry of North Carolina. Fisher was dead.

She saw her first casualty, a man with his side blown away. He was turning black. She thought the temperature must be near one hundred. Any hotter and the dead would fry instead of rot.

They trotted into woods to hide their movements. Geneva heard bullets, and once she thought she felt a whizzing by her temple, a little streak of air. But she dared not give it a thought.

What did rivet her attention was the odd slapping sound—wicker, nicker, wicker—that the cannonballs made. She imagined she could hear them revolving in the air.

As they came out of the woods, suddenly there was the conjugated power of artillery and rifles. Nash's teeth chattered uncontrollably. Geneva, heart pounding, felt only the urge to go forward, to fight. She felt no fear. Banjo's face was thoughtful, but he didn't look afraid. Mr. Poist, slightly ahead of her, chewed his tobacco furiously.

The breathtaking sight of men in flaming red pantaloons thrilled Geneva. They were the Zouaves, infantry who went into battle wearing a Turkish costume that provided excellent target practice for the Confederates. Fighting alongside and equally conspicuous in bright red trousers were the Fourteenth New Yorkers. Geneva laughed out loud.

Out of the corner of her eye, she saw her first Federal. He couldn't have been more than twenty years old. Whether he was handsome or not, she didn't know, for his entire lower jaw had been shot away. He walked mechanically in no particular direction like a bizarre windup toy.

"Charge!" Mars bellowed.

Geneva put the reins in her left hand and squeezed Gallant's flanks. Yelling at the top of her lungs, Geneva Chatfield Hart joined the carnage. A sheet of flame leapt up before her as Zouaves fired. Men and horses tumbled. Between clouds of smoke she could see Mars ahead of her by perhaps twenty yards, his saber drawn, riding his animal with the grace so peculiar to him.

The First Virginia hit the Federal infantry with a shock. If the Yankees formed a square, they might have withstood the charge, but they were green. Artillery crashed around everyone. The Yankees could not reload their rifles in the melee. They jabbed and parried with their bayonets. Geneva saw one large blond man plow his bayonet under David Poist's rib cage and throw him onto the earth.

Nash brought the end of his saber down on a man's head, knocking him unconscious. Banjo, cool and steady, rode down one Yankee after another, slicing them like bacon.

A Yankee tried to grab Gallant's reins, but Gallant suddenly swerved to the right, knocking him over. Geneva thought she might jump the man, but he was smart and rough. He rolled under the belly of Gallant and grabbed her boot from the other side. He was powerful, but she was as crazed with battle lust as he was. She drew her pistol and without a second's hesitation blew a hole in him as big as a silver dollar. Her left leg was black with powder burns. He held on to her boot, his fingers locking like steel.

"Die, you son of a bitch, die!" This time she fired straight into his skull. Although clearly dead, his fingers did not release their grip for another few seconds.

She jammed her gun back into its holster and drew her saber. Two men ran up to her on foot, their bayonets filthy with blood. She knew she could save herself, but she wasn't sure she could save Gallant.

She pressed with her left leg, and he spun right, flinging the dead body out. She slashed at the advancing man as Gallant jumped over a dead soldier's body. The Yankee fell with a scream.

Suddenly a steel saber burst through the chest of her remaining attacker. "Banjo!" Banjo put his foot on the man's shoulder and pushed him off his blade.

Geneva looked about and saw her regiment thundering back into the woods. Banjo and Geneva wheeled their horses and headed after them at a full gallop.

Sweating and euphoric, Geneva found Nash unharmed.

"We broke 'em!" She grabbed her cap and swung it over her head.

Nash glumly asked, "Are you all right?"

"Yes, thanks to Banjo."

Mars looked back on the field from where they had just come. A man was walking among the dying Yankees.

Mars grabbed the field glasses from Sam Wells, whose left

forearm was bleeding badly from a vicious bayonet slash. "It's a priest!"

Mars cantered back into the field toward the priest. He had to be careful because the dead cluttered the earth and his mount, like all horses, hated to step on bodies.

Cannonballs flew over Mars's head. The Zouaves and the Fourteenth New Yorkers were regrouping, but there were enough occasional shots to make the place still murderous. There was no way to tell if they would come back across the field.

Mars pulled up beside the priest, whose bald head shone cherry in the blistering sun. "Father, leave this place."

"I'm giving these men their last rites, Major." He spoke with a flat Northern accent.

"There's nothing here but crushed intelligence. Your place is with the living. Allow me to conduct you back to our lines."

A cannonball suddenly chewed up the earth and part of a dead Confederate not ten feet away.

"I belong to the Fourteenth New York, sir."

"I can't very well take you there now, can I?" Mars leaned down from his horse to help the older man up. "You'll be quite safe, Father. We are Christian men."

As they rode toward the woods, Mars's men cheered. Mars delivered his human package to a makeshift medical unit. The good man immediately made himself useful by giving what aid he could to the bayonet cuts and bullet wounds.

Meanwhile, Stuart sent off couriers ordering his commanders to regroup their men.

The artillery sounded like God's trombones.

Thousands of men marched—Geneva could see the telltale clouds of dust—but whose men and to where? She didn't much care as long as she could get back into the fight again.

Mars rode up to Geneva. "You're bright as a cigar band. Come with me, let's take another look."

Happily Geneva fell in beside him. They trotted through the woods to emerge near Henry Hill. The house on the hill looked like a piece of Swiss cheese.

Mars skirted the area, for the fire remained heavy.

"Are we winning, Major?"

"Not yet."

"Do you think we will?"

"We could."

"Was it like this in Europe?"

"I was in some skirmishes from time to time, but nothing like this. I suppose I could have gone to the Crimea if I'd begged the British, but I felt I had more to learn from the Prussians."

"So this is your first big battle."

"Jimmy, this is every American's first big battle. Well, except for the fellows who fought in the Mexican War, and I was too young for that."

A cannonball whirled overhead. A spent bullet suddenly severed Mars's left rein and grazed his horse. The animal reared, but Mars brought him down quickly by pulling the right rein straight down. "There, there, fellow. You're in better shape than most." He looked at the battlefield and saw disemboweled horses, decapitated horses, and horses screaming with pain. The artillery horses suffered more injuries than the cavalry.

"Let me see if I can knot the two ends together."

"I can ride without my left rein. We'd better keep moving."

"Banjo says it takes a man's weight in lead to kill him, so we've got time."

"The guns are hot. They're too goddamned hot. I need water if you want me to keep firing," an artillery captain shouted to a courier. They were perhaps seventy yards away, but a momentary lull let the captain's voice carry.

A column was seen in the far distance, but the flag was limp. Mars said, "By God, I hope they're ours. If we've been flanked, we'll crack like walnuts."

They rode toward the column, and the shelling resumed. They dipped down behind the hill and enjoyed a moment free from immediate danger. Mars slowed. "Can you see the flag now?"

Geneva stood in her stirrups. "I think it's ours, Major."

"Damn, if we just had a bit of breeze."

"You thinking it's Patterson?"

"I'm praying it isn't."

They stayed there for what seemed like an eternity. Geneva hated the sounds she heard all around her. Crying men called for their mothers, or they called for some water. Then their bodies would go into convulsions, a grand tremor, and that would be the end of it for those lucky enough to die quickly. Others lay sprawled in the cursed sun while the flies laid eggs in their wounds. Men prayed for deliverance, if they could pray at all. The medical staff couldn't get soldiers off the fields fast enough. Around Widow Henry's house, the fire was so intense that no one dared retrieve the wounded. Their comrades, who were unaccustomed to battle, had abandoned them when they were told to fall back.

A slight flutter gave Mars what he wanted. "Ours! Let's go."

While Mars and Geneva were riding back to the battlefield, Nash, so as not to think about what might come next, assisted the priest.

"Are you a Catholic?" asked Father Quinsberry.

"No, I'm an Episcopalian," Nash replied while holding an unconscious man's leg straight.

The priest was busy picking out cannister. "That's a Catholic without the incense."

Nash smiled. "Yes, I guess it is."

"There's a nasty sliver in here." Father Quinsberry pointed to a deeply imbedded piece of steel. Nash worked on it with his boot knife until he could pull it out.

"I killed today." Nash bent over his task.

The priest replied, "You're a soldier."

"I ask for forgiveness, nonetheless. Doesn't the Bible tell us 'Thou Shalt Not Kill'?" Nash yanked out another hunk of steel. The man moaned. "I know if I hadn't killed those fellas, one of them would have killed me. Did you ever kill a man, Father?"

"No."

"Would you?" Nash asked.

"I'm a man who has given my entire life to the word of Jesus Christ. If God wills that you or any of these men shall kill me, then so shall I die. But I shall not kill."

As Mars and Geneva rejoined the regiment, Nash walked over.

"Nash," Geneva said, "we saw a column approaching us. Ours!"

"You're a born soldier, aren't you?" Nash said with great sadness.

Mars wheeled on Nash. "That's right, Piggy. He is."

Nash said nothing more. Geneva, hurt, dismounted and

walked Gallant to a water bucket, then drank herself from
Nash's offered canteen.

By two o'clock Dr. Jeffrey Windsor had run out of anesthesia. His quinine was also low. Desperate, he sent a message
to his Northern counterpart. The courier, carrying a white
flag, rode behind the right flank of the Federals. He stopped
one of Heintzelmen's men who directed him to the hospital.
Either the Northerners did not care that he was a Confederate or because some Northern troops wore gray and some
Southern troops wore blue, they were confused. Or maybe
they saw the white pennant and decently agreed to it. In any
case, the courier rode back to Jeffrey an hour and a half later.
He handed Colonel Windsor a note.

Dear Jeffrey,
    I too have exhausted my supplies of nearly everything
except human misery. When we were in medical school
together, did you ever dream of anything like this? I
believe we are living in a branch of hell.
                               I wish you well,
                               Colonel Elmer E. Larson

Jeffrey folded up the note and placed it in his leather bag.
If he'd put it into his wet, bloody pocket, the ink would have
run. He returned to his branch of hell.

A battery under Lieutenant Robert F. Beckham joined
Stuart. Convinced the enemy could be beaten here, Stuart
sent a message to Colonel Jubal Early, whose column, the
Sixth Brigade, Geneva and Mars saw. Stuart told Early they
could rout the Federals. While Early came up, Stuart joined
his battery to Beckham's, and they pounded at the mauled
Northerners.
    Geneva, Nash, and Banjo watched the fireworks as did the
others.
    All of a sudden, the Federals broke. They turned and ran.
Mars was immediately in the saddle.
    "They'll head back on Sudley Road. Pursue them, boys.
Drive every last mother's son of them out of Virginia."
    The men cheered, and even Nash gave an old-fashioned
war whoop.

The batteries continued shelling until the cavalry came in range. They then stopped briefly. Geneva felt as though she were sweeping under an invisible victory ribbon. The Federal guns were smashed. A detachment of Confederate cavalry was already on its way to appropriate the guns for the Confederacy. Geneva felt the earth tremble underneath her as hundreds, maybe thousands, of horsemen thundered forward.

The Federals did not retreat in good order. They had no reserve troops to cover for them. As she pressed Gallant forward, she saw men throwing down their rifles as if they were burning hot. She waited to see what Mars would do. Would he cut down these stragglers? He didn't.

One Federal did take aim as the cavalry swept by him. Banjo, his eye like an eagle's, dropped him with his pistol.

Even at a distance, the panic was confusing to Geneva. When her regiment had charged the Fourteenth New York, she had a clear objective. She knew to go in, take the shock, cut them down, frighten them if possible, and then retire in good order to the woods. But this was different. She saw a twenty-pounder pulled by six horses. There were no riders on the team, and the cannon rolled this way and that, crushing everybody and everything in its way. She saw one man shoot another in the back because he wasn't crossing a ford quickly enough.

As her regiment, sowing even more panic in its wake, headed toward Sudley Springs, the task of pursuing became impossible. The regiment itself was engulfed in the Yankee panic. Federals actually clung to Geneva's boot, begging to be taken prisoner. They were terrified that the cavalry would cut them down from behind.

Disgusted, Mars and Stuart rounded up hundreds of prisoners. Banjo took a detachment of fifty men to secure supplies left behind by the panicked men. One well-born aide managed in all the confusion to lodge a complaint to Stuart that Banjo Cracker was only a private and a man of low station at that. Enraged, Stuart promoted Banjo to a first lieutenant, as one rank above that of the complainer.

Geneva worked until darkness. By now the smell of rotting flesh, gunpowder, and fear was nauseating. In the twilight she passed a dead Yankee whose twisted body looked so gruesome and silly like a tumbler playing for the delight of children. On his cap a neatly printed logo read "Richmond or Hell." He got hell.

Geneva and her regiment finally reached camp under a full moon, although the light was sometimes obscured by the still burning fires and smoke. Mars posted a guard around the prisoners, who fell asleep in their tracks.

After tending to Gallant, Geneva sat down and drank the cold dregs of the morning's coffee. She'd eaten nothing since breakfast and was now too exhausted to even look for food.

Nash unsaddled his horse; he moved very slowly, as if he were under water. The clouds spiraling into the moonlight looked to him like dust thickened with blood and souls. He knew he would never feel the same after today. He'd never have the same warm hope for people. Even animals behave better than humans; animals only kill when they're hungry.

Geneva touched his cheek. "I'm glad you're not hurt."

He looked at his wife. When they married she was perhaps two inches taller. She seemed even taller tonight. "Geneva, we have written sorrow on the bosom of the earth."

Geneva saw the sadness in his eyes. She knew Nash did not feel the glory she felt. She was born to this. When she heard the great cannon tear the skies this morning at six, it was as if a new Geneva was born. Nash was born for other things. Could she accept that in him? And could he accept this in her?

He touched her cheek in return and silently walked away with his blanket draped over his shoulder.

Mars clapped his hand on Geneva's shoulder.

She jumped.

"I'm promoting you to sergeant. You're in charge of these men now."

"Thank you, Major."

"You can fight, Jimmy."

"If you lead, Major, I'll fight anybody, anywhere, anytime."

A mighty cloud of blackbirds swirled through the sky and blotted out the moon, an eclipse of death. As blackbirds rarely fly at night, the beating of their massed wings and their cawing was eerie. Knowing their destination, Geneva shuddered.

Banjo also had his head to the sky. "I've seen things on this day I'll never forget."

Geneva nodded. As though pushed by a giant hand, she found herself sitting on the ground by Banjo's boot. He wrapped a blanket around her shoulders. "Jimmy," he said, "Yankees are like potatoes, better underground."

JULY 22, 1861

At 3:12 A.M., Lutie was jolted out of bed by a frantic knocking at her door. Because she slept alone in the big house at night, there was no one downstairs to get the door.

"Miz Lutie! Miz Lutie!"

"I'll be right there." Fearing the worst, but hoping for the best, Lutie wrapped her ancient bathrobe around her. Although it was dark, she hurried down the grand, curving stairway in her bare feet. She opened the fan door. Jenkins, a ten-year-old black boy owned by the Taliaferro family, stood there.

"Come in, Jenkins."

"I can't, ma'am. I got more messages to run."

"Come into the kitchen for a moment. At least let me give you some bread."

Jenkins followed her into the great kitchen. Lutie lit a straw from the warm ashes of Ernie's cooking fire and touched it to the wick of a huge tallow candle. The greasy smell filled the room. She gave Jenkins an entire loaf of Ernie's raisin bread and nervously opened the telegram.

Dear Mrs. Chatfield:
    Please bring your nursing ladies to the train station in Charlottesville as well as any physicians that still might be in your area. Bring all available supplies. I will arrive

with what wounded can be moved. Hopefully I will arrive in the early morning.

> Respectfully yours,
> Colonel Jeffrey Windsor,
> Surgeon, C.S.A.

"Thank God!" Lutie sighed deeply. "I was afraid it might be bad news about Sumner. Do you know who won?"

"Yes, Miz Lutie, we kicked their ass bad up at Manassas Junction. Come over the wire. Whole Yankee army running like dogs for Washington!"

Impulsively she hugged the child. "Praise be to God! Perhaps they'll give up on invading us, and we can make peace."

Lutie, holding the tallow candle, escorted the child to the door. "Here, sugar, take this." She reached into a satinwood basket where she kept her pin money. She handed Jenkins an entire dollar bill.

As the boy rode down the long driveway, Lutie raced through the moonlight to Sin-Sin's house. She burst through the bright red door and found Sin-Sin sound asleep in her feather bed. That feather bed was a bone of contention with Ernie June who slept on a straw pallet. If Sin-Sin could sleep in such luxury, then Ernie June certainly had a feather bed coming, too.

"Get up! We've won a great victory at Manassas."

"Can't we celebrate in the mornin'?" Groggy, Sin-Sin stayed under the covers.

"We must get to the train station. Dr. Windsor is bringing in the wounded."

Sin-Sin shot out of bed. "Why din' you say so?" Sin-Sin threw a shawl around her nightdress and hurried outside in the moonlight with Lutie on her heels. Sin-Sin pulled the rope on the large bronze bell by the kitchen. On a clear, sharp night like tonight, it would be heard for miles around. One by one the cabin doors opened, and servants, some stumbling, some running, others wailing in bewilderment, made their way to the back porch. An owl hooted in disgust and flew over the top of the big house.

Di-Peachy, curled in Geneva's bed, heard the bass command. In an instant she opened the door and nearly fell over Big Muler, who was struggling to his feet.

"What are you doing here?" she demanded.

"I's here every night, ma'am, so no harm kin come to you." His voice was gravelly with sleep.

"I think we'd better get up the hill." She'd worry about him later.

Everyone at Chatfield huddled around the kitchen porch. Ernie, dripping with importance because Lutie had already whispered the news to her, displayed her power by putting up coffee in the winter kitchen next to the bell, so everyone could see her. Boyd was banished to the summer kitchen, some distance from the big house, where she was doing the same. Ernie was preparing to feed everyone at Chatfield before they began their unusual toil.

The children bedeviled Sin-Sin for the news. She shook her head no while pacing on the porch, her arms folded across her bosom. Lutie looked ten years younger with her hair down and the soft light on her face. The Chalfonte beauty was still there, despite the plumpness and the years.

"Dear people of Chatfield"—Lutie's voice quavered slightly —"I have just received a telegram. Our troops have won a most glorious victory."

The children whooped. Most of the adults did, too, but a few remained less enthusiastic.

"Is Marse Sumner alive?" Timothy put it bluntly and received a sound smack from his mother.

Lutie's voice shook. "I am sorry to say I have received no information on my son."

Boyd said soothingly, "Take more than a Yankee army to ketch Mr. Sumner."

"The reason I have disturbed your sleep is that the telegram came from Colonel Jeffrey Windsor. I am to meet him at the train station to receive the wounded. I shall need everyone's help. Braxton, dispatch messengers to Hazel Whitmore, Risé Rives, Miranda Lawrence, and Lillian Philpotts. Tell them to meet me at the station and bring their bandages, medicines, bedding, and any clothes they can spare. We don't know how many men will arrive." She gave everyone instructions, then all left to make hasty preparations.

Lutie and Sin-Sin reached the station before the others. Braxton and Big Muler followed with the big wagon. To be on the safe side, Braxton hitched up a buckboard. Timothy drove while Di-Peachy kept the boy company. Thanks to the moonlight, they stayed on the roads with no problem. They didn't need coach lights or lanterns although Braxton prudently packed them. No sooner had they gotten into town at sunup than a light rain spattered on their heads.

Hazel and Judson Whitmore greeted them. The Whitmores had made arrangements to use the facilities at the local university on behalf of the Confederate troops. If need be, they could even use the lawn for the wounded. They left Charles Duval, a professor of chemistry, in charge of organizing help, then they rushed to the station.

Across from the small train station was the Delevan Hotel, called Mudwall by the older residents of Charlottesville because in their youth one entire side of the building had been a thick mud wall. Judson, in his wheelchair but commanding, woke up John Slingsby, the owner. Slingsby, called Grits because of his fondness for the dish, pulled on his pants over his worn nightshirt and started to work immediately.

Grits crossed the street and personally put Lutie's bright red and gold gig into the stable. Braxton spoke with him, and they hauled out large water troughs and lined the side of the street with them. The horses would be needing plenty of water if the day proved as hot as yesterday. Braxton figured that wagons would line up to cart away the wounded to the university or to Stone Tavern on Market Street or to other houses who would agree to take the wounded.

Jennifer Fitzgerald arrived, her court in tow. She, too, had the presence of mind to bring a buckboard. By 7 A.M., Risé Rives, Miranda Lawrence, and Lillian Philpotts had arrived.

They waited for the train and waited and waited. By now it was raining buckets. Jennifer, never at her best when bored, flounced around asking who hunted with black and tans. She received no satisfactory answer. Lutie overheard and kept her mouth shut, which was difficult.

Finally, under the pretext of offering Lutie some honey cakes, Jennifer said, "I saw people hunting with black and tans last night. I think it's you, Lutie. You keep a pack of those hounds where none of us will ever see them and then tell ghost stories."

"I'm not the horsewoman my daughter is."

"You can handle a team like a driver." Jennifer offered the compliment as an argument.

"No one would hunt at night, Jennifer, and the scent's no

good in such hot conditions. Hounds would get thrown off by nature's richness, if you will."

"And if I don't believe that, you'll tell me that the cubs are half-grown and no one would hunt now anyway."

"I expect you saw the Harkaway Hunt."

Jennifer laughed. "Really, Lutie, really. I am not given to superstitions or imaginary companions."

Sin-Sin cleared her throat. Lutie's face flushed. "The only people who ever hunted with black and tans were the Harkaways. That's the truth."

"You have great respect for the truth since you so rarely use it." Jennifer laughed.

Lutie, enraged, grabbed her driving gloves, which she'd jammed in her skirt pocket, and hit Jennifer full across the face. That stopped traffic. "You offend my honor, Mrs. Fitzgerald. If I were a man, I would call you out. Being a woman, I'll have to be content with the invitation."

Jennifer, rubbing her cheek, growled, "No wonder Henley seeks diversions from you, madam."

Risé Rives, a lady of refinement, stepped in. "Really, Mrs. Fitzgerald, this is—not done."

Jennifer, happy that she wounded Lutie, retired for the moment to the Delevan Hotel. No sooner was she in the door than finally the train whistle pierced the listless air. She rushed back out again. To fall under the wheels, Lutie hoped.

A shudder of excitement passed through the little band gathered on the siding. This was soon followed by a shudder of another sort.

The engine grunted into the station. Behind it were flatcars with only two covered passenger cars; all the cars were crammed with men. The odor was overpowering, even in the downpour.

Hazel Whitmore sobbed, "Oh, my God! Oh, my God!"

Sin-Sin, speechless, grabbed Lutie's elbow. Fearing for Lutie as well as being queasy herself, she whispered, "Miz Lutie, mebbe you'd better not stay here."

Lutie, charged with mission as she had never been before, said loudly, "If they can take it, so can I."

The other ladies and their servants looked at Lutie with amazement. They decided they could take it, too.

Lutie walked the length of this train of agony, soaked to the skin. "Whoever can walk, go and sit over there." She pointed to the side opposite the train. A wooden canopy, painted dark green and white, covered the wooden sidewalk. "We will care for you as soon as we can."

Those that could walk did as they were told, glad for what minimal shelter was offered. Other men were crying like babies, begging for water. Miranda Lawrence, trying not to gag, was lifted up to the flatcar by Big Muler. She carried a water bucket and a dipper. Following her example, many of the other ladies and servants climbed onto the cars and began to dispense fresh water. Out of the rain, the flies settled on the men's faces. Risé Rives noticed as she squashed one that it smelled like the rotted flesh it had been eating.

Colonel Jeffrey Windsor had not slept for thirty-six hours. His uniform was caked with blood, and it had stiffened. His face and hands were covered with the smoke of Manassas and the grime from the train.

"Are you Colonel Windsor?" Lutie asked.

"Yes. Thank God you are here. If you will excuse me a moment, I must attend to something."

He walked to the front of the train and called the engineer down. He pulled the engineer behind the train. Moments later, Lutie heard a pistol shot. Jeffrey shot the man in the head. Stunned, she said nothing. When Jeffrey rejoined her, he said wearily, "Had to be done."

Much later, Lutie and the others learned many of the train engineers were Union sympathizers. They delayed troop movements, created mechanical problems, and did what they could to harass the Confederates. Unless one is an engineer, how could he tell if the problem was genuine? Jeffrey just insured that the three workers left on the train would think twice. The train, which should have covered the ninety miles in four hours, or even less if they shoveled on coal, had been bumping and stopping and scraping since one in the morning. Jeffrey thought to shoot him somewhere around Warrenton, but decided to give the man one more chance. Well, the engineer died for the sake of the Union, if that's the cause he believed in.

The doctor explained to the ladies what the soldiers needed. Those who could walk would be helped after the emergency cases. Those who could not walk, yet needed no surgery, were loaded onto wagons and sent to the university. The cases requiring surgery were immediately taken across the street to the hotel.

Unloaded now, the train returned to Manassas. The wounded were laid out in neat rows, and the overflow were placed on the grassy banks flanking the station. At Lutie's orders, Braxton ran to the closest church, the Presbyterian at 2nd Street and Market, and asked the sexton to ring the bell. When the people came to the church, the sexton directed them to bring towels, sheets, bandages, umbrellas, and anything else that might be useful. Soon, church after church rang their bells as the word spread. First they rang the bell for the victory. Then they rang three rings and silence, three rings and silence, which signaled an emergency. They did not yet ring a dirge for the dead. Casualty reports had not arrived.

The citizens and slaves in the county brought what comfort they could. No one was prepared for the rows of men sobbing, dying, sleeping, and babbling in delirium. Nor was anyone prepared for the smell.

Perhaps it was shameful, but no one wanted to remove the body of the engineer from the tracks. Everyone was happy to have the train back over him. Finally the stationmaster grabbed the dead man by his feet and pulled him over to the side by a switching station.

Dr. Windsor, using Lutie, Sin-Sin, Big Muler, and Di-Peachy as aides, set up an operating table in the Delevan kitchen. Grits sharpened his knives and hacksaw. He also sharpened Jeffrey's tools, which had seen constant use.

Despite the horror and stench, Miranda Lawrence was a happy woman because her husband, Ralph, also a doctor, accompanied Jeffrey Windsor from Manassas. Dr. Lawrence set up a second table behind Dr. Windsor's. They left the back door of the kitchen open so they could toss the amputated limbs outside.

Responsibility for removing the arms and legs was accepted by Risé Rives. The gratitude expressed to that brave woman further infuriated Jennifer Fitzgerald, still angry and somewhat irrational over the morning's conversation. She rushed in to help Risé, and some ladies said later that the sight of Jennifer Fitzgerald heaving arms and legs onto an offal cart during the deluge gave them the creeps. Others said they knew for certain that was when she went off her nut.

When Jeffrey removed his coat, his shirt underneath was

caked with blood. Lutie insisted he take it off. They would find him another shirt and an apron in which to operate. When he took off his shirt, the skin underneath was chafed and blistered. Lutie flinched as she washed him down. Exhausted, Jeffrey drank vats of coffee and kept going. He refused any rest. If he didn't operate on these men immediately, many of them would surely die.

One by one the wounded were slapped on the wet, washed-down table. Some men chewed rawhide strips. Others, unconscious from the pain, slept through their surgery; they were the lucky ones.

Di-Peachy, Lutie, Big Muler, and Sin-Sin took turns assisting. They poured liquor down the throats of some to knock them out. A few endured the surgery clear-eyed with no liquor, only a prayer.

Hearing of the makeshift hospital, ladies drove down from Orange County and over from Louisa and Fluvanna. They came from as far away as thirty miles. Some caught a ride on a train, others pressed on in their wagons.

Late in the afternoon, a young corporal named Mercer Hackett was on Jeffrey's table. His leg was swollen three times its normal size. He'd been hit by a minié ball which blew out the whole back side of the leg and shattered the bone. Try as he could, he couldn't keep the flies from depositing rows of their white eggs in the open wound. Much of the wound was green and black. He was running a fever, but in control of himself. He spoke to the surgeon. "Do your best, sir."

Jeffrey motioned for Big Muler to hold his right leg, the good one. Lutie stood behind Jeffrey and handed him a large scalpel. "I think I can save your knee, soldier," said Jeffrey.

"Good. Then I can sit on a horse and get back to the boys." He glanced away from Jeffrey and looked to his right at Di-Peachy, who had placed her hands on his right arm. Sin-Sin now held his left. They used horse harnesses as makeshift straps, but even so, most men had to be held. If a man struggled, they knocked him out with a drink so strong he'd regret the hangover as much as the amputation.

Mercer's light blue eyes looked into Di-Peachy's green-hazel ones. "Am I dead?"

"No, sir," she answered. "You're alive. You're alive." She

said this again as Jeffrey made the first incision. Black blood spurted over his apron. He cut higher. Now it spurted red.

Mercer grimaced but he didn't cry. "I know I'm alive now, but you must be an angel."

Di-Peachy began talking to him in an effort to take his mind off the horrendous procedure. "You're going to be all right."

"If I live, I'm going to marry you."

"I'm a slave, sir. You won't want to be marrying me."

He smiled. "I took on a whole Yankee army yesterday. By damned, I'll take on the Confederates, too, if there's a man in it says I can't marry you." He passed out.

Di-Peachy tried not to look. Jeffrey had cut away the destroyed flesh around the bone which he needed to expose. Hunks of Mercer's leg lay on the stone floor. The worst part would come now. Di-Peachy prayed the handsome man wouldn't wake up again. He did.

"Is it over?"

"Not yet. soldier," she said.

"Will you take your hands off my arm? Will you hold my hand, dear lady? If you will hold my hand, I know I can bear it. I know I'll live."

Di-Peachy glanced up at Jeffrey. He nodded yes and picked up the saw. She held Mercer's big right hand in both her small ones. He stared into her eyes. Every time the blade bit into his bone, the sickeningly sweet smell of living bone reaching their nostrils, he squeezed her hand but he did not cry out. She willed him to endure. She gave of herself to this suffering man as she never had given herself to anyone, not even Geneva. She gripped his hand with all her strength. The bone dust wafted up into the stale air. Finally, Jeffrey cut through.

Big Muler picked up the leg and walked to the open door. It landed in the cart with a soft thud. Mercer didn't look at his leg. He stared at Di-Peachy. She relaxed her grip.

"The worst is over."

Jeffrey brought a flap of skin he had cut and shaped on the one side of the incision to wrap over the exposed bone. He hoped the tied-off blood vessels would heal. Aside from fever and infection, he feared post-operative hemorrhaging and shock; and in these conditions it might be too late before anyone would notice.

"Thank you," Mercer said to Di-Peachy. "Thank you, Doctor."

Jeffrey patted him on the shoulder. Big Muler picked Mercer up as if he were a rag doll. He carried him to the hotel lobby, found a space for him, and placed a blanket over him. Mercifully, Mercer passed out.

All day people brought what they could and took men home to nurse. Over at the university, Charles Duval put men in the student rooms of the ranges. Once it stopped raining, the healthier ones were laid on the undulating, beautiful lawns. Those men that were able, sat and read or played cards. Others stared at the sky.

Apart from seeing what war does to the human body, the citizens of Albemarle County writhed in anxiety. No casualty lists had come over the wire, and nearly everyone had a relative in the army. No one knew what units had taken part in the great battle. Not knowing, in its way, was worse than knowing.

By 9:30 P.M. the last of the amputations was finished. Jeffrey took a big shot of brandy and fell asleep in a chair, his head on his chest. Big Muler carried the doctor to the best suite in the hotel.

Lutie and the other women washed up the mess. Sin-Sin, physically and emotionally drained, got on her hands and knees to scrub the bloodstains off the stone floor. They wouldn't come off. She started to cry. "Blood, blood everywhere. It comes back like the devil laughing."

Lutie stared down at the red. "I think these bloodstains will be here unto eternity."

Wiping her eyes, Sin-Sin struggled to her feet.

In the lobby, Di-Peachy placed her hand on the fevered forehead of sleeping Mercer Hackett.

Big Muler, Boyd, and Timothy sat on the back bench of the train station. There were still wounded men under the canopy, but they'd all been helped. Hopefully they would be taken to private homes tomorrow.

A train whistle brought the exhausted Lutie up short. "Oh, sweet Jesus, not more. We can't take any more."

The train stopped. The light was still good from the moon although a thin haze spread over the sky like a silvery net. A man in overalls jumped down from the engine. He didn't speak to anybody. He motioned for another fellow to help him. Together they hauled fifteen wooden boxes off the flatcars.

Lutie walked over. "Why are you leaving these coffins here?" she demanded.

"Lady, we was told to drop these ones off in Charlottesville."

"Why weren't they buried on the field of battle?"

"I dunno. A general say to me, put these on for Charlottesville. These are yourn."

Oddly grateful that Albemarle would be able to reclaim her own, she picked up a lantern. No names were on the makeshift coffins. She could smell the contents though.

"Big Muler, Braxton, I think we'd better open these and identify them, if we can."

Casualty lists started to come in late that afternoon. Timothy rushed to tell Lutie that Sumner's name was not on them. She feared for her son and her daughter, yet she was fatalistic enough to believe that if they were dead, she would know in her heart. So she did not fear these coffins as much as she thought she would.

She began her grisly work. Every time a coffin was opened, flies buzzed angrily out to freedom. The men, although already putrefying, still looked like themselves.

Braxton and Big Muler pulled off the eighth lid.

"Oh, my Christ!" Lutie reeled backwards. What was left of Greer Fitzgerald was in three pieces. His head was separated from the torso, which clearly wasn't his since it was clothed in a Yankee tunic. The legs, however, were clad in Confederate cavalry pants that had been proudly sewn by his mother. "Put the lid back on! Put the lid back on!" Lutie ran to the pump and stuck her head under it. Shaking, she returned to the men, also woozy from their task.

Much as she disliked Jennifer, Lutie took no pleasure in what she must now do. Slowly she walked across the street to the Delevan Hotel.

Jennifer was tearing sheets for more bandages.

"Jennifer, I have some terrible news. Greer has been killed, and his body is at the train station in a coffin."

"You're lying!" Jennifer shot to her feet, throwing down the rags.

"I'm afraid I'm not. I'm truly sorry, Jennifer."

"I don't believe you!" Jennifer crashed through the hall and out of the hotel.

"I think we'd better go after her," Hazel said. They hurried out the door after her.

Jennifer was beating on Big Muler's chest. "Open it, open it! Open it right this minute."

Muler kept backing away from her.

Wild, she picked up the crowbar and tore off the lid. She snatched the lantern from Timothy and ran the light up and down the pieces. She seemed confused. Then she put down the lantern beside the coffin, reached in, and picked up Greer's head.

Everyone stood still.

"It's all right, Greer, honey. It's all right. You're home now." Jennifer cradled his head in her arms.

Lutie edged up alongside of her. "Jennifer, I think you might want to sit down and have a glass of water."

Jennifer whirled around, turning her back on Lutie. "You can't have him! He's my baby!"

Hazel and Lillian carefully moved toward Jennifer. She was incoherent now. If anyone tried to get close to her, she backed off, tightly clutching her son's head.

Big Muler pounced. Jennifer screamed bloody hell. She wouldn't give up the head. He held her immobile, but she wouldn't release her grasp. When Hazel attempted to get the head from her, Jennifer snarled and then tried to bite her son's head. She was actually trying to eat him.

Horrified, Lillian picked up a piece of wood next to the stationmaster's cubbyhole and cracked Jennifer over the head with it.

As Jennifer fell, she moaned, but she did not release her prize so easily. Lutie pried her fingers from his skull, then picked up the head and put it in the coffin. She didn't know how she did it, but she did. She had done things on this day she never thought anyone could do.

As Big Muler nailed up the coffin, Hazel observed, "It's not all Greer's body."

"I know," Lutie said. "But the parts belong to some mother's son."

They put the coffin in Jennifer's wagon. Hazel instructed Jennifer's servant to bury the body as quickly as possible. Another servant placed Jennifer in the back of the wagon and drove her home.

Lutie and the women dragged themselves back to the

hotel. Grits apologetically put them in a servant's room that he'd saved for them on the top floor. He hauled in some old corn cob mattresses.

After what they'd been through, they wanted to sleep. They didn't care where.

Lutie wondered if this day would come back to haunt her. She feared worse days lay ahead. She fell asleep without calling for Emil.

JULY 23, 1861

Soldiers, bloody cards in a scattered deck, filled hospitals and private homes from Manassas to Richmond in one direction, Manassas to Lexington in the other.

As the trains brought boys into Howard's Grove Hospital and Chimborazo Hospital, Henley's fury escalated. He should have been there. Any uniformed lad with a bandage on his arm was the darling of the city. Not that the young men didn't deserve praise, but Henley wanted to shrivel in his uniform. Men as inexperienced as Philip St. George Cocke, an unstable character if ever there was one, formed the Nineteenth Infantry from Albemarle and fought with them.

He received a telegram from Lutie, informing him of her labors. He was shocked to realize the war had reached his wife.

Further compounding his discomfort was the continual stream of newspaper reports and special editions naming the commanding heroes of Manassas. P.G.T. Beauregard was hailed as the Confederate Napoleon. Joseph E. Johnston, the overall commander, received praise, though not nearly as lavish as for that Creole, Beauregard, the lion of Sumter. What was even more peculiar, from Henley's point of view, was that the report of victory was signed by Jefferson Davis. He knew that Davis left on a train to see the battle. Since they both lived in the Spotswood Hotel, Henley was apprised of his president's comings and goings whether he wanted to be or not. As of the last two days, he preferred not. Every inebriated nitwit plastered himself to the Spotswood like a spitbug on June grass. The partying, the noise, and the puking were not even diminished by the arrival of the first wounded. If the flotsam of the Confederacy didn't shut up tonight, Henley was going to pass among them with a shotgun. Enough was enough.

But the report from Davis nibbled at Henley's curiosity. He would be up for reelection soon. Clearly the president wished the glory of Manassas to rub off on himself. Davis had military experience, and everyone knew (because Davis made certain they knew) that he'd rather be in charge of the army than be in charge of the government. But he kept his creed, "Duty. Honor. Country." And his creed demanded he be their president. For a man who wanted to fight, he was suspiciously eager to be reelected. Rumor had it that Davis actually feared Beauregard since the latter had won acclaim at Fort Sumter. Henley decided he'd keep an eye on that backstage drama, and perhaps he'd be able to peep behind the wings this Thursday on Kate Vickers's receiving day. As her salon was Richmond's most brilliant, surely one or all of the actors would appear on her stage.

Kate Vickers! Yet another reason to be cast into the jaws of wretchedness. Her husband's name was mentioned prominently in dispatches. "Mars Vickers, aptly named" began one. Another recounted that because he had performed the Herculean labors of a colonel, he was promoted to one. Henley, passionately curious about the man he perceived to be his rival, gleaned bits of information like a mouse hoarding pellets of bran stolen from the feed manger. "Rebellious," "plainspoken," "brave, but no political sense"—these sentiments heated Henley's imagination.

Mars Vickers twinkled, a smaller star in the celestial firmament of Beauregard, Johnston, Bartow, Bee, and the apparently magical Colonel Jackson. Henley Chatfield might as well be a clod of mud. He consoled himself with the fact that Robert E. Lee didn't get to the fight either. No doubt Lee was as condemned to drudgery as Henley was.

Walking across Exchange Alley, Henley was jolted out of his reverie by a tap on the shoulder from Maud Windsor.

"Colonel Chatfield, I'm so happy to see you. I'm still overwhelmed by God's bounty to our infant nation!" Maud's face glowed.

"Yes, yes," Henley said, as enthusiastically as he could.

"I received word this morning that my husband is in Charlottesville tending to the wounded. Your wife has been of inestimable value to him. Jeffrey's exact words were 'She thinks naught for herself but only of the men. Whatever I accomplish here, it is greatly due to this good woman's efforts.' "

"What they all must have endured." Henley worried about the strain of nursing on Lutie. He regarded her as fragile ever since Jimmy's death and the appearance of Emil.

"Well, it's over now, isn't it?"

"We've won a battle, Mrs. Windsor, not the war."

"How could they possibly risk another humiliation like that? And where will they find more men willing to die like slaughtered animals? They must beg for peace."

"I truly wish I could say that will happen, madam, for it would bring me much happiness."

She cocked her head and looked up at him. "Why, what do you think will happen?"

"They will appoint a new general. They will raise and train more troops. They have their pride. They must fight again, if for no other reason than to avenge their honor. Unfortunately, they also believe they have a just cause. It's my belief that they are now aroused as one nation."

She considered this. "But do you really think, sir, that they would hazard another drubbing before the world?"

"If the situation were reversed, which thanks be to God it's not, would we fold our hands and quit?"

"Certainly not."

He smiled. "Remember, Mrs. Windsor, that until a few months ago they were our brothers. As we would act, so will they."

JULY 24, 1861

The Warrenton Turnpike cut straight across the rolling meadows, which got flatter the further northeast one traveled. Mars led a patrol out of the camp. The continued celebrating created its own casualties. A few men shot each other in revelry. One fool blasted his foot off while dancing and firing his sidearm into the ground.

New men arrived every day. More mouths to feed. Provisions couldn't accommodate the ever increasing horde. Mars fumed that even with a railroad running from the valley into Manassas, where in blue hell were the grain supplies, fresh ammunition, even simple medicines?

The Confederate army was sinking into its own filth. No one had considered the effects of over twenty thousand men shitting, vomiting, and pissing wherever they pleased. One would be better off sitting in the paddocks than with his fellow man.

As Mars's small patrol picked its way along the road, rutted from the heavy rain and constant abuse from guns and wagons, Geneva could still see unburied corpses. No matter how people worked, they couldn't get the bodies in the ground fast enough. The Yankees ran, leaving no burial detail behind and requesting no permission for a patrol to return to bury and honor their dead.

Confederate soldiers, assisted by townspeople, started burying Northern dead. Aside from the sweet, overpowering smell, the task was made more macabre by the continuous flock of sightseers who arrived daily. The battlefield often degenerated into theater with more than one polite gentleman or lady observer fainting from the sight and the stench. So much for glory.

Geneva passed a row of hastily dug graves. Bare feet stuck out of the ground. The gravediggers, in compensation for the repugnance of their chore, had stripped the bodies clean. Better that boots be on the feet of the living than the dead. The Confederacy needed every supply it could get.

The big prize, twenty-seven captured cannons, was lovingly attended to by the artillery. Nash commented that the officers seemed less like soldiers than little boys gloating over hard-won marbles.

Mars trotted to the rear of the little column. "Gimme a light."

Banjo plucked the cigar from his mouth and handed it to Mars. Amused that Mars was having a hard time lighting his pipe, Banjo advised, "You'd be better off to smoke a cigar."

"Hate the smell." Mars sucked in mightily. "There!" As Mars handed the cigar back to Banjo, his pipe went out again. "Jesus H. Christ on a raft."

Banjo and Geneva laughed. Nash, who wasn't paying much attention, spotted a wounded man lying on his back, moving his arms. Nash turned out of the column.

"Nash!" Geneva called out. "Where are you going?"

"I think that fellow needs help."

"Get back here." Geneva kept her voice soft.

"Get back here, soldier. Double quick!" Mars snapped. "When your sergeant gives you an order, you'd better damn well listen to him. That body is moving because it's full of maggots. There's nothing left alive here."

Displeased, Nash rejoined the patrol. He glared at the stripe on Geneva's sleeve, sewn on crookedly since Geneva did it herself. He said nothing.

"Piggy, what's your problem?" Mars asked.

Fed up, Nash snarled back. "I don't much like taking orders from—someone half my age!"

"He may be half your age, but he's twice the man you are."

Outraged, Nash hissed through clenched teeth, "If you weren't my commanding officer, I'd lay you to whaleshit!"

Mars, alongside him now, said, "I'd like to knock those funny ideas out of your head."

Outraged, Nash shoved the major hard. He nearly fell off his horse. Mars dismounted, handing his reins to Banjo.

"Piggy, now's your chance." Nash flew off the back of his horse. Mars said to his men, "You aren't seeing anything."

"Nash, don't." Geneva barely controlled her voice.

"Shut up, or I'll knock the shit out of you." Nash glowered.

Both men raised their fists and circled around one another. Nash lashed out his foot and caught Mars by the ankle. The bigger man crashed to the ground. Nash hurtled himself on Mars. As they rolled over on the trampled ground, the arm of the dead body moved again, as though waving them on.

Nash grabbed Mars's neck and choked him. Face red, Mars jammed his thumbs with a sharp upward thrust into Nash's armpits. Nash released his grip, and Mars lowered his head, charging into Nash's midsection.

Geneva bit her lip until it bled.

Nash was on the ground this time with Mars on top of him. He struggled to get up, but Mars pinned him. Furious, Nash twisted his head and sank his teeth into Mars's forearm.

"You son of a bitch." Mars yanked his arm upward.

Nash threw him off and faced him again. Mars punched him hard in the side. Nash retaliated with a blow to the shoulder, but he dropped his guard, and Mars pulverized him with a clean, powerful right to the jaw. Nash sank to his knees, blood trickling out of his mouth. He started to rise, and Mars delivered a withering uppercut. Nash was out cold.

Geneva started to dismount.

"Stay mounted," Mars gasped. He walked painfully to his horse, withdrew his canteen, and poured water on Nash's face. Nash opened his eyes. "That was our get-acquainted fight, Piggy." Mars's side hurt him.

Nash shook his head to clear it. He wobbled to his feet and put up his fists to renew the struggle.

"No more," Mars said. "Do you want to transfer out?"

"Not until I can whip your ass good."

"Have it your way." Mars climbed back in the saddle.

Geneva rode in silence for the rest of the patrol.

Nash had not failed in his duty. He overcame his fear and performed as a soldier during the battle, but he derived no satisfaction from his courage. Nash was slipping away from Geneva. She no longer knew what he thought nor could she divine what he felt.

* * *

Late in the afternoon, Mars sent his detachment back to camp except for Sam Wells. Mars and Sam detoured on the Old Alexandria and Warrenton roads, and finding nothing of much interest, rode across fields to the new Warrenton Road. The stone bridge crossing Bull Run was directly ahead. Three lovely arches spanned the stream, still swollen from the heavy rain. A lone Confederate officer walked up the embankment to the bridge.

Mars stopped. "Hello, sir."

"Hello. A beautiful little bridge, isn't it? Thank God for the Romans, or we'd never know how to construct an arch." The man was handsome in that way women found men attractive: a sunny, open face.

Sam Wells brought his leg around and slid off his horse while the man held his reins. Sam got a much closer look at him. "Captain, you look familiar to me."

"You look familiar to me, too. Bet if we both shaved, the mystery would be solved."

Sam laughed. "What's your name, sir?"

"Sumner Chatfield of Albemarle County."

"Sumner Chatfield! The last time I saw you, you were pushing your first whiskers! It's Sam Wells."

"Sam!" Sumner hugged him. "I thought you were in Philadelphia. My God, it's good to see you."

"I was in Philadelphia. When the war broke out, I went to Richmond to discuss the future with my friend here. Brevet Colonel Mars Vickers, meet Sumner Chatfield."

Mars offered his hand. "Pleased to meet you, Captain."

The three men grazed their horses and sat down by the stream. As there was fifteen years between Sam and Sumner, they did not have the same school friends, but there was enough overlap with brothers and sisters that one tidbit of news led to another.

Mars listened with good humor. Mars interrupted, "Mr. Chatfield, there is a Chatfield in our regiment. Best horseman I ever saw. No doubt he is kin to you in some distant way."

"Looks like your father actually," Sam volunteered.

"Jimmy Chatfield."

Sumner was puzzled. "You must be mistaken."

"No, his name is James Chatfield. He's lying about his age though. Says he's eighteen."

"James Chatfield *was* my brother." Sumner blanched.

Sam chimed in. "I don't remember any brother."

"Jimmy's been dead for some ten years," Sumner said flatly.

"What?" Mars was alert.

"Sam, you left before Jimmy was walking. You wouldn't remember. Terrible the way he died. Almost killed Mother."

"This boy looks enough like Henley, well, as like as spit." Sam realized he may have blundered. What if Jimmy was an illegitimate child and Sumner knew nothing? He quickly added, "But you know how often people seem to resemble one another. And distant members of a family can often look like cookie cutter images of each other."

"Captain, would you do me a favor?" Mars asked. "My curiosity is aroused. Will you come to my encampment tonight and meet this Jimmy Chatfield?" Mars wiped his brow.

"I'll be there."

About an hour after sunset, Sumner Chatfield found the First Virginia Cavalry. He picked his way through the rows of tents until he located Mars Vickers. Together they walked to where Geneva, Nash, and Banjo normally made camp. As it was, the three were in the process of cooking stolen chicken.

Geneva was just going to get some more water when she saw Sumner approaching. She knew she'd better take the bull by the horns or all would be lost.

She set down her pails and rushed to a bewildered Sumner. "Brother!" She kissed him on the cheek and hugged him. "Thank God, you're alive! I'm so happy to see you!"

Sumner recognized the voice, but he was dumbfounded.

She stepped away from him. "You've surrendered your paunch to the enemy, I see."

Sumner automatically looked at his stomach. That voice—his sister's voice! "What in the hell are you doing here! Does Father know you're here?"

"No, and I'll thank you to shut up about it. Mother knows."

"And she let you go?"

"She didn't have much choice, did she?"

"Where's Nash?"

"I'm here." Nash joined the family reunion.

Geneva impulsively took Mars's hand. "Major, I lied to you. I'm not Jimmy Chatfield. I'm the baby of the family, so

I took my older brother's name and hoped I could get away with it."

"I declare! You beat all." Sumner smiled broadly. He just got it.

"What is your name then?" Mars dropped her hand.

"Lucius. I was named for my paternal grandfather."

Sumner, dazzled by his sister's impertinence and sheer brass, laughed. "I wish he could see you now." Somewhat recovered, he gazed into his sister's imploring eyes. "Do you mean to tell me that you fought on Sunday?"

"Like a tiger, Captain Chatfield." Mars bragged as if Jimmy, Lucius, were his own. "You can be proud of your baby brother."

Sumner put his arm around Geneva's waist. "You know, in a funny way I'm not surprised." He turned to Mars. "Thank you, sir, for reuniting me with my brother."

"By the way, how old is he?"

"Eighteen." Sumner told the truth.

Mars shook his head. "Oh well, two liars are better than one. I'll still call you Jimmy."

Mars returned to his tent and thought what a curious creature Jimmy was. Something in the boy tugged at the corners of his heart. Mars was reaching that age where a man needs children. Little hope of that unless he found some outside woman. Lacerated by Kate's presence, he'd begun to fear the whole breed or hate them. He wasn't sure which. Well, he had a war to fight, and Jimmy Chatfield was hardly of paramount concern. Still, he thought of the boy.

Finally Sumner had an opportunity to talk to Geneva and Nash alone. "You must be giving Mother heart failure, Geneva. And what about Father? You've got to tell him sometime."

"That's what I've been saying," Nash agreed.

"Let me work up my courage. Don't tell him, Sumner."

"The old man probably wouldn't believe it if I did tell him."

Nash, with some delicacy, asked if he could take a walk alone with Sumner.

Nash opened his mouth and couldn't stop talking. He finished his tale with, "Can't you send her home?"

"She won't listen to me any more than she'll listen to you," Sumner replied sympathetically. He scratched his chin. "She's bullheaded. And she loves you very much. That's why she's here."

"It's not that I don't cherish her desire to be by my side. I do, I truly do." Nash breathed in. "But I don't think of her as my wife quite like I used to."

Sumner smiled. "She's a woman where it counts." He laughed. "I'd say you're in a better position than anyone in the camp!"

"Yes, I'm probably making too much of it." Nash shrugged.

"Everyone's raw right now."

Nash appreciated that sentiment. "Something else happened you should know about. Do you remember my man Bumba?"

"Yes." Sumner cracked his knuckles.

"When we initially withdrew from Winchester before Manassas, we thought Patterson would strike. We thought we'd have to fight our way to Beauregard. That night Bumba disappeared."

"You mean to say he ran off?"

"Either he was afraid of a battle—or he knew the Yankees were close as hot breath and he crossed over to their lines. He wasn't the only one."

Sumner scratched his stubble. "You said as much before we enlisted."

"Yes, but I didn't think my man would run away."

"Maybe he was a rotten apple, and you never saw it."

"Bumba had been with me since childhood; he was no rotten apple. He left without a good-bye, without anything. I trusted that man with my life!"

"You were lucky your life was never in danger."

"How could he do that? He's not going to be free; maybe, free to starve. No one will take care of him. That's what I hate about those people up north. They delude our simple folk into believing they'll give them a better life. They don't even take care of their own. Why would they take care of our Negroes?"

"People believe what they want to believe. Don't take it so hard. If he left, he couldn't be worth much."

"Yes, I'm probably making too much of that, too."

Sumner cracked his knuckles again. "Can't put scrambled eggs back in the shell."

JULY 25, 1861

Lutie and Sin-Sin returned to the big house early that morning, leaving Di-Peachy and Big Muler back in town. Di-Peachy refused to leave Mercer Hackett until his fever broke. Lutie had sent Braxton and Timothy home yesterday.

Ernie June performed so well that Lutie allowed her to wear the keys for the remainder of the day.

The deeply disturbing news was that Jennifer Fitzgerald had dug up Greer's corpse in the middle of the night. One of the servants had stopped her as she was trying to drag it piece by piece into Greer's room. They had sedated her with an opiate and removed the remains to the Methodist cemetery in town. Being an Episcopalian, Jennifer would never think to look there.

Lutie caught up on her Bible lessons, but as they were in the book of Job, she hurried through them. The story was too depressing to contemplate. Then she thought she would read "The Prayer of Manasses, King of Judah, When He Was Holden Captive in Babylon." Manasses beat his breasts bragging on his sins. Lutie had hoped for something edifying, something to further celebrate last glorious Sunday.

No word yet on a peace settlement. It began to dawn on Lutie that one might not be offered.

Lutie twirled a curl by her ear. She fiddled with it for a few minutes while Sin-Sin waited, hands folded in her lap. "Sin-Sin, tell Braxton to saddle up old Exeter. I think I'll ride on the back acres today."

As Lutie was not especially fond of riding sidesaddle, even though she was a decent rider, Sin-Sin balked. Also, Sin-Sin was a terrible rider, so she'd be left out. "What you want to be gwine back there for?"

"Henley has an old hunting cabin up on the ridge. No-body's been back there since April. Maybe whoever killed Alafin is back there. Or maybe I just need a little exercise."

"Whoever kilt Alafin be somebody we kin see. I knows it."

Lutie trudged upstairs to her closet for her boots. "Don't worry."

Sin-Sin dogged her. "Take a gun."

"I will. I'll take Braxton, too."

As Lutie and Braxton slowly cantered over the back mead-ows, leaving the cultivated areas of Chatfield for its wilder lands and its hidden meadows, she felt good. She was glad to be away from the suffering for a moment. She'd begun to think of the train station as the Nekra Gate, the death gate of Constantinople's hippodrome. During the high days of the Byzantine Empire the chariot racing was so dangerous that contestants died or were drenched in glory and money. The injured and dead were carried through one gate only. Anyone who loved a charioteer stood by the gate and waited for the inevitable, his body. Odd how the mind makes associations. Odd that a nondescript railroad station in Charlottesville would forever be associated with the Nekra Gate in her mind.

The heat baked into her bones. How she loved that heat. Let the others complain. Exeter's smooth gait and quiet ways reminded her how enjoyable a bracing ride could be. She'd gotten accustomed to thinking of the stable and horses as Henley's territory. Her father, Christopher Chalfonte, was quite a fine horseman. Probably that's why she fell in love with Henley. As a young man, Henley was a breathtaking sight on a horse. He reminded her of her father: bold, master-ful, easy to talk to. But then a woman finds that husbands rarely act like fathers. She was glad her father, who was born in 1783 and died in 1849, was not alive to see this war. It would have hurt him terribly. Papa would have cried to think the nation which his father, Delos Reynolds Chalfonte, had fought to create would so soon split apart.

Lutie entertained a vague notion that if the women of the South and the North could have voted, this wouldn't have happened. She believed in her heart of hearts that women had more sense, even though her own daughter challenged that convenient notion. At least Geneva was alive and well, thank the Lord.

"Braxton, look!" Lutie pointed to acres of bright green corn. "Did my husband authorize planting these back acres?"

"No, Miz Lutie. Mr. Henley's always left this in pasture."

The Chatfield estate was four thousand acres. Henley farmed the land closest to the house. The six hundred acres far away had been cleared by his great-grandfather and grandfather for back pasture land. Some of this land boasted apple orchards. The trees needed little attention. Henley pruned them every three years or so.

"Someone's farming our land."

"Yes, ma'am."

"Someone who thinks that because my husband is away, this big place will get away from me."

"It be vexatious."

"We're going to harvest this crop come fall. And, Braxton, don't tell a soul that we didn't plant this ourselves. I'd like to see the face of whoever's responsible for this when he finds out we're about to benefit from his seed and his hard labor."

"Yes, ma'am, I'd like to see that, too."

JULY 28, 1861

The Very Reverend Manlius offered from his pulpit a lengthy thanksgiving scene. Lutie gave thanks when it was over. The Bible was ransacked for examples appropriate to Manassas. Since the Old Testament was one long military interlude, the good pastor suffered an embarrassment of riches.

After services, Lutie, Risé, Hazel, Miranda, and Lillian visited the Delevan Hotel. Throughout the week each lady called on her assigned place, whether it was the university, the old Stone Tavern, or an individual house. They agreed to meet at the Delevan on Sundays. Each woman moved the seriously wounded to her own estate as the soldiers improved.

Dr. Windsor remained in Charlottesville awaiting further orders from his commanding officer. He was happy to see the ladies and even happier that Henley had secured a seat for his wife on tomorrow's train.

Mercer Hackett and Anthony Farr-Jones, an Alabama boy who'd lost both his arms, made sufficient improvement to leave the hotel. Colonel Windsor felt a home environment would lift Anthony's spirits. Di-Peachy's constant attendance to Mercer's health encouraged Lutie to take Mercer and Anthony to Chatfield.

Lutie, delighted that Di-Peachy was rejoining the human race, was quite disturbed because Mercer was white. Fortunately Di-Peachy behaved like a lady, and she knew that men always fell in love with their nurses. Probably nothing would come of it.

As the men were being carefully loaded into the gleaming phaeton Lutie brought for the occasion, Reddy Neutral Taylor appeared on foot.

"Mrs. Chatfield, glad I found you."

"Good afternoon, Mr. Taylor." She slid the leather through her hands. The team picked up their ears.

"I've come to make good a mistake."

"What mistake, Mr. Taylor?".

"Your boy Peter told me I could use your back acres. So I planted them and now I regret that I didn't speak to you or to Mr. Chatfield. I am, however, prepared to make good. I could pay you rent on the land, fifty cents an acre."

"I'll consider your offer, but I must discuss it with my husband first." She tightened the reins slightly and casually touched the long whip on the flanks of the two dapple gray geldings. She missed her high stepping hackney team, now safely boarded in Kentucky. She hoped they'd be back home as soon as the North saw the light. She slid past a perplexed Reddy. "Be home in no time, gentlemen."

Mercer sat next to Lutie, his stump stretched out before him. "Not exactly a princely sum, that fellow's offer."

"Not exactly a prince." Lutie smiled.

Anthony Farr-Jones swayed this way and that. Without his arms, balance was difficult. He fought back tears. Mercer heaved himself on the other side of the phaeton to sit next to him. When they'd hit a bump, Anthony would lean into Mercer. Lutie drove as smoothly as she could, but the roads were rutted. She decided that the New World wouldn't truly be civilized until paved roads were built. Of course, this would leave out entire chunks of the Old World, too.

Lutie instructed Mercer to open the food hamper. Ernie June had packed fried chicken, finger dumplings, fritters, and her specialty, fried okra that was so crispy you could hear it snap across a room. Mercer fed Anthony. Lutie munched on the okra and wondered why Peter would lie to Reddy. She entertained no illusions about Peter's word. He could as easily lie to Reddy as he could to her, but why would Reddy take the word of a slave? That corn was put down toward the end of April. Reddy Neutral Taylor had plenty of time to come forward to Henley, Lutie, or Sumner. Reddy's life revolved around profit, but then he was a tradesman, what could she expect? You can't make a racehorse out of a jackass.

AUGUST 1, 1861

The sound of Washington's church bells floated across the Potomac. Geneva, along with other cavalry, pushed from Centreville up to Mason and Munson Hills across from the northern capital. Wherever the regiment rode, people came out of their farmhouses or their row houses in the town to cheer them on.

Geneva and Mars, outposts, watched the river from the hilltop.

"Let's go on in there, you fox in a henhouse." Geneva egged Mars.

He gazed across the water. "Too many hens in that one house. They may be disorganized, but there are a mess of them."

"What's going to happen to the Union general that commanded at Manassas?"

"McDowell? He's so far out on a limb he can hear the wood cracking."

"Why do we wear gray?" Geneva burst with questions whenever she was alone with her commanding officer.

Mars shrugged. "Some asshole became overimpressed with the Austrian army, and they wear gray. The people in Richmond want their boys to cut a fine figure." He laughed. "What else goes on inside that head of yours?"

"Not much, I'm afraid. I'm a disappointment to my mother. I'm not such a disappointment to my father, but I don't think he expected much."

"You're not a disappointment to me. You're the fightingest creature I ever saw."

"Thank you, sir. Thanks for taking me with you to scout." Geneva spoke a little self-consciously.

"Fun to ride with you. You know, Banjo does right well, too. No form but he can hang on and shoot with both hands. Now if the rest of us could do that and be as accurate as he is, I expect we would become twice as deadly. I have to go to Richmond next week. Want to go with me?"

Geneva, excited, remembered Nash and became less excited. "I don't know if I should go, sir."

Mars darkened. "Because of Piggy?"

"It kills him when you call him that."

"He's so thin-skinned he'd bleed in a high wind."

"He's tremendously intelligent, and he—"

"He doesn't interest me too much, but I can see he sure interests you."

"It's not what you think, Colonel." She started to blush.

"If it's not what I think, then it's a goddamned good imitation."

"You make me sick! I don't know how you could think that about Nash." Realizing she had insulted the colonel of her regiment, she said nothing more.

"Let me ask you this: Have you ever slept with a woman?"

Shocked, Geneva stuttered, "N-n-no, and don't make fun of me."

"I'm not. I know you're young, but you've got to learn sometime. I'm taking you with me to Richmond, and I personally am going to see that you become acquainted with the fair sex." A drop of sarcasm coated his voice.

"No."

Not understanding her refusal, he pressed on. "It's not so bad, Jimmy. Granted, it takes practice, and women are complicated. I had to get drunk to attempt it, and I don't remember a minute of the maneuver. You have to start somewhere, Jimmy. For Christ's sake, no man should be a virgin on his wedding night."

"I don't believe that."

"What's the matter with you? Hasn't your father or your brother talked to you?"

"No!"

"Calm down. You have to grow up sometime. A man has a responsibility to his future wife to be knowledgeable, and it's hardly a chore learning! You also have a responsibility to your wife never to let her find out about your, shall we say, experiments and never, ever to let her find out about dalliances."

Devastated, Geneva practically whimpered. "Have you, have you ever had dalliances?"

"A few."

"Even after you were married?"

"Jimmy, boy, you don't look well. Would you like a drink of something stronger than water?"

"You betrayed your wife?"

"She betrayed me first!" Mars flashed. That was one wound he didn't want uncovered.

"Two wrongs don't make a right."

"And what the hell do you know about it? You haven't even won your spurs!"

"At least I'm not a faithless son of a bitch!"

Stung, Mars pushed her to the ground.

She jumped up, swinging wildly. Mars grunted and backed, away from her. He caught her under the elbow and spun her around. She slid onto the grass. He put his foot on her chest, pinning her down. She grabbed his leg but he had most of his weight on her chest.

"You're gonna wish you were somebody else," he snarled.

"At least I won't be you."

"You make me so mad I can't see straight." He let her up. The fight was over. "You're the only person on God's green earth that gets me mad besides my wife." Mars calmed down. He wished he hadn't said that.

"I hate you, Mars!" She rubbed her aching chest.

"Colonel to you, shit ass."

"Colonel." She folded her arms.

"I'm lucky you didn't bite me. Probably give me rabies." He started to laugh. The tension evaporated.

Geneva laughed, too. Finally he threw an arm around her. "I'm sorry. You get under my skin. You're like a little chigger."

"I'm not saying what you're like."

Mars cleared his throat. "I would appreciate it if you did not discuss anything I may have said in anger about my wife."

"I won't. Colonel," she continued, "let me ask you something. You know Nash Hart was recently married. He says he loves her until death do him part."

"Everyone says that in the beginning."

"Do you think he would cheat on her?"

"If the circumstances are right, any man will wander. Hell, Jimmy, what's the big deal?"

Geneva's face drained. "I guess I want people to keep their promises."

Mars smiled ruefully. "It doesn't seem to work out that way. Love is harder than war. You'll find that out in your own good time."

"I hope not. I hope someone can love me for me."

"I hope so, too. It's too late for me."

AUGUST 8, 1861

Glittering in his finest dress uniform, Henley admired himself one more time in the full-length mirror. A knock on the door brought a quick reply. "Come in."

The door opened and there stood Sumner, equally resplendent in the dress uniform of a captain of artillery. His red collar and facings pulsated with gold trimmings. "Father."

Astonished, Henley hesitated a moment and then rushed to embrace his son. "Let me look at you." He walked around Sumner. "Last time I saw you, you were wearing cavalry yellow and a private at that. What are you doing here? It's good to see you!" Henley embraced him again.

At his father's beckoning, Sumner sat in the wooden library chair. "I came down with Colonel Vickers."

"He's here?"

"Yes, he came to wrangle with the Commissary Department and to attend his wife's social extravaganza. He preferred to stay in the camp, but Stuart insisted he attend."

Henley's heart skipped a beat. "How did you come to know him?"

"I met him at Stone Bridge on Warrenton Road."

Sumner answered his father's questions and related events, the events he himself had seen at Manassas. Sumner requested an assignment with Vickers's horse artillery. He'd relayed the news that Nash was bearing up although he didn't like war. Henley showed Geneva's letters to Sumner, who affected great interest. He would not break his word to his sister.

They discussed Lutie, the murder of Alafin, and Lutie's nursing work. The story of Jennifer Fitzgerald made them both queasy.

Henley recognized that his son had endured a test and passed it, a test that he himself had not endured. He was proud of Sumner and envious. For the first time, Sumner spoke to him as a man, an equal. However gruesome the war might be, it gave Sumner the opportunity to carve out a place for himself, independent of Chatfield and his father.

These new feelings prompted Henley to ask Sumner's opinion about the corn crop and Reddy Neutral Taylor.

"Pay him for the seed and the labor, then take the crop ourselves. I think we can only tarnish our name by a partnership with him, even such a tenuous one."

Henley observed his son as he spoke. The lesson for the day was Proverbs, chapter 4. Henley, like Lutie, knew his Bible. Chapter 4 exhorts the reader to get wisdom, to embrace understanding. "Hear, O my son, and receive my sayings; and the years of thy life shall be many. I have taught thee in the way of wisdom; I led thee in right paths. When thou goest, thy steps shall not be straitened; and when thou runnest, thou shalt not stumble." Could it be that Sumner had absorbed Henley's lessons over the years? For a fleeting moment, Henley thought he may have been too hard on the boy.

He stared into Sumner's eyes, clear, light eyes like Lutie's. "That's excellent advice, Sumner. I'm quite proud of you, son. Truly proud."

As they rode in an open coach to Kate Vickers's party, Sumner confided that when the war was over, he wanted to build gardens and fountains for Lutie. Using the fountains in St. Petersburg, Russia, for inspiration. He made drawings appropriate to Chatfield's topography and Virginian materials. Henley said he'd be happy to examine the plans, but Sumner had better keep cost uppermost in his mind.

Every window and door of the Vickerses' house was flung open to invite visitors. Expensive coaches and teams lined the broad boulevard. Music, conversation, and laughter floated out onto the street, beckoning people to enter.

Henley passed through the huge front door and gave his hat to the butler, as did Sumner. Standing a few feet from the door, greeting her guests, was Kate Vickers. Mars, in dress uniform, stood beside her. Sumner sucked in his breath.

"Colonel Chatfield, I am so glad you're here. Whom have you brought to me?"

Henley bowed and kissed her hand. "Mrs. Vickers, allow me to present to you Captain Sumner Chalfonte Chatfield, who fought of late at Manassas."

"Colonel, I can see the source of your son's manner and manly bearing." Her smile was blinding. "You have not met my husband. Colonel Chatfield, Colonel Mars Vickers."

"I've heard so much about you, Colonel Chatfield, and I've looked forward to meeting you at last. You are a great favorite of my wife."

"The honor is entirely mine, Colonel Vickers. Your exploits on the field of battle are known to the entire Confederacy." Henley smiled, then moved into the crowd.

"Father, why didn't you tell me she was so beautiful?" Sumner spoke rapidly.

"Yes, she is, isn't she?" Henley replied.

"Mother!" Forgetting for a moment everyone, even Kate Vickers, Sumner spied Lutie.

President Davis, hot in conversation with cabinet members

also in attendance, also paused for a moment. A sad smile crossed his face as he thought perhaps of the mothers who would never see their sons again.

Henley, surprised to see his wife, held out his hand to her. "Lutie, what are you doing here?"

"Dr. Windsor told me Sumner was accompanying Colonel Vickers to Richmond to battle with your department, and I decided to surprise both of you." To Sumner she said, "There's someone else who wants to see you."

Kate took Sumner's arm. "Come with me, Captain." She led him to the kitchen. The door swung open, and Sumner beheld twenty servants in various states of preparation and panic. Coolly going about her business, a festive red turban for special occasions on her head, was Sin-Sin.

"Auntie Sin-Sin!" Sumner ran over and hugged her.

Sin-Sin held on to him, tears in her eyes. "My young mastah, my baby boy! God done answered my prayers. He brought you safe to Sin-Sin."

Kate rejoined her guests, and Sin-Sin introduced her hero to the other servants. She also complained bitterly that Lutie had entrusted the keys to Ernie June, but it was either that or Ernie June would accompany Lutie, and Sin-Sin wasn't going to let that fat tick get her butt in Richmond. No, sir, no way, no how. Ernie June cooked up a mess of her specialties for this event, and it took three men to load the hampers on the train. Sin-Sin said she thought they could feed the army.

"Auntie, I've told the boys in my company about you. After the war is over, I'm going to bring them all home just to meet you and Momma. What a party we'll have! And will you make a pot for each one?"

"Course." She put her smooth, warm palm to his cheek. "Now you go on out there and make those ladies fight over you. You gots more important things to do than chew the fat with an old slave woman."

Sumner hugged her again. "You're worth the lot of them." He kissed her on the cheek.

Feigning embarrassment, she shooed him away. "Go on, now, you get out here, you tomcat." Laughing, Sumner returned to the party.

"I tell you, sir, we cannot rely on foreign purchase. We must produce ourselves. We can lean upon nobody." General Josiah Gorgas and Judah P. Benjamin were arguing.

"I am not opposed to your theory, General Gorgas, but I do think we need to employ every opportunity to further bind England and possibly even France to our cause. Trade is one of those methods."

"Then you'd better give me the money for a mess of fast ships, gentlemen." Stephen Mallory, Secretary of the Navy, spoke. "Our Yankee brethren are going to set up a blockade."

"Since they can't fight on the land, they'll try the sea." A menacing smile erupted from the lips of Cassius Rife. He insinuated himself into the conversation. Cassius, a munitions manufacturer from Runnymede, Maryland, Lutie's childhood home, was courting these men. Cassius would have cut cards with the devil.

A gasp went up from the crowd, as General P.G.T. Beauregard, the Napoleon of the Confederacy, strode into the receiving line. Kate curtseyed. "You honor my husband and myself by gracing us with your presence, General. The entire nation is grateful for your exploits."

"I did only what any soldier would do, madam. I went where the fire was the hottest. And with ladies such as yourself to protect, I would go to the very jaws of hell!"

The crowd burst into spontaneous applause. The general accepted it and then walked over to Kate Vickers's grandmother, the eldest lady in the room, to introduce himself as her dinner partner. Naturally, that was fitting since he would have to walk second into the dining room, the host, of course, preceding all with the most distinguished lady in the room and that happened to be Mrs. Jefferson Davis. The fact that Beauregard stopped first to speak to the old lady rather than the leaders of the Confederacy endeared him to every woman in the room.

Sumner, at Lutie's urging, was meeting people, including a somewhat ignored Robert E. Lee.

Lutie, always popular in Richmond society, joined a group of ladies who were discussing Elizabeth Van Lew. "She belongs in Screamersville," said one lady.

Another matron, staggering under the weight of her green emeralds, warbled, "She expresses publicly her many opinions, whether people are willing to listen or not. I tell you, I half expected her to appear today. She may be crazy, but she's well bred. We can't keep her out."

Maud Windsor, Elizabeth Van Lew's neighbor, said, "My

husband feels that she is suffering from extreme overexhaustion or even a form of hysteria. He has discreetly recommended to her relatives that they might consider a rest home for her."

"I think she's bats, plain and simple," green emeralds bellowed.

"She's a spy." This was said with some conviction by a thin, but pleasant looking lady of perhaps thirty.

"Well, whatever she is, I take it she has the personality of a gargoyle," Lutie tossed this off casually.

The ladies laughed. A little bell tinkled, and the music stopped. Time for dinner.

Mars, without a doubt the handsomest man in the room, bowed to Mrs. Davis and offered her his arm. The president jovially said, "She is the Confederacy's most precious possession, sir. Handle with care."

Mars placed his hand over Mrs. Davis's hand, which rested lightly on his forearm. "Mr. President, I shall cherish our national treasure."

The guests, encrusted with braid, rubies, pearls, stars, laurel clusters surrounding stars, gold bars, emeralds, sapphires, and diamonds, promenaded toward the long, heavy table, over which hung a chandelier of perfect proportions. As they stood behind their chairs, the last couple, Kate Vickers escorted by President Davis, entered the room. As each gentleman seated his dinner partner, the rustle of dresses sounded like a high wind in pines.

President Davis could have insisted on political protocol and gone first, but he behaved as a gentleman in society and accepted the honor of attending his hostess. He sat on her right. Beauregard sat on Mars's right. Keeping these two at opposite ends of the table, position intact, was both correct and wise on Kate's part. The President won favor that evening by his modesty. Of course, he was only too delighted to converse with Kate. She cast her spell over everyone. Even women could not withstand her beauty. Behind her back, they carped, but in her presence, most simply trembled.

The additional cold dishes from Ernie June provided the finishing touches to the feast. The food was lavishly complimented.

After dinner, appropriate toasts were drunk, accolades sung, and the President spoke. "Ladies and gentlemen, the Lord has blessed us with a great victory and heroic generals. Let us hope that we can conclude this unwanted but necessary war so that we might establish the old form of government and live according to the ways of our people."

Applause ricocheted off the walls.

After the food, the guests wobbled to their feet. The orchestra began to play, and everyone danced until dawn when the last guests left on the wings of bourbon.

For her services, Sin-Sin was presented with a beautiful French cloisonné vase, blood red with white fleurs-de-lys. A five dollar bill was folded in the neck. For Ernie June, Kate sent a bolt of English cotton, sun yellow, and a small portion of moire silk, robin's egg blue. Ernie would find five dollars pinned inside the silk. While exceedingly generous, this was appropriate, for one never asked another person's servant to assist without paying for the servant's help.

That night, flushed with triumph, Kate indicated she would favor Mars with her body. A nimbus of hope shadowed his brain, but the act itself banished it. Kate made love with an imperceptible conjugal revenge. She did not give herself to Mars; she let him do what he wanted. He fell asleep feeling more alone than ever, cognizant of the supreme irony of his position. Every man leaving the party tonight would kill to be resting where he was now. Sometimes Mars felt that he was dying inside. He was waiting for the war to finish the job.

That same evening, Henley lay next to Lutie.

"I know perfectly well you're in love with her. I only ask, dear husband, that you behave with discretion. Don't drag me through the mud."

Henley sat up. "Lutie! How can you talk like that?"

"Oh, lie down. We've been married longer than Kate Vickers has been alive. We should have talked like this a long time ago."

"I declare you aren't yourself since the nursing episode."

"I'm more myself than I've ever been. If you can seduce Kate Vickers, then I see no reason why I shouldn't seduce Mars." She giggled.

Henley pounced. "That's it! I should have known."

"Shut up, Henley. It's too late for your vapid pride."

He flopped back next to her. "You amaze me. I never know what you're thinking. I never know what you're going to say and when you're going to say it. I'd like to know how

many men at that party have wives who would tell them
to—"

"More than you might think," she cut in, "if they have
sense." Lutie changed the subject to Kate and Mars. "They
can't stand one another."

"Oh?" Henley's voice cracked like an adolescent boy's.
"What makes you think that?"

"Women's intuition."

"Oh."

"Would you like a cracker?"

"No. Why on earth would I want a cracker?"

"You keep saying 'Oh.' You sound like a parrot learning to
talk."

"Oh—I mean, I don't know what I mean."

"Years ago, Henley, you broke my heart. I vowed to put it
out of my mind. Never to talk to you about it. And I haven't,
have I?"

"No." His hands felt clammy.

"I was wrong. First, I can't escape it. I am reminded every
day. But more, it's wrong when two people close the door on
any subject. It's a way to pretend the issue is settled. When
something like that happens, it takes years to settle. Anyway,
in my way, I was wrong, too."

"How could you be wrong? The fault was mine."

"The act was yours. Perhaps I didn't love you enough."

Crushed with remorse, Henley whispered, "You loved me
too much. I was young, and young men are very casual about
such emotions."

Lutie opened up to him. "I did love you, but I was young,
too. When I reflect I wonder did I truly love you as you are or
did I want to control you, to turn you into someone else."

The gray light of morning flickered across Henley's rugged
features. "It's hard to look back. Sometimes I feel that life is
a road and I am shocked to glance over my shoulder only to
find familiar landmarks receding. Sometimes, Lutie, I feel
old."

"I do, too. Which is why I'm happy we had this talk. You
see, I know Kate Vickers makes you feel young. When you
look at me, you see a reflection of yourself."

"You're beautiful, my dear."

"I'm getting old, Henley."

"Not to me."

"Yes, well, I'm delighted to hear it, but my point still stands. She makes you feel young, and I've learned enough not to deny you the pleasure she brings you."

"I haven't—"

"I don't really care. In a marriage as long as ours, I think we have become as brother and sister in some fundamental way. Your body is yours to do with as you please. You always did anyway."

"Lutie," Henley stammered, "in my heart, I loved only you. Always."

"You loved her. Back then." She could see by the stricken look on Henley's face that she touched him to the quick. "But I've been unfaithful, too."

"What?"

"With Emil."

"Surely you don't expect me—"

"Let me finish. You place so much store by the body. The emotions I should have shared with you I shared with him."

"He's not real, you know." Henley was very gentle.

"To me, he is."

"I don't understand you. I don't think I ever did, but I love you."

"I'm not sure I understand myself, and if I did, I'd probably be bored. What's life without mystery?" She kissed him on the cheek.

Exhausted from the party, the hour, and this exchange, they fell into a contented sleep.

Two days later, Lutie returned to Charlottesville by train. Sin-Sin stood next to her and regaled Lutie with stories of the servants at the Vickerses' home.

"She got on a red blouse, a green skirt, and orange earrings. Honey, that ain't no country girl, that's a miracle!"

Lutie laughed until her sides ached. Sin-Sin laughed along with her. Lutie hadn't felt this good since she was a bride. Since Jimmy died. A great weight had been lifted from her. She had survived a tortuous passage. It was a long time coming, more than a decade, but she was herself again. Life was sharp and sweet, and she wanted to live forever.

AUGUST 26, 1861

"Jesus has gone to Galilee,

"And how do you know that Jesus is gone?

"I tracked him by his drops of blood,

"And every drop, he dropped in love."

Sin-Sin sang at the top of her considerable lungs as she polished silver while Lutie arranged flowers.

"How about 'Rassal, Jacob.'"

"Rassal, Jacob, rassal.

"As you did in the days of old.

"Gonna rassal all night til broad daylight.

"And ask God to bless my soul."

Sin-Sin gulped in air. "Let's sing one together. You takes the top line; I takes the bottom."

"What do you want to sing?"

"'Swing Low,' we do right nicely on that one."

The two women harmonized, and the more they sang, the harder they worked. This chorale was spoiled by the sound of dishes crashing on a brick floor. The two women tiptoed to the kitchen door and put their ears to it. Lutie put her finger to her lips, a needless gesture since Sin-Sin dangled on each word.

"You ast her, Momma! If you don't, I do!"

"You be sitting on a block if you do. I doan want Miz Lutie knowin' what a fool I gots for a girl."

"How much am I worth? I gonna buy my way to freedom."

"You ain't worth two straws."

Boyd, clever, tried another tack. "How much you worth, Momma?"

"Miz Lutie say I's worth my weight in gold."

"Lotta gold then, 'cause you sure is fat."

"And you're comin' on right behind me!"

"I been astin' about. You worth five thousand dollars 'cause you so skilled. So I gotta be worth 'bout two thousand dollars 'cause I's learnin'."

"You outta your head! You ain't worth jack shit."

"I's buyin' my way out. I doan wanna be no slave. I takes orders from you, and I doan wanna take no mo' orders."

"You takes your orders from Miz Lutie. She run this place."

"She may run this place, but you run me and anyone else you can!"

This recognition of her power, unwitting flattery though it was, softened Ernie slightly. "We all wants to be free, chile. But we got it good here. You gettin' awful airish. Iffin' I was to slap your ass in Mississippi, you'd whistle a different tune."

"I wants to be free."

"Die then. Thass freedom!"

"You old folks is fools!"

Flaring again, Ernie slapped her across the face with an egg beater. "Zat so? How many old folks you see in prison? We got a place here. Not more than two weeks ago the President ate Ernie June's food, food you helped prepare. You gonna throw that away, girl?"

"I sho' din get none of that cloth!"

"You gots the five dollars. You givin' me aches and pains, girl, you know that? Your brother doan bother me a tad, but you jes like a sweat bee, stingin' with every step!"

"I wants to be free. I gonna hire myself out."

"And have no face? No people? You a bigger fool than I thought!" Ernie was separating egg yolks from the whites. Boyd made her so mad she botched the job. "Now see what you made me do! You gettin' these lunatic ideas from that Grizz over at the Fitzgeralds'. I got eyes in the back of my head."

"Oh, him." Boyd feigned disinterest which confirmed Ernie's accusation. Boyd was not one to dismiss her conquests since she had so few of them.

"You thinks you in love. You gonna run off to Yankee lines and get married and live happily ever after. Ha! Let me do that again. HA!"

Boyd, empurpled, sputtered, "Doan you fun at me! You know what Grizz tol' me? That the Yankees closin' down newspapers that takes the Southern side. Even tarred and feathered some man in Messyshussy!"

"Miss Smart Aleck, what do this mean to you?"

"It mean they is gettin' ugly up there. They gonna free the slaves!"

"They gotta win the war first, and they doin' a piss poor job of it! And what if they wins? What you gonna go and do? Cook for wimmins so trashy stupid they puts they napkins in they wine goblets? Ain't no sech thing as a Northern wimmin what can set a table. Work fo' trash, and you be trash!"

"You chicken shit, Momma. You know that little white dot on toppa the black? Thass you, Momma. You thinkin' you somethin' special, but you still chicken shit, and you still a slave!"

Ernie June threw an egg and hit Boyd's head.

"Stop it, Momma, stop it!"

"I's gonna beat those bad manners outta your skin."

"Ouch! Ouch! Ouch! I's sorry I sassed you."

Ernie let her go. "Sit down. You listen, and you listen good! I work all my life for these people. I knows Henley's father and mother and they father and mother when I was little. They ain't so bad as those people go. They got their ways, but they ain't bad. Doan you go and undo the good your Momma store up. We mean somethin' here. We gonna run Chatfield someday. That witch Sin-Sin can't live forever!"

Sin-Sin's jaw dropped on her bosom. Lutie put her hand on Sin-Sin's shoulder to reassure and restrain her.

Boyd appreciated her mother's position, even if she didn't appreciate taking her orders. "You do a better job than that nasty stinkin' cow. But, Momma, things is happenin'. Grizz heard that Bumba run off and leave Nash. He heard that the Yankees treatin' Bumba right good, and he workin' for them as a sapper."

"Huh?"

"Diggin' ditches. Grizz says Bumba get paid most of what the white man get paid."

"Grizz full of shit! Wild talk!" Still, Ernie was glad to know it. "What else you young sparks talkin' 'bout?"

"I hear tell that Peter stole again."

Ernie stopped toweling Boyd's head. "You hush you' mouth 'bout this."

"Momma, will you give Grizz a chance? Doan belittle him."

"I doan think he good enough fo' you, and you knows what I thinks of the Fitzgeralds."

"Please, Momma."

"An' you gotta stop comin' in this kitchen and makin' yo coffee with Miz Lutie's cream 'fore she get up in the mornin'. You didn't think your old momma knew. Rules is rules, missy."

Hearing footsteps in their direction, Lutie and Sin-Sin tiptoed back to the dining room. They worked a bit in silence. "Sin-Sin, what are we going to do?"

"I be stirrin' my brain 'bout it."

"I don't know if I have any brains left to stir."

Sin-Sin began to hum, and Lutie picked up the tune.

"Moses smote the water, and the children they crossed over.
"Moses smote the water, and the children they crossed over.
"Moses smote the water, and the sea gave way."

SEPTEMBER 1, 1861

Anthony Farr-Jones's people descended upon Chatfield to take him home. Stillwater, Alabama, a pinpoint on the map, was their pinpoint nonetheless. They were good people without much in the way of money, and Lutie, who had grown fond of the unfortunate boy, gave them a team of mules to drive back home. She told them they would be doing her a great favor to keep the ornery things because, as they could see, the men were gone, and she could only do but so much. They gratefully accepted her offer.

During their visit of three days, the war was uppermost in everyone's conversation. Mr. Farr-Jones, an ardent secessionist, declared that the mutiny in the Seventy-ninth New York Regiment and the Second Maine Volunteers boded well for the Confederacy. The New Yorkers were shipped to an island off Key West as punishment.

Young Anthony, however, asked some disturbing questions. On August 27, the Yankees won Cape Hatteras in North Carolina without much of a fight. If the North controlled Cape Hatteras, the future would be bleak for blockade runners.

The old man disagreed. War'd be over before the South missed anything from those snotty Europeans anyway.

Mercer, Lutie, Sin-Sin, and Di-Peachy listened to Mr. Farr-Jones with respect, but the Chatfield household was relieved when the bellicose gentleman and wife finally left with their son.

"You think the sight of that po' chile would tone him down," Sin-Sin remarked.

"Some people never learn. 'Some people have a thousand thoughts, others the same thought a thousand times.' "

SEPTEMBER 3, 1861

Jeremiah cried about his bowels in chapter 4. Geneva thought someone with better manners should have edited the Good Book. Awake before sunrise as always, she put the Bible under her blanket and left the tent. Camp life wore on her nerves. Fighting was better than sitting around, drilling, writing letters, and polishing her saddle.

Nash mumbled in his sleep. Last night they made love, the first time since the big battle. Lately there didn't seem to be much desire on his part, and when there was desire, there was no privacy.

She dipped two buckets into the stream. Seeing no one

about, she shed her clothing and jumped in. The cold bit into her skin with a tingle. She splashed around, ducked her head under the water, and skipped out. Shivering, she shook herself like a dog, then quickly put on her pants and shirt. She carried the buckets back up to the fire pit and started a fire.

"You're the early bird around here, aren't you?" Mars came up behind her.

"I like the dawn to myself. It's the only time I have alone."

"I know what you mean. Come on, visit with me while I shave."

"Colonel, I want to know your beauty secret," Geneva teased. "How do you keep your teeth so white?"

Mars smiled. "I'll show you." He reached into his shaving bag and brought out a tin of baking soda. "First I pick 'em clean. Then I rub this on. Tastes terrible, but scrub hard and your tobacco stains will disappear."

"Is that why the ladies are crazy for you?"

"No, it's my superior intelligence."

"It's your moustache," Geneva offered.

"That, too. In fact, I don't think there's a part of me that isn't pretty."

"Don't think much of yourself, do you?"

"If I don't like myself, who will?"

"There's a difference between like and conceit."

"You're, of course, a walking saint." Mars shaved his throat between sentences.

"Sumner told me you danced with my mother at your party."

"I did, and I flatly adore her. She's that rare creature, a woman with sense."

"Oh, balls. I bet you if I raised a regiment of women" —she thought a minute and then pressed on—"they'd fight like tigers."

Mars paused. "I agree. They'd be the terror of the field until the enemy dropped mice and spiders in the middle of it. Be the end of the battle."

"Georgia peaches maybe or Mississippi belles, but I bet Virginia girls would fight." Geneva was annoyed.

"Now why is it that Virginia doesn't produce belles? You know I never thought of that." Mars toweled off.

"You are revolting mean," Geneva hissed, still defending Virginia women.

"Just the way I am." He shrugged. "You know, Jimmy, if I had a son like you, I'd kick his ass bad."

"You don't have a son, and I'm not applying for the job."

"Let's not start the day with speculation about my reproductive capabilities."

SEPTEMBER 13, 1861

Friday, the thirteenth, set Ernie June and Sin-Sin into a tizz. Ernie carried on so with her superstitions that even Cazzie the cat left. Ernie shrieked about burning her fingernails and making her right eye jump. If the right eye jumps, there will be good luck; if the left eye jumps, there will be tears. Ernie's right eye twitched like Saint Vitus' dance.

Sin-Sin's potions on this blistering day consisted of sassafras tea, drunk while sweet herbs burned in Geneva's cobalt blue pot. Sin-Sin brought the pot up to the big house because she could kill two birds with one stone. Since it was Geneva's pot, Sin-Sin could bring luck to Geneva, and since the pot was inside the main house, Sin-Sin could keep the spirits off Lutie, too.

Lutie ignored this orgy of fluster, just as she ignored the fact that she could be more irrational than either Sin-Sin or Ernie June. Emil was proof of that. She was girding herself to meet Jennifer Fitzgerald on September 20, Ember Day and a fast day at that. The Very Reverend Manlius decreed that it was Lutie's Christian duty to pacify Jennifer, who in her distress thought Lutie could talk to the dead. Under no circumstances was she to bring messages from the dead, even if it would ease Jennifer's mind. However, he didn't think that a chat about the afterlife was out of order, and Lutie might assure Jennifer, in a manner of her choosing, that Greer was with God. Jennifer's suffering, while sad, did not make Lutie like her any more than when Greer was alive. Lutie dreaded the day.

Mercer sat under a tree with Di-Peachy. He neglected to tell her that Big Muler cornered him, threatening him if he trifled with Di-Peachy.

When Mercer replied that he would do no such thing, that he intended to marry her, Big Muler laughed. He said that no white man was going to marry a black girl. Plus, Mercer would have to survive the war. Big Muler wasn't menacing, but Mercer felt certain that if he were not a guest at Chatfield, the huge man would have carried him to Mechum's River and dumped him in it with chains wrapped around his neck.

Mercer told Di-Peachy that he was rejoining Stuart. His commander had written that he'd give Mercer a chance, and if the leg hampered him on horseback, they'd find something else for him to do. Mercer worked with Braxton and Timothy for the last four weeks, and although his wooden attachment still hurt the stump, he was getting used to it. He could grip with his thigh and his knee.

When he told Di-Peachy he would be leaving next week, she cried.

"Will you do me the honor of marrying me? Please consider it. Don't reject me out of hand. I love you with all my heart." She did not reply. Faltering, he murmured, "Did I mistake your kind attentions to me? I thought you bore me some affection."

"You did not mistake me, Mercer."

"Then marry me!"

"You're grateful because I nursed you."

"I'm grateful because Almighty God put you on earth and then allowed me to find you. I want to go through the rest of my life with you and only you." He kissed her.

Di-Peachy put her hand on his chest, holding him at bay. "I'm a Negro woman, and I am a slave."

"I'm a white man who wants to be your slave."

"Don't ever say you want to be someone's slave, Mercer. Not even mine." Di-Peachy smiled sadly. "You want to marry me now, but in the cold light of reason, you will change your mind. I would become an albatross around your neck."

"No, I won't change my mind, and I'll buy your freedom!"

"Who will be our friends?"

"We'll find out, won't we? We'll know who our friends really are. That's more than most people know, isn't it?" Breathlessly, Mercer held her hand. "Please say you'll marry me."

"After the war is over and if you still want me then, yes, I will."

Mercer kissed her passionately and stood up. He hobbled in the direction of the stable. Di-Peachy scrambled to her feet.

"Where are you going?"

"To rejoin my regiment. I've got to win this war!"

SEPTEMBER 14, 1861

"I want to get Italian marble." Sumner was discussing his plans for Lutie's fountains. His drawings were spread on the ground during a brief rest period.

"Why can't you get marble from Vermont? I had a friend oncet worked up there in Barre." Banjo nipped off the end of his cigar.

"At this point, Vermont might as well be Italy." The wind picked up and Sumner put a stone on the corner of his drawings.

"Everyone will go back to trading again once things are back to normal." Nash leaned over the plans.

"I thought the war would be over by now," Sumner mused. "Summer is over, and we're still here. At least I escaped Camp Misery for a few days." Sumner drilled with his artillery crew on their twenty-three-pounders, called Napoleons, until they could fire three rounds per minute. He was, however, going batty with inactivity, as was everyone. When

Colonel Vickers ordered Geneva's company to cook up two days' rations because they were going scouting, Sumner had begged to go along. Mars agreed.

After the rest break, the scouting party rode toward the Leesburg-Alexandria turnpike, the sun behind them, warming their backs. While heat alternated with thunderstorms, proving it was still summer in Virginia, an imperceptible tang assailed the nostrils, warning that fall edged ever closer.

The land was rolling and crisscrossed with streams. They were on the east side of Wolf Trap Run, threading their way through woods. Banjo, first out of the woods, wheeled his horse around immediately and hurried back to Mars. "Yankees on the road down there," he reported.

Mars held up his hand for the others to halt. He trotted to the edge of the trees with Banjo. "I make them out to be somewhere around three hundred."

Banjo nodded. "Enjoyin' themselves, from the look of it. You know, Colonel, the sight of them Yankees, ridin' around with all that blue on, gets on my nerves."

"I was thinking the same thing." Mars grinned.

"We've got forty men. Sun's at our back. Scare 'em so bad they won't have time to count how many we are."

"I expect they need a lesson in etiquette. It's not the correct thing to trespass on another man's property."

"Rude boys always get their noses bloodied."

Mars returned to his scouting patrol. He spread them out at the edge of the tree line. They'd have to gallop down a grade which leveled into a fine pasture. The turnpike bisected the pasture.

"You boys have been bragging how you can whip two Yankees apiece. Now's your chance." Mars nodded to the bugler who sounded the charge.

Geneva closed up next to Nash. She let out a piercing yell. Flushed, Nash hollered as well. The forty voices, joined by the rhythm of hoofbeats, surprised the drowsy Northern column of cavalry. Certain they were being attacked by a large force, they turned tail and thundered back toward Washington. Not a shot was fired.

After ten minutes of thrilling chase, Mars galloped next to the bugler and told him to sound a retreat. Hooting, hollering, and laughing at the top of their lungs, the exhilarated men rallied and closed up ranks. Riding four abreast, they turned back toward the southwest.

They camped out that night. Each man put his rubber blanket roll on the ground and put his blanket over that. Then he'd roll up in the blanket. When it rained, the men slept in twos. One rubber cover and blanket would be on the ground. The two would lie on the ground blanket, then put another blanket and rubber cover on top of themselves.

As it remained warm, Geneva and Nash slept side by side, but not rolled up together.

"You asleep?" Nash whispered. She was. Geneva must have a clear conscience, he thought. She didn't know the meaning of the words insomnia or femininity. She smelled of leather. Last April, just thinking about Geneva gave him a hard-on. Now he had little time to make love to Geneva, but when he did, he thought of other women, women who looked and acted like women. He stared up at the stars. What was happening to him? Was his idea of civilization, of himself as a civilized man so much veneer? He thought of the mangled bodies at Manassas. He'd had nightmares about those twisted limbs and the blood. The stream itself was red from the blood flowing into it where men fell. After the battle, no one would drink from Bull Run. He prayed nightly. "Why, God, do we kill when the Bible tells me I am made in Thy image?" God sent no answer. He sent only more questions.

SEPTEMBER 18, 1861

Henley's commissary department confirmed his opinion that the intelligence in politics was so low that even a mediocre person has to stoop to meet it. The state of Virginia, rich in agriculture, could feed its army. The entire South, blessed by rich soils and the cash crop tobacco, should be able to provide for its fighting men wherever they were defending its border. The problem was getting the food and fodder to the armies.

General Josiah Gorgas in Ordnance proved an ally but he, too, was often hamstrung by the consider-the-lilies-of-the-field form of planning. The Confederacy already showed signs of strain in Kentucky and up and down the Mississippi River. Henley's consolation, which he shared often with Josiah, was that things couldn't be too much better in the northern capital either. A plague of golden locusts had been sent on both their houses.

Henley had read the sixth chapter of Luke in his church almanac before his morning horseback ride. A reassuring and lovely chapter, it nonetheless stuck in his throat when he read the passage, "But woe unto you that are rich! for ye have received your consolation." If this were true, then he was in trouble. Personal trouble was harder to bear than national trouble. As much as Henley worried about supplies, about this strange war and what was to come next, he wondered more about Kate Vickers.

Surrounded by handsome men, wealthy men, adoring and dashing men, even government observers and attachés from foreign nations, rumors flew like confetti. She was rumored to be having an affair with Beauregard. Henley knew that wasn't true. He wasn't so certain about the rumor concerning Baron Schecter, a colonel in the army of His Imperial Majesty Franz Joseph. Sent to observe our spasm of national conflict, the baron had succeeded in observing Mrs. Vickers.

"How wonderful to see you." Henley caught up with Kate and the baron out for a morning ride. He touched his hat and the baron did likewise. They despised one another. Behind Kate rode another fifteen young men in a twitter. They called her the Confederate Venus.

She threw back her head and laughed. The men moved closer to be near the sound of such heaven. "Flatterers!" she accused them.

"But it's true, Mrs. Vickers." Cried one green-eyed lieutenant, "We would follow you to the ends of the earth."

"I'd rather go to its center." She smiled.

"I'll go! Give me a shovel and we can come out in China." This was offered by another empty-headed but good looking boy.

Henley thought to himself, You'd come out in the Indian

Ocean and drown, you dumb son of a bitch. He serenely turned to the baron and asked if he was enjoying his assignment.

Smiling through a tense jaw, the baron replied, "What I enjoyed most was meeting your wife. I don't know when I have ever beheld such a charming, witty, energetic lady."

"Thank you. Lutie is home at Chatfield. Mrs. Vickers, I do hope you'll visit Chatfield soon."

"I'd love to go when the foliage is a riot of color, Colonel. I too have been most anxious to see your Lutie again. She's a fountain of wit and very beautiful." Kate's voice rang true.

"No one is more beautiful than yourself, Aphrodite!" the baron refuted. "You are a generous woman to grant another such praise."

"Why, Baron, do you think all women fight over men?"

"I do not think friendship comes naturally to women." The baron's light accent was gentle, but disdainful. These Americans are so primitive, he thought, but what can one expect of people who still keep slaves?

"I do not think, Baron, that it comes easily to men"—Kate's voice was like an alto scalpel—"else why would we be in a civil war?"

SEPTEMBER 20, 1861

"Good God, Miz Lutie, Jennifer Fitzgerald is comin' up the driveway!" Ernie panted from running to the library from the kitchen.

Sin-Sin hurried into the pantry off the dining room as soon as she heard the news. "I better hide the silver." She began throwing silver into her apron.

"She may be crazy, but she's not a thief." Lutie laughed to hide her own nervousness.

A knock on the door cut short their conversation. Lutie glided through the cavernous rooms into the majestic foyer and opened the door. Jennifer, in riding attire even though she'd been driven in a carriage, smiled weakly.

The two ladies walked to the long, arched window walkway where Lutie liked to receive guests in the warm months.

Ernie presented a tray of her best morning sweets, then ducked around the corner only to find Sin-Sin hiding there. They jockeyed for listening positions in silence. As Ernie was so fat, she had the advantage.

"A man named Cassius Rife," Jennifer was saying, "owns a munitions factory in your original home."

"The Rifes spawn profit and contention and have been doing so since the late 1600s. I know the family only too well since Chalfontes came over with Lord Baltimore. The Rifes claim to have come over on the Mayflower, that overburdened vessel, but I think they packed over with Oglethorpe. Regardless, they founded Runnymede along with ourselves and the Creightons. Thatchers came later."

"Apparently he's in business with Reddy Neutral Taylor for the express purpose of enriching themselves at the Confederacy's expense."

"A scorpion and a tarantula, an interesting marriage of creatures." Lutie observed Jennifer. Aside from pallor and alarming thinness, she appeared lucid.

Jennifer abruptly cut off this subject and moved to the one closest to her heart.

"I can't bear to think of the way Greer suffered! I can't bear my own suffering."

"He was killed instantly. I am certain of that."

Jennifer made no attempt to wipe the tears from her cheeks. "If only I knew that he was safe."

"Here." Lutie handed her a Belgian lace handkerchief.

"I've spent years being snide and nasty to you, and now I'm prevailing upon your good nature to help me." Desperately she bargained. "I know you can talk to the dead. You know somebody from the spirit world. Please, please let me talk to my son."

Prepared for this, Lutie spoke slowly. "I can't speak to the dead."

Miserable, Jennifer sobbed. "Oh, Lutie, I know you can.

Please, I don't care who you talk to, just find out if my boy is safe."

Somewhat frightened by Jennifer's outburst, but also sympathetic to her pain, Lutie fudged. "I know Greer is safe. He's with God."

Jennifer continued to sob uncontrollably.

"Emil says Greer didn't live long enough to store up a peck of sins. Greer's with God and wishes you to leave off your terrible grieving. Just look at you, Jennifer." Lutie now warmed to her embroidery. "You're dangerously thin. You've powdered your face until you look like a bled pig. Forgive me, but I must be blunt. You are trying to deceive my eyes, but powder won't help. How can Greer truly accept his new status, if he worries about you? We must accept death and we must accept life. You must pull yourself together and live. Otherwise, you dishonor your son."

Wide-eyed, Jennifer blurted, "He would say that! That boy worried over me. He would fuss if I missed a meal or didn't take my afternoon nap."

"Yes, I wanted to mention those naps to you," Lutie lied.

Jennifer reached over the table and squeezed Lutie's hand. "I knew you wouldn't fail me."

"Then you must not fail Greer."

After more chat, Lutie walked Jennifer to the front door. She held out her hand to her guest, and Jennifer spontaneously kissed her. Lutie watched her drive away. She turned to find Sin-Sin lurking in the background with a smirk on her face.

"I'm a wicked liar, and I'll go to hell for what I just did." Lutie threw her hands to heaven.

"I woan say you lied zactly."

"What would you say?"

"You has a kind heart."

"Wake up, Miz Lutie." Sin-Sin's voice filled her ear.

Lutie sat up in bed. It was five minutes before midnight. Di-Peachy stood next to Sin-Sin.

"Peter done run off," said Sin-Sin. "And the pass—"

"Gone? I knew it!" Lutie threw on her robe. "You were right, Sin-Sin," she said triumphantly. "He showed his hand."

"He also stole your diamond and ruby earrings," said Di-Peachy with a wince.

"Oh, no," Lutie wailed. "Those were my mother's."

"He won't get far. He can't read, and he doesn't realize the pass has no name or date on it." Di-Peachy offered some consolation.

"He may get far enough to sell my mother's earrings, thank you!"

"I knowed he'd bite." Sin-Sin swelled. Her trap had worked.

"Di-Peachy, come with me. We're going into town right this minute. Let me notify the authorities. For all we know, he may have already been netted in a patrol."

"Iffin' the patters be sober." Sin-Sin despised those men.

"There's something else." Di-Peachy fetched Lutie her shoes. "He took Tincia with him."

"That stupid girl!" Lutie ransacked her mahogany wardrobe for her old riding coat.

"You gots to take a gun," Sin-Sin said.

"Why?"

"Cause Peter got one."

SEPTEMBER 23, 1861

The ringworm of chaos munched on both the Confederacy and the Union. General Fremont freed the slaves in Missouri as well as confiscated property belonging to Southern sympathizers. This hardened resistance in those states clinging to a slippery neutrality. Throughout the South, individuals thought that Fremont acted with the blessing of Lincoln. Their hatred of Lincoln and abolitionists in general reached a new pitch.

Lutie dutifully read the newspapers. However, her concern centered on Chatfield more than the Confederacy. The bodies of Peter and Tincia, ripped apart by wild animals, were found by a farmer early this morning. The two slaves escaped no further than three miles north of town. The earrings of Lutie's deceased mother, Diddy Chalfonte, were sewn in the hem of Tincia's dress. The limbs of the dead couple were chewed, but the clothing on the torso was of no interest to the racoons, foxes, ravens, bobcats, and other animals that feasted on their corpses. Lutie was happy to have her mother's earrings back, but sad that Peter and Tincia came to such a violent end. They'd been shot in the head and then dumped in a hurry. The pass was not on the bodies.

That afternoon their remains were laid to rest in the slave cemetery at Chatfield. Disgusted though she was over the affair, Lutie read from the day's lesson which was Luke 9: 1:37. The story of Jesus feeding the five thousand was a favorite of everyone. After the service, she strolled over to the white graveyard and stared at Jimmy's grave. Buried two rows behind him were the bodies of soldiers unclaimed at the railroad station. Their graves were adorned with simple crosses into which C.S.A. July 21, 1861, was carved. Thick grass, which grew swiftly in the heat and moisture, already covered the earth.

A tremendous thunderstorm was brewing in the west. Wind sliced through the huge oaks lining the driveway. Darkness closed in early on Chatfield. Sin-Sin lit candles while Di-Peachy fastened the shutters. Ernie, rattled from the dual murder, left as soon as her cooking chores were finished.

The house in order, the three women retired to the living room. Di-Peachy sat at Lutie's feet. Sin-Sin, agitated, paced. "What galls me is nobody found the pass."

"Maybe he didn't steal it." Di-Peachy softly spoke as Lutie watched the green-black clouds skim over the treetops. Flashes of lightning cast a pale blue glow on the windowpane. "I remember when we were kids how Peter used to cheat at our games. How strange that in a child character reveals itself."

"Jes wait 'til you has some." Sin-Sin wore a hole in the carpet. "They is different in the womb."

"Sin-Sin, sit down. You're making me dizzy," Lutie said.

"Ants in my pants." Sin-Sin slowed her pacing, but didn't sit.

"At least we know who killed Alafin," Di-Peachy said.

"I gits the feelin' we doan know nothin'," said Sin-Sin glumly.

"You think Peter didn't do it?" Lutie was incredulous. "But your trap worked. You waved the pass about. When he had something to trade for cash he stole the pass and off he went."

"With Tincia." Di-Peachy rubbed her temples.

"Girl din have the brain of a peahen," Sin-Sin grumbled. "My trap caught the wrong rabbit."

"Do you think whoever shot Peter killed Alafin?" Di-Peachy asked.

"Peter crossed someone not afraid to kill."

"Then who killed Alafin?" Di-Peachy asked.

A bolt of lightning illuminated Sin-Sin in the glare. "Thass what I like to know."

"You don't think we're in danger, do you?" Lutie asked.

"No, not yet. 'Member that string of killin's up at Bashton Plantation?"

"That was in '47. A house servant went crazy and killed young women. He'd sneak off at night and get into servants' quarters at other houses, like a fox in a henhouse. Finally got so crazy he started killing them at Bashton. He didn't last long after that."

"Men doan kill wimmins unless another man involved or some lunatic sex thing."

Lutie put her hand to her chin. "I think you're right. But a man might kill a woman if she threatened to expose him in some fashion. Or if he's out of his mind with love."

"Thass my point. We safe unless we gits in the way. Mebbe this man smarter than I thought."

OCTOBER 18, 1861

No amount of drilling salvaged the restlessness in the camp. Scarce food and fodder grated on nerves as did the lack of battle. The war in Virginia, aside from skirmishes, hung suspended like a cocoon waiting for spring. Jefferson Davis, hot on the campaign trail, irritated some of the military men more than others, but the campaign was not greeted enthusiastically by anyone in the camp. Night frosts soured spirits, too. Mars kept his men busy on reconnaissance patrols, harassing Federals who moved too far away from Washington in search of forage themselves. Many times his regiment would ride on the south side of the Potomac only to watch bluecoats on the northern side. They appeared as bored as the Confederates.

The men placed small stoves in the middle of their tents in preparation for winter. Infantry, artillery, and cavalry were quartered separately, the horses behind the cavalry tents. Each branch of the military made claims to being superior, but the cavalry, comprised mostly of wealthy men, bore the brunt of criticism—fancy boys, all powder and no lead.

Geneva scrambled to go out on any mission no matter how small. Camp life didn't offend her, but she preferred the saddle to the tent. The major occupations after drill were cards and drinking, usually followed by a passionate religious revival. J.E.B. Stuart, a devout Presbyterian and now promoted to brigadier general, offered a spiritual as well as sartorial example to his troops. Men stuck feathers in their caps or slouch hats and carried Bibles, but very often the Bible was set aside for a card deck.

Banjo became a legend. Slowly but surely he cleaned out company after company.

One frustrated captain, newly impoverished, encouraged Banjo to abandon his cards and embrace the Lord. Banjo replied, "Piety is like garlic. A little goes a long way." When the remark reached Mars's ears, he sent Banjo a box of his best cigars.

Geneva, Nash, and Banjo sat inside Geneva's tent studying a map of the Confederacy and the United States. Since so much action was in Missouri and Kentucky, they were curious about it and thought the map could offer clues. Wearing an old sweater, Mars walked in and crouched down with them, explaining the situation as he saw it.

Sumner burst through the flap, but didn't notice Mars, who had his back to him. "Food! Heard a sergeant in my company whispering that he found a hidden source of flour and oats in an old well on the back of Flugel's farm. If we hurry, we can beat them to it."

Mars turned around. "Stealing, Captain?"

"Colonel—uh, you see, sir—well, yes. I'm hungry and Flugel's made out right well in trading, I reckon."

"I reckon so, too." Mars's eyes were merry. "Let's go." He put his hat on Geneva's cot. No point in advertising that a colonel was descending to petty thievery.

They made their way through their lines in the darkness. The sentries asked for the password, and Mars, the only one who knew it, said, "Queen Victoria."

"Queen Victoria?" Banjo was curious.

"Don't ask me, I didn't come up with it." Mars shrugged.

The full moon flooded the dirt road with light. A half mile beyond the sentry, a split rail fence in a zigzag pattern announced the rear of Flugel's land.

Nash hopped the fence. Banjo, Mars, Sumner, and Geneva prudently crawled over it.

"This way, Colonel." Sumner directed him toward a field full of corn stubble. Picking their way through stalks, they crossed the field to a cleared meadow.

"Damn!" Sumner swore.

Six soldiers were hauling up food from the unused well.

"I got an idea," Banjo whispered to Mars.

"I'm glad somebody does," Nash groaned. He was very hungry.

"Go to it, Cracker."

Banjo pulled his pistol and fired in the air. "You worthless vagrants get away from my well!"

The soldiers, thinking the farmer had come upon them, dropped the rope and ran back to camp. Banjo fired over their heads again for fun. Those boys moved like a streak.

"Let's go!" Banjo dashed to the well.

Sumner heaved up the rope, harder work than it looked. "Here's one!" A heaven-sent sack of ground flour, wrapped in heavy burlap, landed by Geneva's feet.

"Looks like there's more down there." Geneva got down on her hands and knees to peer into the well.

"I'll climb down and tie the rope around the stuff." Nash, wiry and strong, grabbed the rope and scurried down, using his feet against the walls of the well. "Two more big ones," he called up to the others.

"Okay, we're ready." Sumner and Mars hauled up another sack.

Within fifteen minutes, they secured their booty.

Banjo called down the well, "Can you get back up?"

"Yes." Nash caught the rope and began climbing up, harder work than climbing down.

"You're part monkey, Piggy." Mars praised him.

"Thanks, Colonel."

"Christ, this stuff is heavy." Geneva slung a sack over her shoulder and stumbled forward.

"We'll take turns. There're three sacks and five of us." Mars pitched a sack up on his own shoulder. "This must weigh one hundred pounds."

Spelling each other, the five hauled the sacks to the fence, then tottered another quarter of a mile further.

"We can't go through the sentries with these," Geneva advised.

"I outrank 'em, and they'll do what I say." Mars smiled.

"Maybe they'll know who you are and maybe they won't," Sumner said. "Aside from the stripes on your trousers, you don't have any insignia."

Mars looked down at himself. "You've got a point there, Sumner."

"Besides which, if he's one of those infantry boys, they can get pissy."

"There's always some joker who falls asleep or talks to the

other sentry down the line. Give me a minute, and let me scout the perimeter," Sumner offered.

"Don't you get shot!" Geneva said worriedly.

"In the dark those fellows couldn't hit the broad side of a barn."

The four sat on sacks and waited until Sumner returned. "Come on."

Heaving the sacks, they puffed down the road. Sure enough, there was a gap in the line.

"I'll have that son of a bitch's hide," Mars hissed.

"After we get through." Geneva took a sack from Nash and started for the line. She scooted through, then Mars and Banjo, each with a sack, also made it. Sumner and Nash crossed about a hundred yards distant, just in case it was necessary to create a diversion.

"Easy as pie!" Nash exulted.

They started back for their camp. Before they crossed into the cavalry section, they found themselves confronted by four infantrymen, one of them a Goliath.

"What have we here?" the giant sneered.

"Looks like sister boys to me, Charlie," a thin one sneered.

"Shut up, asshole," Geneva flared.

"You cavalry boys are jes so pretty, it makes my heart beat faster," Charlie continued. "And here you come courtin' with sacks of somethin' special."

Mars stepped forward. "Why don't you forget it. Go back to your tent."

"Who died and made you God?" Charlie asked.

The other infantrymen laughed. Charlie moved to get a closer look. Boldly, Geneva walked right up to him. He recognized her. "It's the sister boy that's such a good rider."

"Don't get ugly," Geneva warned him.

"Ugly? Why, I was hopin' you'd come into my tent and keep me warm tonight."

Geneva socked Charlie in the jaw. "Hell, no!" She ducked as Charlie swung his right fist over her head.

Nash sprang to her defense. "Watch the sacks!" He pushed her out of the way and confronted Charlie. "You know how young he is. It's not fair to pick on him."

"No, but it's fair to pick on you." Charlie hit Nash so hard, they had to peel him off the ground. The men made a circle.

Banjo wisely put the sacks inside the circle so no one would run off with their ill-gotten gain.

Nash, rocky, got to his feet to continue the fight.

An infantryman sidled over to Banjo. "I say you cavalry boys are all cocksuckers."

"Is that a fact? I say that you infantry boys are living proof the Indian fucked the buffalo." Banjo hit him with both fists in the stomach. As the infantryman keeled over, Banjo landed a fierce uppercut on his jaw. The man went down spitting teeth.

"Nice work, Banjo." Mars patted him.

Two other infantrymen, seeing their friend go down, moved menacingly toward Banjo and Mars. Sumner stayed next to Geneva and the sacks. Geneva was hopping up and down like a rabbit. Mars and Banjo put themselves back to back like a trained team and waited for the infantrymen. Seeing this maneuver, the two infantrymen decided to remain as spectators for now.

"I jes want to carry him off." A thin one pointed to the toothless one in the dirt. He hooked his arm under the fallen man and dragged him to the sidelines.

Nash was getting the worst of the fight. Charlie, much taller, outweighed Nash by seventy pounds.

Mars stepped in. "Look here, he's no match for you."

"I can take it," Nash gasped.

"I know you can." Mars put his hand on Charlie's chest. "Why don't we tangle?" Mars smiled at Charlie.

"You ain't much bigger than your fella there," Charlie boasted. "I'll make sausages outta you, too."

As Mars, Nash, and Charlie negotiated who would fight whom, the two healthy infantrymen conferred. The sacks drew their attention at last.

"They're gonna make a run for it!" Sumner picked up a sack.

Geneva and Banjo picked up the remaining two sacks. As the three men came toward them, Banjo and Sumner swung the sacks, knocking their opponents off balance. Geneva swung, but missed. Nash, spattered with blood, moved to Geneva's aid. Within seconds everyone was fighting.

Mars and Charlie started pounding on one another. The huge man had an advantage over Mars, but Mars was heavily muscled and quick, and he could absorb punches. Charlie,

who had no plan other than to keep swinging, had trouble
landing blows on the more agile Mars. "Come on, you
cocksucker," Charlie snarled as Mars moved away from him.

"I'm gonna wash your mouth out with soap," taunted
Mars.

"Dream on." Charlie caught him on the shoulder. Mars
reeled backwards. He sprang up and continued jabbing. Without meaning to, Mars bumped into Nash and fell over. Charlie pounced on him. Geneva, turning from her opponent,
kicked Charlie in the side. Her legs were strong, and she
knew she smashed him square on the ribs. Mars rolled away.
As Charlie got heavily to his feet, Mars blasted him in the
eye. But the large man wasn't easily daunted. He grabbed for
Mars, and Mars leapt away. If that ogre wrestled with him, he
wouldn't have a chance.

Banjo, meanwhile, dispatched his victim. The fellow was a
half-hearted fighter, so Banjo had the advantage. He pushed
his sack behind the heels of the man slashing at Sumner and
motioned for Sumner to advance on him. Sumner did, endur-
ing a crushing blow to the nose. The infantryman tripped
over the sack and went down on his back. Banjo smashed him
on the temple with a doubled-up fist, and the fellow was out
cold.

Sumner and Banjo next turned their attentions to Geneva
and Nash. Nash, wobbly on his legs, leaned on his wife's
right shoulder. He could no longer land a blow, but he was
doing his best to keep the man off her. Geneva was losing the
fight, but not giving up. Her lip was split and blood spilled
onto her shirt. Banjo pulled his pistol from the holster and
cracked him over the head. The victim fell to his knees and
then on his face.

All eyes were now on Mars and Charlie. Mars's shirt was
ripped up the back. A red bruise raised up on his cheek.

"Boy knows how to box," Banjo said admiringly.

Sumner, holding his right hand to his nose, supported
Nash with his left hand. "Yeah, but that ape's a killer."

Geneva lurched forward and jumped on Charlie's back.
She pressed her thumbs into his neck, but he ripped her off
like a burr.

"Stay outta this, Jimmy. You'll get hurt," Mars commanded.

Banjo yanked her by the elbow back to his side.

"We can't let that man beat up the colonel!" Geneva cried.

"The colonel?" Charlie paused for a fatal second, and Mars delivered a punishing right to his jaw. He blinked, and Mars followed with a left. Staggering, the huge man, still game, swung wildly at Mars who brought his fist down on the back of Charlie's neck. The giant folded onto the ground.

Mars wiped blood off his moustache and grinned. "Let's get out of here."

Five bloodied, rubber-legged cavalrymen stumbled into their camp. The sacks felt like iron.

"Your tent is closer," Banjo said to Mars.

"Put them in Jimmy's. How would it look if I got caught with this stuff?" Mars gasped.

Finally inside the tent, they sank onto the cots.

By now their wounds smarted. Half of Mars's face shone a resplendent purple. Geneva's lip swelled so much she looked comical. Banjo, the least injured of the group, had only a cut over his eye, but it bled terribly.

"Nose is broke." Sumner tipped back his head to stop the bleeding.

"We laid 'em to whaleshit!" Banjo crowed.

They spent the remainder of the evening applauding one another's prowess. Everything was going fine until Sumner blundered.

"I don't much cotton to being called a cocksucker."

"You know how jealous they are of cavalrymen." Banjo hoped that would stop it.

"Jealous? They're downright rude and crude. Sister boy? Humph!" he snorted.

"Cause of me, Sumner." Geneva gingerly tried another biscuit.

"They think I'm one, too," Nash said.

"You two do swan about like the Siamese twins of love." Mars wasn't rancorous, just factual.

"I'm a married man." Nash knew that sounded ridiculous. Married men visited bordellos and seduced young men as readily as unmarried men.

"I'd like to see the sorry female you talked into marrying you," Mars flared.

Sumner's face turned bright red and so did Geneva's.

"At least she loves me. I don't see where your wife gives a good goddamn." Nash sat up.

"Leave my wife out of this!"

"Then return the favor." Nash was hot. "I despise you thinking I take advantage of Jimmy."

"I didn't say I thought that. I said you two act like the Siamese twins of love."

"Oh yeah, I notice you giving him the glad eye!"

"Don't be ridiculous, Hart. You don't have both oars in the water," Mars sputtered.

"I'm ready to fight again."

"I don't like you enough to hit you!" Mars raised his voice.

"You both make me sick," Geneva said and left the tent.

OCTOBER 19, 1861

Mars's swollen face testified to the fight the night before. General Stuart upbraided him for it. "I've half a mind to bust you back to major, but that would make you too happy. You'll have to suffer as a colonel." He decried Mars's lack of ambition, for surely he could make brigadier, too.

Mars argued that it was enough to be a colonel. He learned more in the field than he'd ever learned in staff meetings where one was in danger of death by hemorrhoids.

Stuart laughed. He admired Mars ever since they were at West Point together. Mars was in the graduating class when Stuart was a plebe. Mars's good looks, horsemanship, and open manner made him the idol of everyone. It was difficult for Stuart, an ambitious man, to understand that Mars's ambitions rested elsewhere. Perhaps if Mars were a Presbyterian instead of an Episcopalian, he'd snap into shape.

Mars was relieved that Stuart hadn't found out about the sacks of stolen grain. He was also delighted that Stuart granted him three days' leave in Richmond.

OCTOBER 20, 1861

The earth shifting on her axis, away from summer's warmth, seemed to Nash a symbol. By degrees he was moving away from the simple love offered by Geneva. If she had not enlisted, he wondered if he would have been able to pick up the marriage where he had left it.

He listened to other men, lonesome for their wives, imagining the day when the war would be over. They assumed they'd stride through the front door to be greeted by wives and children. But this war was changing everybody. Perhaps the human race backs into the future, unable to see anything save its own past. He knew he was changing. He didn't know how much of it was due to the war and how much of it was due to getting to know his wife. True, he was learning about Geneva in extraordinary circumstances, but he suspected he would have discovered her true personality anyway. At Chatfield it just would have taken longer. She wasn't the wife of his dreams. He knew she was a good person, but she irritated him by her ignorance. She cared nothing for the things he loved—books, good conversation, intellectual respect; and he cared nothing for the things she loved—horses, adventure, and war.

Nash turned the page of *Tristram Shandy*. The oil lamp sputtered. Geneva, unusually quiet for her, was writing a letter. He observed her profile. Knowing that his feelings about her were changing frightened him, and yet he felt a deep affection for her. Over and over he reminded himself she was risking her life to be with him. The least he could do was to be kind to her.

She looked over at him. "Good book?"

"Yes. Who is the lucky recipient of your letter?"

Smiling, she said, "It's hard for me to sit still. That's what I hate about writing. I'm writing Daddy."

"Pretending to be in England?" He kept the book open, a signal he would return to it.

"No, I'm telling him the truth." Nash's eyes widened and she continued. "I can't stand the thought that I'm lying to him."

"Once he gets over the shock, I'm sure he'll be pleased that you did tell him. No one likes being lied to, even when it's for their own good."

She carefully put down her pen and capped the inkwell. "Are you mad at me?"

He closed his book. "Of course not."

"You never want to make love anymore."

Embarrassed, Nash said, "How can we? These are difficult circumstances, and we can't ride off like we used to. Vickers tightened discipline like a noose after Manassas."

She sighed, "I know." She paused. "You still love me, don't you?"

"Yes. I love you." Nash smiled and then opened his book. Liar, he thought, what a liar I am. I love her more like a brother than a wife.

OCTOBER 21, 1861

Indian summer bathed Richmond in a deep orange glow. In the overcrowded city, people complained of bad lodgings and obscene food prices. Coffee was up to four dollars a pound. Supplies dwindled daily, thanks to the Yankee blockade. However, even the most pigheaded resident thought himself lucky when passing Belle Isle. Sitting in the middle of the James River, Belle Isle was a camp for prisoners of war. Since the Confederacy was having trouble feeding Richmond's own sons and daughters, certainly food was not squandered on enemy prisoners.

Mars noticed the camp as he rode along the Kanawha Canal at sunset. He turned his horse toward the city and was quickly home.

Considering the shortages, Kate managed to put together a fine dinner for him. The table was already set when he walked into the house.

"Hungry?" She appeared in the front hall as he unbuckled his sword.

"Yes. I rode past Belle Island. That place makes me doubly hungry, I guess." The last slanting rays of the sun illuminated her golden hair. He could not help admiring how beautiful she was.

"It's just the two of us for dinner tonight, as you requested."

Shorn of her brilliant companions and a salon full of glittering braid and jewels, Kate ate quietly with her husband, trying to conceal the fact that she was bored. "Judah P. Benjamin, an engine of ambition, loathes Alexander Stephens."

Mars broke a flaky biscuit. "I thought Benjamin and the Vice-President were on good terms."

"Alliances are like mayflies in this town."

Clearing his throat, Mars said, "Speaking of alliances, have you given further thought to our having children?"

Kate fixed him with a cobalt stare. "No, I haven't thought about it. There's a war on. It could get much worse. This is no time to have a child."

"What if I don't come back?"

"You?" She laughed. "You're indestructible."

"I appreciate the compliment but—"

"I'm not even thirty." She threw down her napkin. She loathed this subject.

"You're getting damn close." His eyes narrowed.

"Let me have my youth, Mars Vickers. You had yours."

"It's not the same for a woman." His face reddened.

"Precisely. Once I have children, I'll be freighted down for twenty years."

"Why is it such a burden? We have help."

"You don't understand anything!" she said, raising her voice.

"I understand plenty. The thought of bearing my children, of bearing any children, displeases you."

"I am not yet ready to ruin my figure, just so you can have some hostages to the future."

"Hostages? Is that how you think of children? My God, woman, I want to love somebody. I want somebody to love me. I'll never get it from you. At least my children might love me."

"If they're like you, they'll prove incapable of that much lauded emotion." Kate icily got up and left her husband to finish his meal. She hoped he'd choke on it.

OCTOBER 22, 1861

Early the next morning, Mars left his house. Kate bade him good-bye and kissed him like a poisoned chalice.

A few blocks away from the Vickerses' house, Henley Chatfield prepared for another day's work in the miserably entangled Commissary Department. A letter was delivered to him, and he absentmindedly placed it inside his tunic. Then he walked out into the bracing air.

It wasn't until later that evening, after he retired for the night and took off his tunic, that he saw the letter. Wearily he propped himself on the bed and opened it.

October 20, 1861

Dear Daddy,

I'm giving this to one of the men going into Richmond tomorrow. I trust he'll drop this off to you.

I'm a sergeant in the First Virginia Cavalry. I have so much to tell you. I don't know where to start, and I'm not much of a letter writer. I'll tell you everything when I see you, whenever that might be.

What it comes down to is everyone believes I am Jimmy Chatfield and I like the cavalry. I couldn't stand being apart from Nash, so I joined up.

I know from time to time Di-Peachy wrote to you and pretended it was from England. I got to thinking about that more and more and decided I can't lie to you. I never have, so why start now? And I thought if something were to happen to me and you found out then what I had done, that would upset you.

So that's it, Daddy. Mother knows. She says I look like you with my hair cut off.

Please don't give me away.

I love you.

Geneva

Henley reread the letter two times to make sure he wasn't hallucinating. Then he helped himself to a liberal shot of whiskey.

With the curtains drawn back, the smokey lamplight gave the night a hazy look. The clatter of hooves and carriage wheels filtered through the window. How long he sat there he didn't know, but he finally got up and sat down at his secretary. He pulled out a page of his white stationery and began.

October 22, 1861

My dearest daughter:

You must live. Using the name Jimmy, you will break your mother's heart twice over if you don't.

I am not a man unacquainted with passion, and I know throughout history women have contrived to follow their men. If you love Nash Hart that much, so be it.

However, allow me to point out that your mother is alone at Chatfield and I would prefer you were there to help her. I'm sure she would prefer it as well.

I take the blame for this caper of yours. You were more my son in many ways than Sumner. You have an exalted sense of adventure and enough willpower for two people. Instead of trying to curb those traits in you, I encouraged them. This is the outcome.

Of course, I will not give you away. You're old enough to take responsibility for your actions.

My other word of caution is that war is not a game.

However, if you serve with the First Virginia Cavalry, I expect you know that.

You are my only daughter. You are the gladness of my heart, my dear child. I hope you will exercise a little caution, an emotion, I know, that has been foreign to you. Your father could not bear the thought of life without you.

Love,
Daddy

Henley folded the letter and sealed it. To his astonishment, tears rolled down his cheeks. He was torn apart by the fear that his daughter could be killed, and yet at the same time, he was terribly proud of her. Wiping his eyes, he knew that she probably didn't believe she could die. She was young and believed all her oysters would bear pearls.

NOVEMBER 17, 1861

"I doan hear you talkin' to Emil no more." Sin-Sin stirred the fire into action.

"I think he was insulted." Lutie sat next to the fire and opened the Bible. Today's lesson in the Old Testament was Proverbs, chapter 11, and in the New Testament, it was John, chapter 11.

"You did the right thing," Sin-Sin pulled her heavy shawl around her shoulders, "settin' Jennifer Fitzgerald's mind to rest."

"She seems to have improved." Lutie commented on Jennifer's lifted spirits.

"Even give up bein' a cottonmouth."

"If she's going to bite, she's taking her time about it. Maybe she has changed. People do."

"I overslept." Di-Peachy quietly came in.

"It's hard to get out of bed before the sun comes up." Lutie thumbed through the thin, crisp pages. The *Episcopal Church Almanac* rested on her left knee while the Bible was on her right.

A loud noise downstairs temporarily halted the morning's devotion. Ernie June screeched, "You better has nine lives, you varmit!"

Four little feet could be heard padding on the smooth floorboards. The cat, a small plucked hen in its mouth, streaked through the room with Ernie, broom in hand, following close behind. "I's sorry, but, Miz Lutie, that cat be the devil hisself."

"It's too late now, Ernie June. You'll have to kill another chicken." Lutie mollified her. Wasting food did not please her, but seeing Cazzie get the better of Ernie June was amusing. "Why don't you sit down and join us?"

Lutie read from Proverbs. " 'As a jewel of gold in a swine's snout, so is a fair woman which is without discretion.' "

"Amen," Ernie June added. "Tincia be alive today iffin' she exercised discretion."

Sin-Sin glared at this religious outburst. Ernie lapsed into silence.

Lutie then read about Lazarus of Bethany, dead in the tomb for four days. " 'I am the resurrection, and the life: he that believeth in me, though he were dead, yet shall he live: And whosoever liveth and believeth in me shall never die.' " Lutie smiled. "That's one of my favorite passages."

"How could Lazarus walk out iffin' he had a napkin over his face and his hands and feet was bound up?" Ernie, of literal mind, was fascinated.

"Hobbled out, I 'spect." Sin-Sin was content with the story as it was.

"How you know he doan stink? Says he was resurrected; doan say he repaired." Ernie, not contentious, was truly curious.

"Jesus restored him to health," Di-Peachy answered. "It wouldn't make sense to bring him back otherwise, would it?"

"But it doan say so." Ernie was stubborn.

Lutie interceded. "You're supposed to take it on faith, Ernie June."

"Thass hard, Miz Lutie." Ernie was forthright.

"Yes, I'm inclined to agree. It's very hard."

Sin-Sin warmed up for her rapture. Lutie, Di-Peachy, and Ernie June got to listen to this tale once a year, sometimes twice. It was Sin-Sin's revelation. "Faith. Yes. Faith kin move mountains but we blind most times. We thinkin' only of usselves. I had me a mean streak in my youth."

Ernie thought, What do you mean, in your youth, you old bat? Prudently, she held her tongue.

Sin-Sin's melodic voice rolled like the tide. "My selfishness was big as a waddymellon. I growed with self-regard. I had no peace in my head. I wisht to be exalted before my kind. I wisht I could fly. I thinks only of myself. This conceit was an injury to me. I see it now. On the outside I say Christian things, but on the inside I say nothin'."

Lutie observed Sin-Sin's dear, familiar face with contentment. Her oft-repeated tale provided reassurance, a sense of closeness.

"My soul swam away from me like a gracey fish. Then a little white man come to me. He say, 'Follow me.' I walked a path no wider than a spider web. Down I scurry on my main lines of sorrow 'til I come to the center. A light blind me. I fall on my knees. Then a voice come to me outta the light, and it say, 'You find God in people's heart.'" Finishing her story, she put her hand on the Bible. "Thass the truth."

Ernie ran her apron between her thumb and forefinger. "Why it be a little white man?" What she wanted to say was, Why not a black man? Why was everything good supposed to be white?

"I doan know." Sin-Sin loathed Ernie anew.

Ernie, irritated, looked at Di-Peachy. Mercer's letters were under Di-Peachy's dress next to her heart. As there was now quite a packet, her left breast looked both huge and square. "You gotta growth, girl?" Ernie asked with annoyance.

"No." Di-Peachy blushed.

"Nothing good comes from mixed blood," Ernie intoned.

Furious, Sin-Sin kicked Ernie in the shin. "Doan be talkin' that way."

Lutie held her breath.

"That girl achin' her heart over that white boy!"

"Thass none of our business."

"Trouble be my business, and we gonna have a peck of

it." Ernie turned her round face to Di-Peachy. "Give him up. You gonna break your heart."

"He's not mine to give up. I'm not married," Di-Peachy said.

"Doesn't matter if a cat be black or white as long as it catches mice." Sin-Sin's teeth flashed.

"The mens always foolin' with the wimmins. You wan this boy to spoil her, after all the learnin' and work? 'Zat what you want, Sin-Sin? I kill my Boyd iffin' she make sech a fool of herself! And I knows the white man kill Braxton iffin' he try it!" She stamped her foot and then delivered her cruelest blow. "But why I think you'd watch over her I doan know. You nobody's momma."

Enraged, Sin-Sin pushed Ernie off the chair. "You shut your trap."

Lutie's sharp voice surprised them. "That's enough! Love is like malaria. You never know when you're going to catch it. It's not her fault if she's infected."

Di-Peachy, horrified, did not think of love as a disease. Ernie and Sin-Sin kept still.

"Furthermore," Lutie continued, "you could no more keep white men away from Boyd than I could. Stop such foolish talk." Her voice increased in volume. "Do you think I like sitting in this house knowing what goes on? What has gone on? Do you think I live without anguish? I will not have us fighting about it!"

Tears ran down Di-Peachy's cheeks. "I'm sorry, Miss Lutie."

"There's nothing to be sorry about. If you've fallen in love with Mercer Hackett, then God help you, because I cannot."

"I gots work to do." Ernie, humbled by Lutie's outburst, picked up her broom and left the room. Di-Peachy, her doe eyes large with tears, left, too.

Only Sin-Sin remained. The two women glared at one another. "That was quite a show you put on, old woman," said Lutie finally.

Sin-Sin crossed her arms over her ample bosom. "That fat tub Ernie June's so ugly she's an elephant fart!"

Despite herself, Lutie laughed. "You're mean and hateful to say such a thing."

"When she start flappin' her gums 'bout no good comin' from mixed blood, I sees red!"

"I don't understand it. Ernie's never been ugly like that before."

"Work her on Sunday. Show her!"

"I am not going to work her on Sunday, Sin-Sin. Aside from the scandal, what would it show her?"

"She doan know who's boss 'round here."

Lutie, clutching her Bible more tightly than she realized, replaced it on the smooth, inlaid satinwood table.

"You gots to talk to Di-Peachy," said Sin-Sin softly.

Lutie stared into Sin-Sin's dark, disturbed eyes. "I know I do. I don't know if I have the courage."

"Anyone can work like you did over them sufferin' mens got courage."

"Thank you."

Sin-Sin rewrapped her shawl in preparation for her own day's work. "You know what I really hates about Ernie June?"

"No, what?"

"She so petty she could find flyshit in pepper."

Around six-thirty that evening the rain crow hollered, and within the hour, silvery beads of cold rain beat down on the meadows, stables, and houses of Chatfield. The temperature was in the high thirties and caused the damp to cut to the bone. It would have been more tolerable had it snowed.

Lutie was down at the main stable. One of the mares was giving birth, and she wanted to be there. If the foal was female, Lutie told Braxton to name it Elizabeth since this was Elizabeth I's coronation day in 1558. Lutie kept odd dates in her mind, strange pieces of information. She thought that her brain was a catchall like sawgrass in fall. If a milkweed floated through, it stuck on the blades. The foal, strangely white, was male. Lutie dubbed him Count Blanc and left to return to the big house.

Behind those low, fluffy rain clouds beamed a full moon giving the evening a noctilucent quality. Lutie felt that she parted silver curtains as she slipped over the wet grass. Despite the chilling damp she enjoyed evenings such as this; their magical quality excited her imagination.

A strange light coming through the raindrops interested her. She stopped for a moment and peered skyward into the billowing mass. Overhead, she thought, the planets are a cosmic parasol, and the earth is no bigger than a teardrop in an inky sea.

Suddenly a hound dashed before her. She hadn't heard it. Then another followed and another and another. They were black and tans.

"No. No!" Lutie cried out.

The hounds bayed, leaping in a ballet of the chase. Out of a pool of liquid shadows thundered the huntsmen. Handsome men, laughing men, pressing their heavy-boned horses faster. Casimer Harkaway, his great chest to the wind, led the way. He cut away from the pack and rode to Lutie.

She stood still, calmly facing this muscled phantom.

"Is it my time?" she asked.

Casimer removed his hat courteously and bowed. His horse pawed the ground. "You shall live a long life."

"Whose time is it then?" Her heart was in her mouth.

"I don't come to predict death, madam, but merely to prepare you for life, for the yoke Fate lays upon your back." He replaced his hat.

"Wait!" Lutie reached out to touch his boot but she withdrew her hand. "Do you believe in prayer, sir?"

"Your existence is a prayer." He smiled and rejoined his huntsmen, then disappeared into the rain.

NOVEMBER 18, 1861

At sunrise, Lutie hurried back onto the vast rolling lawn between the big house and the main stable. The rain stopped and curls of thick, white clouds clung to the sides of the Blue Ridge mountains like baby possums clinging to their mother's tail. The sun turned them soft pink and deep pink and scarlet before banishing them.

Breathlessly Lutie ran to the spot where she had seen

Casimer Harkaway. She searched the earth and found the place where his horse dug into the soft turf.

"It could have been one of our horses," she thought. "I'll bet Braxton or one of the boys exercised them out on the lawn." However, she knew the horses were never exercised on the verdant expanse where she one day hoped to have fountains.

She glanced back at the house. The first full day of brilliant sunlight assaulted Di-Peachy's harp, and it glittered like the torn wing of a golden butterfly. It was true. Last night was true. Lutie pleaded, "Take me, dear God. Take me and let my people live." She saw Sumner in her mind as well as Geneva, Henley, and her adored sister, Poofy. She saw her younger brother, T. Pritchard Chalfonte. She saw the people she loved, even Sin-Sin. She would willingly put down her life in exchange for their lives, especially her children's lives. But she knew the dice were thrown. It was not her turn.

Lutie thought of the women from the icy coasts of Maine to the sticky swamps of Florida. She thought of the women along the Mississippi from its northernmost waters to its exultant release into the gulf below New Orleans. And on the other side of that great river there were women weeping. Two nations were weeping for their dead, for what was lost, and for what would never be.

Carefully she put the toe of her shoe into the churned earth. "I won't weep," she vowed. "I've been down this road before, and I won't weep. I'll fight!" She was determined to bear the yoke Fate laid on her back.

DECEMBER 20, 1861

Frost coated Gallant's whiskers. A scarf knitted by Di-Peachy was wrapped around Geneva's throat to ward off the cold. The regiment rode on the Leesburg-Alexandria Pike toward Dranesville. Wagons were spread out along the road like square pearls in a long, frozen necklace. Food supplies had become so scarce that Brigadier General Stuart was ordered to cover this foraging expedition to the west of Dranesville, a small town about seven miles inland from Coon's Ferry on the Potomac and fifteen miles west of Washington, D.C. The land, good for cultivation, yielded results even when the army couldn't pay for the hay and supplies.

About sixteen hundred infantry troops, one hundred fifty cavalrymen, and four field pieces protected this vital chain of food. Mars wanted to bring his entire regiment, but higher powers deemed it unnecessary.

As the sun heralded the day at 7:10 Geneva and her company were ordered toward Dranesville. The Yankees were reputed to have set up advance posts there, and if they got wind of the forage wagons, they would try to steal them for themselves. Winter was impartial as to its victims, and the Yankees were hungry, too.

Banjo rode on one side of Geneva; Nash was on the other. On the east side of the little town the two turnpikes, the Leesburg-Alexandria and the Georgetown, intersected. As the regiment neared the town, Geneva saw that Dranesville was a cavalryman's nightmare. High hills, a spur before the Blue Ridge mountains, blocked the south side of the town. Much of the ground was covered in thick woods. Banjo was first to see that the Yankees already had the ridge. "Look," he said, "caissons moving up one of the pikes."

Nash pulled on his cigar. "We can't charge in this terrain."

"No," Banjo said, fingering his card deck, "but if they've got cavalry, we could be back and forth all day."

"Why?" Geneva wanted to know.

"To draw them off the wagons."

Mars ordered his small detachment of one hundred fifty men to ride back on the Leesburg Pike. The bugle sounded, and the detachment split as neatly as if cut by a wedge.

Four artillery pieces, twelve-pounders pulled by draft horses, roared by. "Make way! Make way!"

"We're gonna hit them," Nash said.

"Off the road!" ordered Mars again. Again they moved out of the way as the infantry ran forward on the double-quick.

"Halt," a major called.

The infantry stopped, removed their blankets and personal effects, each laid neatly on the ground like rows of large cotton.

"Forward, double-quick!" he shouted again.

The sound of feet on the frozen road sounded like thousands of walnuts being crunched underfoot. Despite the cold, these men were already sweating.

Geneva heard the first cannon fire. This was followed by rhythmic bursts from the other three. Company after company of sober infantrymen hurtled forward. She thought that the artillery boys were wizards the way they could limber guns, get their angle, and fire. Sumner taught her that a twelve-pounder had a maximum range at 50° of 1,700 yards. They used ball for the long range, cannister for shorter range, and grape against infantry at two hundred yards. Geneva didn't mind artillery duels, but she thought the antipersonnel cannister and grape horrible. She'd seen horses and men disemboweled by the stuff.

Boom. The deep-throated Federal guns began to answer the South. One after another, they sang like murderous children. Boom! Boom! Boom! Boom! Boom! Their register increased.

"How many batteries do you think they've got?" Geneva asked.

"I counted twelve guns," Nash answered.

"Either that or some Yankee genius devised a new firing pattern," Banjo said.

"We only sent up one battery," Geneva called to him.

Mars, riding back to check his rear, heard her. "We can make hell with what we have." The sound of battle gave Mars a wild energy. He was larger than life and utterly fearless.

Once Banjo asked Mars if he was ever afraid. Mars replied that he was afraid of disease, insanity, the terrors of the hearth, but not battle. He knew he wouldn't die on the field.

Banjo allowed that whether that was true or not, worrying wasn't going to do him much good, so he might as well soldier on. If nothing else, it gave his companions courage.

"Close up!" Mars bellowed. "The infantry is through. Close up! We've got to get to the wagons." He wheeled and came alongside Banjo. "Cover the rear, Banjo. If you see any Yanks, tell Mandy here to blow."

The bugler came alongside Banjo, too. "We'll do what we can."

For two hours, they heard the cannon fire and rifles crackle. The sound grew more tinty as they turned the wagons and nudged them back toward Leesburg. The cannon stopped.

By late afternoon every wagon was accounted for and secure in camp. Mars and his men waited, but the Yankee cavalry never showed its face. Men attended to their mounts, and Mars paced, but no further orders came. Finally the men dismounted at sunset.

An hour after sunset a courier arrived. The cavalry was to advance upon Dranesville at daybreak and harass the enemy's left flank.

Mars read the dispatch and said to Sam Wells, "We might be able to do some damage on the left. The right's impossible. The men have withdrawn to the railroad station, and Stuart's at Frying Pan Church. What do you think?"

"I'll tell the men to cook up a day's rations, just in case."

"Sam, they were unusually clairvoyant knowing where our supply wagons were heading."

"It wasn't us. Goddamned Richmond cabinet leaks like a sieve."

Mars folded the dispatch and slid it into his breast pocket. "Not a happy thought. Soldiers take the risk, and politicians reap the rewards. I think I'd rather sit in a room full of maggots."

DECEMBER 21, 1861

Dawn hovered on the eastern horizon. Deep frost covered the fields. Every sense alert, Mars and his men rode into Dranesville. The Yankees evacuated. Dead bodies from yesterday's fighting randomly covered the ground. Neither side got all their dead off the field, although they did take care of their wounded.

The lone artillery battery took a beating but the surviving men withdrew the guns, in good order, to shelter.

The small cavalry detachment walked over the broken ground, regrouped on the Georgetown Pike, and trotted east to see if they could pick up the enemy. The infantry was left with the task of burying the dead which did not further endear the cavalry to them.

As Mars questioned people along the Georgetown Pike he learned that the Federals had withdrawn fifteen regiments of infantry and seven companies of cavalry along with several batteries. It was a godsend that the Federal cavalry did not flank Dranesville and come out on the Leesburg Pike. Mars began to wonder about their leadership.

Badly led or not, they had retreated in fairly good order. No signs of panic, discarded clothing or goods, cluttered the road.

Around three in the afternoon, the Virginians turned back toward their camp. If they didn't have to give up the roads for infantry or artillery, they would make it in two hours.

Riding back, Mars wondered what would happen when the first twelve-month enlistments expired. The war was far from over, and it had not proven to be a glorious game. Men were often hungry and cold. Those that were not from Virginia grew increasingly nervous about military activities in their own states and desired to return to protect their homes. Pay appeared like roses in December. Mars didn't worry about the cavalry. Their esprit de corps would hold them together. They were mostly rich boys, and they had a lot to prove. The infantry and artillery were another question.

A biting northwesterly wind prickled his cheeks. The landscape, stripped of foliage, looked desolate, and even the comforting roll of rich meadows could not compensate for the barrenness of winter.

He thought about Kate and her cobalt blue eyes. No doubt she was unbuttoning Baron Schecter's impeccably cut trousers. He no longer cared. What he wondered about these days was not so much Kate but himself. Could he ever love again? Would he know it if he did? He feared that he had grown away from that part of himself. He had hardened his heart to women. Well, no one ever died of lack of love, he thought.

DECEMBER 22, 1861

Having written a letter to both Lutie and Di-Peachy, Geneva read Matthew, chapter 3. She learned that John the Baptist ate locusts and wild honey. If she got hungry enough, she'd try it, too.

The flap of the tent opened and Nash, his face drawn, entered and sat next to her. "I have bad news." He handed her a folded paper spattered with blood.

She unfolded the paper. It was Sumner's drawings for Lutie's fountains.

"Your brother couldn't stay out of the fight. He went forward with the horse artillery commanded by Cutts. The fire raked them for two solid hours, and they were severely outgunned."

"But we beat them!" Geneva shook.

Nash touched her hair. "We beat them, but Sumner's gone." He did not tell her that when they reached Sumner's body, the grass around him was torn up. The man died in hideous agony.

Sobbing, she put her head on Nash's chest. "Not my big brother!"

She cried for hours. Banjo quietly came in bringing Sumner's guns, sword, articles of clothing, and his engineering books. He sat beside Geneva and patted her hand, but she sobbed uncontrollably.

That night, Banjo motioned to Nash to come out. "The little fella's takin' this powerful hard." Banjo squinted.

"Death's etched the first wrinkle on his skin."

Banjo appreciated poetry but would have preferred a solution. "He'll make hisself sick, and that's dangerous in this wicked cold. You think some whiskey would stiffen him?"

"I tried that. He throws it up."

"I'm gonna get the colonel. He'll know what to do."

"He'll come in here all gunpowder and bluster," Nash flared.

"I know you don't like the colonel, but Jimmy does. He'll know what to do. You can't let him carry on like this."

Nash reluctantly agreed. "It's worth a try."

When Mars turned up the tent flap, he saw Geneva lying facedown on her cot, Nash sitting helplessly next to her, his hand stroking her hair.

Mars knelt on one knee next to the cot. "Jimmy, I'm very sorry to hear about Sumner. He was everything a young man should be. The best blood is poured in the ground."

She turned over. "I hate them. I'm gonna find the men who killed my brother and kill them. I want to make them bleed, damn their black hearts!" Her eyes were glazed.

"Jimmy, war is nothing personal. Those Yankees were doing their job, just like we're doing our job. The selection of victims is impersonal."

Geneva sat upright, breathing convulsively. "It doesn't make sense."

"I'm not arguing for it, but that's the way it is. It's not a duel. It's business."

"I don't want to live," she wailed and bent over, her head in her hands.

"You have to live. You've got a mother and a father that love you, and they'll need you now more than ever. You've got Nash." That was hard to say. "You've got Banjo. You have to live."

She looked up at him.

"Come on, now. Pull yourself together. The regiment needs you. I need you."

Her sobs slowed, but her body still shook.

"You need some sleep. It's a terrible thing to lose someone you love. You'll come through."

"Do I have to write Mother and Father?"

"No, I'll write them both. Will you go to sleep now, soldier?"

"Yes, sir, I promise." She crawled under the covers and fell asleep before the tent flap closed behind Mars.

Mars and Banjo walked down the quiet rows of tents, white ghosts in line after line.

"We're just bloody cards tossed on the table," Mars said. "That's all a soldier is, a bloody card."

III

THESE
BLOODY
CARDS

JANUARY 20, 1862

"Most merciful Father, who hast been pleased to take unto thyself the soul of this thy servant, John Tyler: Grant to us who are still in our pilgrimage, and who walk as yet by faith, that having served thee with constancy on earth, we may be joined hereafter with thy blessed saints in glory everlasting; through Jesus Christ our Lord. Amen."

Henley, in full dress uniform with Kate Vickers next to him, watched as the body of the tenth President of the United States, John Tyler, was borne out of St. Paul's Episcopal Church. The "Dead March" from Saul mournfully played.

Baron Schecter, sitting to Mrs. Vickers's right, wore the blazing white tunic of imperial Austria. The fringe on his gold epaulets swayed as he breathed. Schecter, a bold Adonis with a thin blond moustache, accompanied Kate everywhere, as did Henley.

Henley could no longer ignore the condition of the Confederacy whose great victory last summer evaporated like a venomous vapor. The news, unilaterally bad, added to the depression that the funeral of this eminent man produced.

John Tyler died at seventy-two. His coffin was followed in the blasts of icy wind by his second wife, the former Julia Gardiner, and his nine-year-old son, Lyon Gardiner Tyler. Mrs. Tyler held her head up. She knew many a widow's eye was upon her, and she had no right to falter. Lyon held his mother's hand; taking his example from her, he did not cry.

As Henley, in the third column of official mourners, marched with Kate and the baron, he noticed that the sidewalks were crowded with people in obvious distress. The path, lined with mourners, wound the entire distance from Ninth and

Grace streets to Hollywood Cemetery. One hundred and fifty carriages followed the body. The people mourned not just the passing of an ex-President but of an era. There were no more John Tylers left in political life.

Henley wondered how many people also knew of the unseemly squabble over presentation of the casket. Should it be draped with the flag of our present enemy, our former nation? Some members of the cabinet, with disregard for the grieving widow, said absolutely not, his casket should be covered with the flag of the infant Confederacy. This display of smallness continued until Julia Tyler told them in so many words to go to hell. So President Tyler rolled to his freshly dug grave, a feat in itself since the ground was frozen, with a bare casket, save for his dress sword in remembrance of the company he raised in 1813 for the defense of Richmond against the marauding British. Before his casket, a single horse was led, boots reversed in the stirrups, the only sign that the leader of a nation was passing.

Tyler had done what he could to prevent the bloody rupture, but once it occurred, he served the Confederacy and his native Virginia literally until his last breath. He gave us Texas, Henley thought, an icon of independence. John Tyler kissed nobody's ass, Democrat or Whig or the brand-new Republicans. He was able to disagree with a man as formidable as Andrew Jackson as well as make common cause with him when his conscience permitted him.

What troubled Henley was his own shyness about public life. It wasn't just himself, he knew, but a generation of Virginians abdicated public life, leaving it to the second-raters and ultimately to the younger, radical elements of the Delta and coastal South. Virginia had a lot to answer for and so did Henley. Perhaps the richness of Virginia's drowned river valleys from four great rivers, the Potomac, the Rappahannock, the York, and the James, invited people to wealth, not public service.

Jefferson, Monroe, and Madison had wealth, although they squandered much of it. After that triumvirate passed, Jackson and Tyler, both Virginians, took over. And then nothing. The youngbloods drove west because the valleys were tied up by rich and comfortable men, men like himself, Henley realized. Rash temperaments superseded temperate judgments, and slavery sucked away the talent of men of genius like John

Calhoun of South Carolina. The effort spent in justifying slavery, the foundation of rural economy, sapped people. They began to look to the past instead of to the future, and Henley cursed himself because he looked only to Chatfield. He abandoned the great issues of the day to become the best breeder of horses in the country. While it was a worthy achievement, it wasn't enough. Now he, like thousands of others, was paying in blood for his complacency.

In meeting after meeting Henley marveled at the infinite capacity of the human brain to withstand the introduction of useful knowledge. Looking ahead as the six perfectly matched black horses pulled Tyler to the beyond, he wondered, how did the old man do it? How did he sit in endless meetings, listening to people avoid problems or puff themselves up like broody hens. In order to be successful in politics, one must suffer fools gladly. The Richmond soldier killed more enemies sitting around a conference table than in battle. Hell was a bureaucracy with twelve devils arguing at a conference table. Henley renewed his efforts to achieve the uptown of afterlife as opposed to the downtown.

As the procession passed by, Henley thought of Sumner's funeral. They couldn't have a graveside ceremony for Sumner, but the Very Reverend Manlius had arranged a service at the church. Henley and Lutie were gratified at the number of people who came to pay their last respects. Jennifer Fitzgerald had one of her servants, a man highly skilled with marble, carve a beautiful cenotaph with Sumner's name, dates of birth and death, his regiment and brigade numbers. Over this were two crossed sabers.

Lutie had amazed Henley. He worried that she'd fall to pieces as she did when Jimmy died. Instead she bore it like a Roman matron of the Republic. Her only comment was, "If my son can die for Virginia, I can live for Virginia."

Sin-Sin covered her face in ashes and kept to her house for two days. Di-Peachy cried continually. But Ernie had surprised them all. The enormous cook went down like the crumbling of a seawall.

Kate Vickers had come from Richmond. Henley was touched by Kate's concern for himself and his wife. Kate was particularly solicitous of Di-Peachy who was wont to break into tears.

Poofy managed to smuggle a letter through the lines urging

Lutie to come to Bedford, New York, where she would care for her. Lutie answered her sister with a long letter. Lutie handed the document to Henley, telling him to get it on the other side of the Potomac. Once he returned to Richmond, Henley sent it by government courier, and it passed through the lines. He often wondered if anyone, zealous in his duty, read it before it reached Poofy's hands.

What Henley could say to no one was his anguish for never having understood his son. He would awaken in the middle of the night feeling as though he had extricated himself from a black whirlpool. The pain pierced him because he feared his son was a braver man than he was. He failed as a father. He failed as a husband, and now he was failing as a soldier. Sometimes he would wake up to find his pillow wet. One terrible night he crawled out of bed, his knees hitting the cold floor, and he prayed to great God Almighty to forgive him and grant him atonement. He could never make it up to Sumner, but if he felt God's grace, perhaps he would have the courage to make it up to the other people in his life whom he had ignored or hurt. The sins of omission began to loom as large as the sins of commission, and Henley knew he'd committed both. His only comfort was Geneva. Her love for him was the slender thread upon which dangled his self-respect.

Geneva haunted him day and night. He couldn't stand to lose her, but he had given her his word that he wouldn't tell.

"You're so quiet, Colonel Chatfield. I'm afraid this funeral is distressing to you." Kate's low voice brought him back to the present.

"Memories."

Kate, wisely knowing no conventional sentiment could ease him, said, "I know that we can live with deprivation, with war, but I sometimes wonder can we live with our sorrows?"

Baron Schecter, while he disliked Henley for obvious reasons, was not an unfeeling man. He added, "We must all live with our losses—and under God's unblinking eye."

"Right now, Baron," Henley replied, "I feel as though I am seeing God's hind parts, not his eye."

FEBRUARY 2, 1862

A howling ice storm rattled the windows of the Livingston mansion. Bedford, New York, far from the fury of war, could not escape nature.

Wrapped in a fur blanket, Poofy Chalfonte Livingston read her sister's letter which miraculously had arrived by government courier in this winter tempest.

1 January 1862

My Dearest Sister:

Words fall from my brain like leaves. I am becoming spare; perhaps I have the weariness of winter. Let's hope I have the austerity and sinew of winter as well.

Thank you for your letter. It was a great consolation to me. Please give my tenderest affections to Daniel for informing you of what happened to Sumner. His expressions of sympathy for myself and Henley only confirm my belief that while our husbands fight on opposing sides of this repulsive war, nothing will ever shatter the bonds of love forged in our family.

Grief so numbs the senses that I am not always sure what I feel. Sometimes I think I can bear that pain, and other times I think it will crush me. I see around me, as you must in Bedford, other women in like anguish. How can I falter? This grief is not mine alone. We each suffer. We all suffer. Alone, I ask myself, is any cause worth the price of one human life? Do you harbor such thoughts?

I think of our brother. I think of my daughter. She's quite lost her mind. She's with Nash, and she's been in the army disguised as a man since the beginning of the

246 RITA MAE BROWN

war. I've kept it from you as she wished, but now I can't hold it in any longer. Must I surrender my remaining child to the bloody jaws of hell, too?

You used to complain, dear Poofy, that you and Daniel had no children. Rejoice. You will never know the agony of birthing them, raising them, only to see them die before their time.

You asked me do I pray. Yes. But I look at the cross, and I no longer see a symbol of salvation, I see an instrument of torture. I feel I am sailing on a black river to midnight.

And yet, today I looked at Sin-Sin's sweet face. I saw my friends gathered around me to help me though this time. A few of them secretly worry that like a tree, I'll die from the top down. I won't. Don't worry, Poofy. I will not lose my mind. But I looked at them and realized that through my friends God has loved me. And that ray of hope, of comprehension, begins to work on my soul.

I don't say that I shall immediately be restored nor that I shan't continue to ask myself deeply disturbing questions. And grief will pull me like a slumberous undertow. But that radiant moment, lifting me quite out of myself, gives me hope. Perhaps the only way to heal, to find happiness, is to forget one's self. Perhaps, too, we must even forget all that we know. We know too much; we feel too little. Perhaps we must become children again, and try and see the world as a bright new toy despite our suffering, despite the blood, the cruelty, the betrayals we call history! "Suffer the little children to come unto me." This may be the only way to God.

I love you, Portia. You have been a good and faithful sister to me, and I long for the day when we can once again be physically reunited. Until then, know that my heart is with you every moment.

Lutie

Poofy put the letter next to her breast and pressed it against her heart. In the back of her mind like God's whisper was the incantation "Love."

MARCH 19, 1862

Henley returned for a few days to Albemarle County to reach an agreement with Reddy Neutral Taylor over thirty-five horses Taylor was offering for sale. The lunatics running the army decided that when a cavalryman lost his mount, he would drop out of his company and fall in with a specially designated Company Q. There he stayed until he could purchase another mount as the state had no intention of supplying him with one. Granted, most cavalrymen were from well-to-do families, but yanking a man out of the ranks and sending him on a wild goose chase for a horse was stupid. Henley thought his heart would stop when he heard the news. Then, too, some cavalrymen lacked funds. What were they supposed to do, fall in with the infantry?

General Gorgas, no friend of the scheme, did stand by the notion that individual contractors had a right to sell horses. He thought that encouraging businessmen would get the job done. Henley agreed with him there. Christ, set up another government bureau to do a job, and they'd all die, choked in red tape. These enterprising types were to sell at approved government prices. Reddy Neutral Taylor, presenting himself as a friend of both Henley and the Confederacy, offered thirty-five horses at $150 a head. The nerve of the man galled Henley. After loathsome bargaining, he reduced the price to $100 a head, still highway robbery, but Henley paid the thieving skunk and arranged for the horses to be shipped to Colonel Vickers at camp. Through Kate he learned that Vickers was preparing for a major battle next spring, probably in defense of Richmond. Company Q was anathema to Mars so he collected monies from his men for a pool of horses. For those that could not pay, Vickers made up the difference.

Henley strode into his library, appalled at his dealings with Reddy Neutral Taylor and chilled from the cold weather. Snow clouds scraped the cupola atop Chatfield's main stable.

"I could scoop the sky out with a spoon today," Lutie said, as she took a seat next to him by the fire. "Henley, you look so tired. I know having to pass the day with Reddy is unpleasant. He's swelling up like a slug in beer, that one! Try to put him out of your mind."

He pinched the bridge of his nose between his thumb and forefinger. "It isn't just that. We're losing this war, Lutie. Ever since Sumner passed on, the portents and the events spell doom."

"It's always darkest before the dawn."

"This is dark indeed. I think I knew following President Tyler's funeral cortege that darkness was enveloping us. And when Captain O. Jennings Wise was carried through the town, people were distraught. I tell you I've never seen such an outpouring. You couldn't get within a block of St. James Church, even in the slush and the snow. People shivered and wept."

"He was a popular boy and a hero."

"A hero? My God, we asked him to fight off seventy-five hundred Federals at Roanoke Island with one-third that number. He was a lamb led to slaughter! So many lambs." Henley's eyes clouded.

"Over so many centuries."

"What, Lutie?" Henley blinked.

"The human race puts one bloody foot in front of the other and calls it progress." She furiously knitted, her needles clicking. "History is a vile mess."

"But this time we're part of it. I'm part of it! Sometimes I wake up and I think of the Revolutionary War. Was it my father's nightmare? Was it like this? Could the leaders have been as foul, as degraded, as monumentally stupid as that gaunt idiot in Washington?"

"I expect some were."

"I knew we were on the way down when we lost Tennessee and Kentucky. Richmond is flooded with refugees. I don't know where they sleep at night. The Union controls the Cumberland and Tennessee rivers, and Judah P. Benjamin tries to weasel out of the blame. To think I once thought there was genius in that man!" Henley, disgusted, slammed his hand on the arm of the chair. "They made the damn fool Secretary of State after he failed as Secretary of War. Fremont in Missouri is warning enough. Fremont's ravings about emancipation ought to chill us to the bone, and he stole the property of any pro-Southern individual. Confiscation. People are thrown out in the streets in the dead of winter, their personal belongings ripped from them! That's what's going to happen to us if we don't wake up."

"It's not going to happen to us."

"I'd like to know why not?"

"Because I will stand at my bedroom window and fire until every last shell of ammunition is spent, that's why. And then they can come and kill me, because I don't think I'll care anymore. I tell you this, husband, my pacifism died the day Sumner did. I am not going down without one hell of a fight. I owe that much to our son."

"And our daughter." Henley's lips compressed.

"I have moments when I think I'll dress up and join, too."

"With your ample bosom I don't think you'd get far." He smiled.

Happy to see him smile, Lutie called, "Sin-Sin."

Sin-Sin appeared in an instant. "Yes."

"Standing around the corner, Sin-Sin?"

"No, I jes happen to be passin' by."

"What a notoriously rotten liar you are. Might you inform Ernie June that Mr. Chatfield and I would appreciate two toasty hot toddies?"

"Might could." Sin-Sin walked toward the kitchen.

"I miss her," Henley sighed.

"I know there was a time when I didn't know Sin-Sin, but it is now so far back in my memory that it's irretrievable."

"You know what else worries me?"

"Henley, if you'd rest your mind."

"It was suspending the writ of habeas corpus. Oh, how Jefferson Davis huffed and puffed like the big bad wolf when Lincoln did it at the beginning of the war. Not us! Not Southerners! We are a civilized people who respect the laws. And then he claps martial law on Norfolk and Portsmouth to boot!"

"Norfolk is very rowdy. It'll get the drunks off the streets."

" 'Extraordinary times call for extraordinary measures.' Ha!

Even if we can end this war without losing too much territory, how we can repair the damage to our laws?"

"Henley, I have always thought that men paid entirely too much attention to law instead of to behavior. Take dueling for instance. You could outlaw it tomorrow, but the law isn't going to stop it."

"That's a special case, Lutie. Dueling allows a man to defend his honor without going bankrupt in a court of law."

Sin-Sin returned. "Hot toddies, jes the way you likes 'em."

"Thank you, Sin-Sin." Henley grabbed the cup and quickly put it down because it was hot.

"You can leave us." Lutie smiled.

"I's 'fraid I might miss somethin'."

"Sin-Sin, that's the point, isn't it?"

Sin-Sin, grumbling under her breath, retired. Lutie leaned forward. "I hope they don't know how bad it is."

"Di-Peachy reads the newspapers and tells them."

"Henley, how can you say such a thing?"

"Why wouldn't she?"

"The less they know, the better. It'll confuse them."

"Lutie, she's one of them, after all. If you were a servant, wouldn't you want to know how the war was progressing? If the North wins, the Negro race might be freed."

"Lincoln is not Fremont. He knows such an action would harden the resolve of the South and turn ordinary citizens into fanatics," Lutie replied.

"If we win, who is to say that this curse might not be lifted?"

"You and I will never see eye to eye about our special problem."

"We have to free the slaves, Lutie. I don't know what they'll do in Louisiana or Alabama, but here in Virginia we must do it or be in peril for our immortal souls." His chest heaved.

"Henley, where will they go? What will they do? Who would have them?"

"They can stay right here, but we've got to set them free."

"For God's sake, Henley, wait until this wretched war is finally over. You can't leave me here without any authority. What if they leave?"

"You yourself said, 'Where would they go?' "

"Be sensible! How can we pay them? Do we even know

what their labor is worth? How can I run this place? Answer me that! Let sleeping dogs lie."

He ran his big hand through his thick hair. "I am drawing up manumission papers, effective December 25, 1862. I will instruct our servants that if they wish to leave us, to do so immediately and to be quiet about it. There's no need in arousing the ire of our neighbors at this delicate time nor in raising false hopes in their servants. Those that wish to stay will be paid half the wage that a white man would get for the same labor. Under the circumstances I think that is fair."

"Under the circumstances," Lutie replied, "I would say it's extraordinary. I don't agree with you, Henley, but I have no way in which to stop you."

"I must do this thing. I have talked about it since we were married. I must take the bull by the horns, and may God forgive me if I am mistaken and if I expose you to ridicule."

"I can take the ridicule. It's poverty I'm not so sure I can take."

"We aren't going to be poor."

"Even if we are, we'll manage," Lutie said without enthusiasm. "You know what my mother used to say: 'Worse things have happened to nicer people.' "

"Your mother also said, 'What if God is a vegetable?' "

"Maybe we have to be crazy to be happy on this earth." Lutie smiled ruefully.

"In the balance, my dear, have you been happy?" Henley swallowed his drink.

"I have enjoyed isolated moments of great happiness, some of them with you."

"I think that's all there is, Lutie. Isolated moments."

"That's good enough for me."

APRIL 12, 1862

Picket duty irked Geneva, but she didn't complain. She, Nash, and Banjo watched the column as it rode in fours, followed by infantry, down the road to Yorktown. The three of them sat where a narrow wooded lane intersected Yorktown Road. Procedure was procedure.

When in hostile territory, a mounted man rode forward a half mile in front of an infantry or a cavalry column. Halfway between him and the column marched an advance guard, usually a squadron composed of two companies followed by the main column. Behind the main column about a quarter of a mile rode a rear guard. Once the rear guard passed, the soldiers on picket or vidette duty rejoined the rear guard. Pickets were always posted at intersecting roads and wooded areas.

Standing around made Geneva restless, but when her turn came up for this, she performed it without much complaint. The surrounding low country was good for cavalry except where swamps were located. The smell of brackish water assailed her nostrils. How anyone could live in this kind of terrain mystified Geneva. She pitied people who had no green rolling hills or mountains to guard them.

McClellan was reputed to have one hundred thousand men. Geneva knew, as did everyone, that if the Confederates under General Joseph Johnston had thirty thousand men, it was a miracle. The South waited anxiously behind an eight-mile front sparsely populated with redoubts, rifle pits, and whatever else the engineers could throw up. The situation appeared hopeless, although reinforcements trickled in daily. A drop in the bucket was better than no drop at all.

The lowlands, laced with rivers, streams, and swamps,

provided interesting territory in which to fight. McClellan, his headquarters less than one mile from the house in which Cornwallis had agreed to surrender to Continental forces, boasted that he'd drag Johnston and Davis to that very same house and reenact the surrender. Meanwhile, he talked instead of moved.

Geneva knew that outnumbered though they were, if they could get enough men to dig in and make life unpleasant for McClellan, Gorgeous George, as he was contemptuously called, might lose the opportunity for his desired historical reenactment. She figured that the cavalry would be used like a terrier to nip at the Federals' heels.

The rear guard passed with the usual compliments concerning the vidette. "That's right, sit on your butt, cavalry boy, while I get fallin' arches!"

"Think we've seen the last of them?" Nash asked.

"Why don't we wait a bit, as we're downwind from the swamps." Banjo knocked the dust off his cap. "If the Yankees don't kill you, the smell will."

"Do you hear something?" Nash was alert.

"More cavalry," Banjo replied.

"I thought the rest of the cavalry was forward."

"Maybe we're getting units outside of Stuart's brigade," suggested Geneva. "Why don't we catch them up?"

"Shouldn't we notify the rear guard?" Nash was a stickler for rules.

"Take us fifteen minutes to reach them unless we go flat out," said Banjo. "Let's be hospitable. After all, these wretches might be from some outlandish unit like the Sixth Virginia Cavalry." Banjo trotted toward the direction of the sound.

"You're right. Let's greet them and show them how to behave." Geneva enjoyed the sun on her face.

Nash, less than enthused, trotted after them.

The sounds of soldiers drew closer. The three turned off of Yorktown Road onto a dirt road. About twenty Federals on a scouting mission bore down on them. They were surprised, too.

Just as Banjo pulled both his Colts, his horse shot toward the Yankees.

"There they are, boys!" Geneva shouted. She looked over her shoulder as though more Confederate troops were behind her.

Nash spurred his horse to join their wild attack. The Federals turned with difficulty on the narrow road, fired a few desultory shots, and beat a hasty retreat. Geneva, Nash, and Banjo chased them for a few hundred yards, then turned and bolted down the dirt road and onto Yorktown Road. They galloped back to the rear guard.

The major in charge of the rear guard posted fifteen additional mounted men in case the Yankees should return.

Riding with the rear, catching his breath, Nash sputtered, "Damned bravest thing I ever saw, Banjo!"

"Brave, hell. My horse ran away with me."

That night as she made camp, Geneva watched each man perform his pre-battle ritual. Benserade polished and sharpened his sword repeatedly. Sam Wells became unusually hearty. Nash withdrew. Banjo whistled "The Bonnie Blue Flag." Whether he knew it or not, the only time he whistled that tune was before a fight was coming. Mars studied maps and questioned anyone his men brought in who lived in the area. He wanted to know about every cow path. Geneva read and reread the Lesson of the Day. It was the 34th day of Lent, and Judges 2: 1–11 filled her eye but not her mind. She did note that Joshua lived to be one hundred and ten. She didn't know if she'd live to be twenty. Her nineteenth birthday, December 21, had been lost in Sumner's death. Twenty was a number not a reality.

It wasn't until she curled up in her bedroll that she remembered it was her first wedding anniversary.

APRIL 13, 1862

"She's still a relentless gossip, but other than that, I'd say she has enacted a remarkable transformation." Lutie was writing to Poofy about Jennifer Fitzgerald among other subjects. The sun peeped over the horizon.

"Miz Lutie!" Sin-Sin barged into the room. "Boyd's run off!" Sin-Sin reported this with equal measures of delicious malice and worry.

"What are you talking about?"

"Picked her room cleaner than a chicken! She's packed up and gone!"

Lutie capped the inkwell, threw back her shoulders, and headed for the kitchen. The door hung open like a broken jaw. Ernie was kneading, her tears falling into the dough.

"Ernie, is it true?"

"Uh huh."

"I can't believe it."

Sin-Sin, arms crossed over her bosom, leaned against the table like a grim, obsidian caryatid. "As is the way of Barabbas!"

Ernie picked up the dough and slapped it on Sin-Sin's face. Sin-Sin, helpless while removing the stuff, was then knocked onto the floor by Ernie, who held her rolling pin over Sin-Sin's head for the crowning blow.

Lutie grabbed Ernie's huge arm and hung on with every ounce in her. "Don't you dare, Ernie! You harm one hair on her head, and I'll whip you before God and Chatfield."

"I doan care!" Ernie screamed.

Sin-Sin rolled over, still frantically peeling the dough off her face. "You outta yo' head!"

"Ernie, give me that pin," said Lutie firmly.

Ernie pulled her arm away. "How do I know that nigger witch ain't comin' fo' me?"

"Because she is leaving the kitchen this instant."

Sin-Sin did not budge. "I can't leave you 'lone with a crazy woman."

"She's not crazy. She's suffered a terrible shock. Go on now. Please!"

Sin-Sin made a great show of storming out the door. She planted herself firmly on the other side, ear to the crack.

"Tell me what happened," said Lutie in a calm voice.

"I gets up like always. I comes up and starts the bread. Calls my girl and she gone."

"You must have had a warning."

"My tongue too short to tell you all that I knows."

"Would you like me to stretch it for you?" Lutie's voice stiffened.

"Things go wrong since Sumner gone. Boyd, she got herself mixed up with that no-good buck Grizz over at the Fitzgerald place. Every time Miz Jennifer come to call upon you, he finagle a way to come along. He stuffs her head with crazy ideas. She like a rag doll, and he jes jammin' in straw. That boy was carryin' her fast."

"What made her think she wouldn't get caught?"

"When she talk crazy to me, I tell her 'member Peter and Tincia and she laugh and say they dumb. Her Grizz got everythin' figgered out. He gonna get to the Yankee lines and offer hisself to do whatever they needs. He say if Bumba can do it, he can do it." Ernie took a deeply ashamed breath. "And my girl done took that pass."

Sin-Sin's eyebrows flew up to her turban. She whispered to herself, "All this time she had it." Boyd would never again be underrated by Sin-Sin.

"You know if she gets caught, I'll have to make an example of her."

"Doan beat her! I wants to do that myself!"

"I'm not going to beat her. She'll be severely restricted. Naturally, I think Big Fitz, when he catches Grizz, will have that boy stretched on four stakes and whipped raw."

"I hope he kills him." Ernie snarled. "Foolin' with my girl."

"Where's Braxton?"

"He got sense. He down at the stable." She wiped her

eyes. "I knows Boyd was up to no good. She sweep out the house after sundown. She know that mean bad luck. She invitin' bad luck."

Lutie said in a resigned voice, "I suppose I had better check my jewelry and see what she stole."

"She din' steal nothin' from you." Ernie's voice was raw.

"How do you know that?"

"'Cause she took every penny I save instead." Ernie, devastated, began to cry again. "She took one thousand and two hundred dollars. Been savin' for twenty-three years. Every time I gets a dime or a thank you, I puts it away, 'cept for the five dollars from Miz Vickers which I give to Boyd outright so as to encourage her."

Stunned, Lutie's voice cracked. "Twelve hundred dollars?"

"And some odd cents."

"What were you going to do with that money?"

"I was gonna talk to Mr. Henley when the time be right. I was gonna buy Braxton free. Then he can work for Mr. Henley, save like I saves, and buy land. Back up where that trash Reddy planted corn. I was hopin' Mr. Henley see things my way."

Until now, Lutie had never appreciated the full extent of Ernie June's ambition. "I believe that Mr. Chatfield would have agreed to your plan. He admires foresight and hard work." Her throat was cottony. "Tell me, Ernie, did you hope to be free, too?"

"No, Miz Lutie. I's too old."

"Did you ever confide your plan to Boyd? Perhaps she was angry that Braxton would come first."

"I never tell her sech a thing. Braxton the first born. Thass the way it is. She born to be the cook in a great house, the greatest house in the South."

"Did you ever mention your plan to Braxton?"

"Yes, but only oncet."

Lutie figured that he had told his sister in a weak moment or during a sibling fight. "I see. Ernie, would you like to rest today? We can manage."

"No, if I sits home alone, I feels worse."

Lutie handled the rolling pin. "Does this have anything to do with Reddy Neutral Taylor?" It was a hunch.

"No. My girl not mixed up in his scheme! Peter pay for messin' with that man with his life."

"Maybe Braxton was dealing with him."

"Oh, Lawd, Miz Lutie, don't say that!" Ernie trembled.

After further consoling of Ernie, Lutie withdrew to the library. She set aside her letter to Poofy and wrote one to Henley. Alafin, Peter, and Tincia were murdered, perhaps by the same hand and perhaps not. Now Boyd and her lover escaped. Furious though she was with Boyd, she didn't want her to wind up dead. The next thing she did was to write a letter notifying the authorities that a servant from Chatfield had been abducted. Why condemn Boyd out of hand? Love, sometimes, is an abduction.

APRIL 20, 1862

Dearest Mother:

I write to you on Easter Sunday. We are only out of the saddle to sleep, but I went to a sunrise service given by a Lutheran minister for our troops today.

We fought at Yorktown. Perhaps the papers mentioned us because on April 14, Colonel Vickers, together with General Stuart, covered the rear for our commander, General Johnston. We were in constant contact with the enemy.

Around three o'clock we were surprised by a superior force of cavalry. I heard their officer yell "Draw sabers and charge!" Our colonel kept us in tight formation, and we trotted toward the enemy who was galloping at us in full force. I thought Colonel Vickers had lost his mind. Just as we were about to receive the shock of their troops, the colonel ordered us to separate. We peeled away like a banana skin, and we fired a terrific, galling fire into them. It was like shooting fish in a barrel.

To the Yankees' credit, they did not panic, despite their disadvantage. They blew the retreat, and the men tried to extricate themselves from our withering cross fire. I became overzealous in my duty and chased after a laggard lieutenant. I received a slight wound as a result of this foolishness. My face was cut from my right eye down to my mouth by his saber. Guess I deserved it. I succeeded in shooting him out of the saddle. Other than that I am well, but I thought I should warn you that I will bear a nasty scar as a result of this action.

Our colonel said afterward that putting factory boys on horses was a crime. Banjo, my best friend out here, told the colonel to give the Yankees time. I myself do not believe the Union boys will ever be a match for Virginians on horseback. We outshine and outperform every other state in the Confederacy, so you know the Federals have no hope. They do good on foot though, and their artillery is fearsome.

We survey our enemy daily. I expect there will be another fight, but I don't know when and where. I don't much care because we'll beat them wherever we find them.

I have read every one of Sumner's engineering books. Will you send more? Sooner or later someone from our company will get to Richmond. I will return the ones that I have to Father.

I saw Di-Peachy's sweetheart. He was riding next to General Stuart, being one of the general's favorites because of his special courage. He's a handsome man, Mercer Hackett. Stuart is not, but he's as flashy as a peacock and possesses the heart of a lion. He surrounds himself with singers, a banjo player, and even a man who makes music with bones. It's hard to believe that such a well-born man would carry on like that, but he doesn't drink or swear, which is more than you can say for the rest of us.

Colonel Vickers refers to battles as "engagements on our cotillion card." He says General McClellan can't work up the nerve to ask anyone for a rousing dance. He also said that Yankee generals get promoted after every failure so he wonders who will get what after Yorktown.

I miss you, Mother. Give my regards to Sin-Sin, Ernie June, and Di-Peachy.

Love,
Geneva

P.S. Nash fought bravely and received a special commendation by Captain Sam Wells for it. He won't tell you himself.

Lutie put down the letter. Geneva's letters were more precious to Lutie than her jewelry collection.

She opened another letter. This one was from Colonel Jeffrey Windsor. He apologized for bothering her, and he knew that the loss of her son must still sadden her daily. However, he needed her if she could be spared. A great battle would be fought to defend Richmond sometime this summer. McClellan had to move up the Peninsula. Would she come to Richmond? He would send a telegram when he thought the contest was near at hand. Would she also ask her invaluable lady friends, too?

Scribbled on the bottom of Jeffrey's letter was a postscript from Maud Windsor: P.S. Sir Walter Scott has a great deal to answer for!

Lutie agreed with her. Romances glorifying personal combat infected males of all ages, to say nothing of the ladies who thought themselves damsels of purity inspiring their heroes.

Folded in Jeffrey's letter with apologies for not being sent under separate cover was a brief note from Kate Vickers. Lutie didn't mind. Getting mail anywhere was hit or miss. Mrs. Vickers offered Lutie hospitality, and the other Charlottesville ladies were equally welcome. Her husband estimated that there would be a few thousand wounded from the projected battle. Experienced nurses would be a godsend.

"Sin-Sin," Lutie called.

"What?"

"How would you like to go with me to Richmond? It will be more of the Delevan Hotel when we get there. Won't be a pleasure visit."

"When does we leave?"

"Whenever Jeffrey Windsor sends a telegram telling us the battle is nigh."

"Why doan I pack today 'cept for the best dresses? Iffin' we has to go in a hurry, we be ready." Sin-Sin, thrilled to go on a trip no matter how hard the work might be, thought a second and then carefully asked, "Does you think you wants to see more torn-up young mens?"

Lutie placed the letters on her desk, one on top of the other, and walked over to Sin-Sin. She put her arm around the older woman's waist. "Nurse our sick, not our sorrows."

MAY 1, 1862

Outside of Williamsburg, where King's Mill Wharf Road intersects with the road leading into the College of William and Mary, were a handful of good clapboard houses and a small school. Mars halted his men near these dwellings where the tree line met the meadow. They could melt into the woods if necessary, but since McClellan moved at the rate of two miles per day, no one was immediately worried.

At the foot of the meadow, the children erected a maypole, gaily skipping around it, colorful streamers in hand. When they saw the cavalry, they jumped up and down, waving and shouting.

"I believe we are being summoned by the next generation." Mars's teeth glistened underneath his auburn moustache.

"Ain't gentlemanly to refuse a lady's invite." Banjo waited for Mars to order him forward or to dismount.

"Why don't we go down and water the horses?" Geneva suggested, riding forward. "Besides which, children know secret paths and swamps that adults never think about."

"That's right," Banjo agreed. "The cavalry is the eyes and ears of the army."

"Those are little eyes and little ears. Come on." Mars briskly walked forward.

The regiment followed, and the tiny village was swallowed up in soldiers to the children's delight.

"Horse soldiers! Horse soldiers!" shouted the children at the maypole. They couldn't decide whether to drop their streamers and run to the soldiers or to keep singing.

Banjo was drawn to children like a fly to molasses. "How would you like to help the Confederate army?"

"Yay, yay!" they hollered in unison.

"You all finish runnin' around the maypole and sing. You'll make us right happy to see your celebration this day."

Enthusiastically the children danced, their bright ribbons behind them. One by one, the men drifted over after seeing to their horses. Soon the children were surrounded and watched by several companies of silent men. A few swallowed hard. Most of them had not seen their own children for months. The poorer men had not seen their children for over a year.

When the children finished wrapping the maypole, they crowned their queen, a blonde girl of perhaps nine. The men applauded. An awkward moment of silence occurred when the planned festivities were over. The men stared at the children, and the children stared right back at them.

Benserade spoke up. "Thank you."

"When I grow up, I'm gonna be a horse soldier just like you! I'm gonna kill hundreds of Yankees," a husky boy called out.

"I hope you never have to kill anyone," Nash replied. "That's why we're fighting this war."

The husky boy, however, nurtured fevered dreams of glory. "Oh, please don't end it yet!"

The men laughed.

Mars, having questioned a man at the dry goods store, rode into the group. The little May queen bounded toward him. "You are the first best!" Her crown wobbled on her curls.

"Why, thank you, queen."

Her adoring eyes grew larger. "You are the handsomest man in the world!"

The men howled with laughter and catcalled. Mars held up his hand. "The lady exhibits peerless judgment."

They laughed even longer.

"May I get on your horse?" she inquired.

"If you tell me your name."

"Elizabeth Pember." She curtseyed. "And what is yours, sir?"

"Mine," Mars said, grandly sweeping his cap off his head,

"is Mars Elige Vickers. Now if you hold my hand, Lieutenant Cracker will lift you up."

Banjo picked her up as if she were a treasured heirloom. Mars put her in front of him in the saddle.

"Can we charge now?"

The other children crowded around. "Let's play cavalry! Oh, please, Mr. Vickers."

"I am hopelessly outnumbered. I surrender," Mars gaily called out. "Banjo, Nash, Jimmy, hey, Sam, come on! Grab a little Confederate, and we'll show them maneuvers." He called to a few others until each of the seventeen children was sitting with a cavalryman.

They walked, trotted, and cantered. The children squealed with delight. The men showed them how to ride in a line, in twos, in fours, and what a regimental alignment was. They drew sabers and mock charged one another. Mars told Elizabeth that when in danger if you could wheel right, and he executed the maneuver, you had a chance because you could fire with your right hand. After a half hour of this, he trotted to the schoolhouse door.

Geneva rode up next to him with the husky boy.

"Jimmy, what do you think of my youngest recruit?"

"I think she proves, Colonel, that a lady can fight as effectively as a gentleman."

He kissed Elizabeth on her head. "This lady can."

Elizabeth twisted around and wrapped her arms around Mars's neck. "I love you, Mr. Mars Elige Vickers, and when I grow up, I'm going to marry you."

He kissed her in return. "Honey, you can do better than me."

MAY 8, 1862

Kate Vickers's rooms emitted a golden glow. Filled with officers bedecked in gold braid, gold epaulettes, gold sashes, red
sashes, green sashes flecked with gold, her world reeked of
riches. Here and there a Richmond lady in her finery, wearing a spot of mint green or lively peach satin, stood out like a
sugared gumdrop. Contrasted to this brilliantly dressed crowd
were the politicians, correctly dressed in evening black. They
looked like undertakers.

Henley managed to extricate himself from an inebriated
general who was decrying the fact that his wife, a simmering
volcano, at last overflowed when the price of tea hit $18 a
pound. Calico was $1.75 a yard. The general's domestic
battle occupied him more than anything in the field.

Moving quickly away from the old windbag, Henley backed
into Kate and almost knocked her down.

"We seem destined to collide," she said with good humor.

"I'm a clumsy ox." He smiled apologetically.

"You have met our esteemed Vice-President, Alexander
Stephens, I trust."

The Vice-President, a man much shorter than the titanic
Henley, nodded perfunctorily, then launched into his favorite
subject to Henley and a small group of officers whose faces
glistened with ambition and self-congratulation.

"Our President, a physically courageous man, lacks the gift
of administration." Alexander Stephens, a ruthless monolo-
gist, dropped his poison in the well. The Vice-President
implied that he himself possessed vast administrative skills.

"I cannot presume to judge a man when I lack the essential
knowledge of his task," Henley demurred.

The other men liked that reply. Stephens did not.

"Modesty may be a virtue in other times, Colonel, but in this crisis where we have lost everything gained last summer, those men who can lead must come forward." He frowned, then remembered Kate and added, "And our ladies, too. If we had a political leader to equal your social majesty, I should harbor no fear for our fledgling nation."

A dazzling smile was his reward. But before the Vice-President could continue, Henley firmly said, "We must each play our part." He glanced at the other officers. "For myself, as a soldier, I am removed from politics. I believe firmly, sir, that the military must never influence the civilian branches of government."

Vice-President Stephens sighed mockingly, "Ah, the military—every man a hero."

"You're in no danger," Henley replied. "If you'll excuse me, gentlemen."

Kate followed him. "You can't expect any assistance from him in the future."

He was grateful she liked him enough to be direct. "Mrs. Vickers, even if I had the brains to be a politician, I don't have the stomach."

"People are imperfect instruments, but they must be coordinated for the greater good, even the pompous buffoons."

"That man is not a pompous buffoon, he is a virtuoso of discontent!"

She touched his sleeve. "You're worried, Colonel Chatfield."

"The Yankees are moving toward us like a cloud of gilded locusts. I don't know how we can withstand their superior numbers or their wealth," he whispered.

"We're living inside a question mark." She smiled seraphically.

MAY 15, 1862

Lutie finished reading chapter 25 in the first book of Samuel. David takes the heroic Abigail to wife as well as Ahinoam. Michal, his other wife, was given away by Saul to another man, Phalti. The chapter ended there, so Lutie tried to remember from past readings if David had done anything about this. She could understand a man going to bed with different women, but marrying them! The feeding and care of multitudes of wives and subsequent children must have brought more worries and squabbles than happiness. She thought that monogamy was the beginning of democracy. Monogamy might go against nature, but it certainly made one's social and emotional life infinitely easier. Easier on the purse strings, too.

The news from the front was finally turning for the better. The exciting episode on everyone's lips was General J.E.B. Stuart's ride under the broadside of Federal gunboats on the York River. His cavalry was blocked by a large force of Pennsylvania cavalry on Telegraph Road between Yorktown and Williamsburg. He and his men escaped by brazenly tearing along the beach under the noses of both the army and navy.

Geneva wrote that she was on the other side of Telegraph Road and her unit had missed the fun.

General Joseph E. Johnston, in charge of all Southern troops on the peninsula, faced two-to-one odds. But he still held his ground, giving the people hope.

Henley wrote that last Thursday at Kate Vickers's soiree, the Vice-President of the Confederacy, Alexander Stephens, publicly criticized President Davis to such a degree that Henley felt compelled to defend Davis even though he himself loathed the man's policies. The Confederates had one party, namely the government. The Union had two parties, Republican and Democrat, the defunct Whigs scattering according to personal preference. Since the Confederacy lacked a party out of power, there was no effective way to channel criticism or develop alternate plans. Lutie thought in jest that she could form a ladies' party. They couldn't do any worse than the men in power.

The other concern for Henley was the state's tobacco crop. Hard currency vanished, and Virginia needed tobacco to trade with Europe.

Her evening lesson read, her mail attended to, Lutie donned her shawl to go for an evening stroll. A light cool trend followed a day of rain, and Lutie hated to be cold.

The huge weathervanes on top of the stable pointed east. Foals nuzzled their mothers' flanks, the light breeze flopped their little tails.

She wandered down to Sin-Sin's kiln. After three days of firing, Sin-Sin was ready to remove her new pots.

One of the little girls assisting Sin-Sin stumbled.

"Slue-foot!" Sin-Sin barked. "Watch yo' step!"

"Good crop?" Lutie peeked inside the long oven.

"Oncet I gets the ash off—well, mebbe." Sin-Sin never counted her chickens before they hatched.

A monumental pot, four feet high, sat on a ledge at the end of the kiln. "How are you ever going to get that monster down?"

"Braxton and Big Muler'll do it."

"I love the shape. You must have been an ancient Greek in another life."

"Well, I's an old woman in this one!"

"You'll be pleased to know that Ernie June soaked burdock roots in whiskey. She'd perish before she'd admit she was trying your cure for headache."

"Ha!" Sin-Sin clapped. "I'd soak it in hemlock fo' her."

"You two are like oil and water."

"No, us two's like right and wrong. I's right and she's wrong."

"Sin-Sin, you're incorrigible."

"Ow wee!" Sin-Sin gazed with joy at the huge pot. The glaze, a streaked blue over dragonfly green, was perfect.

The sound of running footsteps brought both women out of

the kiln. Timothy, out of breath, grabbed Lutie's hand. "Miz Lutie, Miz Lutie! Come to the big house. Di-Peachy been hurt!"

They found Di-Peachy seated at the kitchen table. Big Muler, scratches over his face, was dabbing at the corner of her mouth which was bleeding. As it was after sunset, Ernie was in her cabin.

"What did you do to her!" Lutie screamed to Big Muler.

"He didn't do anything," Di-Peachy replied. "He saved me, Miss Lutie. Don't yell at him."

Muler, mute, kept dabbing at her mouth.

"I'm sorry, Big Muler."

"Thass all right," he said in his curiously soft voice.

"You look like the dogs got at you under the porch," Sin-Sin blurted.

"Let me get some alcohol to put on your mouth, and Muler could stand some on his face, too." Lutie hurried upstairs, grabbed her medicine kit, and came back to the kitchen, where she took care of Di-Peachy and Sin-Sin doctored Big Muler. "Can you tell me what happened?"

"I was on the way back from town," Di-Peachy explained. "Reddy Neutral Taylor, in his delivery wagon, drove out of the Fitzgerald road. He stopped his wagon, then he stopped mine and wouldn't let me pass. He said ugly things to me, and I slapped him. Then he grabbed me and tried to have his way with me." She began to cry. Lutie patted her shoulder. "Big Muler was down at Rives Mill and heard me screaming. He flew out of the woods and pulled Reddy off of me . . . and then . . ."

"Is he dead?"

"Yes. Big Muler broke his neck." Di-Peachy began to sob.

"Mercy of God!" Sin-Sin knew if Big Muler was found out, he'd be killed himself.

"Did anyone see you?" Lutie asked Big Muler.

"No, ma'am."

"What did you do with the body?"

Di-Peachy regained control now. "We rolled him off the road. I told Big Muler to drag him through bramble to make it look like he was caught in his own traces. Then we drove the wagon off the road, twisted the traces, and Big Muler turned the wagon over on top of Reddy's body. We tried to make it look like an accident as best we could."

"Even if it was an accident, the constable will ride up this hill." Lutie sat down.

"Go to Richmond," Sin-Sin said. "He can come with us."

Lutie turned to Big Muler again. "We'll have to get you out of Richmond eventually, Muler. If anyone puts two and two together, you're very hard to hide."

Lutie observed Di-Peachy's mouth. "Here, hold this on. Doesn't want to stop bleeding. Do you think you can travel?"

"Yes."

"Did Reddy—force you?"

"Big Muler got there first."

"Tell me, whose idea was it to make this look like an accident?" Lutie probed. Sin-Sin grew alert.

"Mine," Di-Peachy lied.

"You showed great presence of mind."

Lutie and Sin-Sin looked at one another. Both knew in their bones that Muler was the one who had killed Alafin.

MAY 19, 1862

"They're like ants swarming up a hill." Lutie was commenting on the mob shouting and pushing outside the passport office.

"You should have seen them last week before you arrived." Kate interlocked the fingers of her right and left hands to tighten the soft ivory gloves. "Odd, Mrs. Chatfield, that so many are clamoring to escape Richmond while you and your ladies clamor to get in."

"These aren't real people, Mrs. Vickers. These are the flotsam and jetsam of the Confederacy."

Kate laughed. "Our cabinet couldn't scurry away fast enough."

"Just so."

"President Davis made Varina leave, of course, because of her delicate condition."

Lutie said, "It's bad enough to bear a child in tranquil circumstances. I'd hate to do it with bombs bursting all around me. The little thing would be blown out like a percussion cap!"

"I regret that your daughter isn't here so that we could all go to the pedigree parties before McClellan descends upon us with his hordes."

"The Lees, the Randolphs, the Harrisons, Cabells, Ritchies, Standards, and Valentines—I wouldn't miss it for the world. I haven't seen Martha Pierce Standard since I was twenty-six."

"Do you know she boasted that she had never read a book!"

"As I said, Kate, I haven't seen Martha since I was twenty-six."

"Lutie, why don't you move to Richmond? You could spend half the year here and half the year at Chatfield. You affect me like a tonic."

"Better a tonic than a purge, my dear." Lutie cherished the praise. Kate Vickers was twenty years younger than Lutie if she was being honest about her birthday, thirteen years younger if she was not. Being friends with such a young woman gave her a lift. She'd grown weary of being the august matriarch of a great estate, and if she heard one more woman her own age complain about gallstones, fallen arches, or tipped female organs, she would surely perish of tedium. "Is it true that poor Mrs. Lee is a martyr to arthritis?"

"Must be a trial for her and for him, of course. What a handsome man, and he stays quite faithful to her. Do you know that when this war started, he had more dark hair than gray?"

"Show you what worry will do to a man—or woman, for that matter."

Kate glanced over her shoulder to check on Sin-Sin and her own servant, Evangelista Settle Egypt, a fine-looking woman who spoke with a French accent and told everyone she was from Haiti, even though she was born and bred in Augusta County. "Mars says he thinks Lee might prove to be an inspired man in the field, but Johnston is thorough. Lee will never get the chance, of course. President Davis finds Lee is the only man who can talk to our conflicting and ambitious officers."

Lutie worried about Johnston's slow pullback of troops from Williamsburg, but for some unexplained reason, she wasn't panicked. She could not imagine Yankees walking down Broad Street next week. And if she couldn't imagine something, she was certain it wouldn't come to pass. "I do hope I will have the pleasure of your stupendously handsome husband's company again."

"He adored you, of course. You're his kind of woman."

"Oh? And what is his kind of woman?" Lutie preened.

"Gay, forthright, ready for anything. I would say that describes you in a nutshell."

"Which is perhaps where I belong." Lutie laughed at herself.

Kate laughed with her, then her tone changed slightly. "I'm sure you fathom that my husband and I are not quite suited for one another. Perhaps I expect too much of him. I think to myself, 'I want more.' "

"I, on the other hand, have had quite enough." Lutie also looked backward as they walked and saw Evangelista and Sin-Sin in animated discussion. "Your Evangelista's vanity would have been more fairly distributed among five or six women."

"Her self-infatuation is astonishing, isn't it?" Kate's voice registered that world-weariness tinged with pride which women reserve for luxurious troubles. "She drives me mad but what can I do without her? She is in charge of my wardrobe, she has a better sense of seating for dinners than I do, and she finds bargains."

"Sin-Sin was impressed when Evangelista guided her through your labyrinthine closets and showed her every gown for which you've marked a card stating when you wore it, where you wore it, and what shoes, hat, gloves, and parasol you wore with it. Even people's comments."

"What are they saying?"

Lutie and Kate became silent and slowed their pace to hear the chatter. Sin-Sin was ringing like the clapper in a bell.

" 'Dah,' she say she called 'Dah.' No good can come from a Gullah girl, I tells you, Evangelista. Thass when Greer Fitzgerald's troubles start, when his momma give him over to that wet nurse. One day Miz Lutie havin' a party so big it last three weeks; so big, Evangelista, that folks comes from Russia! Naturally, Jennifer Fitzgerald come with her man and her baby and that Gullah girl. A big buzzard flies over, and she carry on. She say the turkey buzzard gonna puke on her little Greer, and it be so nasty that he take sick from it. I got no time for this 'stitious foolery and I tell her that no buzzard gonna puke on Greer Fitzgerald unless she out there tryin' to steal its rotten meat. Pah!"

Evangelista nodded and then launched into her own tale, designed to represent her equal authority. She possessed an edge due to her French-accented English. "Miss Kate had a cook that was so violently stupid, she neglected to boil black-eyed peas on New Year's Day. I ordered her to do so immediately lest someone should die in our house in the New Year. She did it, of course, but the pot was not on the fire until sunup. We lost those hours! The pot should have been on at midnight of New Year's Eve."

"Thass right!" Sin-Sin agreed.

"Before four months passed, Mars's enchanting, enchanting mother died. I informed Miss Kate of how angry I was. Surely it was the cook's fault. She removed her, of course." Evangelista swelled with importance.

"No sech thing as a right-thinkin' cook. Always meddle in the 'fairs of the house."

"I'd like to put a halter on the one Miss Kate uses now. She run to the mistress every time my back is turned!"

"Thass what Ernie June do. Evangelista, I can tell you got your hands full with the cook and high-tone folk coming to this house. Uh huh!"

"I paraphrase Napoleon. Kate Vickers is Richmond and Richmond is Kate Vickers."

Lutie paused to admire a high spring garden overflowing with azalea, wisteria, rhododendron, and late blooming tulips. "I detect an affection between yourself and Evangelista. Sin-Sin is part of our family, of course. I have a friend, a woman I like very much, but she lives cheek by jowl with her servants and maintains poisonous detachment. I could never do it."

"I can be detached from my husband, but never from Evangelista, even though she is horrendously spoiled and I should thrash her for it."

"Someday we must discuss husbands, but not today. I want to collect my thoughts." Lutie put her finger to her lips.

"Is it true, Kate, that Quartermaster General Myer's wife called our Mississippi Varina Davis a squaw!"

"In front of God and everyone."

The two women allowed the deliciously awful comment to simmer and continued their majestic procession down Franklin Street. Who cares if the Yankees are at the door?

MAY 20, 1862

The tempestuous, erratic nature of May weather bedeviled Confederate and Yankee alike. One day would be cool and breezy. This would be followed by a stinker which usually gave rise to a thunderstorm of Biblical intensity. However, one or two hot days couldn't shrink the swollen creeks and swamps. The land became a large bog. Infantrymen would sink up to their ankles, and after a punishing rain, the wagons would halt, imprisoned up to their axles in mud. Artillery men, lashing their draft horses and pulling and pushing the guns themselves, suffered the most because of the weather.

The sound of rifle fire punctuated the air. Mars and his men covered the pullback of the army along the Williamsburg Road. Since the battle of Williamsburg, his regiment had kept just out of range of Federal skirmishers.

Up ahead lay the sinister waste of the Chickahominy River sandwiched on both sides by a swamp which even in stifling August heat was two feet deep. Hooking off of that like a spur was the White Oak Swamp.

Despite the extreme changeability of the weather, Mars could not believe that McClellan, with his superior forces, was allowing himself to be sucked into the Chickahominy. The intelligence received by cavalry units operating in the north of the state said that McDowell was moving out of Fredericksburg to reinforce McClellan. McClellan didn't want to fight until he had a force of seven to one. How could the man not know the Confederates would attack before those reinforcements came, no matter what the ground, no matter what the weather? He must have thought that every Southern commander was as loathe to attack as himself. If Southerners had been that cautious, they would never have seceded in the first place.

Whatever the reasons for McClellan's sloth, Mars was confident that McDowell would never make it to Richmond. Stonewall Jackson would throw up a shout and a handful of gunpowder, and McDowell would withdraw to protect Washington. Two could play the game of threatening capitals. The fact that Richmond and Washington were only an anxious 115 miles apart made this tactic easy. Mars's personal preference would have been to place the capital of the Confederacy in the geographic heart of the new nation, far enough away from Washington that the Yankees would have to march for weeks through hostile territory, risking annihilation wherever ground favored the defenders. Spiritually Richmond was the center, but Mars cared more for defenses than spirit, and right now Richmond trembled, exposed.

Geneva and Banjo rode with Mars. He enjoyed their presence, since the sight of Yankees emboldened rather than frightened them. He often wondered if cowardice was inborn. Perhaps a man should not be punished for it. Better to take a man fearful of battle and put him behind the lines where he could be useful.

A bullet smacked into a tree.

"A little closer and I'll get a shave." Banjo puffed on his cigar.

"You could use one, too." Mars glanced at Banjo's unkempt stubble.

"Those boys couldn't hit a squirrel in a year."

"You're bigger than a squirrel," Geneva said.

"Let's trot back about five hundred yards." As they withdrew, Mars shook his head. "This crawl has got to be driving some of those boys crazy. How can they stay in sight of us like this and not push forward? If they don't have a decent general, at least they've got discipline."

"Like a beautiful horse with no rider." Geneva patted Dancer's neck.

"I've been meaning to tell you, Jimmy. I received a letter

from my wife two days ago, and your mother is now in Richmond. Preparing for hospital work, I take it. I saved your brother's sash because I wanted to present it to her myself. Why don't you take it to her?"

"I could take it to her afterwards." Geneva was nervous about seeing her mother. She wondered if it was the red scar on her cheek that made her shy, or maybe it was something deeper and unexplored.

"I want the sash given her by hand from a member of this regiment." Mars was determined about this. "Banjo, you can do it."

"I've never been to Richmond, sir."

"Never been to Richmond?" Mars exploded. "You're going tonight. I'll give you precise directions so you won't get lost. Stay the day, and spend the night at my house. Kate will make room. Rejoin us tomorrow."

Banjo paused momentarily. "Are you su.e there won't be a fight? I'd rather stay if there's hope of knocking them one."

"We've got a while. Clean up, and change into your dress uniform before you get to the house."

"Company." Geneva pointed to a fine-looking man, early sixties, riding down the road to meet them.

The major general stopped in front of Mars and saluted. "Sir, that was a damned foolish thing you did, asking your division commander to arm the servants in your regiment."

"I didn't think so, General. They're men, and they want to fight."

"I don't give a good goddamn what you think now or ever, Colonel!" The general's gray beard quivered with anger. He set his jaw. "I also want to compliment you for your fine performance in the rear guard. It's the most difficult position, and you are executing flawlessly."

"Thank you, General."

He put his mustard colored gloves on the pommel of his saddle. "Another thing. If I do not survive this war, you'll more than likely be made a brigadier and asked to take command of a portion of my forces."

"I'm happy where I am, General."

"I don't care where you're happy; I care where you'll be most effective. Who doesn't want to command light cavalry, sir?"

"I think, General, you'll live forever." Mars smiled but there was no warmth in it.

"Sometimes I'm afraid I won't, and sometimes I'm afraid I will." A flash of humor illuminated the general's harsh but handsome features. "I'll relieve you of my presence in the sweet bye and bye, and I'll relieve you of it now." He saluted. Then he spoke again. "And I do wish you'd stop riding around with your tunic and shirt open like that. We are an Anglo-Saxon army, sir, not an Italian one!" He saluted again and rode off.

"Who's that old fart?" Geneva spat.

"My father."

Geneva blushed. "Colonel, I'm sorry."

Seeing her discomfort, Mars bellowed with laughter. "I don't like him either."

MAY 21, 1862

King David told his men to kill his enemies, the Jebusites, even the lame and the blind. Lutie thought he was horrid to be so cruel. Her Bible lesson nibbled on her mind throughout the morning.

Lutie, Sin-Sin, and Di-Peachy, together with Hazel Whitmore, Miranda Lawrence, Risé Rives, and Jennifer Fitzgerald, stocked and kept inventory of medical supplies. Kate Vickers worked harder than anyone would have thought possible. It was assumed that being so beautiful, she would be useless. Lutie knew better, but slowly the other ladies granted her their heartfelt respect instead of the usual polite pieties. Kate enjoyed Di-Peachy's presence, but shrank from Big Muler. She told Lutie that he made her skin crawl.

That morning Baron Schecter, impeccably attired as always, called upon Kate. While being pleasant to him, she told him she must continue working. He helped her wind bandages which set Jennifer Fitzgerald into a minor tizzy. She found Baron Schecter terribly attractive and told him he reminded her of her gorgeous Greer, fallen hero of Manassas. The baron flirted with her which made her work harder, and Lutie thought if the baron could have known the late and now sainted Greer Fitzgerald, he would shoot Jennifer on the spot.

Kate's liveried butler interrupted their work. "Miz Vickers, a lieutenant here to call upon Miz Chatfield."

"Show him in."

Banjo Cracker stepped into the foyer. Stiffly bowing, he cleared his throat. "Mrs. Vickers, I have something for Mrs. Chatfield. Is she here?"

Lutie came over, and the butler ushered them into the small, fragrant conservatory.

"Mrs. Chatfield, Colonel Vickers wanted to present this to you himself, but he can't leave right now." Banjo carefully handed her a small package.

Lutie unwrapped it. There, neatly folded with a note, was Sumner's red officer's sash. She held it up. Deep brown bloodstains were splashed over much of it. She put her head in her hands and started to cry.

Awkwardly sitting, Banjo wanted to console her. He felt ridiculous. "Ma'am, your boy was a pistol! He'd walk down the line and people felt better for lookin' at him. He stayed with his guns, and he had but three and they had six. What a man!"

Tears falling on her soft, yellow dress, she replied, "He was, wasn't he?"

"Did he tell you about the time we stole the grain?"

"No. My son stole grain?"

Banjo told her stories about Sumner and his escapades. Before long, Lutie's laughter bounced off the glass walls of the conservatory. Hearing Banjo talk of her son in such an unaffected and pungent style brought Sumner back to life for her.

After a few questions, she discovered that Banjo had never seen Richmond. "Well, you are going to see it today, if you will allow me to be your guide."

"Oh, I don't know, ma'am. I have never been in the

presence of such a fine-looking woman. I'm afraid I'll make a fool of myself. You're so far above me." He meant it, too.

Rejuvenated by his assessment of her person and his obvious love for Sumner, Lutie smiled. "Nonsense! We know one another through Jimmy's letters, and I shan't be frightened for a single moment on our crowded streets, filled with riffraff, if I have such a warrior by my side."

Kate came in with Baron Schecter. "Lutie, you look radiant."

"The lieutenant has been entertaining me with news of both my sons!" Lutie clapped her hands together.

Schecter narrowed his eyes. The man was clearly a peasant, an illiterate, ill-bred peasant. "Tell me, sir. How can your army be in retreat? If it had been up to me, I would have stayed in Williamsburg as long as there was hair on my head!"

Banjo swept off his cap and bowed to the pretentious foreigner. "Colonel, we did."

Banjo's bald head, fringed by brown hair, shone in the light. Lutie and Kate laughed until they cried. The baron tried to put a good face on it by laughing, too, but he didn't much take to being outsmarted by a rube.

The next day when Banjo rejoined his regiment, he happily told Geneva everything. He praised Lutie and said, "She's a handsome woman, a handsome woman, indeed."

Incredulous, Geneva replied, "My mother? She's as old as the hills."

MAY 29, 1862

Standing on the Chimborazo Heights, Lutie surveyed the lands to the east. Below her flickered a carpet of light, the fires of the Confederate and Union armies. As far as she could see, pinpricks of fire, blazes of life, gave evidence to the mass of humanity preparing to tear out one another's throats. She thought of those campfires as lit by Lucifer's matches.

Ascension Day, a feast she enjoyed, brought her little solace. Nor did the day's lesson, 2 Kings 2, which told of Elisha watching with satisfaction as two she-bears destroyed and devoured forty-two children who had made fun of his bald head. Peering into the night's valley, knowing what must befall it, brought dread. However, Risé, Hazel, Miranda, and Jennifer were her troops. She wasn't going to lose heart in front of them.

Kate Vickers, standing next to Di-Peachy, stared at the scene below with a shiver of anticipation.

"My husband says that geography is destiny."

"My husband," Lutie replied, "says it all comes down to firepower and food."

Risé, an incurable romantic, murmured, "The hearts of our men count for more than anything."

"Yes, as long as they continue beating," Lutie dryly replied. Risé was a good woman but she'd taken to trailing glorious clouds of chiffon recently as well as quoting liberally from the tale of Arthur and Lancelot.

"It's an unforgettable sight." Miranda spoke for them all. "When I'm a very old woman, I shall tell my grandchildren and my great-grandchildren what this looked like, how it felt, the tantalizing light wind and the violently scarlet sunset which preceded this unquiet night."

"My new friend, Lieutenant Banjo Cracker, thinks the Yankees hope to come through like birds of passage, enriching themselves in the process."

"I'm sure Lieutenant Cracker said no such thing," Jennifer sniffed.

"His exact words were, 'They're so greedy, they'd skin a maggot.' I just softened it a bit for you," Lutie replied.

"What's that?" Hazel heard a bugle.

"Tattoo. It means it's time to go to bed, and I suppose we ought to retire ourselves." Kate returned to the two open carriages. Lutie hopped in next to Kate. Di-Peachy and Hazel sat behind them. Lutie rolled the reins between her fingers, two sets on the left hand and two sets on the right. She felt the lead horse nibble on the bit, asking, What do I do now? Are you ready? She glanced over her shoulder. The four ladies in the other carriage sat across from one another, driven by Kate's liveried servant. Lutie nodded to him, and they started down the hill.

"Do you think a great battle will commence tomorrow?" Hazel called forward.

Kate turned her head. "Who knows? It's worse not knowing than knowing. If I were out there tonight, I'd pray for it to start tomorrow just to get it over with."

"I think that's why there's been such a frenzy of gaiety in the city. Everyone laughs a little harder, dances a little faster. Every moment is so precious," Hazel added.

"I've been guilty of it," Kate solemnly replied.

"Guilty? I thank God for it." Lutie asked the inside left horse to mind her pace. "When our boys have a moment behind the lines, they should be entertained. Let them forget for a night. If it makes us look silly, so be it."

"Croakers spoil the stew for everyone." Kate referred to those citizens who found everyone and everything a portent of doom. Fortunately, there weren't too many croakers left; most of them snatched their passports and fled. "Where has your husband been these last few days?"

"Henley rides between the lines and his office. The commissary is trying to provide for roughly thirty-five thousand men as well as horses. I think the strain will kill Henley before the war." Lutie frowned.

Hazel piped up. "I miss his presence. I want this battle over with, so I can visit with your husband, Lutie."

"Good. You visit with him! He needs a break from me."
Lutie smiled, and her curls bobbed in rhythm with the carriage's motion.

"Just thinking about feeding an army makes me think about Yankees." Kate's profile was brought into relief as they passed by a lit shop window. "Do they suffer a pang of conscience when they eat sugar, molasses, or rice? Have they given up smoking? They curse slave labor, yet they're quite happy to enjoy the fruits of it."

"I never thought of it that way," Hazel replied.

"Sometimes the strangest thoughts flit through my mind, quite unconnected. Other times I see pictures, or I remember places that I've visited. I often wonder if I'm sane or not." Kate bounced as the carriage wheel hit a poorly laid cobblestone.

"Everybody does the same," Lutie reassured her.

The Vickerses' imposing house came into view on the corner of Eighth and Franklin. Another bump tossed Kate onto Lutie's shoulder.

Lutie whispered in her ear, "Do we have a chance? Really, what do you think? McClellan has one hundred thousand men, and we have so few."

As Lutie reined in, Hazel and Di-Peachy leaned forward to hear every word.

Kate replied steadily, "Mars says the only battle you lose is the one you fail to fight."

MAY 31, 1862

Yesterday both armies had withstood not fire but flood. A raging thunderstorm had poured throughout the night. The dawn of the day saw leaden clouds skimming the skies and threatening more rain. The Chickahominy raged. The men joked that conditions favored ducks, but Johnston, the Confederate commander, asked for an attack.

Mars knew from attending staff meetings that yesterday was to be the day of attack. Nothing would prevent the Confederates today, if for no other reason than pent-up anxiety. Since the ground was impossible for any kind of cavalry maneuver, Mars requested permission to attend Major General Longstreet together with Brigadier General Stuart.

At 8 A.M., Longstreet received the order to move. He commanded the center of the Confederate line, right on the Williamsburg Road. He tarried until 2 P.M. waiting for General Huger's division to move up and support him in what would be a deadly frontal attack. Huger didn't appear, so Longstreet went in without him. As usual, he sent out a regiment of infantry skirmishers, followed by regular infantry. Mars, itching for action, beseeched Longstreet to let him ride forward to correctly ascertain the enemy's fortifications.

This request granted, he moved toward the cannonade. Slipping and sliding, he cursed the ground. He could see infantrymen wading midthigh in the filthy water and mud. The closer he drew to the firing, the more he felt like an inviting target, a solitary mounted man amidst the muck and mire. He got within sight of an abatis, trees felled with their branches sticking out to impede progress.

Mars asked a struggling captain, "Do you know what's ahead?"

"Our scout went out last night in the torrent. He said that one-third of a mile behind the abatis are rifle pits."

"From the sound of the artillery, I'd say they've brought up a battery in front of that," offered Mars.

"There's also supposed to be a five-sided redoubt, and that could be evil in these conditions."

"Do you believe they are behind that in force, Captain?"

"I do, and I think they have rings of redoubts on this road. It'll be one obstacle after another."

The gunfire grew fiercer. Suddenly Mars was pitched onto the ground, his horse shot from under him. The animal screamed and kicked its legs, blood gushing from four separate bullet holes.

Mars shot the suffering animal through the skull, wincing as he did so, then quickly untangled his tack and moved to the rear, as the artillery fire was becoming more accurate from both Confederate and Union batteries.

He watched the infantry move inexorably forward, as if pulled by powerful invisible strings. Men would holler and then fall onto the flooded ground, many to drown.

A major rode up to him. "Colonel, do you need a horse?"

"I've got to get back to Longstreet." As Mars spoke, a ball came close. Both men icily refused to notice when it blew earth and water in a geyser not two feet from their heads.

"Come forward, Zimmer!" the major ordered. "Give this man your horse. He needs it more than you do."

"Yes, sir."

Mars leapt into Zimmer's saddle, throwing his own tack on the animal's withers. He handed the man all the money he had in his pocket. Zimmer hesitated. "Go on, man," said Mars. "Otherwise you'll wind up in Company Q, and that's a fate worse than death."

As if to mock Mars's own words, a cannonball whistled and exploded into Zimmer. The poor youth was killed instantly, but the fact that his body had absorbed the force kept Mars and the infantry major alive.

"Good Christ!" Mars shouted, the animal rearing under him.

"Get going, Colonel. The next one might be for you." The major touched his forefinger to his hat and rode into the withering fire.

Mars returned to Longstreet without further incident, but he paced uncontrollably. A light drizzle, which lasted until just before sunset, irritated him.

By nightfall, the Confederates had driven the Federals from their entrenchment positions two miles down the Williamsburg Road. General D.H. Hill ran out of ammunition and could proceed no further.

When the Federals retreated, they left behind six cannons which they did not spike. These guns were turned upon them with murderous result. However, the Federals had their moment when General Joseph C. Johnston, severely wounded, was carried off the field.

President Jefferson Davis appointed General Robert E. Lee to take over the fallen Johnston's position as Commander of the Army of Northern Virginia.

JUNE 1, 1862

Lutie's bel canto carried over the blast of cannon, seven miles from the city. "Behold at that time I will undo all that afflict thee: and I will save her that halteth, and gather her that was driven out; and I will get them fame and praise in every land where they have been put to shame.

"At that time I will bring you again, even in the time that I gather you: for I will make you a name and a praise among all people of the earth, when I turn back your captivity before your eyes, saith the Lord."

"Amen." The ladies from Albemarle County gathered on the sweeping back porch of the Vickerses' house. Baron Schecter and Maud Windsor were there also.

"I never knew cannon could fire for such an extended period of time." Hazel Whitmore squeezed a lace handkerchief in her hands.

"They can go for days, red-hot," Kate replied. "But the firing is desultory. Listen to it."

"I thought we won yesterday," Rise said.

"Apparently we have to win today." Miranda Lawrence wondered how men endured the shelling.

"And tomorrow and the day after that." Lutie closed her Bible.

"I thought it would be over by now." Jennifer rose.

"The battle or the war?" Kate asked her.

"Both, I suppose."

"It's getting dark. Surely they'll stop." Miranda walked the length of the well-built porch.

"I saw night cannonades when we lived in Europe," Kate informed the others. "The balls have a luminous flight. If it's a heavy dose of shot, the entire sky lights up—oddly terrifying and beautiful."

"How does anyone stand it?" Hazel's nerves were frayed.

"Our boys are made of grit and sand," Lutie said.

There was a commotion at the front door. Henley, covered from head to toe with filth, walked onto the porch. "Good evening, ladies."

"Henley!" Lutie embraced him and became muddy herself.

"Can you ladies be ready to receive wounded late this evening?"

"Of course we can." Kate spoke for all of them.

"The hospitals can't take them all, and we were able to evacuate precious few yesterday." Henley looked tired.

"What are you saying?" Lutie's voice was steady.

"I'm saying we've lost one-third of our army; God knows how many they've lost."

"My God!" Hazel couldn't quite believe it.

"So far, we've counted sixty-one officers dead and two hundred and nine officers wounded. Richmond will be remembered as the slaughterhouse of heroes."

"Henley, won't you sit down and take refreshments? You need some sustenance." Kate soothed him.

Just then Sin-Sin sailed into the room. She saw Henley and shrieked. He turned to her, smiling. "It's all right, Sin-Sin. I'm dirty, but I've got daylight in me."

"Have you seen my husband?" Maud Windsor's eyes registered fear.

"Yes. He's with Surgeon-in-Chief Cullen. They'll probably get into the city tomorrow morning unless the Yankees put up another fight."

"Did we win?" Lutie was still reeling from Henley's assessment of dead and wounded.

"Yes, but at a dear price. I've been asked by General Cullen to beseech shop owners along Broad Street to receive wounded in whatever space they have available. Northrupp figured we should keep a large measure of supplies here should the Federals begin a siege. This will make it easier to care for the wounded once we get them here."

"How bad is it? Out there, I mean." Hazel's chin trembled.

"Be glad you are here, Mrs. Whitmore. Even here, you'll see enough horror." His fierce eyes fell on the resplendent

Schecter. "I thought, Baron, that your government sent you here to observe our military operations, not our ladies."

Incensed, Schecter said in clipped tones, "His Imperial Majesty did not instruct me to go on the field of battle."

"Perhaps he did not, sir, but I should think that honor would have compelled you forward."

Schecter stepped up to him and slapped him across the face with his snow-white gloves. "I demand satisfaction, sir!"

Kate, livid, pushed between them. She turned her wrath on the handsome Schecter. "Baron, this is unforgivable! Consider the circumstances of Colonel Chatfield's visit and his last two days. A displacement of decorum is not without understanding!"

Empurpled with rage, Schecter spit. "Decorum? This gentleman, madam, has taken it upon himself to belittle me at every possible opportunity."

"Perhaps you deserved it!" Kate let him have it.

Alternating between rage and terror that he had precipitously fallen out of favor with Kate, he stammered, "Do you think I fear battle? I, who have the scars to prove otherwise?"

"I think, Baron, that our current war is rather different from those dressed-up affairs you participated in on your empire's borders."

A pin could drop, the assembled ladies were so still.

Schecter bowed low before Kate. "Then I shall join General Hill's staff immediately. I may be many things, Mrs. Vickers, but I do not think a coward is one of them." He spun on his heel to glare at Henley. "I will have satisfaction, sir, when time permits."

"Indeed, you shall! Pistols or saber?" Henley couldn't handle a saber to save his life.

"In view of your years, Colonel, pistol seems only fair." Schecter bowed to him and stormed out.

Lutie grabbed Henley's hand. "Honey, he'll settle his tail feathers. You can approach him then."

"Approach him?" Henley roared. "I'm going to give him the third eye of prophecy! Isn't that what your mother used to call that dot she put between her eyes?"

Kate stood behind Lutie. "Baron Schecter's vanity is offensive in the extreme, but in time I'm sure he will withdraw his outrageous request for a duel."

"He might, but I won't. Now, I must be getting on."

Discreetly the other ladies withdrew from the porch.

Lutie asked, "Did you see Geneva?"

"No, but she's safe. The cavalry couldn't operate because the ground was an evil bog." He sat, suddenly exhausted, on a painted wooden bench. "Lutie, after what I've seen yesterday and today, I know our son died a hero. Anyone who stands his ground in that hailstorm of killing fire is a hero. We spawned two warriors." A weary smile played on his lips.

"Three."

"What?"

"You, darling. You faced the test unafraid."

"I faced the test, but I prayed. I was afraid, and I was relatively safe."

"But you did your duty." Lutie held his hand.

"I am a Chatfield."

"And so am I."

"Four warriors then." Henley put his arm around his wife, who was now half as muddy as himself.

Kate returned to the porch, the light fading. "Everything is prepared for you, Colonel." Lutie and Kate walked Henley to his horse.

"That's not my horse." Henley was surprised.

"I asked my stable boy to give you one of our horses. We'll take care of yours. I don't think the poor animal could have taken another step." Behind him, clattering over the cobblestones were wagons, carriages, and buckboards.

"Where everybody goin'?" Sin-Sin watched the procession.

"Mr. Henley!" Di-Peachy raced out of the house.

"How are you, my girl?" Henley embraced her, covering her with filth.

"I didn't know you were here. I was in the back winding bandages. Otherwise I would have come immediately. Are you all right? Should we go out to the battlefield to retrieve the wounded?" One question spilled into another, Di-Peachy was speaking so fast.

"No, don't. Ambulances are overturning in the mud. The roads are a mess once you get out of the city. You'll do more good for more people if you stay at your post and let the wounded come to you. Colonel Windsor knows you are here, and he may have already sent back wounded to you. You might get some Yankees, too."

"Can't they take their own wounded?" Lutie asked.

"Not all of them. The ones most seriously injured stay
with us. I believe Lee will work out an exchange of prisoners
over this. I hope so anyway. Thank you again, Mrs. Vickers.
Good-bye, Lutie." He moved off through the din and
confusion.

Despite darkness, Geneva, Nash, Banjo, and seventeen
men from the regiment picked their way through the fields
riding in an arc from Williamsburg Road to Charles City
Road. Mars knew the back roads and footpaths. The Federals
stopped, moving neither forward nor backward. A series of
landings on the James River provided them with a way out if
they decided to leave. No one knew what would happen
next. If McClellan dumped his army in the lap of the navy,
sailing them back to Washington, D.C., it would be the end
of his career and the end of the war in this part of the country
for at least a year. Even with horrendous losses, McClellan
still fielded more men than the Confederacy.

The horses slipped on the soggy ground. The meadows,
woods, and swamps choked with the dead. Men carrying
torches looked like huge fireflies as they walked over the
ground, trying to recover the wounded.

Geneva shuddered at the cries of the suffering. Battle she
could take, but it was torture to hear those screams. Every
now and then the horror would be punctuated by a single
shot. She didn't know if the search officer compassionately
put a hopeless sufferer out of his misery or if he shot a thief.
Molesters of the dead scurried among the bodies, vultures of
the battlefield. Catholic sisters also walked among the fallen,
sometimes bending to give succor, other times making the
sign of the cross. Private citizens from Richmond, the fearless
ones, also helped the wounded, giving them food and water.
The human vultures, upon seeing a sister or a ministering
citizen, would crouch and slink away.

Some of the wounded lost their minds. "A ring-tailed ferret, a ring-tailed ferret!" one insane man shouted over and
over. Other times Geneva could make out a part of the Lord's
Prayer whispered through cracked and bloody lips.

What frightened her, too, was the sorting system the sur-
geons used for determining who to help. Those who were
certain to survive despite current pain were laid to one side to
wait; those who were likely to die no matter what was done

were laid aside to be helped last. But the men whose lives hung in the balance were slapped on the operating tables first. She wondered if she were badly hit would she have the presence of mind to know what group she'd fall into. She could still feel the surgeon's needle digging in her cheek as he sewed up her face in April. That seemed like a year ago although the bright scar testified that only weeks had passed.

Her horse snorted and danced sideways. He hated stepping on dead humans.

Geneva looked down. "Can't tell if that's one of theirs or ours, he's so caked with mud."

"I hate the way they stare at you with their eyes wide open. My hair stands up on the back of my neck. I think those glassy eyes reproach me for living," Nash quietly said.

"Poor devil, whoever he is. He got his quietus." Banjo placed his hand on his horse's hindquarters and twisted around to see Nash.

The jingle of sabers and spurs was interrupted only by the pop, pop of pistol fire at disjointed intervals.

"Jesus, save me!" a voice called far from the road.

A torchbearer moved closer to the line. "Hear that one?"

Banjo pointed toward bramble. "There, I think. Night plays tricks on the ears."

"Thanks, Lieutenant." The torchbearer, his face shining in the light, walked into the field. Two other men carrying a blanket to use as a stretcher followed him.

As they approached Charles City Road with no sign of the enemy, Captain Sam Wells halted the squadron.

"What in God's name is that?" Nash exclaimed.

They sat silently and listened to wheels creaking, animals straining to negotiate the terrible roads, and voices, far enough off to be a low stream of sound. Dots of light stretched down the road as far as they could see.

Banjo was the first to figure it out. "It's the people."

"Can't be. Nobody in their right mind would come out in this quagmire." Nash shook his head.

Sam rode forward. Within fifteen minutes he returned. "Nine Mile Road, Williamsburg Road, and this one, too, are full of people with whatever vehicles they have, coming to claim the wounded and bring them to safety. Fellow I spoke to said that even the gambling parlors, gin mills, and whorehouses are closed down in Screamersville. They're out here, too." He paused for the weight of his words to have their effect. "Let's go, boys."

Banjo said in a low voice, "Bless them."

Nash found himself profoundly affected. "Any nation that can produce such people is worth dying for."

"Or living for," Geneva quickly added. She hated it when he spoke of dying. He wasn't going to die. No one was going to die. When she found her own thoughts becoming morbid, she'd say to herself, Try not to think about it. God took Sumner. That's sacrifice enough.

JUNE 2, 1862

At four-thirty in the morning twenty wounded men, most of them from the Twelfth Alabama, arrived at Kate Vickers's house. The eight women, including Sin-Sin and Di-Peachy, began washing the mud out of their hair and beards, then stripped them and washed their bodies as well. A few weakly protested, but given the circumstances, no one could afford to be modest. Evangelista Settle Egypt refused to touch the "filthy things" as she called them, but she braced herself for duty in the kitchen, a vile step downward.

A few of the men were in terrible pain, and the women had no morphine. Kate quickly dispatched her stable boy to Phoebe Yates Pember at Hospital No. 2 of the Chimborazo Hospital for morphine. The Chimborazo was equipped for forty-six hundred patients, but within hours that number was doubled, and the hospital was running out of all supplies. Lutie, encountering shortages before, told Kate to give brandy to the ones in pain. It would have to do.

One poor devil had part of his face shot away. His right eye was exposed, much of the cheek was gone revealing a smashed cheekbone, and his nose was ripped off his face. His lips were torn and part of his teeth were smashed. He had no other wounds. If they could keep his facial injuries from festering, he might have a chance. The sight of him was so repulsive that Lutie, after cleaning him, covered his lower face with a large handkerchief.

He motioned for a pen and paper, then wrote: Brittle Smith, Twelfth Alabama. Next of kin is Margarite Hawsley Smith, Mobile. I know I look hideous. Thank you for taking care of me.

Lutie kissed his good cheek, which made him cry, and she forced him to lie down. She lifted the handkerchief, already bloodied, and poured a shot of brandy down his throat, chasing it with cool water. He thanked her by sign, and she moved to the man next to him. He was dead. Without calling attention to it, she motioned for Big Muler to carry the body outside. Several days ago Lutie had taken Muler to the outskirts of Richmond, given him money and papers, and told him to go. He had reappeared at the Vickerses' that same night. He wouldn't leave Di-Peachy. Furious as Lutie had been then, she was glad to have him now.

By six-thirty in the morning, every man was clean and as comfortable as possible. Another wagon pulled up in front of the house. Kate walked outside hoping Colonel Windsor would be there. Instead she found another wagonload of wounded. "Sir, we have our share," she said to the fatigued driver.

"Everyone's doubling up, ma'am. We got tobacco warehouses full of men."

"Of course. We'll make do," she said. The driver and his assistant, wobbly with exhaustion, began to carry in the wounded.

"Big Muler! Hurry and help these men," Lutie called.

Hazel Whitmore, hand on her bosom, watched. She had the sinking sensation that Charlottesville had been only a rehearsal.

Kate fed the driver and his helper and gave them food for they were returning immediately to the field hospital. Thomas Freeman was his name; he had a cobbler's shop on Market Street on Spring Hill. Said he'd started out last night at sunset.

At nine in the morning, the day warming considerably, the women heard the muffled drums of a funeral procession.

"I wish they'd stop," Risé complained between clenched teeth. "How can we keep up morale with that?"

Another wagon came to the door. "Dear God in heaven," Miranda whispered. Most of the men in the wagon looked dead. As they were unloaded, a few were discovered to have died during the jolting, punishing journey.

Kate turned to Lutie. "We have no more beds, bunks, or mattresses of any sort."

"No blankets neither," Sin-Sin added.

"We can take the cushions off the church pews." Lutie was forceful.

Kate spun on her heel. "Let's go!" A light cart was hurriedly hitched, and Lutie drove around the block to the austere and socially correct St. Paul's.

Kate knocked on the sexton's door. A haggard gnome of a man answered. He'd been up all night, too. "Mrs. Vickers, enchanting even in the face of misfortune."

"Mr. Gibson, we are here to relieve you of the pew cushions." His face registered horror. "We're out of beds, bunks, mattresses, even blankets. If you can give us old vestments, old anything, we'll take it."

"But I must ask permission of Father—"

"There isn't time to worry about him. Help us, Mr. Gibson."

"Father John will be most upset."

"For the love of God, Mr. Gibson, men are dying!" Lutie exploded.

"Yes, yes, I take your point." The sexton hurried into the church to gather what the women needed, thinking he'd rather face the Yankees than Lutie.

The two-wheeled cart brimmed with long pew cushions, old vestments, and sheets, as Lutie and Kate spun around Grace Street to head down Eighth. As they passed the Catholic church on the corner, a group of ladies known to Kate flagged them down. She explained what she had done, for they too were desperate for supplies.

As Lutie clucked to the horse, one lady, Deborah Castle, said a trifle loudly, "Well, if the Episcopalians can do it, we can do it better!" Within seconds the good ladies were ransacking their church.

"Better, my foot!" growled Lutie.

JUNE 3, 1862

The Yankees fell back on the roads like sand sliding through an hourglass. Neither army moved toward the other, but McClellan did not evacuate. Reports were that he was digging in and would attempt to capture Richmond sooner or later. Lee, quiet and thoughtful, seemingly everywhere on his horse, was scorned by many of Richmond's armchair generals and intellectuals before he took over for Johnston.

Criticism was a Richmond vice practiced from its first discovery. A Captain Christopher Newport in 1607, finding the rapids of the James River where Richmond now stands, also found himself in an argument with Powhatan, son of the chief, who was not thrilled at the sight of Englishmen. A few men in Newport's party also offered abundant criticism of their captain and the site at the rapids because they thought they were going to find the South Seas or, at the very least, El Dorado, the city of gold. Continuing Richmond's ancient tradition of finding fault and proclaiming so loudly, people moaned that Robert E. Lee, a handsome and genial man, was good for engineering and little else. Behind his back they called him the King of Spades.

Between the muffled drum rolls, the cursed "Death March," and the mournful clatter of wagons still bringing in wounded, Lutie caught snippets of the criticism. She had to laugh. How did she know if it was true or not? She wasn't on the field with a rifle. But she did know that if God had perfected the human being, he would have left out the tongue. Wide awake, Lutie stared into the night. What time was it? She tiptoed across the richly inlaid floors. Two-thirty in the morning. She'd fallen asleep sitting next to Brittle Smith.

As her eyes adjusted to the darkness, she saw that every

lady there was asleep in a chair. Even though Evangelista, bitching at high pitch, kept the food coming, the women's energy had flagged.

Time folded like a spyglass collapsing in on itself. So much frenzied activity and emotional drama in such a short sleepless span gave events a hallucinatory aspect. She padded upstairs and washed herself in the large basin in her room. She changed her bloodstained dress for a clean, navy blue cotton one. Perhaps the blood wouldn't show so much. She thought it must upset the men to see the women splashed with red. She returned to Brittle Smith and felt his forehead. It was cool. She checked his pulse. He was dead. Poor fellow, she thought, perhaps he's better off.

A low moaning caused Sin-Sin to stir. She sat between a Yankee from the One Hundred Third Pennsylvania and a strapping Southerner from the Palmetto Sharpshooters. The two, when put beside one another, gave no indication of a cheerful convalescence as they continued the war verbally. Hazel mediated, questioning each man in turn about his home, until she plucked the common thread which would allow them to get along: Each man kept bees. They babbled about clover versus blooming trees and how to keep the black snakes out of the hives. Later, when Hazel returned, the South Carolinian remarked, "He's a fine fellow for a Yank!" These compliments, with disclaimer, were returned by the Pennsylvanian.

"Am I gonna die?" the South Carolinian asked, fright clinging to each word.

Sin-Sin, roused, whispered, "Shh, you ain't gwine to die. Auntie Sin-Sin be right here. She shoo away Old Satan who wear a big shoe. No one comin' for you."

Lutie gave Sin-Sin a cup of hot coffee. The two sat next to one another and kept an eye on the South Carolina man. "I makes pots," said Sin-Sin to him. "You have anyone on yo' place makes pots?"

He shook his head no. His mind wandered, and he became more frightened. Sin-Sin gently spoke to him, hoping he'd get a grip on himself. "When I was a sprig, Mammy Rachel ran the show."

"Mammy Rachel," Lutie murmured, remembering that ancient departed major domo. Memory is the true function of age, she thought.

"Mammy was the head womans of the dyein' room. Nothin' that woman didn't know 'bout dyein'."

"I'm not going to die, am I, Auntie?" He clutched her hand.

"No. Thass why I tellin' you 'bout the only dyein' gonna happen. Mammy Rachel knew every kind of root, bark, leaf, and berry that made red, blue, green, whatever color she wanted. She'd set the dye pots over coals, fill 'em with water, and then she put in her potions—roots, bark, her secrets. Then she boil the juice out, and then she strain it and put in salt and vinegar to set the color. After the wool and cotton carded and spun to thread, Mammy take 'em hanks and drap 'em in the boilin' pot. She stir 'em up and lift 'em out, and she hang 'em up on the line to dry. Every color of the rainbow. Then when they dry, she take 'em in to the weavin' room where more magic happen. Thass how I come to pots. I love Mammy Rachel's colors, and I want to make colors on somethin' that last longer than clothes."

"He's asleep." Lutie squeezed Sin-Sin's shoulder.

"Must mean I doan tell a good story."

"Let's walk down to the capitol. The smell gets fierce in here."

"Put on yo' shawl."

"Don't tell me what to do, Sin-Sin. I hate it when you tell me what to do." She threw on her shawl.

The light flickered in the street lamps. They heard the roll of wagons a few streets over. Soon they stood in front of the Virginia state house, a Greek revival building drawn up by a young Thomas Jefferson.

"I wonder if he knew when he was young how great he was?" Lutie stared up at the Ionic columns.

"Mebbe when God give you a great gift he protects you from knowin' 'bout it. Otherwise you get lonesome. There be no one to talk to."

Lutie put her arm around Sin-Sin's waist. How easy it was for Lutie to forget just how deep Sin-Sin's mind was. She wondered how many white people had stopped to listen to what was actually being said by their servants but then she wondered how many people, white or black, have frank communication with one another. "I wish Colonel Windsor would come. I don't know how much longer we can hang on without him."

"We jes do what we have to do."

"Did you know that the hotels sent out their biggest carriages to gather the wounded? The Broad Street Hotel, the Powhatan, the American, all of them. Bet the interiors are ruined. But who cares anymore? If a sick boy can lie down and feel a little comfort under his bones, so what if he bleeds on the rug."

"Well, it's not yo' rug." Sin-Sin smiled.

"Why do I talk to you?"

" 'Cause we friends of the heart."

JUNE 5, 1862

Rain slashed at the windowpanes. It was ten-thirty in the morning, and still no medical officer had called at the Vickerses' house. A big, handsome man, Joseph Rutledge from the Sixth South Carolina was hemorrhaging badly. When brought in from the battlefield, he had a hole in his bicep the size of a cherry tomato. Two hours ago the artery burst—why, nobody knew—but they had to stop the bleeding or he'd die. The women pressed on the exposed artery to cut off the blood. Every twenty minutes they changed places because they'd lose strength after that. His lower arm, not having received blood for those two hours, was cold. Essentially that lower arm was dead. It would have to come off, and if a surgeon didn't get to the house within the next twelve hours, the lower arm would begin to putrify. Jennifer, on duty with Rutledge now, fingers deep in the wound, was keeping up a cheerful round of stories. Clear and composed, Joseph betrayed no sign of panic.

Lutie and Kate retired to the kitchen.

"This is nigger work, Miss Kate, and I am no nigger," announced Evangelista. "I am a quadroon born on the island of Haiti!"

"Whatever you are, Evangelista, if you don't pull your weight, you're going to be black and blue."

Sin-Sin pushed through the door for a pot of boiling water.

"Where are you going with that?" Evangelista demanded.

"We got a situation!" Sin-Sin snatched hotpads and picked up the pot. In so doing, she pushed a dishrag on the floor. Seeing it, Sin-Sin said, "Somebody coming who be hungry."

"That's one superstition bound to come true," Lutie said.

Evangelista stomped on the dishrag. "I refuse to continue in this degrading work!"

"Fine. How would you like to take out the bedpans?" Color rose in Kate's cheeks.

Sin-Sin reentered the kitchen and put the pot of water on the stove. "You gonna wear yourself out with this grexin' and groanin'. You sure can tote yourself, girl!"

"How could you understand, Sin-Sin?" Evangelista tossed her head. "You were born to this."

"Horse shit!"

"Evangelista, you do not possess a useful temperament, and I haven't the time to fool with you. Stay in this kitchen, or I'll beat you within an inch of your life, so help me," Kate snarled.

Evangelista, sullen, chewed her lip.

"Miss Kate!" Di-Peachy shot through the door. "Colonel Windsor is here with another gentleman." Lutie hurried out the door with Kate on her heels.

Sin-Sin and Evangelista eyed one another.

"You got the big head talkin' to the missus that way. But I know you too refined for this grubbin'." Sin-Sin honeyed her.

Her high opinion of herself confirmed, Evangelista renewed her rapport with Sin-Sin. "I know you have to take up for them when they're in the room."

"Uh huh. Naught is naught and figger is figger, all for the white man and none for the nigger."

"I'm a quadroon." Evangelista turned up her nose.

"Jes a figure of speech. Can't expect the white ladies to understand yo' position. They used to rough-hewn women such as myself." Sin-Sin's eyes gleamed. "Why doan I takes yo' kitchen duty for the next few days? I can still tend to my mens if I has authority over the other servants 'round here."

"Well . . ."

"Like I said, you too refined and delicate for this work." Evangelista puffed up as Sin-Sin continued to talk. "The other girls is jealous! I seen it in their eyes and the way they moves about. Jealous 'cause you be a quadroon. Jealous 'cause you speak pretty. Jealous 'cause you good-lookin'. Why, honey, that po' girl, Dinah, they have to put a sack over her head for her to catch a man." Evangelista beamed with pleasure. "And you closest to Miz Kate. You got the power. That be the hardest rock to carry."

"Don't I know it." Evangelista sighed the sigh of the powerful, temporarily weary of her burden.

"Iffin' I takes yo' place in the kitchen, you can be more useful elsewhere. You got to keep yo' nose close to the others. No tellin' what trickeration they up to, times being what they are."

"I'll speak to Miss Kate this minute."

"Jes one little thing. You know them dresses Miz Kate give you?"

"She never keeps a dress for more than a year." Evangelista inherited Kate's giveaways.

"I like you to give me one."

"Sin-Sin, excuse me for saying so, but I believe your figure is a trifle fuller than Miss Kate's."

"Oh, I knows that. I wants to give it to Di-Peachy for a present."

Evangelista wrestled. She desperately wanted out of the kitchen, but Di-Peachy was beautiful and Kate already showed too much favor toward the girl. After a few minutes' struggle, she said, "All right."

As Evangelista left in search of Kate, Sin-Sin laughed to herself how Evangelista was so easily weaseled out of her place. It had not occurred to Evangelista that Sin-Sin would now be giving the orders in this house.

Joseph Rutledge was being operated on in the back room off the large supply room. His arm hung over the edge of a tub, the fingers curled upward.

Major Bullette, the assistant surgeon, silently observed Lutie and Kate. They performed well but he thought these high-born women would get tired of the daily drudgery of nursing soon enough. Their life of opulence and luxury did not equip them for hard labor. Once these two women grew tired of being useful the others would follow like glamorous sheep. He sighed as the rain came down in sheets accentuating the misery of the suffering men.

Colonel Windsor and Major Bullette operated the entire afternoon. Gangrene nibbled at some of the wounds. The doctors cleaned them with nitric acid, an excruciatingly painful process.

A tray full of bullets taken from the men rested on a table. Another bullet hit the porcelain tray with a clatter, rolling to the center with the others.

"Using soft lead," Jeffrey grunted.

The bullets were bent, twisted, and in some cases split. He didn't remember many being like this at Manassas or at Charlottesville. The base of the bullets had three concentric rings, clearly marking them as Yankee. When a bullet was extracted with two rings, the doctor knew the South had shot one of its own. The wounded soldier was never told the truth.

Big Muler carried in George Dawson, Lynchburg Artillery. A bullet had entered through the upper left portion of his back and was lodged somewhere within.

Major Bullette held a rag with chloroform over Dawson's mouth. Lutie was grateful that they had anesthesia. Layer by layer, Jeffrey's scalpel carefully followed the progress of the bullet.

"Colonel," Lutie said, holding Dawson's wrist, "we've lost him."

"Goddammit!" Jeffrey threw his scalpel in the pan. "I beg your pardon, ladies."

"No apology necessary, Jeffrey." Kate addressed him in the terms of their long-standing friendship.

"I thought we could pull him through." He wiped his face. "Maybe I should have cut in faster instead of trying to make such a neat job of it. Gone in and gone out."

"You did everything you could," the major consoled him. "He couldn't take the shock. Many can't."

"I hate losing a man on the table. You think I'd get used to it. I just hate it." His jaw clenched.

Lutie skirted a pile of bloody bandages and motioned for Big Muler to remove Dawson's body. Whoever died in the night was covered and laid in the small stable behind the house. The dead carts would come once a day to pick up the bodies and body parts. No matter how hard they worked, and the city praised their organization and efforts, the stench became appalling. To make matters worse, flies were everywhere.

Jeffrey gulped a hot cup of coffee brought by Di-Peachy. Bullette requested tea.

Patting his lips with a small handkerchief, Jeffrey warmly said to Lutie, "Seems to rain whenever you and I have our work to do, doesn't it, Mrs. Chatfield?"

"Let the weather do its worst, Colonel. We'll brave it."

Di-Peachy brought in a camphor bottle to disguise the smell. Kate told her to take it and open it in the hallway. Perhaps it would freshen the rest of the house. This room was hopeless.

"I say, Mrs. Chatfield, are you kin to the horse Chatfields?"

"She *is* Chatfield, Major." Jeffrey smiled at Lutie. "I'm sure you miss your beautiful estate, but God bless you for coming here."

"I'm a soldier in the shadow army of the Confederacy." Lutie quietly smiled back at him. "But I don't have the sash of an officer. I get to tie an apron around my waist instead."

"Shadow army?" Bullette asked.

"I think of the women of Virginia as a shadow army. You have your duties, and we have ours."

Kate smiled in agreement. "Are we ready? We've got three left."

"Let's get on with it." Jeffrey cracked his knuckles.

JUNE 6, 1862

The two synagogues closest to the capital formed a Hebrew Military Aid Society. Kate almost cried for joy when she opened her front door early in the morning to behold two ladies carrying bedding, bandages, and a crate of medicines.

"We hope this will be of help, Mrs. Vickers," a good-looking woman of about thirty said.

"Won't you come in, Mrs. . . ."

"Mrs. Reisman, and may I introduce my dear friend, Miss Roth."

"I am very pleased to meet you both. Please come in."

The moans in the background were not inviting. "Thank you, but we must complete our rounds." The women returned to their huge supply wagon.

Lutie joined Kate on the front step. She waved to the women driving off. "The smell is strong this morning."

"I feel like I'm living in the charnel house of the nineteenth century."

"We are." Lutie lightly touched Kate's elbow. "Jennifer Fitzgerald is sick. I put her to bed, so now we're short a pair of hands. Everyone's ready to drop as it is. Can you think of anyone we can petition to help us?"

"What about Miriam Gallard?"

"She is rather an elderly blossom."

"Perhaps you're right. Surely, Kate, there must be someone."

A milk wagon pulled up across the street. Kate crossed her arms against the doorway. "Actually, I do know who might help us. Bebe Austin and her girls."

"That's cutting cards with the devil."

"I think it only fair that I ask the other ladies."

Kate explained to Hazel, Risé, and Miranda the nature of

Bebe Austin's business. Maud already knew Bebe ran a house of ill repute. This was met with stony silence.

"Some people already think that nursing is not proper for a lady." Risé spoke first. "I hear that in the Delta, they won't even let a lady near a hospital."

"Are we willing to work side by side with these women or not?" Hazel had neither the patience nor the humor today for a long ramble.

Maud Windsor said, "If it's our reputation or a man's life, then I vote for life."

Put that way, no one could disagree.

"I'll go then." Kate dreaded being a supplicant before such a woman, but it was her idea in the first place.

"Wait, I'll go with you." Lutie was already half out the door.

The huge, oiled walnut door with a shiny brass knocker glistened on Grace Street. Taking a deep breath, Kate cracked the knocker against the brass plate underneath.

An overdressed servant opened the door. His eyes bugged out of his head. Everyone in Richmond knew who Kate Vickers was.

"My card. May I please see Miss Austin?"

Bowing low, he replied, "Won't you ladies please have a seat in the waiting room?"

"Wait a moment," Lutie called. "My card, too."

As the butler retreated at a fast clip, Kate whispered, "You needn't have done that."

"She can have proof positive that I was here, too, and I don't give a fig whom she shows it to!"

A flustered Bebe Austin slowly walked down the hall, trying to compose herself. She could converse with cabinet members, senators, and generals, but a lady of quality was a horse of a different color. Nor was this a chance encounter where the lady did not immediately know Bebe's identity and profession. Bebe nervously appraised herself in the ornate, oblong mirror in the hall. Her fancy dress was the calling card of a courtesan. In vain she tore off some of her jewelry. Why could she never master the art of the exact right combination? Bebe knew she loaded herself with too much jewelry, too many petticoats, and indiscreet colors. She couldn't seem to help herself. If she didn't have "papers," by hell, she had money. Right now, she was acutely embarrassed by her twenty-carat sapphire necklace. The huge center stone was flanked by diamonds in a lacy pattern that drooped clear down into her cleavage. She silently motioned for the butler to bring her a glass of ice water. She drank a sip, put a dab on her wrists and her forehead, then walked into the room. "Misses Vickers and Chatfield, I am speechless at this honor. What may I do for you?"

"Miss Austin, we are here to ask you if you will help us. We cannot properly care for the wounded in my house. One of our number has taken sick, and the house already has thirty-five men in it." Kate was polite.

"Thirty-four," Lutie corrected.

"Who?"

"Private Theodore Ingram, early this morning."

"As you can gather, we are desperate."

Bebe was stunned. "Do the other ladies know who I am?"

"Yes. We voted that you be invited to help us, help our men."

"How many of us might you need?"

"We'll take you all, Miss Austin. We can train your girls, and within the week I will ask other ladies in our predicament if they could use assistants. I will, of course, tell them the source. But I will ask you not to inform the wounded."

"I understand completely." Bebe's sapphire rose and fell with her breathing. "I may be a whore, but I am a patriot!"

"Which is why I came." Kate smiled.

JUNE 7, 1862

Rains washed away the flimsy covering of earth over the trenches of the dead. Henley, gagging, refused to vomit. Good sense told him not to look but the fascination of horror on such a grand scale kept his eyes riveted on the rows of bodies, partially or fully exposed, bloated and stinking. Mud filled their eyes, their opened mouths, and the holes in their bodies where steel ripped them open like rag dolls.

Philosophy, he suspected, was a weakling's vice, but recently Henley found himself questioning everything he believed in. The only rock which withstood his tidal wave of doubt was Jesus Christ. He did not think that Jesus failed, but rather that man failed. A message of love and brotherhood looked simple enough when read in Matthew, Mark, Luke, or John but here on this soggy earth, it was proving nigh to impossible.

Witnessing the rotting corpses did not make him a better Christian. He loved his enemy less than ever. What man could look upon such a sight and not hate the perpetrators of the loathsome deed? The army of the North was a ruthless invader sent by Lincoln and his vulgar henchmen. Hundreds of thousands would suffer. A pang of fear shot through his side. He knew the figures as well as any cabinet member. The South had one million men between the ages of eighteen and forty-five. The North had many more. Would this be the first war in which millions died? A million dead men. Henley, paralyzed with the thought of a crisis so huge he could not grasp it, put pressure on his horse's flanks and cantered. Even cantering, he could not escape the mass graves.

They mocked him, those dead. They stretched out their arms, pointing to heaven in supplication. Were those pieces of rancid meat now with God? Were the twelve thousand Federals who fell at Fair Oaks now in hell? Many of those men were Episcopalians, the same as Henley. Did they not pray to the same God? Men on opposite sides of the war claimed to be good Episcopalians and Christian soldiers.

"I have lived a life of ease," Henley thought to himself. "Does God mock me now?" He passed the last of the graves. "I am fifty-two years old, and I don't know much at all. But I know I'm right about this war. Did I subjugate the North? Did I try to take away their liberties? Did I meddle in their means of livelihood and saddle them with tariffs and embargoes? I only asked to be left alone with the sin of slavery on my own shoulders! To go to housekeeping on my own hook."

These questions haunted him. Yesterday he told Lutie that he was going to find Geneva. There were things he had to tell her. An undeniable force propelled him forward; the same force that directed him to prepare the manumission papers for this Christmas.

Finding his daughter proved difficult, for a cavalry stays in the saddle, fluid and swift. He finally located her riding within sight of the Federal army. Henley marveled at her coolness in the face of the enemy.

"Daddy!" She rode toward him. "What are you doing this far forward?"

"I've come to get you. You're coming with me to Richmond tonight."

"I won't leave my regiment."

"I'm not asking you to leave your regiment. I'm asking you to return with me to Richmond. You can come back here tomorrow. I want you to see your mother. You haven't seen her for a year and two months."

"You won't tell Colonel Vickers who I really am?"

"No."

Mars and Banjo pored over army maps. Mars was using a red pencil to show cow paths, footpaths, or unmarked short-cuts between roads. He was also marking fords in the creeks. He granted Geneva a day's leave and asked Henley to give his regards to Lutie.

Banjo intently studied Henley. His distinguished face, courtly bearing, and perfect diction depressed him. No wonder Lutie married him. Henley made Banjo feel like a wiry brown squirrel. However, he was cordial to Henley for Jimmy's sake.

"Lieutenant," Henley said to Banjo, "my wife told me she spent such a happy day in your presence. I think it did her a world of good. Thank you."

"Sure." Banjo offered Henley a cigar.

"Should I not survive this war, will you watch over her when all is past?"

"I will, Colonel. On my honor." Banjo wondered what in the world had gotten into Lutie's husband. After all, Henley was a noncombatant.

Riding back toward the city, Geneva puzzled over her father's extraordinary behavior. "Daddy, are you sick?"

"No, I don't think I've ever felt better." He puffed on his cigar. "That's why I came for you today. I want to tell you something. I have not always been a brave man. Nineteen years ago I fell in love with a gentle, beautiful woman. Obviously, I was married to your mother. Sumner was eight, I believe, and you had not yet peeped on the horizon. I broke your mother's heart. I don't know what happened to me, Geneva. I was possessed by that woman."

"Those things happen, I guess." Geneva felt awkward.

"They happen all the time, but some men are wiser than I was. I cried to your mother. I told her I couldn't live without this woman. To make matters worse, the woman bore a child, a daughter. Your mother was praying for a little girl of her own at the time. She must have suffered very much. I finally saw what I was doing to her and promised to give up the woman, who was a slave. She insisted I sell her. That was the hardest thing I have ever done in this life. I can still see that woman's eyes when she was led away. Her only fault was that I loved her."

"Daddy, why do I have to know this?"

"Because my life is more painful than you can imagine right now and much of that pain is within. I'm not putting it very well. Di-Peachy is your half-sister."

Geneva rode quietly for a while. "I think I've always known inside. Why did Mother keep the baby?"

"She found out she was pregnant with you. She said she knew she was going to have a girl, and she wanted you to have a playmate. What she didn't count on was Di-Peachy growing up to be the spitting image of her mother. By then you two were inseparable. Every time your mother looks at that blameless child, she sees her own humiliation."

"I am my sister's keeper then?"

Henley threw away the cigar butt. "You were always responsible for Di-Peachy."

"Does she know?"

"No, but I'm going to tell her tonight. She deserves to know the truth. The only truth I ever told her was that she was named for Diane De Poitiers, the most beautiful woman in sixteenth-century France. As a child, you shortened all that into Di-Peachy." He paused. "Don't be as big a fool as your father. Learn to see reality as it is, not as you wish it to be."

"Are you referring to my marriage?"

"I have given it some thought. Nash is a young man, and you are outshining him at the things men are supposed to do. That's asking a lot of him."

"It's asking a lot of me to flounce around in starched petticoats. I'm a good soldier."

"So were they." Henley gestured toward a trench of mass graves.

"If I can stand, I can fight. And if I die, well, I won't know about it, will I? I found something, and I won't ever give it up!"

"You found that you love your country and that you are brave." He pulled his neckerchief up over his mouth.

"No, I found myself."

JUNE 8, 1862

"Friday, all the jaybirds go to see the Devil. You see, there's jes one Good Friday in the year. The others is given over to the Devil, his imps, and the jaybirds. This being Saturday, you safe as a lamb!" Sin-Sin triumphantly declared to Joseph Rutledge. He survived the amputation, but now he suffered with fever and flies. It was touch and go.

The two beekeepers, Beverly Fyffe from South Carolina and his Pennsylvania counterpart, Gunther Krutzer, were recovering nicely, due in part to one another. Their animated spirits lifted the other men.

Bebe Austin and her girls worked like Trojans. Lutie took it upon herself to give the women demonstrations of cleaning wounds, binding, removing bullets if visible to the naked eye. One hour after sunrise was the appointed time for lessons.

Meanwhile Kate rode from makeshift hospital to makeshift hospital. Sally Tompkin's hospital was run the best for a household operation. Some ladies refused the assignment of Bebe's girls, but most, unnerved by the suffering and physically frazzled by the backbreaking labor, agreed so long as it would be kept a secret. By the time Kate got back home, she was freighted down with secrets. She no longer cared. What would ruin a reputation before the war shrank to insignificance now, but she appreciated shrewdness. Every woman knew the war would end eventually, and they projected into the future. They had reputations to protect. Kate really didn't give a damn about her own, since she knew she would leave her husband.

She'd gone over it in her mind. Seeing these men bleed to death, listening to them talk about their wives, sweethearts, and mothers, smashed into her own heart with the force of a bullet. She and Mars were killing one another with indifference, punctuated only by a flare-up of hostilities. He deserved the kind of love these poor men spoke of in their agony. There was no reason to burden him with her insights now.

Years ago she had hated Mars so much she placed a thorn in his heart. Every time he pressed against her, he would bleed. She never knew she could be so cruel. She didn't want to be cruel any longer.

If Mars survived the war, she would approach him then about a divorce. If he did not survive the war, the issue would be settled. She hoped he'd survive, even though a divorce would permanently shatter her reputation. Even if no lady of society would receive her after a divorce, she knew perfectly well she could make a brilliant marriage. After all, it was men that asked you to marry, not women.

Sweet with fragrance, the air clung to the Vickerses' expansive back porch. Lutie and Geneva read from the first book of Kings, chapter 11. Solomon had seven hundred wives and three hundred concubines.

"I thought he was supposed to be wise," Lutie commented when the lesson was finished. She broke off further discussion when Henley joined them.

"Di-Peachy's in her room," he said. Geneva immediately left the porch.

"You told her?" Lutie pulled the silk ribbon markers in her Bible.

"Yes." He exhaled. "She showed very little emotion."

"Since when do Negroes show their true emotions to us?" Lutie so took Sin-Sin for granted that she blurted this out.

"Sometimes you is disgusting mean!" Sin-Sin glared at

Lutie. Her feelings for Di-Peachy ran deep. Her love for Lutie had never prevented her from seeing Lutie's correct coldness to the girl. She stormed off the porch.

Lutie, without thinking, tore a ribbon out of her Bible. "See what you've done."

"You insulted her, I didn't," Henley logically replied.

"I hate it when you're reasonable!" Now Lutie stormed off the porch.

Henley sat alone in the rocker and lit his pipe. Old emotions, like old scars, savaged his face.

When Geneva walked into Di-Peachy's tiny attic room, she closed the door behind her. For an awkward moment they stared at one another, two half-sisters separated by the chasms of race, temperament, and war.

Geneva, always the more demonstrative and impulsive of the two, rushed to embrace Di-Peachy. They clung to each other like frightened children.

Finally Di-Peachy stepped back and looked at Geneva. "You don't look like yourself. I don't even know you anymore."

"I'm still me." Geneva smiled.

"We've both changed."

"You and I will never change with regard to one another." Geneva's conviction was pure.

"I hope not." Di-Peachy took her hand. They sat at opposite ends of the bed, facing one another, as they had done so many times at Chatfield.

"It's a relief to know. I always suspected."

"Me, too, but I was too afraid to say anything. I felt like my birth was enshrouded in a poisonous mist. No one ever spoke of it. I never knew what I did wrong."

"Nothing."

"Are you ashamed?"

Geneva shook her head. "Why should I be?"

"You have a sister, a half-sister, who is illegitimate and black."

"Me and half the Confederacy." Her grin was infectious.

"Lutie's been a little better since Sumner died. I don't know why. And we hardly ever hear her talking to Emil anymore."

"She probably doesn't have the time. Mother was always embroidering her woes. Now she's seeing everyone else's."

Geneva exhaled. "Away from her, from home, I see things differently. It must have been miserable for her."

"Disappointment seems to be a standing feature of marriage," Di-Peachy quietly said.

"Not mine! Mine's perfect," Geneva lied.

"I'm glad to hear it."

"What about you? Are you really in love with Mercer?"

"I think so. I've never been in love before. Once the war is over, you'll get to know him."

Geneva, relaxing in the company of her oldest friend, spilled over. "My marriage isn't perfect. He doesn't love me anymore. I went into the army to be close to him, and I succeeded in driving him away. But I can't leave him, and I can't leave my regiment!" Tears filled her eyes.

"I'm so sorry." Di-Peachy's eyes glazed over, too. "Things will be fine when you get home, when life is normal."

"You're smarter than that, and now, so am I." Geneva shook her head. "I don't want to spoil your love, but, Peaches, marriage isn't what you think it is!"

"I know. I see it all around me, and it scares me."

"Plus, Mercer is white. That adds one more burden to it."

"I know that, too. Does it bother you?"

"Some." Geneva hastily added, "But I'll get used to it. I'm getting used to a lot of things."

"Me, too. Geneva, everything is happening so fast. I used to have a dream for the future. I kept it to myself. I didn't even tell you or Sin-Sin. I used to dream that I'd be free, and I would go to college. Then I would come home and teach my people. Living in ignorance is as bad as being a slave!"

This sentiment didn't offend Geneva. Di-Peachy never pretended to like her status for Geneva's sake. "It might come true."

"It might, but from the things I see and hear in Richmond, it seems to me that whether you win this war or whether you lose it, the fate of my people, of me, is going to be one thunderstorm after another. I don't see any rainbows."

Geneva very quietly said, "Your fate is with Chatfield. We're sisters; we rise or we fall together!"

"God, I wish I believed that." Di-Peachy squeezed Geneva's hand, and they cried anew. They cried for their new knowledge, for their lost childhoods, for their fear of loss and of death. They were women now, and they knew that not every story had a happy ending.

JUNE 12, 1862

"Gentlemen, in ten minutes every man must be in his saddle." Geneva sprang to her feet, along with the other twelve hundred men under Stuart's command, for a mission as yet undisclosed. After making that announcement, the twenty-nine-year-old brigadier general left them to their hasty preparations.

Mars Vickers, leaving most of his men with Benserade, now a major, came along because J.E.B. valued him and because companies of the Fourth Virginia, augmenting the First Virginia and the Ninth Virginia, were without a regimental officer. Colonel Fitz Lee, a nephew of Robert E. Lee, commanded the rear guard, mostly made up of the First Virginia. Rooney Lee, the general's son, commanded the advance guard. Rooney was described as too big to be a man, but too small to be a horse. Lt. Colonel William Martin commanded the Jeff Davis Legion with the South Carolina Boykin Rangers, and Lieutenant Jim Breathed had two units of Stuart's Horse Artillery.

Geneva and Banjo, on being selected by Mars, cooked up three days' rations and were issued sixty rounds of ammunition. They assembled at Kilby's Station on the Richmond, Fredericksburg, and Potomac Railroad line outside of Richmond.

Mars handpicked twenty of his own men to come along. Nash was not chosen. This precipitated a small crisis when

Geneva hotly contested that Nash was an excellent trooper. Mars said that he was aware of Nash's skills, but he didn't think Nash was suitable for a mission which might prove extremely punishing. One needed a touch of Murat or madness was how Mars put it. When she asked why he wanted her, he replied, "Because you weren't born. You were foaled."

Nash took the news surprisingly well. While he didn't shirk responsibility, he didn't seek it either. He assumed, as did Geneva, that the cavalry was going to reinforce Jackson in the Shenandoah Valley. She said that three days' rations seemed thin gruel to get over to the Shenandoah Valley. Nash replied that there was nothing to prevent Stuart from foraging after three days' time or, once far enough away from Richmond, to putting everyone on trains. So she left him without tears. As she bedded down for the night near Mordecai's by Kilby's Station, she felt strangely relieved that she was on this mission without Nash. They didn't argue much, but sometimes the tension between them crackled. She felt protective of him and tried to keep her eye on him. He felt the same way toward her, but the task was more difficult for Nash because he lacked Geneva's reckless daring. Once he accused her of liking to kill people. She said that she'd rather kill the Yankees than have the Yankees kill her.

One thing did trouble her, however. When she rode over fields dotted with enemy dead, she wanted to laugh. She was glad they were dead. They had no business marching into Virginia. Even more, she was glad she was alive. Was it so wrong to be happy to be alive? To be happy in a victory of arms? If it was wrong, then everybody would go home, wouldn't they? She didn't understand Nash.

Forming up in columns of fours—Mars immediately up ahead, Banjo on one side of Geneva and Sam Wells on the other, Private Parker outside of Sam—the regiment trotted out in the dazzling moonlight onto the empty Brooke Turnpike. As they pulled out, an old army friend of Stuart's called out, "When will you be back, Beauty?"

"It may be four years and it may be forever," he replied, a piano-wide grin in his bushy beard.

Riding north they sang "Kathleen Mavourneen, the gray dawn is breaking, the horn of the hunter is heard on the hill." The music swept from the head of the column to the rear. At Turner Tavern, five miles later, the column, which at close ranks stretched out half a mile, cut left. Geneva was certain they were heading north to the Louisa County Courthouse where they were going to relieve Jackson, who was contending with three separate Federal armies. She reckoned he could use a little help.

Before noon the heat rose up off the meadows of undulating grass in little waves. Good-bye spring. Hello summer. Geneva thought how pleasant the summers were at Chatfield. Here in the Peninsula, shot through with three strong rivers and countless creeks, streams, and swamps, summer was a steambath made even more uncomfortable by the great variety and ferocity of winged irritants that inhabited the place. The mosquitoes flew, fat as yellow hornets. If she never saw a Peninsula mosquito again, she would count herself lucky.

By late afternoon the force crossed the Richmond, Fredericksburg, and Potomac Railroad, west of Ashland Station.

The column veered right. At first Geneva paid little attention, assuming the road was better and they'd soon turn back north.

After an hour of this rightward direction, she said, "Banjo, we're heading east."

"Maybe the bold general is lost," Banjo replied.

"With Mars in the line? You know he can be a real maiden aunt about roads. If a pissant walked over a meadow, he'll declare it a shortcut."

"I heard that," Mars called over his shoulder from up ahead.

"I thought officers had better things to do than eavesdrop on us lowlies," Geneva said to tease him.

"I eavesdrop on you all the time, Jimmy."

"Is that a fact? I had no idea my conversation was so fascinating to you."

"It isn't. I'm waiting for your voice to crack." At this, titters rippled through the ranks.

"You know, Colonel, I have an Auntie Sin-Sin. She says if you take a strand of a person's hair and nail it to a tree, it will run that person crazy. When you're asleep tonight, I'm gonna snatch a piece of your curly hair and do just that."

"Don't bother. You're already driving me crazy."

The good-natured banter went on until the men stopped for the night. They were on Winston Farm near Taylorsville, twenty-two miles from Richmond. No fires. No bugles. As

Banjo rolled up in his blanket, he said to Geneva, "We aren't going to the valley."

"Maybe we're going to the dogs," Mars said, rolled up behind Banjo.

Geneva stealthily crept around Banjo and yanked a hair right out of Mars's head.

"You little shit." He grabbed her wrist. "Gimme that."

Banjo propped himself up to enjoy their horseplay.

"Let me go."

"Give me that hair."

"Why, think you'll need it? Afraid you'll go bald?"

"You're the one going to be bald in a minute."

"Bully." She tossed the hair on the ground.

Mars let her go. "I'm no bully; I just don't want you to nail my hair to a tree. I wouldn't mess with Sin-Sin's potions and spells."

JUNE 13, 1862

An hour before sunrise, Geneva was awake. She drank cold tea from her canteen and pulled out her Bible. The lesson for the day was 1 Kings 20:1–22 and Acts 18. The travails of St. Paul made good reading. In yesterday's lesson, Acts 17, St. Paul told the Greeks at Athens that their altar with the inscription TO THE UNKNOWN GOD was to worship the only God. He was proclaiming that God was the true God. St. Paul was a clever man. Many of the Greeks had a tough time believing the resurrection. Geneva sometimes did, too. Why did it apply to only one of us? Although right now she was rather glad the dead stayed dead. Imagine if those rotting soldiers rose out of their mass graves to turn on one another anew, or worse, to turn on her?

She noticed that Mars's bedroll was made up. Banjo stirred.

Mars spoke to the other officers, then they all scattered to their units.

Mars strode up to Geneva. "We are going behind McClellan's right! General Lee wants us to gather as much information as we can about entrenchments and disposition of troops. Then he's going to attack." Mars was jubilant. "There's nothing between us and one hundred thousand Yankees! Can you beat that?" His eyes sparkled. The sheer impudence of their venture outweighed the danger for him.

Geneva picked up Gallant's feet after Mars left her. Shod a week ago, the shoes fit him perfectly. Good, she thought. The last thing I need on an assignment like this is a horse that throws a shoe. Gallant nuzzled her behind as she held his foreleg between her knees.

Banjo joined her and inspected his own sturdy roan, which had a touch of Connemarra in him. "Ever ball a horse for worms?"

"Sure." Geneva moved to the left foreleg.

"I'd hold the ball between my first three fingers and pull his tongue out with my left hand. Then I'd shove that ball down there as far as I could and zip my hand out! Stand there until I could see it go down his gullet. Course, if I were to be nervous, oh, what a mess!"

"Ever use a big peashooter to shoot the pill down?"

"Tried that once. Horse blew back first."

"Well, at least you didn't have worms that season."

"Mount up." The call came down the line.

As the sun edged over the rolling horizon, Stuart's men rode toward the Hanover Courthouse five miles east. When roads narrowed, they passed in twos. The rest of the time they stayed four abreast.

Sam Wells remarked on the enemy. "Fitz-John Porter is at Mechanicsville, or so we've heard."

Private Parker, who lived in these parts and was therefore very valuable to the expedition, replied, "If he is, then his outposts will be along the Virginia Central Railroad toward the north. I mean, if he has any sense, that's where his outposts will be."

"Bluebirds!" Banjo shouted, pointing to the crest of a hill. They hovered on the rim, wheeled, and disappeared. Hanover Courthouse was within sight.

At the crest of a wooded knoll, Stuart halted his column.

He called Colonel Fitz Lee forward and instructed him to take his rear guard and swing right to flank the Federals, cutting them off further down Courthouse Road. Satisfied that would do it, the rest of the men turned south a mile past Hanover Courthouse, riding past Taliaferro's Mill and Erron Church to Hawes' Shop near Totopotomy Creek, bloated with the recent rains.

"This road gets right evil." Banjo squinted ahead.

Geneva noticed that the road dwindled into a narrow ravine, the sides studded with pine and laurel. If infantry was in there, they'd be blown to bits in a matter of minutes.

A disappointed Fitz Lee soon rejoined the column. He'd bogged down in swampland and hadn't cut off the small force of Federal cavalry.

Mars turned in the saddle. "You know, those boys—"

A shout interrupted him.

"Sabers!"

Geneva drew her saber, the rattle tinkling in her ears. No one uttered a word.

Lieutenant Robins called to his advance guard. "Prepare to meet an attack!"

Mars's moustache twitched upward on the left. "Goddammit, I hate it when I can't see."

He did see Rooney Lee quickly send out flanking parties on both sides, but in this terrain they were useless.

The lead squadron, under Captain S.A. Swann, cantered forward. The column behind them moved up. "Close ranks!" an officer in the front shouted. The men kept their rows as though a center axle ran underneath each team of four. If the lead squadron broke, then the next row would take the attack, and so on down the line until the rear guard was called into action.

Shouts, pistol reports, and the wild neighing of horses made Geneva's heart race like an engine. The Yankees retreated without a fight.

"Dammit to hell!" Mars cursed. "Those boys broke. No dance for us."

Captain Swann chased the fleeing Yankees one mile down the road and then sounded recall. The road was too narrow ahead; maybe that easy victory was bait to reel them in.

The column rode forward to Old Church two miles away.

They knew there'd be trouble there because the Federals ran in that direction.

"Nobody's here." Banjo held his hands, palms upward, as he scanned the river crossing. Totopotomy Creek, a natural defensive barrier, surged on its way, no rifle pits, redoubts, or abatis on its banks.

"They're up in the air." Mars wiped his lips with his sleeve. "I think McClellan's putting his marbles in the center and paying little attention to his right. Let's find out how far his line extends." He rode down his line. "Dress up, dress up there. No reason to get raggedy."

The Confederates trotted toward Old Church. So far, so good. Geneva's senses were razor-sharp.

"Battle form!" Again the call came down the line.

"I knew they'd be back." Banjo nonchalantly lit a cigar. "No reason to let a few Yankees get in the way of a good smoke."

Immediately ahead, dust swirled up in the road. The front of the Confederate column blasted into the Yankee cavalry, which was waiting for them four abreast. Geneva strained to hear.

"Move up!" Mars ordered.

Geneva squeezed Gallant, and he picked up his trot. Now she could see. The Federals broke and ran, but not for long. They must have had some Old Army officers with them because they wheeled about, re-formed into fours, and galloped back toward the Confederates. The Confederate squadron attacked them again. Steel clinked against steel. The combat was hand to hand and in tight quarters. There was precious little room to maneuver.

"We're next," Mars called. "Move up! Move up! Steady!"

Again the Yankees broke and ran. Geneva saw a scattering of bodies on the road. A few riderless horses plunged back into the retreating Federals, adding to their confusion. She could plainly see the sergeant's stripes on one Yankee as he held his bleeding arm and ran off the road. The Northerners turned and re-formed one more time. She heard their captain curse them and bellow, "Cut those secessionist sons of bitches to pieces!"

"Steady." Mars trotted forward, his saber resting on his right shoulder. He lifted his saber and hollered, "Let's go, boys!"

Geneva whooped. Banjo emitted a piercing rebel yell, sending shivers down her spine. The thunder of hooves pounded in her head. She stood in her stirrups, racing forward as far as she could, saber poised at a forty-five-degree angle to her body so she could slash downward. With a terrific slam, her line hit the Yankees and was hit in return. She couldn't see for the dust. Gallant, a dependable rock, kept his head. The Yankee coming toward her didn't have as much success with his animal, and he pitched off under the metal hooves, more dangerous than the saber. A puff of dust blew up before her, then subsided. She saw Mars stick a Yankee between the ribs, withdraw his saber, and lash out at a ferocious man coming straight at him. Another swirl of dust obscured him.

"Get out of here!" someone shouted in a nasal, Northern accent.

Amidst the screaming and choking dust, she felt more room around her, and she pressed a lathered Gallant forward. The Yankees scooted away and were about ten yards ahead except for those on the ground.

"Come on, get 'em!" Mars, his face streaked with dust and sweat, appeared amidst the confusion. He looked terrifying and beautiful. Banjo, on his left, shot forward, his saber level to the ground and straight out, riding for all he was worth to catch the rear of the Yankee line. Geneva overtook him, and they rode side by side, but the bluecoats pulled further and further away. Recall sounded.

"Slow down, Jimmy boy."

"Shit!"

"Don't be ugly." He sheathed his saber.

"Your cigar went out," she casually told him.

Men were picking up discarded guidons. The few Yankees that lost their mounts and couldn't get away surrendered.

A lifeless body was put on a horse.

"Who's that?" Geneva asked Sam Wells, slightly ahead of her as they returned to form in fours once again.

"Latane, five bullet holes in him," the trooper answered.

Mars rode up and down his line. Everyone was accounted for and in one piece.

The few Yankees who surrendered were put on their horses and tucked in at the rear of the line between the artillery and the last of the rear guard.

*   *   *

After 4 P.M., the column halted at the house of Dr. Brocken-borough. General Stuart dismounted, removed his hat, and went inside. Mercer Hackett and Heroes Van Borcke, formerly of the Third Dragoon Guards of the Royal Prussian Army, dismounted also. Geneva knew who Mercer was, but as yet she had not introduced herself. She didn't know why she hung back, but the more she pretended to Di-Peachy that it didn't bother her that Mercer was a white man, the less she wanted to meet him.

Heroes hypnotized Geneva. The giant wore boots like Casimer Harkaway, huge leather ones that, if unfurled, would cover the knee and a portion of the thigh. Heroes rolled the boot top over once. A heavy dragoon sword, longer than a light cavalry sword, dangled at his right side. He sported expensive gauntlets, a campaign hat with a luxurious ostrich feather, a wide red officer's sash, and a fierce, waxed moustache that nearly reached his ears. She tried to imagine what the fighting would have been like if the Yankees were dragoons, encased in shiny breastplates and metal helmets, riding thick-boned horses. Just bumping into a heavy cavalryman like that would send an opponent flying off the road. But what they gained in weight, they lost in maneuverability. Light cavalry was exactly where she belonged.

"Wore a pink coat, white breeches, and those top boots, did he?" Banjo unceremoniously pointed to the Prussian.

"It worked. Stuart noticed him."

"He'd be hard to hide," Private Parker chimed in.

"Colonel," Geneva asked Mars, "do they look like that in Prussia?"

"Some do." Mars rested his hands on his saddle pommel. "Some units have long horsehair manes dyed in regimental colors flowing from their helmet halfway down their back. You should see it when they ride. Male Valkyries!"

"What's that?" Banjo inquired.

"One of twelve female warriors from Valhalla, the Teutonic heaven. When a warrior dies on the battlefield, a Valkyrie rides down to bring him to the hall of heroes where he feasts with Odin."

"Do they fight, too?" Geneva let a hint of a grin flicker across her face.

"The fiercest warriors in Teutonic mythology are the

Valkyries. They ride naked from the waist up except for
breastplates."

Parker's ears picked up. "Say, think we might enlist a
few?"

"Just for you, Parker," Mars replied.

Heroes removed the body of Latane from his horse and
swiftly carried him into the nicely kept house. Stuart emerged,
remounted, and the column moved on. The ladies and ser-
vants·of the Brockenborough place came out on the porch to
wave to the men as they passed by.

"Where are we headed now?" Banjo asked, after another
sixteen miles of fighting and marching.

"Tunstall Station," Parker said. "About eight miles from
here. That's where we're going unless the general changes
direction."

"The Yankees have to know we're here." Geneva unbuttoned the top of her tunic, revealing the shirt underneath.
The sun was blazing.

Mars called back, "They know we're here. The question
is, Where are they?"

From a slight distance it sounded like Chinese firecrackers.

Mars fished his gold filigree watch from his back pocket.
The chain, fastened to his belt, was long enough so he could
bring the timepiece around his waist. The sun fried him.
"Someday someone will figure out how to make an accurate,
light watch, and that man will make a fortune."

"Sure 'nuff," Banjo agreed, "but you'd lose a valuable
weapon. Twirl that thing over your head, Colonel, and you
could decapitate offenders."

"Parker, up front," Mars ordered the young private. "They're
ready for you to scout." Parker tipped his hat to Banjo,
Geneva, and Sam and cantered forward.

"That's the life," said Geneva, "being a scout, jumping
ditches and fences, a life of adventure."

"If we fight around Charlottesville, you can be our scout,"
Mars promised.

"Think we will?" Geneva's high voice climbed higher.

"No one knows where armies will collide, especially when
commanded by peculiar generals like that Yankee Hooker,
for instance. But I think Charlottesville is safe. No important
railroad junction or precious material will lure them that way.
Course, if they want horses, you might get raiding parties."

Geneva thought of Yankees riding up the long driveway. What would her mother do? Well, it couldn't happen.

"Firing stopped," Banjo laconically noted.

"Think we'll turn back, Colonel?" Sam Wells asked. There was an army between him and Richmond. Not that he minded.

"We know where their right stops. But if we turn back, they'll be waiting for us at every crossroads along the way. If they aren't that alert, you'd think they'd have the sense to burn the bridge at the Totopotomy and bag us there," Mars replied.

"This is most interesting. I don't think I've ever been in this situation." Banjo grinned mischievously.

"Tunstall's Station is McClellan's main supply line, according to Parker."

"There ought to be infantry there." Sam removed his cap and ran his fingers through his sweating head, hair sticking out between his fingers. "What's to prevent the Yankees from sending troops down the York River Railroad to intercept us there?"

"Nothing," Mars replied. "Except everything we've seen indicates these boys are sloppy as hell."

"Isn't General Stuart's father-in-law commanding?" Banjo enjoyed personal gossip.

"If he is, he's doing a piss poor job of it."

"It's this heat." Banjo appeared philosophical. "Those fellows can't stand the heat. That's why they wear blue coats. Makes them dream of ice and snow. They'd be better off if they'd go home, poor things."

Mars called ahead and put Sam Wells in charge. Sam cut out and moved ahead of the unit. Banjo and Geneva, side by side, rode behind him. The column spread out longer than its formerly tight half-mile span. News came up from the rear that the firing was from advance Federal units who withdrew after harmlessly discharging their rifles.

Geneva turned and looked behind her. A fantastic red ball seemed to be advancing upon her or the earth. Sunset and the long, summer, Virginia dusk would soon envelop them in pink light.

"First firefly!" She pointed out the blinking light to Banjo.

"Just think if we could light up our rear ends like that. Never get lost in the dark."

"Banjo, who knows what you'd attract?" Sam jibed him.

A commotion rumbled up from the rear.

"What in the hell are they doing back there?" Sam twisted in his saddle.

"Well, they've got that big rifle and the howitzer. Guess they have a right to commotion. This road has seen better days," Geneva reminded him.

"Captain, may I go back?" Banjo said.

"Yes, but then come forward." Sam thought this would give him relief from Jimmy and Banjo's incessant chatter. If a fence rail was down, one would point it out to the other. If a red-winged blackbird flew overhead, Jimmy would relate some superstition about it. A squirrel brought forth a torrent of culinary advice from Banjo.

Banjo soon reported back to Sam. "A party of about twenty-five Federals plus a captain and one assistant surgeon surrendered to Lieutenant Colonel Martin. They think we're advance guard for a large body of infantry. Ignorance is bliss."

"Thank you, Banjo."

Banjo fell alongside Geneva. The gossip started again, as inevitably as the sea returning at high tide. Wells thought, it's a terrible death to be talked to death.

Geneva noticed that two squadrons detached themselves from the main body when they halted at Wynne's Shop and Hopewell Church. While watering Gallant, Geneva inquired about the squadrons. She was informed that Garlick's Landing by the Pamunkey River was two miles east. Supplies and horses were supposed to be there, and Stuart aimed to have some. Peeved, Geneva mounted up. Why was everyone else getting to have the fun?

As they moved toward the railroad station, Geneva encountered overturned wagons, their goods spilling out along the road. The Yankees were running from them fast and light. A sack of potatoes beckoned her but she sighed, kept in line, and beat back dreams of richly scalloped potatoes, cut thin and swimming in cream sauce. Ernie June slowly acquired the proportions of a saint.

Great plantations, many of them founded long before the Revolutionary War, invested this part of Virginia with special significance. In these rolling lands, washed over by the Atlantic Ocean millions of years back, and today laced with rivers, the English began the slow, brave, and oftimes cruel process of cultivating the New World. Henley's people began here in the mid-seventeenth century. One bold, dissatisfied Chatfield struck out from the Tidewater and headed for the bloody frontier, the Blue Ridge Mountains. He found the site for Chatfield, traded with Indians, fought when he had to, and eventually found a woman to share his hardships and triumphs.

The ladies of these hallowed plantations reposed in open carriages where their private road cut into the road to Tunstall. Parasols swaying, they waved, carried out food and drink, and even pressed scented handkerchiefs into the hands of those considered handsome. Their servants perched on the fences and shouted out encouragements to the troopers.

As Mars rode back to his men, he was particularly favored by a dark-haired beauty. He politely chatted with her and eventually his men caught up with him. He bid farewell to the lady and joined Sam Wells.

"Oh, Colonel, you are just the handsomest man in the Confederate States of America. I do think I may faint from the sight of you." Geneva waved her hand over her nose, imitating a lady taking the vapors.

Mars laughed, then spoke to his regulars. "Well, boys, we're going to ride around them! We aren't turning back!"

"Holy shit!" Sam exclaimed. "Excuse me, sir."

"I don't mind but if Stuart hears you, he'll give you a speech about temperance and the Methodist Church. It's worth leaving off creative abuse to be spared."

The sky turned velvet cobalt blue, the color of Kate Vickers's eyes. Another detachment under Captain O.M. Knight separated itself from the column. Von Borcke, John Mosby, and a detail surged ahead to Tunstall's Station. Geneva wondered if the enemy squared off along the road. If they did, there wasn't much choice but to try and flank them or bull straight through. Exasperated that she was lodged in the main column and not with the squadron sent to Garlick's Landing or with the advance party to Tunstall Station, Geneva became sullen.

"Halt!" Mars ordered.

The column of tired men and horses lurched to a stop. Another ripple passed from the head of the column to the back. "Bring the guns up."

A ripple passed from the rear to the front. "The guns are stuck."

They waited.

Finally Lieutenant Breathed put a keg on the gun and told

the men they could have it, if only they would pull. They pulled the guns through the mud and were rewarded with a whiskey keg captured at Old Church earlier in the day.

Frayser, one of the scouts who lived but a few miles from the road, dashed in from the direction of Tunstall's Station and reported to Mars. Moonlight now flooded the fields, and the young cornstalks shone like small, silver spears.

"Form platoons!" Mars impatiently hollered. "Draw sabers! We're going in!"

Geneva heard the head of the column break into a gallop. Within minutes Gallant, excited by the sounds of hoofbeats running, happily shot forward.

They roared into Tunstall's Station. Nothing. The advance guard had scattered the Federals.

Mars let his saber fall to his side and spat on the ground. "Unbelievable! If I were Abraham Lincoln, I'd court-martial every son of a bitch over the rank of major in this army! Look at this!"

The station, a ripe plum, was virtually undefended. The two Yankee companies assigned to defend Tunstall Station had made no effort to secure the town. Mars wondered how the Yankees could ignore the fact that the railroad was their lifeline to supplies and to Washington itself. Did they think their opponents would be as lax as themselves? It seemed McClellan's idea of a campaign was for an occasional shelling in the direction of Richmond or up in the air to give the gunners practice.

"Look up there." Banjo pointed to Lieutenant Robins dangling atop a telegraph pole cutting the wires.

"All right. Dismount. Put the horses where they can graze."

Men began to chop down poles and drag them on the tracks. Mars yanked off his tunic and removed his shirt. Barechested, he lit into a telegraph pole. Banjo and Geneva grabbed axes and did the same. While they were sweating away, about eight men pulled a fourteen-foot-long oak sill across the tracks.

"Heads up!" Mars cupped his hand to his mouth.

The telegraph pole crashed across the track. Within seconds, Banjo's pole fell and then Geneva's also.

A train whistle sang its piercing, eerie song. It was about quarter to eleven.

"Colonel, should I fetch the horses?" Geneva asked.

"No, enough of the men are in the saddle. If it gets thick and we have to make a run for it, we'll take our chances. Come with me, Chatfield. Let's roll this baggage cart alongside the track and turn it over. We can fire from behind it."

They ran, their legs rubbery from eighteen hours in the saddle.

"Take the front and guide. I'll push the rear," Mars shouted.

Geneva and Mars pushed and pulled the cart away from the station, then with help from Banjo and Sam, they turned it on its side. Using a second cart, they created a small barricade about two hundred yards behind the obstruction on the track.

"Here she comes!" Mars pulled his gun.

The train slowed, then ripped forward at full speed as the engineer saw the ambush ahead. There were flatcars and a wood car behind the engine. The men on these cars shouted as they were jolted forward.

Geneva dumped lead into the men on the flatcars as they sped past. A few couldn't fathom what was happening to them, and they stood straight up in the moonlight. Most of them, upon hearing the shots, wisely dropped flat on their stomachs. Others jumped off, screaming as they hit the tracks.

"Look at Will Farley!" Sam Wells pointed to his right.

Will Farley, a young man known for his almost insane disregard for danger, was galloping next to the engine. He put a rifle to his shoulder and fired into the cab. "I got him! I got him!" Farley yelled, waving the rifle over his head. The train pulled away.

Mars rose. "Let's see what we've got."

They walked along the tracks. Several Yankees were crumpled on the sidings or crawling to get away from them. Geneva easily caught up with one whose legs were broken. He rolled over and pulled his pistol, but she shot him. He twitched and then relaxed. "I wasn't going to kill you." She nudged him with the toe of her boot. "What'd you draw for?"

Banjo was dragging a sergeant major under the arms. "Here, help me with this one. His legs are folded up like an accordion."

The Yankee moaned as they dragged him to a waiting bench under a chalked-in train schedule. "What are you going to do with me?"

"Nothin'," Banjo replied. "One of your own will find you soon enough. We've got to get out of here."

"I thought we held this side of the river." The Yankee tried to straighten his leg, but couldn't do it.

"That's a matter of opinion." Geneva looked up and saw billows of smoke curling skyward to the east. "We've been successful there, too."

Banjo motioned for a trooper to give the Yank a light off his cigar.

Mars walked over. "Take what food you can out of the wagons over there, burn the rest, and then let's go. It's neck or nothing."

After looting the wagons, Geneva and Banjo stopped at a small house. An older woman was contentedly sitting on her big, hanging swing. "Hellzapoppin!"

"Might we ask you a favor, ma'am?" Banjo removed his hat. "We put the Yanks with broken bones by the station office. Would you bring them water? I think it will be a time before their people return."

She nodded. "I'll do it."

The column formed up and rode out of Tunstall's Station. Stuart sent out scouting parties and a detachment to New Baltimore Store but the bulk of the column rode, stumbled, and fought to keep awake as they threaded down the dirt roads.

JUNE 14, 1862

Geneva, because of her youth, didn't get as sleepy as the others. Gallant was worn, but not blown out. Banjo curled his right leg around the pommel of his saddle and slept.

Mars bobbed to one side and then the other. Finally Geneva rode up next to him. Every time he'd fall over, she'd hold out her arm to right him, then he'd mumble and doze off again.

The moon was on the other side of the sky when they stopped at St. Peter's Church.

Mars dismounted, groggy but willing himself awake. "Boys, take a break. Water your mounts, wrap the reins over your shoulder when you're done, then lie down for a spell."

The men thankfully did as they were told. Geneva dropped on the ground lying on her back with her arms outstretched. She wrapped the reins around her wrist. She didn't know how long she slept, but it was still dark when she was ordered to her feet. "Mount up!"

A flicker of gray glowed in the heat. The column turned down the lane to Sycamore Springs, the house of Lieutenant Jonas Christian. They passed the house and came to a blind ford. Forge Bridge was a mile away, but had been destroyed. Stuart figured that's where the Federals would head. Stuart knew the Yankees were two hours behind his column, and this ford would get his men across unnoticed. By now the Yankees were aroused at Stuart's encirclement of their entire force. They were determined to catch the twelve hundred Confederates and save face.

Mars, wide awake, walked up and down the banks of the raging Chickahominy.

"It's never been this bad," Christian mournfully said.

Rooney Lee stripped and swam across. Swimming back, the half-drowned man was hauled out of the gurgling water by John Easten Cooke. "What do you think of the situation, Colonel?"

Dripping wet, Rooney shook himself and began putting on his clothes. "Well, Captain, I think we are caught."

"There's got to be a way over!" Mars hunkered down. "What if I swam across with a rope and pulleys, and we rigged a tram?"

"We'd get the men over, but not the horses," Rooney replied.

"Some of us could swim the horses over."

"Too many of them. We've picked up over two hundred and fifty besides our own. And there's mules, too."

"Let's walk downstream to see if we can find another ford," Mars pressed.

Christian, knowing the land like his own palm, said, "Colonel Vickers, this is it."

Stuart rode up from the rear of the column. He looked over the Chickahominy and twisted his beard. Banjo unconsciously imitated Stuart. "I am giving this river my bright regard."

"I say we swim for it." Geneva crossed her arms.

The general must have agreed with her because men that were strong swimmers pushed their horses into the water to swim with them, a few hanging on to their tails.

Mars motioned for a handful of his men to follow him. They chopped down trees hoping to make a rough corduroy bridge, but when the trunks splashed into the water, they washed away like toothpicks.

"Doswell, get this to General Lee." Stuart handed Turner Doswell a message, and Doswell plunged into the torrent with his horse. The tangled banks on the other side made getting out difficult, but both man and horse managed. Turner shook off water, crawled into the saddle, and headed for Richmond, thirty-five miles distant.

Stuart asked General Robert E. Lee to create a diversion on the Charles Town Road. If Stuart got his men on the other side of the Chickahominy, he could keep General Hooker and the Federals on the other side of the swamp.

The sun began her majestic ascent while the troopers and their animals collapsed at Sycamore Springs. After trying everything, Stuart commanded the thirty-five men who'd gotten across the river to go downstream. The rest mounted up and headed for Forge Bridge where the Yankees were certain to appear on the road from Providence Forge to Charles City Courthouse.

Forge Bridge leapt the Chickahominy, deceptively narrow and deep at this place, to an island in the middle of the river. From the south side of the island was a second bridge leading to the safety of dry land. Both bridges had been destroyed, but there was a swampy ford off the island if one could get to it.

When they reached the bridge, only the abutments were standing. Videttes were posted, the artillery swung to face the road. An abandoned warehouse, a gift from the gods of chance, stood near the bridge. The men immediately ripped planks out of it. A skiff marooned on the bank was pushed into the water and used as an unsteady pontoon. The planks were laid from the abutment to the skiff and then from the other side of the skiff to the far abutment. The first troopers crossed, fighting to keep their balance as they held their saddles on their right arms and with the left, held the horses' reins, urging them across.

Geneva, working in the warehouse pulling off planks, said, "There's another way. Let's bring out the support beams and lay them from abutment to abutment, then nail the planks across. We'll have a strong bridge, strong enough for the guns. What they're doing out there now will take half the day. We'll never get twelve hundred men and two heavy guns across in time."

Mars, also yanking out planks, said, "If the beams reach, it might work. If they don't . . ."

"Nothing ventured, nothing gained."

Within minutes, crews of strong-backed men feverishly bent to remove the main support beams without shortening them unnecessarily.

Ten men, wavering under the weight, lifted the monster upon their shoulders and got it to the first abutment. Using the skiff, they slowly slid and coaxed the beam across. Every man held his breath.

"Made it!" Banjo jumped in the air. "You're magic, Jimmy Chatfield."

"No, I read Sumner's engineering books."

The second timber came out from the warehouse. Once these main supports were across the Chickahominy, Vickers's men pounded down the planks. Even Stuart removed his gilt encrusted jacket and hammered like a carpenter.

Their entire time at Forge Bridge was three hours. Once men, horses, and the guns had crossed, Fitz Lee, the last man over, fired the bridge. As the flames began to eat at the morning's hard work, the Federal cavalry galloped into view. They shot at Colonel Lee. He waved his hat to them and rejoined his men.

Geneva now threaded her way across the island. The ford on the western side of the island was a bitch but within the realm of the possible. They even got the guns across. However, the trying succession of swamps bothered the one hundred sixty-five prisoners more than the cavalry. The prisoners went first, many of them two to a mule.

"We're on solid ground," Banjo rejoiced, when his little roan's hoofs touched the right bank of the Chickahominy.

"Solid ground and twenty miles of the Federals' left flank to ride through." Mars laughed. "But, hell, we got this far."

General Stuart put Rooney Lee in charge. With one scout and one guide, Stuart moved on to Richmond. At Thomas Christian's house he rested for two hours. From there he went to Charles City Courthouse to Judge Isaac Christian's plantation. Another brief rest and then on to Rowland's Mill where he stopped for a cup of coffee. By the next morning, June 15, he reported to General Lee, turned around, and returned to his men.

JUNE 16, 1862

Covered from head to toe with caked mud, Geneva, Mars, and Banjo rode their exhausted horses into Richmond. The column kept in good order. General Stuart led his men through city streets thronged with shouting, singing, crying citizens.

Flowers crushed underfoot gave off a sweet, heavy scent. Women threw flowers, rice, and confetti. Young men looked on with pea-green envy; older ones looked on with pride.

At the head of this column, Stuart threw back his head and started a song: "If you want to have a good time, 'Jine the cavalry." The column picked it up, and soon the melody ricocheted off buildings and cobblestones.

John Easten Cooke remarked to Stuart, "That was a tight place at the river, General. If the enemy had come down on us, you would have been compelled to have surrendered."

"No, one other course was left."

"What was that?" Cooke inquired.

"To die game."

*   *   *

The men were given two days' leave. Mars led his detachment of twenty to his house. Kate, Lutie, and the other women, plus all of the wounded who could sit or stand, were waiting for him when he rode to the house. Franklin Street and Grace Street, mobbed with people, put up a cheer when they saw Mars.

"Dismount." The men obeyed. As Mars walked up the long steps of his house, the patients cheered. Mars saluted them. He noticed that a Yankee in their midst saluted also.

Kate threw her arms around his neck. "Welcome home!" He kissed her on the cheek. "We'll stay in the barn."

"Nonsense, you'll stay in the house. The men can double up in the ladies' rooms, and we'll go up to the servants' quarters."

Lutie didn't recognize Geneva until she spoke. "Mother, it's me and Banjo."

"Oh, my word. You two look like gingerbread men."

"Gentlemen, we'll take our horses to the back, and we can clean up out there." Mars led them behind the house.

Lutie organized a washing brigade. The pumps in the stable brought up clean water. She delivered towels, soaps, scrubbing brushes, hair shampoos, and ointments. Risé and Hazel scoured the neighborhood for shirts and trousers that the men might wear until their uniforms were cleaned and repaired. Jeffrey Windsor checked everyone. Aside from bug bites, splinters, bruises, and small cuts, they were fine. He walked back to the house, his green sash swaying. "Let them sleep. By supper they'll be as good as new."

Most of the men, once cleaned up, didn't make it back into the house. They dropped onto horse blankets in the straw-filled stalls and slept like babies.

Kate and Lutie, flying about, arranged a feast. Treasured coffee was brewed. Neighbors were invited. The wounded that could walk laid out damask napkins. Those still unable to move were carried into the massive dining room and put against the walls, propped up with pillows so that they might hear everything that happened. Kate invited Mrs. Reisman and Miss Roth as well as Bebe Austin. This was no time to be petty.

That night fifty people sat down to dinner, not counting the men against the walls. After dinner, another seventy people paid their respects. Hundreds of bystanders crowded around the house, hoping for a glimpse of their heroes. Sin-Sin, voice booming, pressed the stable boys into service, and they passed punch among these people. The Vickerses' popularity shot into the heavens after that.

Kate procured a small orchestra at an exorbitant rate. The ballroom was packed with those guests invited for 10 P.M. General Stuart dropped in with his staff. Mercer Hackett was with him, and when he saw Di-Peachy at the harp, tears rolled down his face. He had no idea she was in Richmond. She couldn't leave her post, so he told her he would call at eight in the morning. Geneva, as Jimmy, was finally introduced to Mercer. She could see that Mercer loved Di-Peachy, and she knew he was a good man. She was also happy to see Di-Peachy in love, but in her heart, she felt no good could come of it, and she hated herself for thinking that.

Lutie, the belle of the ball, giggled when Geneva asked her to dance and they stepped all over one another's toes. Banjo partnered Lutie as many times as was permissible. Her little curls shook with laughter, and her face turned up to his. "Lieutenant Cracker, I am not often in the arms of a hero."

"Mrs. Chatfield, it isn't often that I have in my arms an angel put on earth."

Lutie blushed. "Thank you." Her beautiful skirt, pale peach trimmed with maroon, billowed as he turned her. "I am so happy tonight, so very happy that I want to live forever!"

A strange look passed over Banjo's face. "My late wife said that to me the night we were married."

"What a strange coincidence," Lutie said gently. "I hope I didn't upset you."

"I want to live forever, too." He smiled.

Brigadier Hannibal Vickers entered the room. The music played on, but for a split second the revelers fell silent. Mars, in his dress uniform, excused himself and walked over to his father.

"How good to see you, sir."

"I have come to salute a valiant officer." Hannibal saluted his son, and the guests cheered. Poor Hannibal, hard as nails. This was as close as he could get to telling Mars he loved him.

Around two in the morning the last of the excited guests left. Gunther Krutzer, in his blue uniform, approached Mars.

He walked with a severe limp, and his left arm was heavily bandaged. He held out his right hand. "Colonel, I am happy to meet you. I wish you were my commander, and even more, I wish you were a Union man."

"Under the circumstances I'd say that was the most generous compliment I received tonight." Mars squeezed his hand.

Mars strolled through the rooms to see if any guests were stone drunk on the floor. Not a one. That was unusual. He heard laughter on the back porch and poked his head outside. Lutie, Banjo, Henley, and Geneva were having their after-party party.

"Colonel, this is one of the most wonderful nights of my life, and I owe it to you." Lutie radiated joy.

"Thank you, Mrs. Chatfield. I was ably assisted by your son. In fact, it was he who suggested we use the beams of the warehouse, and that's how we finally got the men over the Chickahominy River."

"I read Sumner's books," Geneva explained to Lutie.

Lutie, her voice heavy with both sadness and rejoicing, said, "In death there is life, and in life, death. But in love, there is only life. We did love him, didn't we?"

JUNE 17, 1862

The baby green shoots of a trumpet vine climbed up one side of the back porch. In another month the leaves would be large and bright green. By early August the brilliant flowers, shaped like orange trumpets, would festoon the porch along the right side.

Sin-Sin boiled up "life everlasting," also called rabbit tobacco, and was applying the plaster to Joseph Rutledge's chest. His stump still oozed, though the bandages were changed daily and the wound washed. Slowly he was gaining strength.

"Sin-Sin, do you think any girl will marry me now?"

"They gonna knock one another out runnin' to grab you."

He smiled weakly. "You're full of flattery."

"Now you listen to me. 'Men fall in love with they eyes, womens with they ears.' " Sin-Sin quoted Jennifer Fitzgerald. "You thinks about that. Lotta truth in old sayin's. No good woman gonna push you out cause of yo' arm. But you can't be layin' about like a king jes waitin' for the girls to come to you. When you back on your feets, you go out there and you calls on those Richmond gals. And when they speak, listen. Quickest way to a woman's heart is to listen. Doan let that gal try and throw a net over you with girl talk neither. You ask her 'bout 'portant things, and I promise you, you gonna be married 'fore this time next year."

"You really think so?" His earnest brown eyes sought hers.

"I know so!"

"Why are you putting this stuff all over me?" He itched underneath the hardening plaster.

"Prevent pneumonia. When folks get colds or pneumonia, this is what you puts on them. So iffin' I slaps this on you now, you safe as can be."

Less than convinced, Joseph said, "Does Colonel Windsor know about this?"

"Colonel Windsor too busy to know about everything."

Joseph's right eyebrow twitched upward. Before he could reply, a woman's scream from behind the barn startled them. He started to rise.

"Doan you dare get up!" She held her hand on his chest.

Banjo, sleeping it off in the barn, jumped up. He glanced around. Everyone was gone except for a cowering stableboy, who wouldn't go out on the back street where the commotion was. Banjo ducked his head in a bucket of water, shook himself alert, grabbed his Colt, and hurried outside.

Di-Peachy, dress ripped on the shoulder, was pummeling Big Muler on his back. Muler had Mercer Hackett from behind by the throat. Mercer, a powerful man, was at a disadvantage because he was being attacked from the rear, plus he had a wooden leg. Muler brutally pushed his knee into Mercer's bad leg. Banjo fired overhead. Muler loosened his grip for a fraction of a second, which allowed Mercer to shake free.

Di-Peachy ran in front of Big Muler. "Don't touch him! I love him! I'll never love you!"

Big Muler started to circle the two of them, ready to strike again at Mercer.

"Di-Peachy, please get away from here." Mercer pushed her toward Banjo, who with catlike reflexes grabbed her by the elbow.

Muler pounced. He came at Mercer on his weak side, but the white man spun and deflected the blow. He couldn't move fast on foot, but he could keep his balance. Muler was six feet eight inches. Mercer was barely six feet. Muler had the advantage of reach as well, but Mercer bobbed his head and most of the blows glanced off his shoulder. He ducked in and smashed the giant on the rib cage. Muler didn't even grunt. Di-Peachy sobbed. Banjo forcibly held her.

The two antagonists traded blows for fifteen minutes when suddenly Muler flung himself at Mercer's legs and toppled him on the ground. Once down, Mercer couldn't get up quickly. They rolled over and over, each one intent on killing the other one. Big Muler grabbed Mercer's wrists and slowly bore his great weight down on Mercer. Mercer gave inch by inch, knowing the giant would have him soon enough.

"Boys, that's enough fun for now." Banjo cocked back the hammer on his gun. "Come on, Big Muler, let him go."

Muler ignored Banjo.

"I said to let him go!"

Muler pressed down, finally pinning Mercer, then began to choke him.

Bam! Fire spit out of the muzzle. Big Muler halted and looked at his left arm. Mercer with one mighty heave pushed him off. Di-Peachy ran to Mercer.

"Doctor can fix that in a jiffy." Banjo kept his gun pointed at Big Muler.

Di-Peachy cried in Mercer's arms. "Big Muler," she said between her tears, "you can't keep men away from me. I don't belong to you. I never did."

He turned his back on her and walked into the barn.

"Let him cool off," Banjo advised. "You can talk to him later."

"I don't think talking will do any good," Mercer said. "He's killed two men already. Di-Peachy has told me everything."

"Let's go up to the house and drink a little coffee. This will sort out." Banjo wondered if Lutie knew that Di-Peachy was in love with Mercer. He could well understand Mercer being in love with Di-Peachy.

After a light breakfast, Banjo went back to the barn to spruce up. He found Big Muler hanging from a cross beam. Unnerved, he swallowed and fetched his saber. He clambered up the ladder and cut him down. Then he went in and quietly informed Lutie.

"We shall have to bury him," Lutie said. "Big Muler didn't have an evil heart, but when it came to Di-Peachy"— she paused—"he was quite insane."

Di-Peachy, upon hearing what Muler had done to himself, cried again. She was glad to be free of him, but she felt guilty for his misery. It was Kate Vickers who set her straight. "Never feel responsible for what men do to themselves over you. If you've been honest with them, you have nothing to worry about. If a man wants to hang himself over a beautiful face that never loved him, so be it."

As the unconsecrated burying ground was some distance from the house, Lutie read the lesson for the day over Muler's body. Di-Peachy, Mercer, and Banjo stood with her. Geneva and Nash were still out on the town.

The lesson was a hopeful one. Chapter 4 of the second book of Kings tells how Elisha laid himself on the body of a dead boy and breathed into his mouth. The boy came back to life. The New Testament, Acts 20, said that St. Paul revived a youth, Eutychus, who tactlessly died during one of his long sermons.

After the brief service, Mars invited Mercer into his office and asked him how serious he was about Di-Peachy.

"I intend to marry her. I'd marry her now, but she says we must wait until the war is over," Mercer said.

"I see." Mars watched a jade-green hummingbird hover near the window, then dart away.

"Big Muler was crazy."

"I don't doubt that." Mars flicked ashes into the huge crystal ashtray. "Corporal, what if our legislature repeals manumission when the war is over and makes it retroactive?"

"That's not going to happen." Mercer was puzzled. "Once the war is over, we'll phase out slavery."

"Virginia, perhaps. Maybe a few other states but not the

coastal states or the Delta." Mars shook his head. "Some men are already talking about reopening the slave trade."

"Never!" Mercer exploded.

"I agree wholeheartedly but consider this, Corporal. Suppose six or seven years from now these men strike a bargain for Virginia's votes. Naturally there would have to be something vital to our interests involved, but it is possible." Mars wanly smiled at him. "I only wish for you to be aware of the insecurity into which you might be placing yourself."

"You sound very formal, Colonel." Mercer was testy.

"I suppose I do. I am not your commanding officer, and perhaps I have no right to speak to you this way. But I have come to know the Chatfield family, and I thought perhaps I could help."

"Are the Chatfields against this marriage?" Mercer took a deep breath.

"Mrs. Chatfield feared you would fool with the girl and abandon her. Apparently Di-Peachy has told her very little."

"Well?"

Mars cleared his throat. "Mrs. Chatfield seems to be grateful that your intentions are honorable, even if they do present a thorny situation."

Mercer exhaled. "Thank God." He stubbed out his cigar. "Does it matter so very much that she is black and I am white?"

"I'd be a liar if I said it didn't." Mars looked him square in the eye.

"I love her, Colonel! If we have to flee to the North once this war is over, I'll do it. If that's no good, then we'll go to Brazil or Peru. I don't care where we go as long as we are together!" His eyes flashed and his cheeks burned.

Mars said nothing for a few moments, then he, too, stubbed out his cigar. "I envy you, despite what lies ahead. If she loves you as you love her, good luck to you. Come now, let's join the others. Tomorrow morning we report back to duty, so let's enjoy the day."

JUNE 22, 1862

A smoky haze, golden peach, enshrouded Richmond at sunrise. It remained in the sky at matins when Lutie, Kate, and the other Charlottesville matrons attended early services at St. Paul's. The war provoked an upsurge in church attendance, not that St. Paul's, being the most fashionable church in the city, needed new parishioners. But St. Paul's popularity was hotly contested by St. James Episcopal Church. When the war started, the first funerals were elegantly orchestrated by each congregation for its fallen officers. By now, death among the high born was so commonplace that neither church could spend much time on a man's last social engagement.

No one said anything on this First Sunday after Trinity, but sharp concern rippled through the people. The Old Testament lesson was Genesis, chapter 3. In normal times Father John might have woven a delicate but dogmatic theme from the pulpit on the subject of Adam and Eve and the serpent. Instead, the sumptuously robed priest talked about the flaming sword and the cherubims who guarded the east of the Garden of Eden. As Lutie listened, she mused on the situation in which she, and everyone around her, found themselves.

McClellan received seacoast siege guns at White House Landing, his headquarters on the York River Railway not far from Tunstall Station. He also received reinforcements, rumored to be another ten thousand men. Richmond needed not only a cherubim at the east, she also desperately needed one at the west. General Stuart's dashing exploit had proven what everyone felt passionately: that any Southerner could outride and outfight any Yankee. But the South needed more than superb cavalry to win this war. The statistics slowly gathering in Richmond like marbles rolling into the ring were sobering. The North had superior artillery and more men. The South had no chance to catch up. The entire white population of the eleven Confederate States was five million. The equivalent population of the North was twenty million.

Lutie prayed less for cherubims and more for a great leader. As yet, no one man had emerged to save the infant nation. She hoped it would be Robert E. Lee who now found himself commander of the entire Confederate army. But how rarely in history does the right man find himself in the right place? Was that race of giants, Washington, Jefferson, Madison, Monroe, and Mason, the last of a breed? Patrick Henry, too, who walked the streets of Richmond, arguing as he went, was he the last? Was Virginia so impoverished intellectually and morally that she bore no more great men or women? Lutie nursed an abiding affection for Dolley Madison, her childhood heroine. Thomas Jackson showed himself a master in his fighting in the Shenandoah Valley. Was he the one? She fidgeted in her seat. Whoever he was, he'd better show himself fast because the wolf was dozing at the door, and sooner or later that wolf had to wake up.

"May the Lord bless thee and keep thee. May the Lord lift up His countenance upon thee and make His face shine upon thee and give thee peace. Amen."

"Amen," Lutie and the congregation answered in unison.

The organ rumbled its throaty pipes. The rustle of skirts and the shuffle of boots filled Lutie with a strange premonition. The men walked down the aisle, ladies on their arm, to the rear of the lovely church. There they shook the hand of Father John and immediately outside, in the small vestibule, they retrieved their swords.

Lutie thought, Christ is an hour and a half a week plus a few prayers in the morning or the evening. We go through the motions and conveniently forget Him the rest of the time. Small wonder we fall into such evil. One hundred years from now every person in church today will be dead. Will anyone remember us? Even my own blood kin? Will my great-grandchildren and great-great-grandchildren know who I was or care what I did? Will anyone remember Sumner? He left no children. We'll be shadows, shadows dispensed with their sunlight, their problems, their triumphs. They won't believe that we loved, fought, sung, cried, and died nor will they care. Maybe we're already shadows and we don't know it. What if

my soul should awaken one hundred years from now? I fear
my sorrows would awaken with it, but then so would my joys.
Yes, I'd like to come back. I'd like to see these new people.
Dear Jesus, why did you give me but one life to live?

Hazel Whitmore, walking next to Lutie as they paraded
past the Catholic church on the corner murmured, "You're
unusually pensive."

"I was wondering, what would it be like to come back here
to this very spot one hundred years from now?"

"That would depend upon whether we won the war or not,
wouldn't it?"

"If they win, I don't think they will do as Rome did to
Carthage. They won't sow the land with salt," said Lutie.

"What are you two talking about?" Kate skipped a little
faster to catch up to them, dragging the other ladies along.

"Whoever wins, I'd like to see better streetlamps and less
traffic," Jennifer said. "But we'll win, of course."

"If the North wins, it means we'll all end up so relentlessly
commercial." Risé Rives turned up her nose.

"It is vulgar. I think anyone who discusses money publicly
should be locked up for one month's time." Miranda was
adamant. "A nation of shopkeepers. I can see it now."

"Who knows what kind of hideous machines they'll foist
upon us? They are machine mad, and if you want my opinion, the downfall of the human race started with the spinning
jenny!" Jennifer was on a roll.

"I thought this mess started with Adam and Eve," Kate
drolly commented.

"Oh, that." Jennifer's hand fluttered.

"It is a disturbing story." Hazel waved to parishioners
leaving other churches. The neighborhood, filled with churches,
gave every Sunday a festive air because after service, people
strolled up and down Grace and Franklin streets and often
onto the capitol grounds.

"As a child I had a mammy," Kate interjected, "Mammy
George. Her real name was Georgianna, but we called her
Mammy George. Her story of creation was that when God
made man, the earth cried. Taking a handful of clay hurt her.
So God said, 'I will repay you.' When we die, we must go
back to Mother Earth lest our Father be a liar. The spirits of
those who accept Jesus fly up to heaven. Those that don't get
mixed up with old tree roots. I can tell you that as a little girl

I'd go to bed at night and pray to Jesus, 'Dear Jesus, I accept you. Please don't let me be mixed up with tree roots.' "

Lutie laughed. "That's a charming story. I do so love to hear their stories."

"I get more stories than work out of mine," Risé ruefully noted.

"A Negro is a Negro and nothing more." Jennifer said this without rancor. "They have to be told the same thing every day and watched to see if they do it then."

"I never have to watch Sin-Sin," Lutie said.

"She's the exception that proves the rule," Risé said.

"Yes," Jennifer piped up. "Certain Negroes are exceptional, but I think that goes back to whatever tribes their African ancestors were from. Obviously, some tribes were far more intelligent than others."

"Like the European tribes?" A light smile played over Hazel's lips.

"Just what do you mean by that?" Jennifer demanded.

"Anglos, Saxons, Jutes, Welsh, Irish, Gauls, Romans, Etruscans, Austrians, Prussians, Russians, Montenegrins, Czechs, Rumanians, Norwegians"—she breathed in—"the list could go on."

"It's not the same," Jennifer said.

"Why not?"

"Because those are Caucasian peoples."

"Oh, I forgot." Hazel, of course, had forgotten no such thing.

"There does seem to be differences in intelligence among the Caucasians," Kate remarked.

"I know what you're driving at." Jennifer spoke clearly. "But it won't wash, ladies, it won't wash. I have spent a lifetime with servants, as has each of you, and my entire experience has taught me that you can't let those people out in the world. Why, they're babes in the woods!"

"That's what men say about women." Lutie swung her purse, the velocity of that object being the only clue as to her inner feelings. Perhaps Henley was right about freeing Chatfield's slaves.

"Have you turned into an abolitionist?" Jennifer surveyed her with horror.

"No! I don't believe the Negro can go into the world as it now stands." She paused for dramatic effect. "But I think

with planning, schooling, moderation, they could be grad-
ually taught the responsibilities that go with freedom."

"Piffle." Jennifer dismissed this. By this time the women
had reached Kate Vickers's house. A smug lieutenant stood
there.

"Good morning, ladies." He bowed. "Allow me to introduce myself. I am Lieutenant Barbizon Hun. I understand
you have a wounded Yankee here."

"Yes, we do." Kate extended her hand to him.

"Is he well enough to be taken to Belle Island?"

"Certainly not!" Lutie rushed forward. The purse was
really swinging now. "He suffers terribly, especially at night
when his fever shoots up alarmingly."

"Might I see him?" Lieutenant Hun asked.

"Of course, if you would be good enough to give us one
moment to change his bandages," replied Lutie.

"I would like you to see him in the best possible circumstances." Kate's voice wavered with insecurity.

"Mrs. Vickers, you have one of the best home hospitals in
the city," he said. "I do understand your desire to have
things perfect."

Hazel and Risé chatted with the lieutenant while Kate and
Lutie hurried inside. Miranda casually walked Jennifer around
to the back porch. Jennifer wanted to know what the fuss was
about.

"He'll die over there in his condition. He needs good food
and attention."

"We aren't starving them." Jennifer's patriotism burst forth.

"How do you know? Have you forgotten last February and
March?" Miranda's voice fell low. "Even we couldn't get
enough to eat. Why would we feed prisoners before we feed
ourselves?"

"But he is the enemy!" Jennifer could be stubborn.

"He's a sick young man deluded by the thought that he is
preserving the Union."

Sin-Sin silently slipped into the sick room and wrapped
Gunther Krutzer with boiling towels. As soon as he looked
feverish she whisked them away. Lutie prepared him.

"Here he is, Lieutenant." Kate stood close to Barbizon
Hun's side.

The lieutenant, not fond of any sick man much less a sick
Yankee, said, "He does look feverish."

"It comes and goes." Lutie mournfully glanced at him while seated next to the suffering fellow.

The other wounded men viewed this ruse with some amusement. As enlisted men, they had no special love for officers; so it was fun to see this pompous banty rooster bested.

"What was your unit, soldier?"

"The One Hundred Third Pennsylvania, sir," Gunther answered through parched lips.

"Do you know you are a prisoner of war?"

"Yes, sir. When do you think I can be exchanged?"

"Your President Lincoln, in his vast wisdom, is now refusing to exchange prisoners. Be glad you are in Richmond and not in one of your own prisons, such as Elmira." The lieutenant glowered at the red and sweating man.

"I am glad, sir. These women have been angels of mercy." Krutzer was sincere.

Kate steered the lieutenant to the front door chattering about how difficult his duties must be and how she and the other women were forever indebted to men such as himself, the only bulwark between themselves and the bayonets of the enemy. He left in a cloud of compliment.

Kate reappeared in the sick room. "That ought to give us another two weeks."

"Thank you, Mrs. Vickers." Gunther's eyes misted.

Kate said, "I'll do what I can to keep you here, Private. Perhaps you can stay as an orderly once you're really back on your feet. I hope so. But if you try and escape, so help me God, I'll shoot you myself."

"Yes, ma'am, I believe you would."

JUNE 23, 1862

"Those two are thick as thieves again," Mars grumbled to Banjo. Geneva and Nash were once again on very friendly terms.

"I pay it no mind."

"What stuck in my craw was that Henley Chatfield let Jimmy have his room for two nights. And I take it Nash stayed there, too."

"Where'd the good colonel sleep?" Banjo picked burrs out of his horse's mane, deliberately seeming uninterested.

"Over at the Windsors'. Our house, as you know, was like the depot."

"Best party I ever attended." Banjo grinned.

"Except for that black devil hanging himself."

"Love takes a man in strange ways," Banjo continued as they rode up the Richmond, Fredericksburg, and Potomac Railroad track. They were right outside of Richmond, waiting for battle orders. "Knew a schoolteacher oncet. He explained to me that in ancient Greece an older man would love and care for a younger man until the young one grew a beard. He said it was a noble love. I said it might be noble in Greece, but you won't get far with it here."

Mars threw back his head and roared. "Go tell that to Jimmy!"

"Think I'll wait for the beard first."

JUNE 24, 1862

Phoebe Yates Pember sent a message to Kate to evacuate the strongest of the men. By nightfall, with tearful good-byes, every man was out of the house except for Joseph Rutledge and Gunther Krutzer. Beverly Fyffe and Gunther were distraught at having to part, but Beverly promised once the war was over they would visit one another.

Lutie bought a church almanac for each wounded man. She read them Matthew, chapter 3, as it was the Feast of the Nativity of St. John the Baptist. She loved the part where John calls the Pharisees and Sadducees a "generation of vipers."

Richmond was breeding its own generation of vipers, and no doubt Washington was, too. Lutie was especially disturbed at the behavior of the Vice-President, Alexander Stephens, who criticized Davis with spiraling vehemence. If you're going to be a man's Vice-President it would be prudent not to stab him in the back.

Watching the wounded men climb into carriages and wagons which would take them west of the city, Lutie overheard a soldier remark, "Heroism at the front; opportunism in the rear." Surely these brave boys deserved better than that, or at least a Vice-President who kept his mouth shut.

Life changed like fluffy clouds. A puff of wind and the clipper ship in the sky turned into a dragon. Another puff and the dragon was a frying pan. Lutie had grown up in a society where individuality was prized above all virtues, individuality and courage. Now the government was secreting power to itself from the states. The Confederacy was becoming centralized. Lutie knew that once power was accumulated it would never be willingly dispersed. Her world was disappearing.

"Good-bye." Kate waved to the last carriage.

"When do you suppose we'll receive more wounded?" Lutie asked her.

"Soon. Both cocks are in the ring and spurred. They have to fight."

"I think it'll be worse than last time."

"I do, too, and we have only a small surplus of medicines. I've asked Colonel Windsor for more."

"We could break up a few large buckets of charcoal. If all else fails, putting that on the wounds might retard gangrene."

Kate sighed. "Gangrene is what Richmond and Washington have. A plague on both their houses for the corruption those politicians have spawned."

"Corruption is the beginning of change," Lutie replied.

"What do you mean by that?"

"I don't know what I mean—but I mean it."

A light drizzle imprisoned Sin-Sin and Di-Peachy in the house. Both were stir-crazy from the absence of the men and the sudden gift of time on their hands. Everything was done that could be done. Bandages had been counted. Old sheets and fabric scraps had been searched out although there were few left since the onslaught of wounded from Seven Pines. Medicines had been catalogued and organized.

They sat in a gabled window high on the third floor overlooking Franklin Street. People carrying large umbrellas looked like black mushrooms as they hopped over puddles.

"Wasn't that funny when Kate's mother came to the party and criticized Varina Davis to Kate's face?" Di-Peachy leaned forward conspiratorially.

"Uh huh." Sin-Sin wore a violet and gold turban made from a piece of exquisite material Kate had given her.

"Said Varina aped royalty by putting her servants in expensive livery."

"She knows Kate tight with the first lady. Jes needlin' her."

"Kate said, 'What are we to do, Mama? Are we to level down or raise up? If servants don't wear livery in the President's house, they should go naked.' I thought the old lady would pitch a fit, but instead she laughed. Odd family." She paused. "I've always thought of you as my family, Auntie."

"I loves you."

In a sudden outburst, Di-Peachy said, "I wish I'd known my mother."

Sin-Sin stared out the window. "She was a kind soul and very beautiful."

"Do you remember your mother?"

"I see her face plain as I sees yours but it is queer to me, I cannot 'member one word my mother spoke to me, not nary a word. I 'member she brought me hot pot licker and bread in the mornings when I was small; but I been tryin' to 'member some words she spoke to me and I can't."

"Was she sold away?"

"No. Lucius Chatfield, Henley's father, din' believe in breakin' up families. Momma was killed in an accident with one of the horses. She was standin' by the big carriage—"

"The coach-in-fours?"

"That one. Arnold, Ernie June's daddy, dressed to sparkle, hung on the back. One of the horses went crazy rearin' and screamin', and the traces tangled up. He knock Momma down. She drug under those traces before Arnold could get her out. He was brave, that Arnold, 'cause he went right for the horses."

"I'm sorry." Di-Peachy rested her hand on Sin-Sin's.

"Honey, that was a long yesterday—"

"And a far tomorrow," Di-Peachy cut in.

"You gots the far tomorrows, not me. Tell me now, I knows you from little on up. What's workin' on your mind that you askin' me 'bout the past? We haven't had one minute to put our heads together since Mr. Henley told you the truth."

"Auntie, I feel I have the sin of both races in my face." She covered her face in her hands.

"Hush. I doan want to hear such talk! You got no stain on you. He got the stain. Yo' poor Momma got no stain on her neither."

"I knew, I always knew. Do you know what it's like to be loved, but never to belong?"

"You belong. You belong to Chatfield. You belong to me."

Tears ran from underneath her hands. She pulled her hands away from her face to wipe her cheeks with the backs of her hands. "I'm not black, and I'm not white."

"Thass a hard road. God provided you for it by giftin' you with a wondrous mind. Solomon was black. Simon of Cyrea, he was black and he bore Christ's cross as he wagged up Calvary Hill. You not useless. That brain in that body, no, thass not useless. Yo' think you the only café au lait on this earth?" A light tone crept into Sin-Sin's voice.

"No."

"You be here to do good. Doan be wastin' yo' time cryin' that you neither here nor there. You gots me and you gots Geneva and yo' beau." Sin-Sin wasn't so certain about the beau.

"I know I have you. I love you." More tears fell through her hands. "But Geneva—she's changed. We're in two different worlds now."

Sin-Sin noticed a gust of wind pull an umbrella over a man's head. He stood in the rain, furiously trying to bring it down.

"Geneva told me," continued Di-Peachy, "that Henley is going to free everyone at Chatfield on Christmas."

Sin-Sin took this quite calmly. "Zat a fact?"

"But you know," Di-Peachy spoke, "much as I want that for everyone, I think Henley's doing it for his vanity. He's more worried about his soul than he is about us!"

"See what I mean 'bout your brain? Don't hate the man for why he's doin' it. Good always mixed up with bad. He's doin' something! Thass more than you can say for most."

"And Lutie doesn't want him to do it. She thinks someone like Braxton could go and make a living, but someone like Frederica would be crushed. Lutie's subordinating the larger issue to individual people. Henley subordinates people to the issue."

"Who cares so long as we be free."

Di-Peachy wiggled in her seat. "If we were treated the way people in the North think we're treated, it would be easier. We're not bound by chains, Auntie Sin-Sin, we're bound by ties of love. You love Lutie, and I love Geneva!"

"I loves Lutie."

"Don't you see, it would be so much easier if we could hate them."

"Hate's cancer. Eat you right up. Listen to me, it take a long, long time to develop mother wit." Sin-Sin smiled. "Lutie be worth my love. You worth it. I could no more break my invisible chains than fly! Love be my honor."

Di-Peachy said, "They say niggers and women have no honor."

"This nigger woman does!" Sin-Sin blazed. "Don't envy the whites. They got chains, but they thinks they free. Least I knows my chains."

"I don't want any chains!"

"Then you don't want to live, girl. We bound to one another hand and foot. This whole human race, I don't give jack shit 'bout they color nor they sex, we bound hand and foot, and we goin' to walk to glory or we goin' to walk to hell! I used to cry 'bout bein' a slave. Oh, yes, you wouldn't know it now. I hated it. I still care but I'm an old woman. Makes no sense fo' me to care too much. One day I heard God. I heard his sweet music in my soul and ever since then, I doan care like I used to 'bout what happens to this husk. No one owns my soul. You gettin' like the white folks. You gettin' seduced by they money and they power and they land, but they have no peace."

"The war will be over soon."

"For a smart girl you sure dumb. War be on the outside. Peace be in the heart. I pity white folks. Doan be imitatin' them else you lose yo' heart and you lose yo' soul."

"But I'm swept up in their madness."

"Even Jesus swept up in madness, chile."

Di-Peachy looked at Sin-Sin's dear face. "I think I have to live more before I can accept, if I ever can."

"You thinkin' I laying down like a wiped dog? You think thass what I'm talkin' about? We each climbin' a mountain, and the top be where God and his angels waitin' for us. Everybody climbin' this mountain, Di-Peachy. Even little Chinamen climbin' this mountain. The rich man, he stop to admire or grab glittery rubies and diamonds and whatever he can. He ain't gettin' too far. But I climbs straight up. This mountain is in our hearts. Acceptin' doan mean you lie down. I ain't no weak woman. I changes what I can. What I can't, well, I prays for another day or another person someday, when I dead and gone, to change things. I can't do everythin', but I can climb. You can climb. We can redeem ourselves. Jesus shine a light for you on that mountain, but you gotta climb it!" Sin-Sin finished. A silence.

"I'm thinking."

"Must be that whirrin' sound I hear."

"Sometimes I feel such a sadness wash over me. It's like a tidal wave of grief, but I don't know where it comes from."

"It means somebody dyin' way off somewhere, and we doan know it."

"Someone I don't know?"

"God give each of us little pieces of other people's souls even when we doan know them. When you sad like that, one of 'em dies. You see, honey, we all part of one another. Thass white folks' terrible curse. They cuts off everyone from them. They thinkin' they superior but they jes alone, and when they hear that coffin's hollow moan, it too late."

JUNE 25, 1862

Just before sunrise, Lutie, Kate, Di-Peachy, Sin-Sin, and the other ladies of the Vickerses' home hospital were awakened by the boom of cannon. The windows shook in the house. The ladies, together with the servants, Joseph and Gunther, quickly assembled in the conservatory. The cannonade rattled the glass with consistent rhythm.

"It sounds quite close," said Jennifer, who was observed talking loudly to thin air before she descended the curving stairway.

"We knew the battle had to begin sometime." Hazel sniffed the odor of redeye gravy coming from the kitchen.

Bebe Austin entered the room. "I rushed over here as fast as I could. My information is that our men under John Bankhead Magruder have opened fire upon the enemy."

Risé whispered into Miranda's ear. "Last night's pillow talk."

"We might as well get used to the sound. It'll go on all day," said Lutie.

The ladies dismissed for breakfast. They thought by night-fall the wounded would begin to arrive.

Sin-Sin counted and recounted supplies. She couldn't stand being idle. Di-Peachy finally pulled her aside.

"I've been thinking about what you said yesterday."

"Good." Sin-Sin beamed.

"Does that apply to Ernie June? Is she climbing a mountain to God?" A malicious twinkle danced in Di-Peachy's eyes.

Sin-Sin bristled. "Even the Good Lord's allowed a few duds!"

Geneva and the regiment picked up General Stuart as they rode north on the Brooke Turnpike. The territory was familiar to everybody. This time the force was two thousand sabers plus Captain John Pelham's battery. Another force of cavalry was assigned to watch the right flank of the enemy. These men covered the road to Charles City, Williamsburg, and the James River.

Geneva again had three days of corn and bacon in her haversack and tea in her canteen. No baggage trains followed the column, so Geneva knew they'd be traveling light. If anything went wrong, they'd live off the land. If they were fortunate in battle, they'd live off the enemy.

No Federals were in sight. The column, marching through intermittent rain, passed Yellow Tavern, perched in the middle of fields. By the afternoon they'd crossed the Chickahominy at Upper Bridge alongside the Richmond, Fredericksburg, and Potomac Railroad. An entire brigade of infantry waited there. The men hollered at the horsemen. The cavalrymen usually didn't deign to holler back, but they waved their caps.

They bore left. The sound of cannon was faint now. "I heard that an entire block of Locust Alley has been given over to an army of scarlet women," Geneva chatted.

Nash hoped this war would be over soon. The longer Geneva was in it, the worse she got. Nash pushed his horse up next to hers and growled under his breath, "You disgust me. You're not here because you love me. You're here because it suits you. If I left, you'd stay."

She snarled back. "I joined because of you, and I'm staying because of you. Don't say that you'd leave, because you won't. I used to look up to you, but you're not the end all and be all. I'm out in the world now, and I've got a mind of my own."

"That's exactly why women should stay at home."

Banjo, riding behind them, noticed the mounting anger. "You two are like oil and water today. Jimmy, go on up and ride point." Point was first man, ahead of the advance unit.

"With pleasure!"

Furious, she trotted forward. She neared Ashland Station and saw low clouds. These were dust clouds. She wheeled, cantering back to the advance guard. Fitz Lee was up front today. A reward perhaps for his tenacious covering of their rear during the three days' ride.

"Colonel Lee." She saluted. "Jackson's coming, sir. I saw the dust clouds. They should be at Ashland Station in time to bivouac for the night."

"Thank you, Sergeant. You may return to duty." What Fitz Lee didn't tell her was that Jackson had been due at Ashland Station at sunup, not after sundown. The less the troops knew, the better. Why force them to bear the anxieties of a senior officer? If a man is captured, the less he knows, the less he can blurt out or unwittingly reveal to the enemy.

Mars knew as well as Fitz Lee that the plan was for Magruder to make a demonstration on the center of McClellan's line. Stuart was to screen Jackson's advance on the left, once that general arrived from the valley. The other generals, D.H. Hill, A.P. Hill, and Longstreet, together with Jackson, would roll up McClellan's right. There's an old saying, Between a rock and a hard place. McClellan was between a swamp and a swamp and two rivers. The York River could afford him naval assistance; the James River could not. The only thing about the terrain was that the Confederates had to move through it as well as the Federals. Nature didn't take sides.

Before sunset a large, bright rainbow arched over the Confederate camps immediately outside Richmond. The raindrops sparkled like diamonds falling through sunshine.

"What do you think it means?" Banjo asked Nash.

"That we're all dumb beasts on Noah's ark."

JUNE 26, 1862

From far away a toy bugle sounded. An army of elves was blowing reveille. Riding point along the Virginia Central Railroad, Geneva and Nash heard it.

The pearl-gray haze grudgingly revealed an orchard here, a meadow there, a lean-to shed on a dewy meadow. Husband and wife were the two points on the railroad. Mars had fanned out scouts on every road and path. Their mission was to keep alert for Yankees.

At sunrise, the advance of Stuart's column was at Merry Oaks Church on the Ashcake Road. One mile east of the road ran the Virginia Central Railroad.

The crackle of carbines told Geneva and Nash that they were lucky not to be riding down the railroad.

The cloudless sky shone a robin's egg blue.

"I thought we'd hear cannon by now," Geneva said.

"Maybe we're too far behind the line. Here, chew some hickory 'bacca. Takes your mind off food." Nash handed her a strip of hickory bark, thin and sappy.

They moved on. Two squadrons were about one mile behind them. If they ran into resistance, the squadron would be up quickly. If the resistance proved formidable, two squadrons ought to be able to hold them until the column hurried forward.

Ahead lay Taliaferro's Mill, a familiar landmark that they had passed two weeks ago.

"Wish we had some of that ground fog back." Geneva's nerves sang a warning. A sudden hail of bullets tore into the trees and kicked up the dust around the horses' feet. Nash wheeled and turned the squadrons with Geneva right behind him. "Bluebirds!" Nash sang out.

Von Borcke, riding halfway between Geneva and the squadron, signaled them to move up.

"They're deployed along both sides of the road. They've dismounted." Geneva reined in next to the Prussian.

"How many?"

"At least a squadron," answered Nash. "They know we're coming."

Mars rode up. "Dismount, fan out, and press forward. By the time the column comes up, they'll be pinned by fire. When they break for their horses, we can mop them up."

Geneva crawled on her belly between Nash and Banjo. She fired her Henry rifle. "I'm not hitting the broad side of a barn." Dust up her nose and in her mouth further irritated her.

"Little whizzing over their heads ought to keep those boys honest. Doesn't matter if you hit any or not." Banjo squeezed the trigger.

"There they go!" Geneva stood up.

"Keep firing!" Mars bellowed as he stood and motioned for the men to run forward.

The Yankees leapt on their horses and were quickly out of range, but the head squadron of the column now pursued them.

Geneva kicked at the soft earth.

Mars laughed at her. "Did I ever tell you about Epaminondas?"

"No." She walked next to him as they returned to their horses.

"Up until the time of Epaminondas, whenever there was an armed dispute, men just ran at one another pell-mell and that was it. But Epaminondas developed the echelon, a column of men who would obey orders—turn right, turn left, go forward, fall back. When he did that, war became a science. You're still at the pell-mell stage." He clapped her on the back.

Henley Chatfield stayed at a respectful distance from General Robert E. Lee and President Davis. Headquarters for the army was the Dabbs' House, on the north side of Nine Mile Road, perhaps one and one-half miles from Richmond. It was two o'clock.

Apart from Magruder's continued demonstration at the center of McClellan's line, there seemed to be an ominous lack of activity on the enemy's right.

Henley hovered in the background on the Mechanicsville Turnpike. The earthenworks protecting the permanent gun positions rose out of the ground like red shoulders of half-buried titans. On either side of the road, men stood at attention by their guns. Most artillerists acted like old men, fussing at ammunition boxes, checking and rechecking harness, testing spokes of the gun carriages for light artillery. Heavy artillery men, though equally fussy, had the starch burnt out of them. Standing at their posts since sunup, they felt wilted by two in the afternoon.

President Davis, a blackbird amidst gray catbirds, stood out among his entourage of staff officers. He wasn't saying much.

On the other side of the road, General Robert E. Lee affected a glacial composure. He betrayed neither anger nor irritation, but his glance swept to his left. Nothing was happening.

General Magruder, for the second day, blasted away at McClellan's center doing exactly as he was asked to do and in good form.

Henley wondered if it was usually this calm at field headquarters. Sharp rifle fire snapped him out of his stupor. Officers quickly stared through field glasses. A young major with prodigious brown sideburns offered a pair of field glasses to Henley, pointing to the rolling hills dotted here and there with woodlands.

"Over there, Colonel."

Henley observed figures of blue in a ragged line falling back from Meadow Bridges. This bridge over the Chickahominy was one and one-half miles from the village of Mechanicsville toward the northwest. The road leading to it was roughly parallel to the Mechanicsville Turnpike. The red Confederate battle flag unfurled like a tongue in the slight breeze. "We're coming on in columns of four," said Henley.

"A.P. Hill," the Major commented.

"I need a courier," called out Charles Venable, an aide-de-camp to General Lee.

"I can take that." Henley stepped forward.

"Colonel Chatfield, I'm sure one of the boys will be up in an instant."

"An instant might be too late." Henley smiled.

The general noticed this exchange. "Never was a message in such capable hands." A fleeting smile crossed his bearded face.

"Find A.P. Hill at the Meadow Bridges, Colonel, and wait for him to reply, if you will. Oh, Colonel Chatfield, take this extra paper and pencil. The officers have a habit of losing them."

Henley carefully slid the material into the inside pocket of his tunic. He gracefully swung onto a big gelding and moved off toward the roar of the guns.

By the tollgate he had to decide whether to press on the Mechanicsville Turnpike or to cut over on one of the side roads and take his chances. If he pushed straight ahead, he'd smack into the Yankees eventually. If he rode off to the side, perhaps he could circle them without losing too much time.

The rich fragrance of June filled his nostrils. He asked the gelding for a strong canter.

The sounds of battle grew louder. His heart raced. He thought to himself that his daughter had faced this as had his son. For a second, Henley felt his heart might burst with fear, excitement, grief, and pride. Those emotions, for himself and his children mixed together, stirred in him as he swept closer to danger.

Cutting across a meadow, a swarm of milk-white butterflies appeared out of the grasses, hesitated, and then darted off, a parasol of winged happiness. Henley noticed them out of the corner of his eye. Immediately up ahead was Meadow Bridges Road. Once on a solid road, he urged the gelding to a gallop.

As he cut across a meadow, noise burst in his ears. He began passing over bodies. Ahead of him he could make out the last of a column of infantry moving up double-quick, discipline holding tight.

He clattered over the bridge, slowing the horse. He couldn't charge by the column. He held a fast trot on the outside of the men. Most of them were looking at some point off in the distance. Their energies focused on what was about to happen. Each man seemed absorbed in his private world.

The horse snorted and reared. A disemboweled corpse frightened the animal. For the first time in his life, Henley smelled hot blood. The odor was strong. He'd smelled it when pigs and cattle were slaughtered, but he'd never smelled human blood. It smelled sweeter. For a moment he felt woozy. He shook his head vigorously and passed along the moving brigade. A stern infantry colonel rode ahead of his men.

"Colonel." Henley saluted smartly. "Where might I find A.P. Hill?"

"Up ahead, sir. The fat's in the fire!"

A ball whistled overhead, exploding about fifteen feet away. The men didn't flinch, but pressed on.

Henley now heard shouting and screaming. The fire grew hotter. His heart pounded so hard he thought his ribs would break.

The late afternoon heat caused moisture to glisten on bayonets, on foreheads, on the flanks of horses.

Ten minutes later under heavy fire, Henley found A.P. Hill, a handsome man in his late thirties who was eager to fight.

Henley dismounted, handing the reins of his lathered horse to a placid sergeant. "From General Lee, sir." Henley saluted.

Hill read the note. A lieutenant handed him a small lap board. Hill wrote a reply, put it in an envelope, and gave it to Henley.

Henley saluted and ran toward his horse. He felt himself float up in the air and then crash to earth. A cannonball removed his right kneecap from his outstretched leg, passed between his legs, and blew off his left leg completely from the knee down. He was tossed in the air, then dumped like a doll.

"Colonel Chatfield! Colonel Chatfield!"

Henley pushed up on his elbows. He struggled to clear his mind.

"You are hit, sir."

Another voice leaned over him. "I'll take the message, Colonel."

"Yes, of course." He handed the envelope over. "Take the horse, too. Headstrong. Belongs to Mrs. Vickers."

"Yes, sir." The man vaulted into the saddle and spurred away.

"Stretcher!" the first voice shouted.

Henley saw his boot about eight yards from him. "That is my leg, is it not?"

"I'm afraid it is," replied the sergeant who had held his horse.

He looked down and saw his legs. He trembled violently for an instant, then forced himself to be calm. "Sergeant, carry me to that tree, will you? And bring me a lapboard."

"A stretcher will be here in a moment, Colonel."

"I'll bleed to death before they get me to the field hospital. Please do as I ask."

Two men carried him to the tree. The hum of bullets darted around them.

"The lapboard, sir."

"May I ask you, young man, to do me one last favor? Will you see that these letters reach my wife in Richmond?"

"I will do that, Colonel."

"You are most kind." Henley, wishing to make use of what energy he had remaining to him, pulled paper out of his tunic. He wrote quickly.

My Dearest Wife,
    I never knew what I had in you. Forgive me. Until we meet in heaven, I love you.

Your husband,
Henley

He smoothed out another piece of paper on the board.

Dear Geneva,
    Remember, the mare is sixty percent of the horse. The speed comes from the stallion, but the heart comes from the dam. Carry on our breeding program. Take care of your mother. You are all she has now. I live in you, my child.

Your loving father

Hands beginning to tremble, he wrote another letter.

Dear Di-Peachy,
    You brought me only joy.

Love,
Your father

He forced himself to write one last letter.

Dear Baron Schecter:
   I regret not being able to give you satisfaction. It seems I satisfied a Yankee first.
                    June 26, 1862
                    Colonel Henley Chatfield, C.S.A.

Ebbing fast, he handed these folded papers to the sergeant. He watched men hurry past him with slight interest. A locust sputtered for an instant. The boom of another cannon convinced the insect she couldn't outsing that roar.

He thought of Chatfield and the seventeen-year locusts. Once every seventeen years, each tree, bush, and building would be crawling with the large green-black bugs, their eyes popping. Harmless, the cacophony of those millions of joined locust trills was enough to drive him crazy. Yet he looked forward to each seventeenth year. Next one would be in 1877. He had seen the seventeen-year locusts three times in his life. When he sold Di-Peachy's mother, in '43, translucent tan locust shells were everywhere. Like a dead soldier, a locust shell, the essence is elsewhere. "Did she love me? Did she ever really love me?" He felt pain, but no self-pity. Rousing himself for one last look at the world, he noticed the lacy pattern of the leaves, the handiwork of a master. "Our Father who art in heaven, Hallowed be thy Name. Thy Kingdom come, Thy will—"

"Curious," Kate remarked to Lutie. The cannons belched for two days, but few wounded filtered into Richmond. Every now and then an ambulance cart would clatter past the house, but an odd silence prevailed.

"I think this battle may not be fully joined," Lutie said.

"Yes," Kate replied. "My husband once said that danger has a bright face. I expect he's seeing it now."

"Ever notice how in times of trouble, people invent reasons for it?"

"Such as?"

"A woman loses a valuable shawl. She says to herself, 'This is my punishment for being short with dear Aunt Helen.' "

Kate chuckled. "I do that all the time."

"Humans are unwilling to believe that great suffering and disaster can be inflicted without moral justification."

"I usually have the strength to bear great suffering, some-one else's great suffering." Kate smiled.

"Where is the baron these days?"

Kate's eyebrows twitched upward. "I do hope, Lutie, that is a non sequitur."

"Well, of course it is, Kate."

"Miss Kate, someone is here to see you," Evangelista softly interrupted.

"At eleven-thirty? It must be the wounded at last. Let's see."

"Miss Kate, Miss Lutie should stay inside for a minute."

A cold spear burrowed in Lutie's stomach. Kate put her hand on Lutie's shoulder. "Let me go first. Wait here with Sin-Sin."

Kate nervously hurried outside. The ambulance cart had one body in it, Henley. A blanket covered his wounded right leg and his severed left. His face was completely white. "Oh, no!" She buried her face in her hands.

The ambulance driver was distressed to see such a beauti-ful woman in tears. "Fine-looking man. The general told us to bring him here soon as we could get away. Terrible fight today, ma'am. Couldn't go out for the wounded 'til long after sunset."

Kate composed herself. "I thank you for bringing him here. If you wait a moment, I shall have him carried in."

Jensen and the stable boy quickly ran to the wagon. Kate instructed them. "Put the colonel in my room. We may need the other rooms for wounded. Jensen, find some ice if you can. We'll pack him in it."

She squared her shoulders and walked into the house. Lutie and Sin-Sin, motionless, waited. Di-Peachy had joined them.

"My dearest Lutie—"

"It's Henley, isn't it?"

Kate broke down and cried. She had so wanted to be a source of support for Lutie. "Yes. But wait, let us get him upstairs before you look at him."

"Lord God, no!" Sin-Sin's throaty voice shook.

Di-Peachy remained silent. A father found and a father lost.

"Please step into the kitchen until Jensen prepares him."

Twenty minutes later, Lutie, Sin-Sin, and Di-Peachy followed Kate upstairs.

Lutie walked into Kate's bedroom. Aside from his marbled whiteness, he didn't look that bad. Silvery curls framed his face.

"He looks like the boy I married," she whispered. "Death stole his years."

"Don't lift up the blanket, Lutie." Kate moved between her and the body.

"What happened?"

"Lost his left leg and part of the right. There's no need to look."

"I've seen worse."

"Yes, but those men weren't your husband."

Lutie leaned forward and ran her fingers through his curls. Sin-Sin came behind her to catch her if she fainted.

"The ambulance driver also handed me these letters," Kate gently informed Lutie.

"He wrote one to Baron Schecter, too. The driver told me that half the army is talking about it. The other half will find out tomorrow."

"What?" Lutie forced herself to stay reasonable.

"Schecter is with A.P. Hill. Henley couldn't have known that the baron was perhaps two hundred yards from him. His letter was delivered minutes after he died."

"What did it say?"

" 'Dear Baron: I regret not being able to give you satisfaction. It seems I satisfied a Yankee first.' "

Lutie laughed until her laughter turned into tears. "He never broke stride." She placed her face next to his cold cheek and sobbed.

Even *The New York Times* carried Henley Chatfield's obituary. They called him "the greatest horseman of modern times." The London *Times*, *Le Matin de Paris*, the St. Petersburg paper, and papers throughout Europe noted his passing. But the event in his life that passed through time was his note to Schecter. Whenever an outsider would ask what it meant to be a Southern gentleman, inevitably the story of Henley Chatfield writing a note while he lay dying on the Mechanicsville battlefield would be recounted.

JUNE 27, 1862

Old Cold Harbor Road, deeply rutted, was intersected by numerous farm roads in equally deplorable condition. Geneva rode toward the noise in front of her. A hot battle raged and cavalry was not a part of it.

Stuart's force, spread out, was sweeping a wide front from Old Cold Harbor Road as far north as Old Church Road, almost to the Pamunkey River.

Mars cast his men out like a net, and they picked over the fields, each man within sight of the other. Occasionally an overturned wagon would break the monotony, but the Federal cavalry eluded them. So did the Federal infantry who had withdrawn in the night to superior defensive positions.

Geneva tried to put together the pieces of this scattered puzzle based upon what she had seen with her own eyes and what she had heard from others. Used for information and to screen Jackson, the cavalry hadn't been assigned a combat role. This infuriated Geneva. She also knew Jackson lagged behind. The guns barked perhaps three miles distant from where she rode. Someone was mixing it up in the direction of the Chickahominy. Why didn't the Yankees come out into the open fields where everyone could maneuver? The temperature in the swamps was five to ten degrees hotter than on the meadows. Artillery men nearly fried, for their guns also produced heat. Vines grew thick amidst the trees, choking movement in swamps and bogs.

The gentle farmlands along Old Cold Harbor Road would make an excellent battlefield as well as a splendid place for cavalry to wheel, clash, wheel, and clash again. A cluster of woods or a glistening pond added interest to the rolling wheat fields and corn. She passed a lovely peach orchard and was sorry it was too early in the season for the gnarled trees to bear fruit.

"What's he doing up there?" wondered Geneva aloud, to herself. Mars was about two hundred yards ahead of the thin line.

"Ants in his pants," Banjo declared.

Nash, riding on the other side of Banjo, was less kind. "Wants everyone to notice him, the conceited ass."

Geneva, accustomed to Nash's consistent antipathy to Mars, said nothing.

"Good land," said Banjo. "Appears the farmer built himself a spite fence." He pointed to a stone fence about six feet in height. The gray fieldstones, carefully positioned, fit into each other like interlocking fingers.

A sheet of flame startled them. Federals appeared from behind the fence. More Yankees, mounted, spun around outbuildings and the farmhouse.

Mars grabbed his left arm.

"Colonel!" Geneva screamed.

"Stay back here!" Nash ordered.

Geneva spurred Dancer with Banjo right beside her.

Another burst of fire hit Mars's horse. A bullet passed about one inch below the animal's eyes. Crazed and dying, the animal charged the fence, then surged over the high barrier. More gunfire spit.

Geneva and Banjo were now fifty yards behind Mars. "I'm going over!" Geneva shouted to Banjo, her head resting low near Dancer's outstretched neck.

Banjo nodded, wondering how the hell she could clear that stone fence. Colonel Vickers's horse had done it only with a burst of superior, final strength.

"Dancer can clear anything! Cover me!" With that she grabbed Dancer with steel calves, leaned forward with her seat deep in the saddle, and fed the bay the bit. Dancer, ripping huge hunks of earth as she ran, gathered her bulky hindquarters under her and shot over the solid fence with a foot to spare. Banjo's jaw dropped on his chest. He skidded to a stop at the fence, tucked his feet on his saddle, and sprang to the top of the fence as gracefully and economically as a gray cat. He fired both pistols into the scattered Yanks, oblivious to his exposed status.

Mars was stumbling away from his dead horse who collapsed on the other side of the jump. His mare's feet didn't touch the ground, she folded like an accordion. Blood covered Mars's left side.

"Swing up, Colonel." Geneva leaned over and helped him up. Banjo cursed the Yanks and continued to cover them.

"You can't jump back over with me. Save yourself, Jimmy," Mars commanded.

"Can't hear you, Colonel." Geneva galloped along the wall looking for a way out. Bullets slammed into the stone.

"Get back, you walleyed sons of bitches!" Banjo screamed. A bullet tore his cap off. He didn't miss a beat.

"Flaming hell!" Nash jumped up beside Banjo. The two men ran rightward on top of the wall, firing and cursing together.

Out of the small, enclosed apple orchard, a Yankee captain ran forward, waving a white handkerchief. He stood still and motioned with his left hand that there was a turn up ahead.

As she approached him, Geneva slowed.

The Federal captain, clear green eyes, called up to her, "Anyone who can jump like that deserves to live! Get out of here!"

"Jimmy Chatfield, Charlottesville, Virginia. Find me when this war is over!" She dug into Dancer's flanks and barreled through the small opening in the wall where a portion had fallen into disrepair.

Banjo and Nash, seeing the escape, vaulted off the wall.

"By God, you're a fine fellow!" Banjo slapped Nash on the back, exuberant at their exploit. Banjo ran underneath the wall until he found his cap. Jubilantly he picked it up and stuck his finger through the hole. "Those factory boys are improving their marksmanship."

Geneva thundered to a nondescript little crossroad, then cut hard left toward the sound of artillery. She knew a field hospital would be stationed somewhere behind the main line of infantry dispute.

Mars's head leaned on her back. She glanced down. Dancer's left flank was deep red with the Colonel's blood. She felt hot liquid soaking through her left side where his arm swung up and back as they flew onward.

When she saw the yellow hospital flag, she sent up a silent prayer. Arms and legs lay outside the tent. The earth was slippery with blood. She reined in her grateful horse, slid down, and gently pulled Mars off. He was conscious but foggy.

Two orderlies met her and put Mars on a litter. She followed them to where they laid him. For a moment she didn't notice her surroundings. The screams and sobs meant nothing to her. She leaned over Mars, tears splashing on his face. "Don't die, Colonel, please don't die! I love you! I never knew how much I loved you!"

His eyes fluttered open as he whispered, "But I did." He closed his eyes.

She put her head to his chest. His heart was beating.

A major, covered from head to toe in blood, knelt beside Mars. He took his pulse. He pulled an eyelid back. "On the table!" he shouted.

"I'm not leaving him," Geneva cried.

"Do as you please, Sergeant, but don't pass out or vomit near me. I've got enough to do." The surgeon brushed by her.

Mars was slapped on a table after a fresh bucket of water was thrown on it. Behind him was another table and one was behind that, a row of torture. Immediately behind the Colonel, she saw a foot being tossed on the pile as though it were a ham hock. A bloody stump confronted her. The surgeon feverishly tied off the artery with waxed thread.

The surgeon and his assistants worked like a well-oiled machine. They cut off Mars's tunic and the shirt underneath. They examined his upper body to see if he'd taken any more wounds.

An orderly rapidly washed the left arm.

"No chloroform," the surgeon said. He stared into two holes on Mars's bicep. Then he pulled the arm away from the body. "One in. One out. Forceps!"

A master sergeant handed him the long steel instrument after wiping it on his bloody apron. Another man held the arm down. Plunging into the ugly tear, the surgeon probed for the bullet. He saw no signs of shattered bone, but he couldn't feel the bullet either.

"Do you want the scalpel, sir?"

"When I want it, I'll ask for it!" he snarled. He probed again, none too deliberately. "Ah!" He played with the forceps and extracted a bullet, perfectly shaped.

"May I have that?" Geneva tearfully asked.

"Huh?" The surgeon had forgotten she was there. He tossed it to her.

"Will he live?"

"He's lost a great deal of blood, but he ought to make it." He spun to face the next case, a man shot through the throat. Mars was carried away from the field tent and put in a grove of trees. Geneva followed him. Once she was sure he was still alive, she fetched Dancer. Removing her tack, she led the exhausted mare by throwing the bridle reins around her neck, then put her on the other side of the grove. Geneva brought her a bucket of water and a bucket of corn. The orderly chatted that they'd taken supply wagons from the Federals and the corn was one of the prizes. After Dancer drank her fill, Geneva pumped up more water and gave the horse a sponge bath.

A wounded man called to her, "Blooded, ain't she? Where'd you get her?"

"My father, Henley Chatfield, bred her."

A cloud of dissatisfaction blotted his serene composure. "I'm sorry 'bout him."

"Why, what happened?"

Terribly upset that this tall, skinny boy didn't know the truth, the wounded man quietly said, "He was killed yesterday at Mechanicsville. Took it calm. Wrote letters."

Geneva stared at the kind face of the battered man. She touched her finger to her cap by way of thanks and walked back to Mars. She sat cross-legged beside him and buried her face in her hands. Racking sobs convulsed her. Those wounded who were conscious whispered one to another. Soon they knew Henley Chatfield's boy, a young one at that, was among them.

One man, considering himself luckier than the rest because he'd lost only three fingers from his hand, came over. "Sergeant, would you like a belt of whiskey?"

She wiped her nose on her sleeve. "No, I'll be all right. Thank you."

He touched her shoulder and walked back to the others.

Mars moaned and twisted. He opened his eyes. "I'm alive?"

Geneva bent over him. "You're gonna pull through, Colonel."

"May I have a drink of water?"

"Here." She held her canteen under his lips and told him about her father.

Mars reached up and put his right hand on her cheek. She rested her head on his hand for a moment. "Don't you die, Colonel."

"I'm not dying." He fought to stay awake, but fell asleep again.

Geneva curled up next to him as night came. She could still hear guns. She thought about Henley. It didn't seem possible that he was gone. She wondered if her mother was holding on. She vaguely remembered Lutie's hysteria when Jimmy died. The aftermath she remembered only too well. But when Sumner was killed, Lutie seemed to grasp life more firmly instead of letting it slip away. There were no men left in the family.

She remembered her father's face, the deep creases alongside his mouth, his huge hands, the sprig of gray hair that sometimes peeped out from under his unbuttoned shirts on a sultry summer day. Henley smelled of tobacco and horses. It would be difficult to imagine Chatfield without his scent, without his heavy tread shaking the floorboards, without him falling asleep in the peach room with a newspaper over his face.

The face of the good-looking Yankee captain jumped into her head. That man could have killed them both. When he held up his white handkerchief, his men held their fire. Why did he do that? Why am I fighting such a man?

For the first time Geneva had an inkling of what she was doing, of what they were all doing. It was wrong. It was so profoundly wrong that she felt cold sweat trickling down her armpits. Gripped with a fear unlike any she had ever known, she curled up beside Mars, seeking an answer in his animal warmth.

JUNE 28, 1862

Throughout the night columns of transport rattled over cobbled streets. A new army of wounded invaded the city. Roughly nine thousand men had fallen by yesterday evening. The hospitals, overwhelmed with even greater numbers of wounded than before, pitched tents on the lawns for the soldiers.

Clearly the battle wasn't over. McClellan, never defeated conclusively, would withdraw and then turn to fight again. Rather his generals on his right fought, for McClellan apparently waited for Joshua to be sent down from heaven, trumpets and all.

Lutie, Sin-Sin, Bebe, Di-Peachy, and the ladies worked "from can until can't."

Kate pleaded with Lutie to rest after they returned from Hollywood Cemetery. Henley's hastily arranged funeral was punctuated by incessant artillery fire. Kate had allowed the colonel to be buried in her family plot. Lutie would have him removed to Chatfield later.

When a gleaming hearse clattered up to Kate's front door in the morning and the undertaker presented her with a mahogany casket, complete with ornate bronze railings, everyone was surprised. Hearses were working overtime, and caskets were hard to find. Even the highest ranking officers were going to their graves in pine coffins.

Lutie, asking no questions, allowed her husband to be placed in the tufted white satin. She kept his officer's sword, his watch, and his red sash. He was buried in the uniform in which he fell.

As the women withdrew from the cemetery, the undertaker surreptitiously slipped Kate a note. The funeral arrangements had been made by Baron Schecter. He galloped into Richmond from Mechanicsville after eleven o'clock at night, made provisions for Colonel Chatfield, turned around and rejoined General A.P. Hill. The funeral director wryly made note that the Baron's dazzling white tunic and other Austrian bric-a-brac were encrusted with blood and dust.

When Kate read Lutie his note, Lutie remarked, "These arrangements were made more for your benefit than for my husband's, but I am grateful all the same. If he lives through this hell, please don't turn him away from your door for my sake."

By the time they got back to Kate's house, they had a new crop of wounded. Gunther Krutzer had already organized the men according to the severity of their injury. Bebe Austin, in charge, rushed to the door when Kate and the Albemarle ladies returned.

She told Kate that Mars's name was posted on the bulletin outside the capitol. He'd been wounded.

"Why don't you sit down?" Now Lutie urged Kate to retire.

"He's alive. My blow is nothing compared to yours."

"I don't believe in comparative pain," Lutie said.

"I wish I had your courage."

A howl from the next room and the figure of Hazel Whitmore running out for more bandages galvanized both of them.

"You have plenty of courage. We've buried our dead; let's do what we can for the living."

The howl came from Frazier Hawkins of Hood's Fourth Texans. He'd been shot through both lungs as well as the thigh. He was slowly drowning in his own blood.

As Lutie washed him, he babbled between bloody gasps for air. "—bent over like I was turkey hunting. We ran down a slope, and General Hood, he was running right on ahead, and, ma'am, the lead was fearsome. I don't know how I saw the sky for the fire, but the worst part was when we reached the bottom of the hill. It was a tangle and a mess, and those Yanks were thick on the other side of that creek. More up on top of the slope. I didn't even stop to take aim and fire. I jumped over and pumped up the side of that hill. I didn't start firing until we got over the breastworks. Must have been one hundred degrees, and those Yanks, they'd been fighting all day, they finally gave it up. Those of us that made it up the hill, we give 'em everything we had. Didn't know I was hit until then. I saw my leg bleeding a little, and then like a mess of hornets, I felt them bullets rip into my lungs. Like a terrible thump. We died like flies in a sugar bowl . . . just like flies."

Lutie put a cold compress on his glistening forehead. "You rest quietly."

He sat bolt upright and grabbed her. "Sister, I want to see you in heaven." He released his grip, then lurched back, dead.

"Jensen," Lutie called. She suddenly thought of Big Muler. Whatever his insanity over Di-Peachy, he had labored like Hercules to help the wounded. Jensen, with difficulty, moved Frazier Hawkins out to the barn.

As heat climbed into the low nineties, the day pulsated with a nightmare quality.

"Glad to see you're back in the saddle, Colonel Vickers," said a soldier.

"Thank you." Mars's lips were white with pain.

Mars and Geneva trotted toward Dispatch Station on the York River Railroad line.

"Let's rest. A drink of water and a little corn and hardtack, compliments of the U.S. Army, will do you good."

"I've returned to duty. I can manage."

"Yeah, you can manage to make yourself worse," said Geneva.

At Dispatch Station the railroad had been yanked up, and telegraph wires swayed like long tendrils.

From Dispatch Station they rode to Tunstall's Station. This, too, was torn apart, although they did notice that the Federals had reinforced it somewhat since their earlier raid.

From Tunstall's Station they rode toward White House Landing. A drift of smoke crossed over the Pamunkey valley.

"Someone's torched the Landing." Geneva sat up straight.

"There's only one reason the Federals would abandon their supply line. They've moving their base of operation."

"Can they afford to lose that much material?" Geneva, never having visited the North, could not conceive of that section's industrial wealth.

"Yes, they can afford to lose it and replace it ten times over."

"Colonel, are you worried?"

"I hope General Lee knows about this. I don't want these weasels to slip the trap!"

"We've got cavalry fanned out everywhere. If he doesn't know now, he'll know by tonight."

They rode up on the rear of Stuart's column at night. The men had halted at Black Creek just before White House Landing. Yankees destroyed the bridge and contested the opposing bank, but a few salvos from Captain Pelham's guns and they left. The men observed cannon along the ridge, but it was not brought into play.

While engineers worked to replace the bridge, the men camped for the night.

Geneva found Nash and Banjo. They rejoiced to see her. After hearing of one another's exploits, Geneva said, "Nash, they killed Daddy at Mechanicsville."

"Oh, no," Nash said.

"I heard it at the hospital." She told them about the letter to the baron.

"I think your father had a premonition." Nash scratched his sandy stubble. "The day he came to fetch you to Richmond, he asked Banjo to look after your mother if anything happened to him."

"That poor lady has known her share of suffering." Banjo slouched on a log. "Don't you worry, Jimmy, I'll keep my promise to your daddy."

JUNE 29, 1862

Geneva awoke earlier than usual. A few sentries were alert at the bridge. Everyone else was asleep. Three days of constant marching and skirmishing had taken their toll.

She waved to the sentries and walked down Black Creek to get out of sight. Lice irritated her considerably. She figured it must be around three-thirty in the morning. The temperature hung in the mid-seventies. The day would be a sizzler.

Crawling down the steep bank, she removed her boots, then plunged into the cool water, clothing and all. She got out of the water, stripped naked, and washed her clothes. Only boiling would kill the lice, but this would help some. She spread her pants, shirt, and tunic over branches and dove back in the water. Dirt and blood washed off her.

She heard a rustle on the bank on the other side of the bend from where her regiment was sleeping. Someone dived into the water. She heard coughing. She realized someone was drowning. She swam around the bend and saw a familiar curly head bobbing up and down in the water. It was Mars. She grabbed him under the arms and across the chest in an instant. Even under the water, she could feel he was burning up.

"Shut up, Colonel," she warned him. The last thing she wanted was a platoon of men jumping into that black water. Black Creek was aptly named.

"Jimmy," he cooed in his semidelirious state. "You hot, too?"

"You near drowned."

"It's so hot, so hot. I could fry an egg on my forehead." He whispered, water going in and out of his mouth.

She pulled him around the bend until she found level ground. Grunting, she heaved him on the bank. "You stay here."

Instinctively she smacked his hand as he picked at his bandages. "Let that be. Wait here. I want to fetch my clothes."

"I'm going back in the water, Jimmy. I can't stand this heat." He slurred his words. "What's wrong with you?" He sputtered.

"Nothing's wrong with me." Furious, she restrained him with both hands. "Stay put!"

"Jimmy," he whispered in shock, "you lost your cock."

"You're delirious." Too late, she realized she was naked. She brazened it out. "Mars!" It was the first time she addressed him by his Christian name. "Stay here until I fetch my clothes."

He blinked. He stared at her. She plunged into the water,

swam to the bushes, then swam back, holding her clothes over her head. She quickly dressed.

She reached down to help him. "Come on, I'm taking you back to camp. We'll find your clothes."

"I want to know why you're a girl."

She felt his hot flesh. "Be quiet about this girl stuff. We'll talk about it when you're right in the head."

He leaned against her. Fevered though he was, he understood what she was saying. "I promise." He paused for a moment. Then he held her in his good right arm and kissed her. At first she tightened, but then kissed him back.

Shaken that she could kiss anyone besides Nash and mean it, she said nothing and hauled him along the banks of the creek until she found his clothes. He stumbled and couldn't get into his pants. She sat him down and had him wriggle into them. He stopped before he pulled his pants over himself. "Shoots blanks," he whispered. "I don't think I can have children."

"You will. After the war," she reassured him.

"Not with Kate, I won't." He was drenched in sweat.

She hurried down to the creek, dipped his shirt in water, and returning, pressed it to his forehead, then wiped his chest with it.

"Jimmy, you could of been killed taking that fence." Overwhelmed, he started to cry. "My own wife wouldn't of risked herself to save me."

Continuing to wipe him, she said softly, "You're sick. You're feeling low. It'll pass." She got him back to his feet and into camp.

At dawn the men were awake and Pelham's guns rolled over the makeshift bridge. The cannon on the ridge was the Quaker variety, painted logs. Geneva, with Banjo, got Mars up and changed his dressing. He didn't say anything about their swim.

Geneva found Fitz Lee and asked him if they could put Mars in a house once they arrived at White House Landing. He readily agreed.

By eight they reached White House Landing. The glow of the fires set by the departing Federals illuminated the sky like an orange halo. The U.S.S. *Marblehead* floated in the middle of the Pamunkey River, firing eleven-inch naval shells at the advancing column. Stuart called for seventy-five troopers to dismount. They aimed their rifles at the gunboat. John Pelham hurried forward and opened with his howitzer from the woods. The U.S.S. *Marblehead* weighed anchor and moved away, losing a small boat in the process.

By noon Geneva had Mars Vickers in Lisette Woodard's small, white cottage about two blocks from the river.

The White House, for which the landing was named, once belonged to Martha Washington. She was Rooney Lee's great-great-grandmother, and he inherited the house from her. Usually happy, Rooney fought back the tears when he saw his beautiful plantation smoking, her timbers charred, her architectural glory burnt away. Not only was a piece of his heart ripped out, so was a piece of Revolutionary history.

Two square miles of depot smouldered. Five locomotives were ditched, railroad cars still crackled with fire, and wagons were scattered everywhere. Barges in flames listed in the river.

Aghast at such wealth and then the destruction of it, troopers ransacked wagons and storehouses at their own peril. A few burned their hands, and another narrowly missed being crushed by a falling timber. Banjo plucked out an official-looking box, opened it, and discovered a dozen pair of spotless, white kid gloves. Disgusted, he lifted his arm to toss it back into the flames.

Mercer Hackett grabbed his wrist. "Don't burn those gloves up. Richmond is full of weddings these days. Every officer wants white gloves to wear. If you save them, you can ask your own price."

Banjo picked up a pair. "Here. My present. You'll get married some day."

"I hope to." Mercer blushed, the glow shining through his soot-smeared face.

"Want my advice?"

Mercer stiffened. "Go on."

"Marry her the next time you're in Richmond. Who knows what will happen? You cart that girl right down to the altar."

Relief spread over Mercer's handsome features. "I will surely try and make her see things my way." He paused. "I don't think many of the fellows would come. Considering."

"I'll be there." Banjo returned to fishing out items from the chaos.

*   *   *

In the small cottage near the landing, Mars was proving to be a handful.

"Stop hovering over me like a blowfly! I'm all right."

"Stop acting like a flaming idiot. You're running a fever, and Fitz Lee says you're to stay put until it comes down."

General Stuart knocked on the door and entered. "Jimmy, thank you for saving this varmint's carcass. You stay put for the night, Mars. If the fever's down, you can catch up with us tomorrow."

"I can ride now."

"I just gave you an order, sir. Jimmy, don't let him out of your sight."

The door slammed.

"Why don't I read the lesson for the day?" said Geneva. She found the Old Testament page, Genesis, chapter 9. "Whoso sheddeth man's blood, by man shall his blood be shed: for in the image of God made he man. And you, be ye fruitful, and multiply; bring forth abundantly in the earth, and multiply therein. . . . I do set my bow in the cloud, and it shall be for a token of a covenant between me and the earth." She finished the chapter. "That's one of my favorites."

She turned to the New Testament and Acts, chapter 3. Geneva read of Peter and John going to the temple called Beautiful at nine o'clock to pray. A man, lame from birth and known to all, sat every day at the gate to the temple begging for alms. Peter stopped and said, "Silver and gold have I none; but such as I have give I thee: In the name of Jesus Christ of Nazareth rise up and walk." Not only did the man walk, he leapt with joy, rushing into the temple to proclaim his happiness with God.

"It's so simple in the Bible," Mars said. "One has only to have faith and miracles follow."

"Mother says that every day is a miracle." A sudden pang shot through Geneva. She thought of her mother, now a widow, at Mars's house, which must be filling up with wounded.

"Maybe it is, but I lost my faith years ago. The last Christian died on the cross."

"How can you say that?"

"How can I not? The human race seems bent on a filthy cycle of destruction, and every advance means we kill one

another more efficiently. Napoleon's troops could fire with
accuracy up to one hundred yards. We can fire up to five
hundred yards, and those big siege guns can loft a shell into
the heavens for a mile or more. Then it crashes on soft flesh.
Those artillery boys never see who they're killing."

Holding her Bible tightly, she said, "That captain who
saved us, I don't want to kill him. I could have shot him at
another time. He'd be a dot in blue."

His clear, light hazel eyes searched hers. "You're a strange
duck, Jimmy."

"I never expected you to have such thoughts—being Old
Army."

"A soldier should have these thoughts. Old men make the
wars, and young men fight them. I'm not a soldier because I
like war. I inherited the profession, and in some odd way I
am suited for it." He lit a cigar and inhaled deeply. "I don't
know what comes over me during a fight. Do you?"

"No. It's like a jumped-up foxhunt."

"Some kind of animal rage, some kind of lust. Why do we
get that excited at the prospect of killing another man?" He
blew out a blue tail of smoke. "Some events, some principles
are so great that we are willing to violate the commandment
and kill for them, and we're willing to lay down our own life.
We're no different than a woman in childbed. She risks death
to bring forth life; we risk death to bring forth a nation." He
looked at Geneva. "You'll have it both ways."

"I thought we agreed not to talk about that."

"We agreed that I wouldn't tell." He crossed his legs
under him. "I've been through two names with you. Now tell
me, just what in hell is your real name?"

"Geneva Chalfonte Chatfield Hart."

He laughed. "I'll still call you Jimmy. And how old are
you? Tell the truth."

"I turned nineteen last December. The day after Sumner
was killed."

"So you did tell the truth about that. When I think about
it, it was in front of me. I didn't see."

"Hard to think the unthinkable. It's so easy, Colonel. All I
have to do is keep my clothes on and keep fighting. Blond
John Pelham has a sweeter girl's face than I do. Men see
what they want to see."

"Yeah, that's the truth." He tugged at his bandage.

"Let that alone."

"Shut up! I hate it when you nag at me. I'm a grown man, and I can take care of myself. I'm sorry. I'm so damned irritable I don't even like myself."

"I like you."

He felt shy but didn't know why. He'd fought and ridden with this woman for more than a year. "You've got me over a barrel, you know. I should chuck you out, even though you are the best soldier I've got. But you've saved my life twice and I gave you my word. But answer me one more question and then I'll let it lie: Do you love Nash Hart that much?"

"Yes." She fumbled. "It's different now than in the beginning. He's good to me. But he doesn't look at me like he used to. I never was pretty, but when I trussed up in a dress he looked at me, you know, that way. He doesn't anymore. He says after the war, when I go back to being normal, that everything will be all right. I hope so."

"When I look at you, Jimmy, I know what a failure I am. No woman has ever loved me enough to risk her life for me or even walk around the corner for me. Somehow that's my fault."

"No—"

Vehemently he interrupted her. "It is my fault. I see it every day, Jimmy. I see love every day, and I have no part in it. I have seen slaves love one another with all their heart and soul. I've seen ignorant white men and women pull together as if God put a golden yoke around their necks. I see Maud Windsor smile when Jeffrey walks in the room. He doesn't have to say anything. He just walks in the room, and she's happy and he's happy. Don't try and make me feel better. I'm missing something. Maybe I don't give enough or—I don't know! I could ignore it before. I knew in a vague way that I was slipping away, missing something, but it isn't vague anymore. I am a human failure."

"You are not!" Her eyes blazed.

"You're not my wife."

JUNE 30, 1862

Stuart pushed forward like the nervous antennae of a large insect. He kept feeling, feeling but the Federals were not where he thought they would be.

A courier informed him there had been a fierce battle yesterday while he was at White House Landing. It was inconclusive, although Lee continued trying to grasp the elusive McClellan in his pincers.

Geneva and Mars rode some fifteen miles behind Stuart.

"This could have been our Cannae," Mars said. "In 216 B.C., Hannibal destroyed the Roman army there. We had a like opportunity, but Hannibal was fighting with an instrument he'd forged over the years. We're too mixed up for coordinated action, too green."

"We hurt them though."

"That we did, but McClellan's like a rabbit that got its foot caught in a steel trap. He chewed off his foot and is crawling to safety."

JULY 1, 1862

At three-thirty in the morning, General Stuart received an order from Lee to cross the Chickahominy. As they moved into the dawn, Nash wasn't worried that Geneva hadn't overtaken them.

"The colonel's fever stayed up, I'll bet," Banjo said. They reached Bottoms Bridge as Jackson's division was crossing over it in an orderly fashion.

Orders were called down the line, and they turned their horses back from the bridge. The roads, curving and tortuous in many places, kept them wide awake. They crossed the river downstream at Ford's Bridge.

Cobb's Legion from Georgia was left to guard White House Landing in case McClellan doubled back.

In the early afternoon, as they heard the massed artillery belching from Malvern Hill, Nash said, "Maybe Mars and Jimmy stayed back at White House."

"Would you want to sit in the hot sun with a mess of Georgians?" Banjo shook his head. "They're somewhere behind us. We've kept up a stiff pace, and the colonel's probably feeling weak."

Forty-two miles from dawn, the troopers bivouacked in oat fields east of Turkey Creek. They were aiming for Haxall's Landing on the James. If a Federal column hoped to get off the Peninsula at that spot, the cavalry would harass them until infantry came up to finish the job. A heavy rain began to fall. The horses were oblivious to it because they munched on the sweet oats. The cavalry had received no further word from either Jackson or Lee.

Banjo, sopping, passed by Mercer Hackett, who had a fresh mount. "Where are you going?"

"Toward the guns. We've got to find out what happened."

"Got any more fresh horses?"

"In the rear. Those Yankees sure are generous with their supplies."

Banjo ran back, picked up his tack, and asked Nash to join him. They cut out two rough but sturdy animals and were beside Mercer within fifteen minutes.

The rain pelted them mercilessly.

"Black as Erebus this night," Nash grumbled.

"Who's Airybus?" Banjo, ever curious, asked.

"He's primeval darkness, fathered by Chaos out of Night, who was his sister."

" 'Zat what they teach you in college? Fooling around with your sister?" Banjo jibed.

"Since it was the beginning of the world, according to the Greeks, there weren't many people to choose from."

"A likely excuse." Mercer watched the red glow.

As they reached the battle site, the low black clouds were illuminated by tongues of orange flame. From the heights of Malvern Hill a small scarlet tornado ripped the darkness each time a cannon discharged. One after another the heavy artillery shattered the rain and what remained of life. The Yankees had been firing their superior guns throughout the day. The metal cannon glowed with heat. At 10 P.M. the firing stopped.

The eerie silence after the relentless fountain of death gave way to the sounds of hell. The wounded dying, trapped under the muzzles of the enemy guns on the steep incline, howled, shrieked, and sobbed into the night. The medical teams could not cover the territory to retrieve the men.

"There must be thousands of them!" Nash cried through the deluge and the horror, and he thought of all that crushed intelligence, all that pitiless waste. "How can they stand it? How can those Yankees sit up there and listen to that? Why can't they send down their own doctors?"

"They don't know that they won't be shot any more than we do." Mercer, too, was unnerved by the massed suffering. His horse stumbled, and he peered down into the darkness to see a bearded jawbone. "Come on, we've got to find a senior officer."

They finally found a colonel, reported their position, and

told him that another small detachment from Stuart was in search of Jackson.

"Some hero." The colonel spit.

"Jackson?" Banjo innocently asked.

"Jackson hasn't done jack shit!" The colonel spit again. The exhaustion and savagery of the day wore off this officer's protective coloration. He spoke freely and with rancor.

Mercer thoughtfully replied, "He fought three separate armies and defeated each of them in turn in the Shenandoah Valley and then turned to march to Richmond. He's probably tuckered out. I am."

"Tell that to those poor bastards up there." The officer pointed in the direction of the slaughter.

"How many men do you think we lost today?" Mercer asked.

"One-fourth of our army."

Riding through the downpour back to camp, nobody spoke.

JULY 2, 1862

Without interruption, vehicles carrying the wounded rolled into Richmond night and day. Until proper shelter could be found, they were placed on the sidewalks. When the rains came, women stood over the men with umbrellas until they could be taken away. With the rain came a jolting drop in temperature. People lit fires in their fireplaces in July. There wasn't an extra blanket to be found. Many soldiers lost or discarded their tunics and jackets in the ferocious heat only to now spasmodically shake with cold.

Lutie worked with snatches of sleep, an hour here and an hour there. Through her fatigue Henley's funeral seemed like years ago.

The United States government declared medical supplies

contraband. The Confederacy's depleting reserves worried Lutie and everyone else fighting to save the wounded. It seemed a particularly barbaric act.

A courier, not more than thirteen years old, delivered two letters, one addressed to her and one to Kate.

"Kate! It's a letter from Mars!" She recognized the colonel's heavy handwriting with its slight rightward slant.

How odd this is, Kate thought to herself as she opened the letter. I'm preparing to divorce the man when the time is right, yet I fear for him.

Dear Kate:

I have been wounded in the left arm but escaped serious injury. One bullet passed clean through the flesh, and the other lodged next to my bone. Jimmy Chatfield saved my life. Tell the gallant Mrs. Chatfield that courage is commonplace in that family. When we are together, I will tell you in detail how Jimmy saved me and, strangely, how a Federal captain saved us both.

Forgive my brevity. I didn't want you to worry. We are leaving White House Landing Station to rejoin the regiment, my fever having subsided.

Love,
Mars

P.S. They destroyed Rooney Lee's house.

"He's alive," Kate said with relief.

Lutie opened her letter. "It's from Jimmy. I want to read this to Sin-Sin and Di-Peachy, too." She found them in the parlor and motioned for them to come out.

Dear Mother:

I heard about Daddy's death. I don't think it will sink in, really, until I return to Chatfield. Forgive me for not being there to comfort you. I know you understand.

The Colonel endured a nasty wound but he's a tough bird. I jumped a six-foot fence to fetch the Colonel from some Yankees eager to make his acquaintance. I would have given anything for Daddy to have seen us!

Nash says that he thinks Daddy knew he was going to die. Just before we rode around McClellan, Daddy asked Banjo to take care of you if anything happened to him.

For the next war, I think both sides should chose doughnuts as weapons and throw them across the Potomac.

After a little tangle with Yankee outposts yesterday, Banjo said, "God created the Yankee, but why?"

I miss you. Di-Peachy and Sin-Sin, too.

Love,
Jimmy

P.S. I almost forgot. Colonel Vickers knows everything.

JULY 3, 1862

"Ground must be paste down there." Mars appraised the land below Evelington Heights, a long ride overlooking the James River. McClellan's army huddled around smoky, sputtering campfires, built with wet wood. William Byrd's mansion, Westover, acquired by him in 1688, was surrounded by sullen Federals. Mars hoped this piece of history wouldn't fall to the torch.

Yesterday's chill made his arm ache, but his fever was nearly gone. He felt terrible, but as he'd always enjoyed a strong constitution, he forced himself back to work. He'd heard when dawn finally came to Malvern Hill, the wounded writhed on the ground like worms in hot ashes. Until certain that the Yankees had evacuated, no one could or would retrieve them. He figured he was in better shape than those poor devils.

The Ninth Virginia Cavalry protected their rear as the remainder of Stuart's force dismounted, pulled out their rifles, and waited for the Yankees to come up the hill. Captain Pelham had dragged up his lone howitzer in the night. Satisfied that the Confederates were as ready as they'd ever be, he was ordered, Let 'em have it.

The first shell spiraled and splattered below, sending teamsters and their horses scurrying. Pelham continued a steady, controlled firing.

"Think they'll come up?" Geneva asked Nash.

"Once they figure out it's just us, I don't see why not. They may be demoralized, but they're not stupid."

"Longstreet and Jackson are movin'. If they get here in time, we'll have 'em dancin' the Turkey Trot." Banjo watched the running figures below.

The gun, while an irritant, did not cause mass panic. Bobbing on the James were Federal gunboats, whose men feared no land force, confident that their shells would blow anyone to kingdom come. The U.S.S. *Monitor* was anchored around the river bend at Haxall's Landing.

Geneva, born for the saddle, exhibited no appreciation or understanding of the navy's role in warfare. As far as she was concerned, they should steam off to the Atlantic or the Chesapeake and sail around one another, firing their big guns. They got in the way of real fighting. But by this time in her passionate embrace of cavalry, she was beginning to think that infantry got in the way of fighting, too.

While Pelham fired his lonely gun, someone below started thinking. A Federal battery rolled up east of Herring Creek, which slogs though marshes across the south face of Evelington Heights. It was about 9 A.M.

"Lining the boys up. You know, I can't abide the color blue. After these unpleasantries between the states are settled, I don't never want to see blue nothing!" Banjo bit off the end of his cigar and spit it as far as he could. "No blue booties on baby boys' feet, no blue ribbons in little girls' hair, no blue dresses on the good ladies—not even sky blue and I was formerly partial to sky blue. I want lots of red and yellow and sea-green. I love sea-green on a woman. No blue jewelry neither!"

"You mean sapphires." Geneva, interest aroused by the activities below, moved over the ridge a bit.

"Yep. What do you call those pretty light ones."

"Aquamarines."

"Well, I don't want to see nary a one!"

"What are they doing down there?" Geneva borrowed Sam Wells's field glasses. "They're going to come on the flank."

"We've got sharpshooters on our right. That'll slow them for a bit." Nash sounded worried nonetheless.

"I'll tell the colonel." She gave the glasses back to Sam, who was showing the effects of lack of sleep.

"What else do you tell the colonel? You two are getting very matey," Nash grumbled. "Why you risked your life to save his bones, I'll never know. That was a damn crazy thing you did!"

Banjo, wearily accustomed to their flare-ups, kept his eyes trained on the Yankees. The three of them were lying side by side over the ridge while Nash and Geneva argued.

"Then you and Banjo were as crazy as I was, running along that stone wall."

"At least I knew who I was fighting for."

"So did I!"

"That's my point," Nash hissed. "God, I hate that man!"

Nash flipped over to find Mars Vickers behind him. He got to his feet. "No point lying about it. I'm as ready to say it to your face as behind your back."

Geneva stood up. The front of her uniform was wet from the damp earth. "Don't fight, you two. Colonel, your left arm isn't any good anyway."

Suddenly boiling over, Nash pushed her on the ground. "Take his part!" A grip like a vise closed around his throat. He found himself not two inches from Mars's face.

"Don't ever do that again." He released Nash, who rubbed his throat. "Now come with me. We aren't going to fight."

The earth slurped at their boots. They walked behind the center of their line.

"You and I will never see eye to eye," Mars began.

Nash, without waiting for him to finish, blurted, "We never will. I can't abide the way you glorify combat."

"If a man's not willing to fight, then he's not worth his salt."

"The ground turns to salt under your feet!" Nash insulted him.

Mars wheeled, his heel sinking deeper into the mud. "Don't provoke me. We serve no useful purpose by fighting. As to this war, Piggy, what the hell is the answer: To kill ten thousand men in one day or to take ten days to do it? That's what it's come to. This is a new kind of war." Noticing that his adversary lapsed into an unagreeable quiet, he said, "The main problem between us, aside from our temperaments, is

Jimmy. I misunderstood your relationship, and I leaned on you pretty hard. I want to apologize."

Nash never expected this. "You do?"

"I know." Mars conveyed his meaning.

"She didn't tell me—but we don't talk much anymore." Nash fumbled.

"You want to know what makes me sick? You've got more love than any man deserves in this life, but you're more worried about somebody thinking you're a pansy than you are grateful for that love."

"What?" Nash was now completely off guard.

"If I had what you have, I wouldn't give a good goddamn what anybody thought of me!"

"What passed between you two at White House Landing?"

"It was more what passed between us at Black Creek. I was delirious, and Jimmy fished me out of the water. Obviously, once she got me on shore, the game was up. I was delirious, but I wasn't blind."

"Why don't you muster her out?" Nash sounded hopeful. "She's got no business here."

Mars laughed. "Best soldier I've got. I'm not sure I could do without her."

"I appreciate your admiration for Jimmy." Nash paused. "Funny how I never call her by her right name anymore. Colonel, this is easy for you to talk about. You're married to the most beautiful woman in the world who is doing what she's supposed to be doing: nursing the sick and behaving like a lady."

"You're a damned fool, Nash Hart, and I reckon you always will be."

Stuart's men fought the methodical pressure on their right as the Yankee infantry pressed them. At two in the afternoon, Captain Pelham fired his last shell. There was no more ammunition nor any relief in sight. Jackson and Longstreet never showed.

With great reluctance, Stuart withdrew two miles to the north and went into camp.

JULY 20, 1862

A carnival of hope infected Richmond. McClellan stayed at Harrison's Landing. He plopped there like a frog full of buckshot. He moved neither forward nor backward, but seemed imprisoned by his own weight. Richmond was saved. Churches offered up services, people shouted, "Gloria in Excelsis," and Lee, instead of being the goat, was now the hero.

While Lutie, like everyone around her, offered up prayers of thanksgiving to Almighty God, she thought of the weeks of battles as the slaughterhouse of heroes. The death lists were appalling. The best families of the South lost their husbands, sons, and brothers. Hardly anyone was untouched, especially since the upper classes led the regiments, brigades, and divisions. The leaders, the wealthy and the gifted, were cut down by the scythe of war no less than the small farmer, the shopkeeper, even the vagrant seeking to redeem himself by military service. They died alike, and Death, as always, impartially selected his victims. She used to think of Death as a personal force, the god of the underworld, Hades or Pluto. Odd, too, that Pluto was the god of riches. Each day you bargained with this god, but in the end he got the better of the deal. She put aside that embroidered, mythical notion. Death these days was a threshing machine. Someone started the blades whirling, and it wouldn't cut off.

She suffered a brief spasm of hope that the North would sue for peace. McClellan was beaten. Even if the general refused to admit it, how could Washington ignore the results of those terrible days?

No peace offer arrived. No courier rode with a white flag from the Federal army. Nothing.

Lutie thought to herself, Here we are in the midst of

death, and we persist in thinking it is something that happens to others, not ourselves. She didn't think, not for one minute, although surrounded by an enemy over one hundred thousand strong that she herself would die. But then she didn't think Henley would die either. Perhaps if she had been at Chatfield, she would have sensed it or heard the baying of those black and tans. Here in Richmond, separated from the coordinates of her life, she wondered if she was able to put events in perspective. She would die someday, but not now. She would die an old lady; like a wave receding from the shore, she would prepare to leave the earth at last. She had much life left in her. She felt it strongly, but where this life would lead her, she didn't know.

She had seen things that decades would not wipe from her mind. It wasn't really the occasional grotesque sight that shook her: a corpse already blowing up with gas or a dog running down Franklin Street with a man's foot in its mouth. Even the bone-throbbing screams could be borne. What seeped into her marrow were the little things, those small incidents that caught her unawares like a bright, shining pool of blood on cobblestones. No body was in sight, yet the blood was as fresh and slick as if someone dumped a bucket of red paint on the street. Those were the things that shifted her inner compass. It was as if a voice incanted, "You who have seen this will never be the same."

No one would be the same. Not the men who fought, or the women who nursed them, or the children who bore mute witness to the carnage. When Lutie was a child, her mammy used to scare her, saying, "Raw Head and Bloody Bones gonna get you." The children of Richmond had seen this devil. What would come of them? What world would they invent when this was over?

A fog rolled up from the James. Lutie was in Kate's stable just to get away from the commotion of the house for a minute. She realized the sweet smell of hay, leather, and horse sweat reminded her of Henley. She felt closer to him here than anywhere. She realized since Sumner had died, she spoke to Emil less and less, and when Henley was killed, she'd quite forgotten her old friend. She wondered if Emil had been her answer to Henley. Once her husband was dead, she no longer needed a confidant. Lutie used to tell herself that she and Emil would travel to Cairo in a pelican's beak.

She laughed out loud and startled one of the horses. "No one can accuse me of lacking imagination."

There was precious little to laugh about outside herself. The chemistry labs at the university were manufacturing gunpowder. The men of enrollment age had all enlisted, and many of them were already dead. People in Charlottesville questioned whether the school could survive the war.

Elizabeth Van Lew performed her "mission work" among the Northern prisoners. Maud Windsor no longer thought her peculiar neighbor was feeble-minded. She thought she was an outright spy and should be marched, silken curls and petticoats, to the garden wall and shot.

Shooting civilians, unbelievable as that sounded to Lutie, might enter the war. The newspapers carried General John Pope's address to his Union troops when he took over command in the Shenandoah Valley. He said that any resistance on the part of "disloyal" citizens would be met with harsh resistance, even death. Up until now, the war was between armed men who chose to fight. A note of bitterness was creeping into conversations. Lutie noticed that the combination of Pope's extraordinary statement and the constant presence of death was hardening many hearts. Worse, some people, reading Northern newspapers that blamed the war on slavery, began to believe it themselves. Instead of feeling shame for their "peculiar institution," they began to express outright hostility against the Negro race. Irrationality was more to be feared than outright cruelty in Lutie's mind. She carefully distinguished between irrationality and suprarationality. The former was illogical, the latter was beyond logic and therefore spiritual. It did not occur to her that this explanation was self-serving.

Poofy had not written, or rather, her letters had not gotten through the lines. Lutie missed her sister and she missed her younger brother, T. Pritchard Chalfonte, though he scribbled a message from time to time. But most of all, Lutie missed her husband. She scarcely believed it possible that she could so long for the man who had once brought her so much pain, the man she subsequently shut out of her heart for years. Well, thank God, she had that good last year with him. She couldn't think of her losses. She put Henley and Sumner out of her mind and concentrated on the enveloping fog, a shroud pulled over the capital.

Humans are unwilling to believe that great suffering and disaster can be inflicted without moral justification. She had often told herself that. Lutie now knew that there was no moral justification for the maelstrom of events. The entire human race was swimming in a night sea of darkness.

JULY 21, 1862

The workload eased. The worst cases had died. Those with minor wounds had been moved to other locations. What remained were men too seriously wounded to move who nonetheless had a chance.

"Were you married?" Evangelista asked Sin-Sin as they sat on the back porch covered with trumpet vines.

"Ha! I wisht I had a halter on that husband of mine. Thass a long time ago."

"I'd better find a man soon." Evangelista wrinkled her pretty nose. "I want a man that's bright. Can't marry an ebony man. And he must have a good trade."

"My Marcus was a blacksmith. Get you a big, strong man like that."

"How'd you land him?" Evangelista thought of love as a form of fishing.

"I sashay 'bout that man 'til I wore out his indifference!" She laughed. "Course if you need love charms, I knows a few."

"Like what?"

"If you wishes a man to fall in love with you, you got to take the small bow from the sweatband 'round his cap. You wears that under your clothes next to your body. That man be yours in no time."

Not exactly convinced, Evangelista changed the subject. "Miss Kate says that you Albemarle people will be going home soon. She says we're gonna come visit in late August or September. Unless there's another battle around here."

"Doan look like it."

"I never knew so many people could die at one time."

"Not since the great flood, I reckon. Everybody died then."

Evangelista watched the cook tend to her small herb garden. "The man I felt sorry for was that one had his"—she paused—"his manhood torn away."

"Man can live without pleasure, but doan know if he can live without the future."

"Do you think about the future, Auntie Sin-Sin?" Shrewdness was written all over her voice. The future meant the hope for freedom. "I do. Constantly."

"Then I sees you at Chatfield. Thass enough future." Sin-Sin smiled.

Evangelista thought, What a crafty old fox.

AUGUST 15, 1862

Lutie, Sin-Sin, and Di-Peachy returned to Chatfield on August seventh. Charlottesville, crowded with walking wounded, had so far escaped any other mark of war.

The drive up to the big house, its huge trees deep green in August glory, brought forth tears to their eyes. Every hand on the estate crowded on the graceful front steps to greet them. Ernie June, as happy to see Lutie as she was soured to see her nemesis, did the honors for Chatfield's people by welcoming Lutie home. When she mentioned Henley's name, she broke down. Even Braxton, a controlled man, cried. What would become of them now that the master was killed and Sumner, too?

Lutie, deeply moved at this outburst, assured everyone that Henley's remains would be transferred to the quiet land he loved. Once the war ended, the horse breeding program would continue under the direction of Geneva.

Walking the grounds with Sin-Sin, she noted with delight that the gardens were luxurious, the stables were as spotless as when Henley supervised them, and not one thing was missing from the big house except for a feather bed. Sin-Sin told Lutie to snatch it right back from Ernie's little cabin, but Lutie informed her that Ernie had done her duty, and she deserved the mattress. No word from or about Boyd. Sin-Sin said she thought she'd come home by Weeping Cross. She meant that Boyd would come home with her tail between her legs.

Frederica was pregnant again, and Timothy had grown a foot or so. The air hummed with bumblebees, honeybees, sweat bees, yellow jackets, dragonflies, damselflies, and every variety of horsefly known to man.

What Lutie did not discuss was the persistent rumors that Abraham Lincoln was preparing a carte blanche document concerning all slaves. He had already made provisions for slaves in occupied territory, and these provisions had grown progressively more radical since the beginning of the war. Lutie knew a servant grapevine carried news quickly. Well, she wasn't going to worry about the effect of such calculated bombast on her people. Much as she was opposed to it, she talked to her attorneys. She would fulfill Henley's wishes on Christmas Day.

Since the Battle of Seven Days, as the battle around Richmond was being called, the Confederate generals squabbled like boys fighting over marbles. General Toombs challenged General D.H. Hill to a duel because he thought D.H. impugned his courage. Only the skillful intervention of the friends of each man kept them from depriving the army of one or both of their services.

A duel she understood. When men got hotheaded, she'd rather see a duel than one man dragging another to court. Henley used to say, "The law allows what honor forbids." Henley was right.

What Lutie couldn't believe was that Colonel H.L. Benning nearly got himself arrested and General A.P. Hill succeeded in getting arrested. The scandal was the talk of Richmond and the entire nation. Benning, violent in his protests against conscription, endangered himself. When it was pointed out to him that the North had been employing conscription, he said that only further hardened his opinion against it. If a man doesn't willingly volunteer to defend his nation, then he isn't worth a damn. The conscripts will get in the way of the real men. The pungent phrase attributed to Benning was, The wheat are in the army; the chaff is at home. Even worse in Colonel Benning's eyes was the fact that conscription was unconstitutional. Were we to become like our enemy? First conscription and then income tax? Lincoln had signed into law on July first a three percent tax on annual incomes of $600–10,000 and five percent on any income above $10,000. That, too, was unconstitutional. The South must keep to its standards of individual initiative and individual sacrifice. Benning's superiors shut him up with difficulty. The unspoken feeling was that conscription might be unconstitutional but necessary.

The fact that the Yankees submitted to income tax further convinced every Southerner that they were a nation of sheep.

The other news from the enemy capital, news met with howls of derision in Richmond, was that on August 4, Lincoln refused to accept two black regiments from Indiana into his armed forces. Ernie June called him a "hippocat."

But the Longstreet affair put every other misdeed in the shade. Generals Longstreet and A.P. Hill shocked everyone by challenging one another in the newspapers. *The Richmond Examiner* printed praise of A.P. Hill. Then Longstreet engaged his adjunct general to write a letter to *The Richmond Whig* that Hill was overpraised. This caused more uproar than McClellan's cannonades. Longstreet, the senior officer, then had Hill arrested. The entire affair flourished out of petty jealousy. To further accent the humiliation, everyone in Richmond knew that everyone in Washington was laughing, too.

Finally, Lee, who didn't have time for personal huffs, took Hill out of jail and sent him to Jackson, hoping those two could pull in harness. General Pope was on the upper Rappahannock threatening northern Virginia. His supply line was the Orange and Alexandria Railroad, and he might mean to cut up the Virginia Central Railroad, which was Richmond's link with the west. The point of the Confederate compass was stuck in Richmond, but the pencil leg was swinging out into northern Virginia.

Jackson attacked Yankees at Cedar Mountain, driving them

off the field. The papers said it was the advance guard of General N.P. Banks.

What concerned Lutie more than the scandal or the battle of Cedar Mountain was the massing of Confederate troops at Gordonsville, just a holler from Charlottesville. Federal cavalry raided Beaver Dam Station in Louisa County last month. That was close, but Gordonsville was closer.

Geneva was out there somewhere. Lutie's thoughts centered on Geneva more and more, not only because she was all that was left of the family, but because she knew her daughter was caught in a cross fire between Mars Vickers and Nash Hart.

Geneva's destiny might be bizarre, but it was hers, and she grasped it. Lutie respected her for that, but she missed her strong presence at home.

Standing in the meadow, ankle deep in sweet grass, Lutie watched the sun disappear in the west, flooding the hills, the plains, the running streams with the pink and golden glow of life. Clouds rose up from the meadows like soft creamy wings seeking the bodies of gigantic birds. Watching the sun rise made her want to soar like the low clouds rising up to meet the sky, the sun, perhaps God.

Poor orphan God, she thought, as a brilliant red cardinal darted out of the struck chestnut tree. We have deserted you, haven't we? Does man first desert God or other men? Where is the initial rupture in accord? Perhaps the initial rupture, the first drifting away from harmony, occurs inside the self.

As a young woman, she thought her marriage would be one long idyll. When Henley began his disastrous liaison with Di-Peachy's mother, Lutie thought Henley's unfaithfulness was her fault. Why didn't she see then that Henley wasn't responsible for her happiness? He could add or detract, but only she could create happiness.

The children brought some happiness, but they also brought trials. In Geneva, she wanted a replica of herself. She wasn't always cheerful when she got it. Her first inkling that Geneva absorbed more than she realized was at dinner one night when Geneva was four years old. Henley led the family in a prayer of thanks for the abundant food. Geneva said, "Me and Sumner didn't pray."

Henley indulgently chided her. "Where is my good little girl?"

"She's not here today." A few mouthfuls later, Geneva added, "But she'll be back in time for dessert." Lutie's irreverence stared at her from the face of her four-year-old daughter.

And I never appreciated her, Lutie thought. She had to find her way in her time. I was young in a different time. Why was I so hard on Geneva? Lutie felt she had no right to look for answers in her children when the answers should have come from inside herself.

As for Di-Peachy, how could she have taken out her hurt on an innocent child? But she had, and she still couldn't warm to her. And as for Sin-Sin, she took her for granted. She never asked Sin-Sin what she wanted, even if Sin-Sin was her servant.

In subtle or blatant ways, she used everyone in her life to give her what only she could give herself: joy, meaning, peace.

Lutie held out her arms to the sunlight. Her anguish had brought her this form of resurrection. Her mistakes had brought her closer to God. She did not know God as much as she felt God.

A loud munching startled her. Decca, one of the big draft horses, had pushed open a paddock gate. "Come on, Decca, let's go back to the stable, big girl." She patted the mighty neck and was rewarded with an affectionate nuzzle on her cheek. "Decca, everything here is the same, but I have changed."

AUGUST 22, 1862

Geneva scrawled "Master Sergeant James Chatfield, First Virginia Cavalry" in the register of the Warrenton Hotel when Stuart allowed his men to rest an hour. She thought she'd be grand and put her name in the register.

She'd ridden hard the last two days, rising with the moon at 4 A.M. Late in the afternoon at Kelly's Ford on the Rappahannock, her regiment skirmished with Yankee cavalry.

From that afternoon and all of Thursday, a series of dogfights entangled both the Yankee and the Confederate cavalry. The Yankees no longer ran at the sight of a gray horseman. Mars said they were watching the fords to catch early intelligence of their troop movements.

The entire cavalry in Virginia was now under the command of J.E.B. Stuart, who'd been jumped up to major general. He had three brigades, fourteen regiments, and two batteries for his cavalry division. Lee was using Stuart more efficiently, and Lee himself was becoming more efficient.

After the Battle of Seven Days, a great many promotions were handed out. Mars was promised a brigade when enough recruits were found to form one. Benserade was a major. Nash, to his surprise, was promoted to a sergeant. Mars asked Banjo if he wanted his name put forward for captain. Banjo said being a lieutenant was about as much officering as he could stand.

Every lady who could run, walk, or hobble under the overcast skies gathered down at the Warrenton Hotel to admire the cavalrymen. Von Borcke, now a major, swaggered to good effect for the damsels. Geneva leaned against the registration desk and laughed at his antics.

When a lady, seeing her alone, offered her a dyed feather

for her cap, Geneva graciously took it and kissed the lady's hand.

Mars walked into the lobby from the serving room. He spied Geneva with the feather in her cap and the fluttering Warrenton girl. "What have we here? A little Stuart? How about a Stuartette? Or Stuart Minor? Why is it everyone wants a plume in their hat just like J.E.B.?"

"What'd you eat in there?" Geneva noticed the girl oogling Mars. "Oh, Miss. . . ?"

"Rebecca Rifton."

"Miss Rebecca, this is Colonel Mars Vickers, a military legend. When he isn't beating up on the Yankees, he keeps in practice on his wife."

Rebecca Rifton was shocked.

Mars bowed to the stupefied girl. "Jimmy has an overactive imagination, ma'am. But I think I'll take a lesson from him and start beating up on this poor, sapskulled boy."

He picked Geneva up under her armpits and carried her to the lobby amidst the laughter of the men. Putting her down, he addressed his comrades and the ladies.

"Boys, let's mount up. Ladies, we will return to you as soon as we convince our former comrades in the United States Army to pay us proper respect and go home to their own ladies. You know, I believe the reason they are trying our patience with their presence is now that they've caught sight of you beautiful Virginia ladies, they don't wish to return to the homegrown variety."

Back on the road, the column turned east toward Auburn, seven miles from Warrenton. Once at Auburn they turned again toward Catlett's Station. The clouds which threatened them throughout the day changed violet-black after sunset, hurling their fury earthward. In brutal darkness and lashing rain, the men halted outside of Catlett's Station. Despite the weather, they kept in tight formation. They were in General Pope's rear. At any turn they might encounter Yankees, and they knew without a doubt that Catlett's Station was loaded with Yanks.

"Aren't we going to attack?" Geneva asked Mars.

"Not until we know exactly where we are. You can't see the hand in front of your face."

The horrendous downpour drowned out sounds. At the front of the column, Stuart questioned a prisoner taken with the few Yankees they'd rounded up today. He was a black teamster, and upon recognizing Stuart, he offered to guide him through this mess right to Pope's headquarters between Catlett's Station and Cedar Run, which by now would be boiling over.

The man was as good as his word. Stuart and his men found themselves at the very edge of a large encampment which they could only see during the flashes of jagged lightning. The Ninth Virginia was ordered to hit Pope's headquarters. The First and Fifth Virginia were to make a diversion at the adjoining camp. Captain Blackford, the engineer with the Fourth Virginia, was ordered to destroy the railroad bridge over Cedar Run.

With a surge Geneva hurtled forward in the blinding rain. As they crossed the tracks, Geneva reined in. Sam Wells, coming up behind her, shouted through the thunder and quick gunfire, "What are you doing?"

"I'll cut the wire. Hold my horse, will you?"

Sam seized the reins, and Geneva shimmied up the telegraph pole like a monkey. At the top, she pulled her saber and slashed the wires. She slid down, leaping off about fifteen feet from the ground. As she swung into the saddle, she grasped Sam's hands for the reins. The searing blue of lightning showed her Sam was slumped forward in his saddle. She pried his reins out of his hand and lead them both forward into the pitch, the screaming, and the commotion.

Banjo almost collided with her in the darkness. "Can't destroy the bridge. Not enough axes." He stretched forward. "Who's that?"

"Sam Wells."

Recall sounded between thunderclaps. "Let's get out of here. We've done all we can do."

Fearing harassment by pursuing cavalry, Geneva couldn't attend to Sam until they were two miles from Catlett's Station.

Nash helped her. "His legs are frozen on this animal."

Mars rode up. "We can't stop."

"I've got to see if he's alive."

"Who is it?" Mars called.

"Sam Wells," Nash answered.

Geneva felt his pulse. "He's dead, Colonel."

"If the Yankees come after us, you'll have to dump him," Mars shouted through the relentless downpour.

"I know," Geneva answered.

By daybreak the cavalry was back in Warrenton.

Geneva removed Sam Wells's personal effects to send to his family. If the army had time to bury a man, the family was told the location in case they wished to remove the body later or visit the grave. Very often there wasn't time for that. Sometimes the body was sent home, although this was usually reserved for officers.

Geneva opened Sam's Bible. A note fell out. The note read: The bearer of this body to Martha Wells of Charlottesville, Virginia, will receive $500.

Nash read it. "He must have had some premonition like your father."

Banjo found a box to use as a casket.

The three of them, before resting themselves, laid Sam's body in the sturdy pine box. They also located a young boy who was willing to drive the body to Charlottesville in his wagon. They put the note in an envelope and addressed it to Martha. They wrote a second note to Sam's infant son, Samuel Wells, Junior.

As the wagon rolled down the Warrenton Turnpike, Geneva thought to herself, "Who next?"

AUGUST 24, 1862

The one thing Geneva liked about hard fighting was that she didn't have to do the dishes. Camp life worked on her nerves. Life in the saddle suited her. A hot meal was a rarity. Often they awoke and leapt in the saddle without even morning coffee, although Banjo, ever hopeful, wrapped a tin coffee pot in his bedroll.

Last night when they bivouacked, they didn't unsaddle their horses although they let them graze. The cavalry pa-

trolled the south side of Hegeman's River which fed into the
Rappahannock. Every ford of the Rappahannock was contested. Pope massed eighty thousand men on the other side
of the river plus he had another twenty thousand at Aquia
Creek. Confederate forces were half that number.

In the faint light of dawn, Geneva consulted her church
almanac. It was Sunday, the Feast of St. Bartholomew, the
tenth Sunday after Trinity. The lesson was Numbers, chapter
23, and Acts, chapter 28. Acts stretched through the summer.
St. Paul relished his misadventures, and Geneva began to
suspect that he might have exaggerated.

Geneva mused to herself that Stuart probably called yesterday's battle a skirmish. No fighting is a skirmish if one is in
it, and yesterday one thousand men rode up to the
Waterloo Bridge from Fords below it, firing, ducking, and
running every inch of the way.

She walked down to the river to fill her canteen. The
temperature was deliciously mild for late August, but then
the sun wasn't over the horizon yet. She saw a Yankee on the
other side of the river, also filling his canteen.

Putting her hand on her holster, she called over, "Yank, I
won't fire if you won't."

"All right by me. I'll get you later." He waved, finished his
task, and left.

An approaching Confederate rider sent Geneva back to the
camp. The men were up. Mars, with field glasses, studied
the bridge. The corporal saluted Mars and asked for Benserade.
Mars pointed to the major.

A courier grinned as he handed Benserade a smudged
envelope.

Benserade nervously opened the message and then let out
a whoop. "Boys, I'm a father! An eight-pound baby girl!" He
leapt in the air. The other men crowded around him, slapping him on the back. "If we ever hit civilization again, I'm
going to buy every man in this regiment a drink!"

Geneva, Nash, and Mars rejoiced with Benserade, but each
was inwardly glum because having children seemed impossible now.

The sun, finally free of the horizon, brought with it artillery fire from the other side of the river.

"The only reason they want this bridge is because it's
named Waterloo." Nash quickly mounted.

"And it's easier to get an army over a bridge than through the fords." Geneva rode beside him.

Mars deployed his men. Most of them had already dismounted, firing across the river. He sent Geneva and Nash northward to check the videttes posted on the upper fords. The lower fords were well covered. Banjo was dispatched back to General Longstreet to inform him that the bridge was going to be hotly contested and might he show his infantry in force as well as bring up artillery?

A small stucco house, painted bright white, at the edge of the bridge already had cannonballs stuck in its side. As Geneva and Nash galloped past it, she thought years from now these souvenirs would add to its charm, the owner bragging about the fight for Waterloo Bridge. Right now though, everyone in that house was either under the bed or running to Warrenton.

At each ford they stopped, learned that no Federals had been seen, and continued to the next one.

Nash, in ebullient spirits, was whistling. "What have we got, one vidette left?"

"Yes, but I heard there was another ford about one mile or a mile and a half above it. To be safe we ought to check it, too."

As they approached, the four men posted on the ford straightened up. A short, stocky man saluted.

"Seen anything?" Nash asked.

"Nothing. What's going on down there? Sounds like a tussle." He was curious.

"Contesting the bridge. Something to do, I guess. Takes their minds off the heat."

"Not too bad today. Bugs are fierce," the stocky man replied.

"Thank you, Private. We're going to check one last ford."

"Nobody's posted up there."

"I figure they've seen our videttes same as we've seen theirs. If they did a decent job of reconnaissance, they may have discovered this ford by themselves."

"Sergeant," he said, addressing Nash, "they're getting tougher, don't you think?"

"No longer novices in killing." Nash saluted and pushed on, the river on his right.

After fifteen minutes at a pleasant curve in the river, they beheld the huge gates to an estate.

The two of them stopped, tilting their heads up. The stones were pale gray and smooth, giving the gate a triumphal appearance. Carved over the left gate in Latin was the following inscription:

SALVE

En age segnes

Rumpe moras—vocat ingenti

clamore Cithaeron

Tangetique canes—domitrixque

Epidaurus equorum

Et vox assensu—nemorum

Ingeminata remuquit.

Carved in the same bold style on the right gate was:

HUNTLAND

Fields, woods, and streams

Each towering hill

Each humble vale below

Shall hear my cheering voice

My hounds shall wake the lazy morn

And glad the horizon round.

"Here's to today's fox." Nash held out an imaginary toast.

"Makes me homesick."

"The gate or thinking of foxhunting?" He stood up in the saddle and stretched.

"Both."

"If you were home, you might see the Harkaway Hunt." Nash teased her.

"I hope not. Might as well go back. I think we've seen everything."

A splashing of water drew her attention away from the gate. Six Federal cavalrymen clambered up on the other side of the bank.

"Nash, let's go!"

He turned from the gate, still saying the Latin out loud, "Et vox—"

A volley of shots rang out. Geneva felt something slide along the sole of her boot. She galloped downstream. Nash wasn't with her.

Pulling her pistols, she turned Gallant and headed back to the gate. The Yankees were gone as quickly as they had come.

Nash was sprawled on the ground, face to the sky.

"Nash!" She bent over him. One small hole, the only evidence of damage, was through his heart. A small patch of blood seeped out of the wound. Numb, she caught her horse and with difficulty threw his body over it. She headed back for Waterloo Bridge. No need to look for a field hospital. Nash was dead.

JUNE 11, 1910

"Then what?" Laura's wide cognac eyes, the color of her grandmother's, were moist.

"I remember riding back into the fight. The colonel went white when he saw me. He accompanied me to the rear of our lines. I could move my limbs, but I couldn't think. He assigned Banjo to take care of me, and Banjo wrapped Nash's body in a blanket. How he found a coffin, I don't know, but he did get one, and we rode the train down to Charlottesville. Colonel Vickers must have wired Mother, because she met us at the station. I only remember that I asked Nash's father whether he wanted Nash buried next to his mother or buried at Chatfield. The old gentleman asked to have his son, and I didn't fight him.

"No one seemed the least shocked at seeing me in uniform when we arrived at Chatfield. Later, I found out that Mother had told everyone."

Pointing to the worn boots standing next to the fireplace, Laura said, "I knew those were your cavalry boots."

Geneva picked them up and ran her finger along the groove the bullet had made from heel to toe. "Look." She handed them to her twenty-year-old granddaughter who held them as though they were a religious relic.

"I'm glad you're finally telling me, Mahmaw, about your first husband and the war. No one would ever tell me anything."

"You were too young to know about such things. Now that you're about to be married, you're ready, I guess."

Laura, who bore a strong resemblance to her great-grandmother Lutie, replaced the boots next to the fireplace. "What happened then?"

"Di-Peachy slept in my room just like when we were children. I stayed in the big house. I don't know why, but I couldn't bear to sleep in the bedroom I had shared with Nash.

"Feeling began to return to me in about six weeks. I remember that. Banjo was already back with the regiment. They'd fought Second Manassas. Mars wrote that for two full days they protected our exposed flank against heavy Federal cavalry attacks. Very hard fighting. I felt guilty as well as desolate. I belonged with the regiment. Mother didn't try to hold me back, but she told me to release my flood of tears first. I didn't know what she was talking about until I was alive enough to cry. That probably sounds strange to you, but you haven't known great loss. It took some time for the loss to sink in. The actual event, for me anyway, wasn't as terrible as the aftermath. When I finally cried, I couldn't stop, and I took sick for a while. Mother nursed me, and Sin-Sin would sit with me for hours telling me stories.

"As soon as I felt physically strong, I wrote the colonel and asked to rejoin the men. He and Banjo were the only ones who knew of my true identity. Banjo never spoke to me about it. He just accepted it with no fuss. In a strange way, fighting was all I knew. I had grown up in the army, and I belonged there.

"While I waited for him to reply, Gunther Krutzer, the Yankee prisoner who'd come back to Chatfield with Mother, and I began to lay out Sumner's plans for Mother's fountains. Little did I know at the time it would take sixteen years to complete the task.

"Well, the colonel wrote back and said that I could return. He offered no explanation other than that he needed the best rider in the Confederacy. And so I met up with the cavalry on November 11 at Culpeper, and there I stayed until April 9, 1865. At the end of the war I was still wearing the same boots I wore on that August day when Nash was killed. I was lucky. Aside from the slash on my face, I was hit only once, on the right shoulder. Took a piece out of me, but no serious mess."

"I wish I'd been alive then!"

"You're alive now. Make the most of it. When people tell about their war experiences, it sounds exciting. It was, but, honey, I saw things I'll never forget. I remember seeing a man at Sharpsburg with two ribs sticking out of his body, flesh dangling on them, and he was walking. I saw men with their brains oozing out of their heads, and they lay for days in agony. I saw beautiful homes destroyed. More horses were slaughtered or suffered on battlefields than you can imagine. And by the end of the war, it was death and destruction, nothing but death and destruction. You didn't see a woman, but what she wore black.

"Richmond was put to the torch. We blamed it on them, and they blamed it on us; said it was criminal elements that did it. It seemed as though the whole world died. Beautiful John Pelham was hit in the back of the skull with a shell fragment at Kelly's Ford on March 17, 1863. Never forget that. Heroes Von Borcke had a metal casket made with a window over John's face because John was such a beautiful man, and that's how they sent him home to Alabama. Benserade was killed in a skirmish.

"I guess the worst death was Stuart's. He was shot up through the liver at Yellow Tavern on May 11, 1864. They got him into Richmond, and Kate Vickers wrote that a crowd assembled outside the house where he was lying. They stayed there all night weeping and through the twelfth, too, which got unseasonably hot. When he died, I think I knew the end was in sight. I believed he was invincible. When Mars heard—he was a brigidier general by then—he put his face on his horse's neck and sobbed like a baby. We knew we didn't stand the chance of a prayer in hell, but we kept fighting."

"Didn't Pahpaw get his father's brigade?"

"Yes, that happened in 1863. Hannibal Vickers died at Gettysburg like the lion he was. Sentiment was such that the brigade, what was left of it, was offered to Mars. He asked Stuart if he could have myself and Banjo. Stuart made a great show of being reluctant to let us go, but he did. He even arranged a dance in Mars's honor before he left. You know, every age and every generation has their heroes, but I don't think we'll ever see the likes of J.E.B. Stuart again. Not now, not ever."

"People say that about you," Laura shyly complimented her grandmother.

"Idle gossip. I wasn't the only woman in the war. Once the dust settled, hundreds came forward. Some, like Loreta Velaques, even wrote books about it. More women fought on our side than theirs. I can't decide if those Yankee girls were less passionate about their men or a damned sight more intelligent than we were!" She sighed and noticed Sin-Sin's blue pot gleaming in the light. "It doesn't matter anymore."

"You must have loved him very much, Mahmaw. Your first husband."

"I did. Who's to say what would have become of us if it wasn't for the war? I know my wanting to be with him drove him away, and yet he tried. He was a good man and so young. An entire generation of men was wiped off the face of this continent, and most left no children behind. It's as if they had never been!"

"The war must have been horrible." Laura couldn't think of another word.

"Yes, but what came afterward was hell. I never knew I could feel so bad and still want to live. We had no food. There was hardly a horse or mule left from Maryland to

Florida. We were so hungry that we boiled the dirt under the smokehouse to get salt that winter. By the spring of '66, we had some crops come up, but from the summer of '65 to that late spring of '66, you chewed sassafras roots if you could get them. Ernie June lost weight. You know, I thought Ernie would leave us once she was set free in '62 according to the last wishes of my father. She was always an ambitious sort, but she stayed. Braxton left, but he came back after a year. Most of the other servants stayed. I think they stayed here because it was home.

"When the peace was signed, Mother called a meeting with everyone at Chatfield and told them she couldn't pay them. Sin-Sin suggested that Mother divide up the land so that every servant had a share of fifty acres each. Then everyone would promise to pitch in to get a crop for Chatfield as well as their own crop. Lutie agreed. After all, if there was one thing we had, it was land. She gave out good land, too, not billy-goat land. When it was said and done, we still had about twenty-five hundred acres. Never sell one inch of it! Not one!"

"I won't."

"See to it that your children don't either. My God, we died for this land. You can't put a price on it now."

"What happened to Gunther?"

"It was Gunther Krutzer that saved Chatfield from being looted and burned when Sheridan's men came through the mountains and swooped down on Charlottesville. We were still fighting. Gunther put on his blue uniform and met the Yankee squad that rode up the hill. He said he was in charge of this place and could he be of service to them. Cool as could be. He offered them what little food we had and they rode off. Now I don't want to imply that Gunther was a traitor to the Union. He wasn't, but he was grateful to Mother for saving him from Belle Island and possibly death. By that time, too, he'd fallen in love with Risé Rives's younger sister, Caroline. After Appomattox, he waited until I came home and then left for York, Pennsylvania. He came back within the year to marry Caroline. He went into the business with Beverly Fyffe, too, the South Carolina man he met at Kate's when they were wounded.

"They started with their honey business and then they put

their money in a machine shop—a factory, really—going up in York. Well, the place made money hand over fist."

"I don't remember Gunther."

"You were too little. I pray for him most every night. A good man. Died of cancer of the throat, and he wasn't but forty-eight."

"When did Pahpaw get here?"

"Ha! That was something. He returned to Richmond, but their gorgeous home on Grace Street was ruined. Only the west wing was inhabitable. But Kate absolutely refused to leave Richmond. Kate asked him for a divorce. It took some time, and it did not go down well in Richmond, I can tell you. She married Baron Schecter, and they left for Vienna. I don't know if Kate ever found love, but she did find power. She knew everybody who was worth knowing in Europe, and Mother said she had great influence. I never liked Kate Vickers. Not from the first time I laid eyes on her. Of course, Mother said that was because I was already in love with Mars, but too dumb to know it. I would disagree with that theory, but Mother's not here to defend herself. Mother loved Kate. I believe Kate was more her daughter in ways than I was, or should I say, more like the daughter she would have liked to have had. I was neither fish nor fowl, although Mother and I got along much better once I was a soldier. Curious."

"Yes, but when did Pahpaw get here?"

"Oh." Geneva inhaled. "He knocked on our door during a wicked snowstorm in February, 1866. February sixth. It was J.E.B. Stuart's birthday. Always have remembered that day because we used to make a fuss over him on his birthday. Well, there he was, cold, hungry, wearing his worn-out uniform. He'd lost everything, you see. Didn't even have the money for a suit of civilian clothes. Sin-Sin opened the door, and he embraced her, and I remember Cazzie the cat jumped off my lap when the door was opened and ran to the front hall. She was a better hostess than I was! Sin-Sin hollered at the top of her considerable lungs, 'Miz Geneva, the general is here!'

"I was in the library with Mother. I remember it as if it were yesterday. We'd been going over the account books, which was like a doomsday exercise. I wore pants, boots, and a shirt. I couldn't see the point of a dress. Mother and I shot out of the library, and there he stood, shivering in the entrance hall with Cazzie looking up at him. He bowed and kissed my mother's hand. He said, 'Jimmy, I guess you know why I'm here.' I said, 'It's good to see you, General.' Mother asked him to please sit by the library fire, and she'd see if she couldn't find a cup of coffee somewhere. It was make-believe coffee. Nobody had the real thing. You'd grind up molasses and other stuff. God knows what Ernie June put in there, but it was hot. He sat next to the fire, and said, 'Kate has divorced me. I have no money. I have no trade. I don't even know if I have a future. But I have two hands and a strong will. I can't promise much in the way of the world, but I love you. I've loved you for a long time, and I'd like to spend my life with you. Will you marry me?'

"Laura, I was struck dumb, and then I cried. I hated to cry, but I did. And the first thing I said was, 'I'm not beautiful.' Can you imagine? He said, 'To me you're the most beautiful woman on earth.' I cried some more, I guess, but I said yes. He kissed me. He'd kissed me once before, during the Battle of Seven Days. He was delirious then, so I discounted that or pretended to. When I kissed him, I felt myself come to life again. It was the strangest thing, but I felt that we were one person, two people with one heartbeat. He cried, too. He got hold of himself and found Mother. He said, 'Mrs. Chatfield, your daughter has agreed to marry me, but I would like your permission and your blessing.' Mother threw her arms around him and kissed him, too. So we were married. Then Sumner was born, then Jeb, then your mother, Merriweather, and finally we had John Pelham Vickers, still the baby, no matter how old he gets."

"Did Kate Vickers ever have children?"

"Yes, finally. She had two girls, and she named the first one Lutie after Mother. They stayed close and when Mother had her final illness, Kate sailed from Austria to be with her. I was fit to be tied, because Kate, who was in her fifties at that time, was still terrifyingly beautiful. Mars treated her like a sister. He said time changes things like that, and after I pitched a fit, he calmed me down. I actually think he was flattered that I could be so jealous. Anyway, Mother loved her."

"Do you miss your mother?"

"Yes. I regret that you didn't know my mother. She was a most remarkable woman. She wasn't happy when I was a child. Socially she was brilliant, but at home she was in the grip of some melancholy. But after the war, when everyone else was falling to pieces, Mother gave off a bright light. She married Banjo. As soon as he arranged his affairs in West Virginia, as it was called after separating from Virginia, he came home for her. He'd bought all that land around Harper's Ferry. He didn't sell it, but he found workers, easy enough then, and put in a crop, found a manager, and then left. He bought more land, too, as his farm was a good producer, so he started speculating. You see, because West Virginia stayed in the Union, it made out quite well after the war. Years later, some of that land he bought had coal on it. I'm putting the cart before the horse. That was long after he married Mother.

"Now those two loved one another. She called him Darryl. She was the only person, aside from his first wife, who called him that. He was besotted with her. She'd come down the stairs in a dress ten years old—who could afford clothes? —and to him she was beautiful, and she was beautiful! Happiness makes people beautiful. Of course, Mother couldn't have any more children. One day Banjo brought home a three-year-old girl. It was Benserade's baby. His wife had died, and so had her people. But before she died, she'd written a letter to Mars asking, as her late husband's commander, would he care for the child or find a home for it? Poor soul, she must have been desperate. Well, this little child with a note pinned to her dress came to the train station. It was pure D luck that Banjo was in town that day. He brought her back up the hill—I can see his eyes dancing— and he said, 'Lutie, we have a baby!' That was how you got your Aunt Rose, which you knew. One thing led to another and before long we had four orphans. Laura, I think those children were the joy of Banjo's existence and Mother's, too. They worked in the fields, and so did we. Even Mother. There she'd be, the lady of a great estate, the sleeves to her dress rolled up, and she'd be hoeing a row of carrots, laughing and talking. Hardships reveal the true person. Strange as it may sound to you, the years after the war made Mother joyful. She had a purpose. She had love. I believe she was blessed.

"It wasn't as easy for your grandfather and me because we were younger. We'd rail against fate, and Mars would cross the street before he'd pass a Yankee soldier. Town was full of them. They threatened to burn Mr. Jefferson's university, you know. Those people had no respect for the past, for traditions. They still don't. Oh, I won't start up on this subject. I've made my peace with the Yankees, but that doesn't mean I want to be like one. They live for profit, those people. You can marry one, but for the love of God, don't become one."

"They're not all moneygrubbers, Mahmaw."

Geneva grumbled, "Most are."

"When was Pahpaw elected to the state house?"

"Years later. We couldn't vote or run for office until the U.S. Congress said we could. We were occupied. Mars didn't run for office until the '80s, and only then because everyone begged him to. Your grandfather is able to see things quite dispassionately. That and his conduct during the war made him a man other people turned to. They turned to Mother, too. In the last decade of her life, nothing important was decided in Albemarle County but what she wasn't asked for her opinion."

"Tell me about Di-Peachy and Mercer."

"Not now, honey, I'm tired. That's a sad story. They did get married, but the Fates and other people were not kind. I'll tell you that one after your honeymoon."

"I wish I'd known Auntie Sin-Sin and Ernie June!"

"Sometimes when I go down to the kiln, I feel Sin-Sin. I know she's there with me. She was a gift from God, Sin-Sin was. As usual, you don't know it until it's too late."

"And Boyd did come back, just like Sin-Sin said."

"By way of Weeping Cross—and so did the Yankee captain who saved us in the orchard." She stood up. "Now look, young lady, you've got plenty to do, and so do I."

"What do you have to do?"

"Soothe your mother's shattered nerves. She thinks she's the only woman who's had to be the mother of the bride."

Laura reluctantly rose. "Did you ever see the Harkaway Hunt again?"

"No. Others have, though, discounting the stories of Jennifer Fitzgerald who claimed to have weekly sightings. She was quite unpredictable, that one. One time she looked me right in the face, it must have been the first year after the war, and she said, 'The other day I met a zulu-tail-of-gold who sings and chants, keeps pennies in his pockets, knows mermaids, and listens to flowers.' Extraordinary! I wrote it down. But aside from the questionable Jennifer, people have seen them. I guess I'll see them when I'm supposed to."

"Mahmaw, why don't you and Pahpaw speak about your first husband?"

"Too painful, I guess. Mars hated him, and I loved him. That didn't foster conversation." She walked over to the windows to look out on Lutie's magnificent marble fountains, their various levels glistening. "People close doors rightly or wrongly. It's easier to keep them shut than to open them again."

"I'm glad you talked to me."

"I am, too." Geneva kissed her. "Go find your mother, and I'll be down in a minute. I just want to put these things away."

"Mahmaw, one more question."

"What?"

"It was so long ago, the war. What do you think of it now?"

Geneva turned from the window. "I think that David flung his pebble at Goliath and missed."

Laura smiled softly, then she carefully opened the door and left the room.

Geneva returned to the window. So many emotions stirred within her. If she closed her eyes, she could hear artillery fire. She could see Gallant's fine head. He lived through the war and died at age twenty-seven. She'd loved him, too. And Nash. His life was a spark caught up in the howling flame of war. Who is to say what he would have given to the world if he'd lived? She did not believe in lost loves or lost causes. The rest of the South could wrap themselves in their imagined chivalry, but it was over. The dead numbered in the hundreds of thousands. What started out as a classic war became something new, something ugly, something that twisted everyone. No one was safe at the end. We all live in the dark shadow of Sherman, she thought.

Geneva could hear the laughter of other lifetimes, and like forgotten sunlight, it still warmed her soul. The love of her husband, her children, her neighbors, and her friends were her lifeline. She knew she had not achieved the transcendent love, the purity her mother had reached. She didn't have the tender forgiveness of Sin-Sin. She'd seen too much perhaps.

"Mother," Geneva whispered, as she listened to the water in the fountains. "I just don't believe as you did. I wish I could, but I don't have much use for the human race. I love a few people, and that's all. I don't have your wide embrace, your high heart. There are other wars out there, Mother. They'll be worse. We haven't learned a thing!" She sighed. "May God have mercy upon us; we have none for one another."

EPILOGUE

On April 3, 1865, most records of the Confederacy were destroyed in a fire in Richmond. Enlistment scrolls burned, making the task of counting soldiers accurately for a historian or this novelist difficult at best.

The county of Albemarle and the city of Charlottesville do not have paid historians or archivists on their roster of city and county employees. This is not a criticism. I wonder if any county has an archivist. While it saves on our budget, it plays havoc with our legacy, our past. We have in our county bits and pieces of information moldering in boxes, stashed in back rooms and who knows where else. Our elected officials are generally too concerned about their political futures to be overly worried about our collective past. I have tried to reconstruct enlistment figures from Albemarle County with the frustrating knowledge that there are probably treasures down at our courthouse or over in old Lane High School about which I know nothing. Does anybody know?

Claudia Garthwaite and I have been able to piece together the following information. Much of this was taken from R.A. Brock's valuable summary of enlistments. This gentleman was secretary of the Virginia Historical Society and the figures were published in 1884 in the *Special Virginia Edition* of *Hardesty's Encyclopedia*. Supplemental lists are from what records remain in the office of the clerk of the circuit court of Albemarle County.

Another difficulty with enlistment figures is that sometimes muster rolls fell into the hands of the Federals. It is entirely possible that some of our papers are languishing in New York, Maine, or where have you.

Fearing Federal soldiers at the war's end, we also destroyed many of our own records. The aftermath of the war was in many ways worse than the war itself, and people's concern for their safety had basis in fact.

This is what we have been able to piece together. The total number of enlisted for which there is record from Albemarle County is 2,189. Those killed during the war numbered 278. We know there were more killed, but sometimes the bodies could not be found.

In the 1860 census, there were 26,625 residents of Albemarle County—12,103 were white and 14,622 were black. Among the black residents, 606 were free.

Roughly half of the 12,103 whites were female. So if we had a male population of 6,050 men, one can quickly see that 2,189 in service is one-third of the male population. Those men not in service were either children or the elderly. In other words, Albemarle County was totally mobilized.

At the University of Virginia, 515 men in attendance out of a student body of 630 immediately joined the service in 1861. By the war's end the University of Virginia gave up 503 dead on the field of battle. Their names are inscribed on a plaque on the south side of the rotunda. Three of these dead were under 16 years of age. They are not listed here since most of the students were not Albemarle residents.

You will not find the name of either my paternal or maternal great-grandfather on this list. Miraculously, they both survived.

This is but one list from one county in central Virginia. Imagine if we compiled a list from every county, from every state. It would be the volumes of dead, mute testimony that once they lived, they were young, they were filled with hope and high spirits.

I do not believe you can read this list without being moved by it. Perhaps you will find a list for your own county and find the names of your people. What I pray for is that neither you nor I, wherever we live, will have to read a list like this in the future.

COMPANY A, NINETEENTH VIRGINIA INFANTRY, MONTICELLO GUARD

Collier, James, killed at Seven Pines
Johnson, W.A., killed at Manassas, August 30, 1862
Wingfield, R.F., killed near Richmond, July 30, 1862
Christian, John J.
Jones, Lucian S., killed at Gettysburg

COMPANY E, NINTEENTH VIRGINIA INFANTRY

Goss, W.W., lieutenant; promoted captain; killed at Gettysburg, July 3, 1863
Mooney, Madison, accidentally shot near Richmond; died August 1, 1864
Sandridge, J.J., color bearer; wounded June 27, 1862, at Seven Pines; killed at Gettysburg, July 3, 1863
Pritchett, William R.
Salmon, James, killed at Hatchers Run, March 1865
Gilvert, Robert M., died at Cold Harbor
Butler, Jacob W.
Carden, William B.
Carpenter, John F., killed at Gettysburg
Eastin, Henry
Easten, Granvills
Hall, Henry J.
Johnson, W.W.
Leake, John W., mortally wounded in battle at Seven Pines, June 1, 1862; died from wounds
LeTellier, William B., wounded, captured, and died in hospital, April 26, 1862
Munday, Thomas Walker, wounded and killed in 1863
Munday, Henry B.
Norvell, Joseph B., captured and killed at Gettysburg
Thomas, Tazewell S.
Thomas, Jerry
Taylor, John R., killed at Gettysburg, July 3, 1863
Wood, William
*Zibinia, Antonia, killed at second Manassas

*COMPANY E, FORTY-SIXTH VIRGINIA INFANTRY, WISE'S
BRIGADE*

Patterson, D.N., killed at Petersburg
Moon, Scarlar, killed at Petersburg, June 15, 1864

*COMPANY I, FORTY-SIXTH VIRGINIA INFANTRY, WISE'S
BRIGADE*

Harris, James O.
Jones, Robert M., wounded at Petersburg, February 5, 1865;
    died March 1, 1865
Jones, W.H., wounded at Petersburg, November 6, 1862
Reeves, Tucker, wounded at Petersburg, June 17, 1864;
    killed April 1, 1865, at Five Forks
Shackleford, William, killed at Petersburg, June 17, 1864

COMPANY II, FIFTY-SIXTH VIRGINIA INFANTRY

Ballard, William
Michie, Orion
Maupin, David G., wounded at Gaines Mills; killed at Get-
    tysburg, July 3, 1863
Ballard, Joseph M.
Ballard, William G., killed at Gettysburg, July 3, 1863
Beddows, Nash
Bellew, John R., died March 1864
Brown, Thomas
Dunn, Thomas W., killed at Gettysburg, July 3, 1863
Dunn, George M., died September 1864
Estes, Robert, killed 1863 at Gettysburg
Gibson, Henry T., killed at Gettysburg, July 3, 1863
Herring, George
Murry, James
McAllister, ———, killed 1863 at Gettysburg
Maupin, Burnett C., killed at Gettysburg, July 3, 1863
Maupin, Carson B., killed 1863 at Gettysburg
Rhodes, Franklin, killed 1862 at Malvern Hill
Sandridge, George W., killed at Gettysburg, July 3, 1863
Sandridge, William

COMPANY H, FIFTY-SEVENTH VIRGINIA INFANTRY

Magruder, John B., captain, killed 1863 at Gettysburg
Rogers, R. Lewis, killed 1864
Ward, J.B., orderly sergeant, died February 1862
Biggins, James A., killed 1862 at Malvern Hill
Ward. J.B., died 1862
Bragg, H.R.
Black, J.T.
Dunn, Leroy E., killed 1862 at Malvern Hill
Eads, James, died 1864
Eddins, Theodore T.
Eddins, Charles C.
Morris, James B., died 1863
Morris, John W., died 1863
Morris, A.J., killed 1862 at Malvern Hill
Mayo, W.B., killed 1862 at Malvern Hill
Marshall, Wesley B., died 1863
Norris, John W., died in Richmond, March 1863
Powell, Edward, captured at Gettysburg, July 3, 1863; held
    at Point Lookout; died 1865
Shiflett, O.M., color bearer, died 1863

COMPANY K, SECOND VIRGINIA CAVALRY

Anderson, M.L., killed near Woodstock, October 8, 1864
Baxter, Thornton, killed 1864 near Trevilian Depot
Carr, James, killed 1864 at Fort Kernan
Good, Albert H., wounded at Gettysburg, July 3, 1863; died
    August 3, 1863
Goodwin, F.C., killed 1865 at Appomattox
Goodwin, William W., wounded at Cold Harbor, June 3,
    1864; died next day
Leslie, J.O., wounded 1862 in the valley of Virginia; killed
    1864 at Front Royal
Magruder, James, killed 1864 at Meadow Bridge
Marshall, William, killed 1862 in the valley of Virginia
Minor, William B.
Nelson, Frank, killed 1864 at Fort Kernan
Newman, Thomas, killed 1863 in Loudon county
Rothwell, J.W.
Sneed, Horace A.

Tebbs, W.B., killed 1862 near Richmond
White, B.T.
Boston, Reuben
Clark, Christopher
Garth, Hugh
Geiger, George H., killed at Gettysburg
Harris, William
Jacobs, James
Lasley, John, killed at Front Royal, September 1865
Michie, Octavius
Robertson, Constantine
Reynolds, Chesney

COMPANY F, TENTH VIRGINIA CAVALRY

Edge, Benjamin
Edge, John E., killed at Reams Station, August 24, 1864
Elson, John, killed at Reams Station, August 24, 1864
Giles, Joseph H., killed at Stony Creek, September 1864
Hopkins, John, killed at Reams Station, August 24, 1864
Wallace, George P.
Walcott, Gideon, killed at Brandy Station, June 9, 1863

COMPANY I, SEVENTH VIRGINIA INFANTRY

Brown, Basil G.
Brown, William A., wounded at Williamsburg, May 5, 1862;
    died May 8, 1862
Walters, W.P., killed at Williamsburg, May 5, 1862
Fretwell, B.
Ambroselli, John B., killed at Gettysburg, July 3, 1863
Ballard, C., killed at Dinwiddie, March 31, 1865
Ballard, Marion, killed at Fraziers Farm, June 30, 1862
Bowen, F.A., killed at Williamsburg, May 5, 1862
Brown, W.G.
Clark, I.L., captured at Five Forks, April 1, 1865; held at
    Point Lookout; died 1865
Clark, Tobias, captured at Five Forks, April 1, 1865; held at
    Point Lookout; died 1865
Cox, N., captured at Five Forks, April 1, 1865; held at Point
    Lookout, died 1865
Dore, David

Fielding, B.F., killed at Bull Run, July 18, 1861
Gardner, Elzie
Good, A.H.
Herring, W.H., killed at Gettysburg, July 3, 1863
Herndon, W.G., captured at Five Forks, April 1, 1865; held at Point Lookout; died 1865
Keyton, W.L.
Lane, J.M.
Lowery, George

COMPANY K, NINETEENTH VIRGINIA INFANTRY

Black, Robert, wounded 1865 at Howlett House; died June 12, 1867
Dollins, Alexander M., died August 25, 1861
Dollins, John A., died February 1862
Dollins, William R., died October 7, 1861
Grimstead, James H., first lieutenant; wounded at Gettysburg, July 3, 1863; died July 7, 1863
Humphries, William, died August 1, 1861
Martin, Joseph N., died March 4, 1863
Martin, Joel A.
Robertson, A.J., second lieutenant; wounded at Cold Harbor; killed at Gaines Mills
Troter, Lewis, killed 1862 at Boonesboro
Woods, John J., wounded and captured at Gettysburg, July 3, 1863; died July 20, 1863
Woods, John J., corporal; wounded at Gettysburg, July 3, 1863; died July 16, 1863
Woodson, James, killed 1862 at Boonesboro
Woodson, James Garland, first lieutenant; promoted captain and major; wounded at Sharpsburg and Gettysburg; killed at Cold Harbor, June 3, 1864
Wolf, George, killed 1862 at Boonesboro
Wolf, William, killed 1862 at Boonesboro
Abell, M.L., killed 1864 at Cold Harbor
Harris, William
Hays, Thomas
Johnson, James
McSparran, Robert M.
Moyer, Jacob
Scott, James M.

Scott, ———
Shepherd, Robert
Shepherd, William B.
Taylor, Randall
Maupin, J.T.
Maupin, C.B., killed at Gettysburg, July 3, 1863
Marshall, T.A.
Sandridge, R., captured at Five Forks, April 1, 1865; held at
    Point Lookout; died 1865
Toombs, William L., killed at Manassas, July 11, 1861
Taylor, J.W.
Thurston, George, fell from team and killed, 1863
Walton, J.W.
Wood, W.T., killed at Gettysburg, July 3, 1863
Woods, W.W., wounded at second Manassas, August 27,
    1862; died in Albemarle County, September, 1862
Wood, William, wounded at second Manassas; killed at Get-
    tysburg, July 3, 1863
Wyant, J.A., killed at Dinwiddie, March 31, 1865

COMPANY D, FORTY-SIXTH VIRGINIA REGIMENT

Bruce, George W., killed at Petersburg
Garrison, Robert, killed 1864 at Petersburg
Gardner, Walker R., wounded 1864 at Petersburg; died from
    wounds
Hall, Ebenezer, killed at Petersburg
Keyton, ———, killed at Petersburg
Lamb, Newton, killed 1864 at Petersburg
Madison, James M., killed 1864 at Petersburg
McGrath, Morris, killed 1864 at Petersburg
Marshall, William H.
Rodes, Walker, killed March 19, 1865, serving as color
    guard
Shiflett, Benjamin F.
Shiflett, Chapman B., killed at Brandy Station
Shiflett, Micajah B., killed at Petersburg
Smith, Theodrick B., killed carrying the colors at Scary Creek,
    1861; first man from Albemarle killed in the war
Shoemaker, ———, killed at Petersburg

COMPANY B, NINETEENTH VIRGINIA INFANTRY

Alexander, William, killed March 29, 1865
Bowyer, L.R., killed at Gettysburg
Cox, Lucien H.
Daniel, James L.
Durrett, James M., killed 1862 at Frazier Farm
Dudley, John W.
Dunn, Edward
Darden, ———
Hamner, N.B., killed at Williamsburg
Hamner, B., killed at Boonesboro
Harris, William, killed at Chancellorsville
Johnson, M.D., wounded and killed at Hatcher's Run
Jordon, John D., killed at second Manassas
Jones, William
Keiley, John
Laine, Thomas E.
Lindenborne, P.
Lumsden, William J.
Leake, Walker, killed at Gaines Mill
Mullen, W., killed at Seven Pines
Morris, Alec, killed at Gettysburg
Noel, John, killed at Cold Harbor
Pearsons, E.J., killed at Hatcher's Run
Points, Polk
Porter, L.R.
Points, Leonidas
Rodes, Walker
Robertson, William J.
Reynolds, R.F., killed at Sharpsburg
Richards, ———
Shepherd, M.J., killed at Boonsboro
Shepherd, D.S., killed at Boonsboro
Thomas, ———
Wolfe, Luther T., killed at second Cold Harbor
Whitesel, D., killed at Gettysburg

CHARLOTTESVILLE ARTILLERY, CARRINGTON'S BATTERY

Bibb, French S.
McCary, Kenneth
Belew, ———

Durrett, William S.
Norvel, William
Terrell, N.A.
Pendleton, Phil
Via, Lyman
White, Thomas B.

ALBEMARLE ARTILLERY, EVERETT REGIMENT, SOUTHALL'S BATTERY

Wyatt, J.W.
Rivers, Charles M.
Bellamy, F.W.
Chimsolm, William
Collins, Tandy
Clements, R.M., killed at Cold Harbor
Delake, William, killed at Petersburg
Dobbs, Ira
Dowell, C.R.
Garth, D.G.
Goodwin, James E.
Harris, David
Harris, J.G.
Hughes, Elijah
Jones, Thomas R.
Kelley, George
Kelley, William
Keys, William
Linkenhawkes, J., wounded and killed at Cold Harbor
Maupin, James R., killed at Gettysburg
Munday, T.H.
Murray, William H., killed at Cold Harbor
McKennie, James
Nimmon, Henry
Perry, J.J.
Pugh, E.A.
Pleasants, P.B.
Pollard, C.T., killed at Cold Harbor
Thompson, Nick, killed at Cold Harbor
Woodson, T.S.

STURDIVANT'S VIRGINIA BATTERY, TWELFTH BATTALION

Reppeto, James T.
Brown, E.P.
Beck, ———
Carver, R.A.
Carver, J.D.
Cobb, George E.
Jacobs, William
Edmondson, B.W
Pritchett, John
Sandridge, J.D.
Timberlake, ———
Yeamains, J.W.
Zimmerman, A.

MISCELLANEOUS SERVICE

Baber, C.L.
Bowen, F.A.W., killed at Williamsburg
Breckinridge, James, killed in 1865
Breckenridge, Gilmer, killed 1865 at Fort Kernan
Brown, Lucian B., wounded May 12, 1864; died July 19, 1864
Cobbs, George E., killed at Petersburg, August 20, 1864
Coleman, Chester C., killed at Spotsylvania, May 8, 1864
Dunn, Edward
Harris, Henry T., captured at Petersburg, March 26, 1865; held at Point Lookout; died May 28, 1865
Harris, William H., killed at Chancellorsville, May 2, 1863
Horden, John
Horden, Mortimer, wounded at McDowell, October 28, 1861; died December 11, 1861
Houchins, George T.
Jarman, Thomas T.
Jones, Allen L., killed near Winchester
Jones, Frank, died from exposure, January 1865
Magruder, John B., wounded and captured at Gettysburg; died in prison in 1863
Rothwell, J.B.
Rothwell, Joseph Warren
Sutherland, Edward
Tapp, Henry L.

DEFINITION OF MILITARY UNITS CONFEDERATE STATES OF AMERICA

An *army* is the largest military unit. Strength varied considerably. The Confederacy had twenty-three such armies, each one usually taking its name from its state. Commanded by a full general, four stars.

A *corps* is two or more divisions from 15,000 to 20,000 men. The South did not adopt this organization until after the time frame of this novel. Therefore, corps is not mentioned here. Commanded by a lieutenant general, three stars.

A *division* is made up of two or more brigades. If they were at full strength, this would be about 8,700 officers and men. Commanded by a major general, two stars.

A *brigade* is made up of two or more regiments. The average Confederate brigade was 4.5 regiments, roughly 1,850 men. Commanded by a brigadier general, one star.

A *regiment* is made up of ten companies. The number of men was usually between 1,000 and 845. Commanded by a colonel.

A *company* was made up of about 100 men.

As the war progressed, the numbers declined. A company might be made up of far less than the requisite number of men. New recruits, rather than being sent into existing regiments, formed new ones. On both sides, therefore, the numbers inside a regiment declined throughout the war.

Anyone seeking more information on the organization of combat units is referred to *The Civil War Dictionary* by Mark M. Boatner III.

BIBLIOGRAPHY

Albemarle County Historical Society. *The Magazine of Albemarle County*. Vol. 25, Civil War issue. Charlottesville, Va.: The Michie Company, 1964.

Andrews, Matthew Page. *Women of the South in War Times*. Baltimore, Md.: The Norman, Remington Company, 1920.

Archives of the Episcopal Church. *The Church Almanac for the Year of Our Lord 1861*. New York: The Protestant Episcopal Tract Society.

Archives of the Episcopal Church. *The Church Almanac for the Year of Our Lord 1862*. New York: The Protestant Episcopal Tract Society.

Archives of the Episcopal Church. *The Church Almanac for the Year of Our Lord 1910*. New York: The Protestant Episcopal Tract Society.

Battlefields of the South, From Bull Run to Fredericksburg. New York: J. Bradburn, 1864.

Beauregard, P.G.T. *A Commentary on the Campaign and Battle of Manassas . . . with a summary of the Art of War*. New York: G.P. Putnam, 1891.

Black, Robert C. III. *The Railroads of the Confederacy*. Chapel Hill, N.C.: University of North Carolina Press, 1952.

Blémont, Emile, ed. *The Memorial Life of Victor Hugo*. Boston: Estes and Lauriat, 189-.

Boatner, Mark M. III. *The Civil War Dictionary*. New York: David McKay Company, Inc., 1959.

Bowman, John S. *The Civil War Almanac*. New York: Bison Books Company, 1982.

Brock, Sallie. *Richmond During the War*. New York: G.W. Carleton and Company, 1867.

Bruce, P.A. *History of the University of Virginia 1819–1919.* 5 vols. New York: Macmillan, 1920.

Byrd, Colwell P. *History and Genealogy of the Byrd Family.* Pocomoke City, Md.: F.W. Byrd, 1908.

Civil War Times Illustrated. 22 vols. Gettysburg, Pa., 1962-   .

Clemons, Harry. *Notes on the Professors for Whom the University of Virginia Halls and Residence Houses Are Named.* Charlottesville, Va.: University of Virginia Press, 1961.

Confederate Soldier in the Civil War, The. New York: The Fairfax Press.

Connelly, Thomas L. *The Marble Man: Robert E. Lee and His Image in American Society.* New York: Alfred A. Knopf, 1977.

Correct Thing in Good Society, The. By the author of *Social Customs.* Boston: Estes and Lauriat, 1888.

Cox, Leroy Wesley. *Memoirs of Leroy Wesley Cox: Experiences of a Young Soldier of the Confederacy.* (Unpublished manuscript)

Cunningham, Horace H. *Doctors in Grey: The Confederate Medical Service.* Baton Rouge, La., 1958.

Dabney, Virginius. *Richmond: The Story of a City.* New York: Doubleday and Company, 1976.

————. *Virginia: The New Dominion.* New York: Doubleday and Company, 1971.

Daily Progress, The. "Generations of Change." Charlottesville, Va. Photocopy.

Daniel, F.S. *Richmond Howitzers in the War.* Richmond, Va., 1891.

Davis, David Brion. *The Problem of Slavery in Western Culture.* Ithaca, N.Y.: Cornell University Press, 1966.

Davis, Major George B., et. al. *The Official Atlas of the Civil War.* New York: The Fairfax Press, 1983.

Davis, William C. *The Deep Waters of the Proud.* Vol. I, *The Imperiled Union: 1861–1865.* New York: Doubleday and Company, 1982.

————. *Battle at Bull Run.* New York: Doubleday and Company, 1977.

Dowdey, C.D. *The Seven Days.* Boston: Little, Brown, 1964.

Edwards, Anne. *Road to Tara: The Life of Margaret Mitchell.* New Haven, Ct.: Ticknor and Fields, 1983.

Encyclopedia Americana International Edition. 30 vols. Danbury, Ct.: Grolier, Inc., 1984.

Foner, Philip S., ed. *The Life and Writings of Frederick Douglass.* 4 vols. New York: International Publishers, 1950.

Freeman, D.S. *Lee's Lieutenants: A Study in Command*. 3 vols. New York: Charles Scribner's Sons, 1934–1935.

———. *R.E. Lee: A Biography*. 4 vols. New York: Charles Scribner's Sons, 1962.

Harwell, Richard B., ed. *Kate: The Journal of a Confederate Nurse*. Baton Rouge, La., 1959.

Hassler, William Woods. *Colonel John Pelham: Lee's "Boy Artillerist."* Richmond, Va.: Garrett and Massie, Inc., 1960.

Hattaway, Herman and Jones, Archer. *How the North Won: A Military History of the Civil War*. Illinois: University of Illinois Press, 1983.

Hayden, Karen. "Confederate Christmas." *Shenandoah Valley Magazine* (November, 1981).

Jones, Katharine M. *Heroines of Dixie*. Indianapolis, In.: Bobbs Merrill, 1955.

Kightly, Charles. *Country Voices: Life and Lore in English Farm and Village*. London: Thames and Hudson, Ltd., 1984.

Kunitz, Stanley. *American Authors 1600–1900: A Biographical Dictionary of American Literature*. New York: The W.H. Wilson Company, 1938.

Liddell, Viola Goode. *With a Southern Accent*. Norman, Ok.: University of Oklahoma Press, 1948.

McClellan, Henry Brainerd. *I Rode with Jeb Stuart*. Bloomington, In.: Indiana University Press, 1958.

McWhiney, Grady, and Jamieson, Perry D. *Attack and Die: Civil War Military Tactics and the Southern Heritage*. University, Al.: University of Alabama Press, 1982.

Massey, Mary Elizabeth. *Ersatz in the Confederacy*. Columbia, S.C.: University of South Carolina Press, 1952.

Maury, Richard L. *The Battle of Williamsburg and the Charge of the 24th Virginia, of Early's Brigade*. Richmond, Va.: Johns and Goolsby, 1880.

Meeks, Steven G. *Crozet: A Pictorial History*. Crozet, Va.: Meeks Enterprises, Inc., 1983.

Miller, Francis T. *Photographic History of the Civil War*. New York: T. Yoseloff, 1957.

Mitchell, Joseph Brady. *Decisive Battles of the Civil War*. New York: Putnam, 1955.

National Archives and Records Service, General Services Administration. *Weather Reports Submitted to the Smithsonian Meteorological Project by I. Ralls Abell, Mount View, Albemarle*

County, Virginia, January-April, 1861. Roll 520, Microfilm Publication T907.

————. *Weather Reports Submitted to the Smithsonian Meteorological Project by Rev. C.B. MacKee, A.M., Georgetown, Washington, D.C., January, 1861-November, 1862*. Roll 81, Microfilm Publication T907.

Opie, John. *A Rebel Cavalryman with Lee, Stuart and Jackson.* Chicago, Il.: W.B. Conkey Company, 1899.

Rawick, George P. *The American Slave: A Composite Autobiography.* 18 vols. Westport, Ct.: Greenwood Publishing Company, 1972.

Richey, Homer, ed. *Memorial History of the John Bowie Strange Camp.* Charlottesville, Va.: Press of the Michie Company, 1920.

Sherman, W.T. *Memoirs of General W.T. Sherman.* 2 vols. New York: D. Appleton & Company, 1875.

Shriver, Howard. *Precipitation by Months, Seasons, and Years at Wytheville, Virginia, 1861.* Unpublished weather records located in the Office of the State Climatologist, University of Virginia, Charlottesville, Va.

Simkins, Francis Butler. *The Women of the Confederacy.* Richmond, Va.: Garrett and Massie, Inc., 1936.

Smith, G.W. *The Battle of Seven Pines.* New York: C.G. Crawford, 1891.

Sommers, Richard J. *Richmond Redeemed: The Siege at Petersburg.* New York: Doubleday and Company, 1981.

South Vindicated: From the Treason and Fanaticism of the Northern Abolitionists, The. Philadelphia, Pa.: H. Manley, 1836.

Stern, Philip Van Doren. *Robert E. Lee: The Man and the Soldier.* New York: Bonanza Books, 1963.

————. *Soldier Life in the Union and Confederate Armies.* Bloomington, In.: Indiana University Press, 1961.

Stout, Dr. Samuel Hollingsworth. *St. Louis Medical and Surgical Journal. Vol LXIV, 1893. Southern Practitioner. vols. XXII-XXV, 1900–1903.* Information from journal articles quoted in *Kate: The Journal of a Confederate Nurse* by Harwell. Original articles not available.

Symonds, Craig L. *A Battlefield Atlas of the Civil War.* Annapolis, Md.: The Nautical and Aviation Publishing Company of America, 1983.

Tanner, Robert G. *Stonewall in the Valley.* New York: Doubleday and Company, 1976.

Thomas, Emory M. *The Confederate Nation*. New York: Harper and Row, 1979.

Thomason, J.W. *JEB Stuart*. New York: C. Scribner's Sons, 1930.

Von Borcke, Heroe. *Memoirs of the Confederate War for Independence*. 2 vols. New York: Peter Smith, 1938.

Welch, S.G. *A Confederate Surgeon's Letters to His Wife*. Georgia: Continental Book Company, 1954.

Whitnah, Donald R. *A History of the United States Weather Bureau*. Urbana, Il.: University of Illinois Press, 1961.

Wiley, Bell Irvin. *The Common Soldier in the Civil War*. New York: Grosset and Dunlap, 1958.

Williams, T. Harry. *The Selected Essays of T. Harry Williams*. Baton Rouge, La.: Louisiana State University Press, 1983.

Wise, Terence. *Military Flags of the World*. New York: Arco, 1978.

Woodard, C. Vann, ed. *Mary Chestnut's Civil War*. New Haven, Ct.: Yale University Press, 1981.